STOP THINKING

The change that came over her was unnerving. He couldn't pin it down exactly; maybe it was the wild glow in her eyes. The shape of her lips changed, her posture, the tilt of her eyebrows. Then she began to shimmy the dress down over her tits, and all coherent thought fled.

He fell back into the chair, shocked into total stillness. Whoa. She was dead serious about this, but he didn't have time to feel weird about it, because right then the corset fell to the floor, and the world stopped.

—from "Meltdown" in BAD BOYS NEXT EXIT

BOOK YOUR PLACE ON OUR WEBSITE AND MAKE THE READING CONNECTION!

We've created a customized website just for our very special readers, where you can get the inside scoop on everything that's going on with Zebra, Pinnacle and Kensington books.

When you come online, you'll have the exciting opportunity to:

- View covers of upcoming books
- Read sample chapters
- Learn about our future publishing schedule (listed by publication month *and author*)
- Find out when your favorite authors will be visiting a city near you
- Search for and order backlist books from our online catalog
- Check out author bios and background information
- Send e-mail to your favorite authors
- Meet the Kensington staff online
- Join us in weekly chats with authors, readers and other guests
- Get writing guidelines
- AND MUCH MORE!

Visit our website at
http://www.kensingtonbooks.com

ALL ABOUT MEN

SHANNON McKENNA

KENSINGTON BOOKS
KENSINGTON PUBLISHING CORP.
http://www.kensingtonbooks.com

CONTENTS

SOMETHING
WILD

Chapter One

There he was again. The Motorcycle Man sped past her for the third time in the last half-hour, shooting her a huge, dazzling grin. Annie Simon's heart gave a startled little leap in her chest, and she forced herself not to smile back at him. It took real effort.

He roared down the highway ahead of her like a bullet, drawing her gaze helplessly after him. His dazzling red motorcycle glittered with chrome, his helmet gleamed, his black leather jacket flapped wildly behind him. He was larger than life, bursting with brilliant energy against the leafless winter backdrop of dull browns and grays.

This was the third day in a row that he had followed her. She noticed him for the first time around Charlottesville, Virginia. At first she had figured that he must be going her way by sheer coincidence and was just flirting with her to amuse himself on the road, but she'd been stopping every day for hours to hike in almost every state and national park that she passed, and he never seemed to outdistance her. She didn't really mind. In fact, the few times she thought she'd shaken him off for good, she'd been surprised at how disappointed she felt—almost angry at him for not trying harder. Then poof, up he popped, flashing her a wild grin so full of rollicking good humor that she couldn't help laughing back.

She knew she should be alarmed at his persistence, young woman traveling alone, yada yada, but the game was actually giving her a tingle of pleased excitement, and it had been so long since she had felt anything remotely like a pleasant tingle. Lately, her feelings had run more along the lines of dread, exhausted anger, or a crushing sense of impending doom. The little buzz that the Motorcycle Man gave her was a refreshing distraction—as long as he stayed strictly in his place.

Annie had whiled away what would have been many long, depressing hours on the road speculating about him, studying the fascinating details of his bike and his wardrobe—not to mention his powerful, gorgeous body. Three years as a fashion buyer had trained her eye to read the silent language of his wardrobe. She had a feeling that the jacket on his back retailed for over $2,000, depending on the season, and how well things were moving on the floor. And her foster brothers had taught her enough about motorcycles to spot the sleek, sensual lines of an exquisitely preserved vintage Indian. The guy was speeding down the highway on a jewel of a collector's item that had to be worth at least fifty grand, if not more. Whoever he was, and whatever he did, her Motorcycle Man didn't spare any expense in outfitting himself. He looked great.

Not that it made any difference what he wore, or what he rode, of course, she reminded herself. From that wild, wicked grin and those broad shoulders right down to the tight, excellent ass and long, muscular legs, the man had trouble written all over him. More trouble Annie did not need. She'd had a lifetime of it. That was why she was running in the first place. But she shouldn't dwell on the past. She stuck her hand into her beautiful black Prada bag, beloved relic of her days in the world of the gainfully employed, and rummaged until she found the velvet sack of silver dollars. She clutched them hard, trying to ward off the sad, sinking feeling in her belly. "Think lucky thoughts," she whispered to herself. That bag represented the future. Another chance.

Five years ago, at the callow age of twenty-two, she'd taken a road trip with her friends to the Black Cat Casino in St. Honore, Louisiana, where she hit the jackpot at a dollar machine and won almost two thousand bucks. She'd seized her chance and bolted from her dreary cashier's job in Payton, Mississippi, straight to New York, the city of adventure. It was scary, in hindsight, to think of how naive she'd been. She should be grateful it hadn't gone any worse.

Maybe it was superstitious and silly, but the Black Cat was as good a place as any she could think of to petition the gods of chance for one more shot. She wasn't beaten yet, in spite of the mess with Philip. That little sack was the last drop of her lucky money. She'd kept it safe and secret, a good luck talisman. It might not have brought her much luck lately, but then again, she'd actually managed to get away from Philip in one piece, although without most of her stuff. And Mildred, her rusty, trusty Toyota pickup, by some miracle of duct tape, spit and baling wire, was still roadworthy, bless her faithful mechanical soul.

New York wasn't the only place in the world to make a life for herself. She would miss the bright lights and the fresh bagels, but on the plus side, she would never have to apologize to anyone for loving country music ever again. She cranked up the volume on her radio and sang lustily along with Pam Tillis, her eyes still helplessly fixed on the sparkling, wind-whipped figure on the road ahead of her.

The Motorcycle Man hung back, letting her pull up alongside him. He gave her a thumbs-up, and made extravagant gestures toward the Food-Gas-Lodging sign ahead of them, just as he'd been doing all day. He was getting bolder. She supposed she should be worried, but her worry supply was all used up. She stared at his bold, laughing grin, savoring the tingling pull of curiosity he gave her; a pull that had nothing to do with his designer clothes or his costly bike. His smile caught her off guard, like a blaze of sunshine piercing unexpectedly through thick clouds. He radiated light and color in all directions. It was incredibly sexy. Almost tempting enough to make her stop and flirt with him in person, just to see if the gooey, melting feeling that his smile had provoked had any basis in reality.

But going gooey was the last thing she should do, after everything that had happened with Philip. She had to toughen up, fast. She shook her head with a regretful smile, blew him a kiss and mouthed "in your dreams, buddy," as she accelerated smoothly past him.

The wind whipped Jacob's shout of frustration into nothing as he pulled onto the exit ramp. He'd decided that today was the day to make direct contact; enough road tag, but the touseled honey-blonde was not complying with his timetable. It was driving him nuts. He was ravenous. Didn't she ever eat?

He parked his bike and stalked into the restaurant, grumbling as he yanked off the helmet. He was restless and jazzed, and that taunting kiss she'd blown him from the pickup had given him a raging hard-on. Something about the way that luscious pink mouth puckered up just got to him. She seemed to like yanking his chain.

He ordered steak, salad and a baked potato, and pulled the crumpled Kentucky road map out of his pocket to gauge how far out of his way he'd gone in his wild pursuit. Not that he'd really had any destination to begin with. He'd kept his vacation plans deliberately vague, figuring that it would do him good to practice spontaneity. Well, he was practicing it now, with a vengeance.

It had started at a restaurant off I-95, right after Philadelphia. The sight of her walking out of the ladies' room had

hit him like a fist. He found himself staring helplessly at the
fit of her jeans, deliciously snug over her round, lush rear.
And those cute little nipples, poking out of the tight
T-shirt, bouncing and quivering as she moved.

She hadn't seen him. In fact, she'd noticed barely anything. She'd walked like a woman in a dream. Something
about the way she swept those heavy waves of honey-blonde
hair out of her pale face was eloquent in its unspoken weariness. She looked tired, rumpled, her big gray eyes haunted
and vulnerable. Like she needed someone to cheer her up,
make her laugh. Chase those shadows away from her eyes.

He'd left his uneaten food on the table and followed her
like a man under a spell. She hadn't even noticed him until
Charlottesville, Virginia. That had been his first victory.
Goofing and clowning at sixty miles an hour alongside her
truck until a smile budded on that lush, kissable mouth—and
then widened to a big, delighted grin. She laughed at him,
and he was ecstatic. That was how bad it was.

He knew where she hiked, where she camped, where she
stopped to pee, where she got gas. He hadn't approached her
yet, sensing that the moment wasn't right, but no one else
had gotten close to her without him knowing about it, and he
was cheerfully prepared to tear any guy who bothered her to
pieces. He'd reflected at great length upon the irony of the
situation while keeping her pickup in full view. He was acting like the guy her mother had probably warned her about;
the guy who couldn't stop dreaming about how her nipples
would taste when he finally peeled off that little shirt and got
her settled on his lap. How he would ravenously suckle her
lush, perfect breasts while she wrapped her arms around his
neck and squirmed with pleasure. How that gorgeous honey
hair would cascade all around them, tickling his face. How
her smoke-colored eyes would glow with excitement when
he tumbled her into the bed of the first motel he could find.

All things considered, he couldn't really blame her for not
stopping. But it still drove him nuts.

This compulsion to follow her was unnerving. He stared idly at the list of dessert specials, telling himself to stop worrying, to just go with the flow. Worry was a waste of energy. He was just following his instincts, like he always had. Following his instincts was what had made him a successful man. They'd just never been this strong, that was all. In the past, his instincts had served him dutifully whenever he'd called upon them. He wasn't used to thrashing helplessly in their grip.

He supposed the situation was funny, in a way. Jacob Kerr, successful architect and entrepreneur, accustomed to calling all the shots, driven out of his mind by one beautiful, mysterious girl who wouldn't stop and talk to him. It was wild, irrational, but he wasn't giving up the chase. He just couldn't.

Thunder rolled, and rain started pouring as the waitress set his steak before him. He scowled out the window, hating the thought of his honey-blonde out there in that rattletrap piece of junk. He'd checked out her vehicle at the campground last night while she was taking her shower. All of her tires were bald.

Worry robbed him of his appetite. He got up and paid for the uneaten food, and stared out at the slashing rain, cursing under his breath. His rain gear was stowed inside the hardcase saddlebags on the back of his bike. And it was insanely stupid to go out into that weather in any vehicle, let alone a motorcycle, the cool, rational part of his brain observed. He hadn't gotten this far in life by being insanely stupid.

Oh, to hell with being rational. Being insanely stupid looked like a lot more fun. He pulled on his helmet and headed out the door.

This, too, shall pass, Annie told herself over and over, clutching the steering wheel in a death grip. The rain had been innocuous at first, pattering down gently, but now it was a deafening roar. Violent gusts of wind buffeted the pickup, shoving her around the road, often into the lane of oncoming traffic. Mildred's bald tires slipped and slid, making the truck fishtail madly, and lightning stabbed down in wild, unnerving bursts. Maybe she was racing toward some freak tornado that would pick her and the truck up and deposit them miles away, in twisted, unrecognizable chunks. Chill out, she reminded herself, swallowing down her fear. Panic is not an option.

But each time she assured herself that this had to be the grand finale, that it couldn't possibly get any worse . . . it did. Maybe there was no end to how bad things could really get. If only she'd pulled off at the last exit. She could've been flirting with the Motorcycle Man right now over pie and coffee. As dangerous forces of nature went, he was definitely the lesser of the two evils, and a hell of a lot more attractive.

The rain was so blinding that she almost didn't see the exit. She had to lunge for it at the last minute, and the rapid swerve sent her into a long, heart-stopping slide. Once she finally got a grip on the road, she drove very, very slowly, hands trembling, toward the nearest diner. She was pathetically grateful for the coffee, chili and saltines the waitress brought her. She hunched over the steaming bowl, listening to sappy Christmas music, but she couldn't seem to stop shivering.

She was just starting to settle down when the string of bells over the door tinkled delicately. She heard the tread of heavy boots, and a fresh surge of adrenaline jolted through her body. She swiveled her head, and her stomach flip-flopped.

It was the Motorcycle Man, his shiny black helmet tucked under his arm, beaming at her.

He was huge. Much bigger than he'd seemed on the bike, now that those long, muscular legs were unfolded. The restaurant seemed small and shabby, dwarfed by his presence.

He was gorgeous. Breathtaking. And drenched. He squelched as he walked toward her. A puddle formed around his boots when he stopped by her table. The waitress was giving him a dirty look, which he ignored.

"Were you out in the rain?" she asked, instantly wanting to kick herself. What a stupid question. The answer was so obvious.

A triumphant grin blazed across his lean face. "Hah! I finally got you to talk to me."

"Don't let it go to your head," Annie snapped. She tried to drag her eyes away from him, but she was riveted by his intense black eyes, sparkling with intelligence. His eyebrows made a bold, slashing line across his broad forehead. His midnight-black hair was long and glossy, pulled into a ponytail. He was clean-shaven, a hint of shadow across his strong jaw. The fascination on his face made a bubble of flattered pleasure pop up to the surface of her consciousness. She actually felt . . . pretty, under his intense scrutiny. Prettier than she'd felt in a long, lonely time. The sensation was like a subtle caress. She began to blush.

"Why didn't you wait for the rain to stop?" she asked.

He shrugged. "I've been out looking for you," he said simply. "I had to make sure you were OK."

She narrowed her eyes in swift suspicion. "Let me get this straight," she said slowly. "You were warm and dry, and eating your lurch, and the storm hit, and you went out in it? To look for me?"

"Yeah, I know. It was crazy," he admitted, wringing water out of his ponytail. His dark eyes danced with silent laughter. "But a guy's gotta do what a guy's gotta do."

It had been so long since anyone had worried about her that it actually took away her breath for a second. Probably it was just a slick line, she reminded herself. My, what big ears you have, Grandmother. Toughen up, little girl. Still, a reluctant smile tugged her mouth. "I'm fine, as you can see," she murmured.

"Can I sit down?"

"No," she said quickly.

He shifted his helmet to the other arm, undaunted. His eyes swept over her appreciatively, and a ticklish, fluttery feeling raced madly across the surface of her skin. "What's your name?" he asked.

She hesitated, as if giving him her name would give him some obscure power over her, a hook into her private self. She decided to give him a fake name. Jill, or Monica, or Brooke. She looked into his intense dark eyes, opened her mouth and said, "Annie."

"Annie." He said her name tenderly, savoring it. "Just Annie?"

She gulped. "Just Annie."

He nodded. "OK, just Annie, I'm just Jacob. It's a pleasure to meet you at last. You've led me on a merry chase."

"You haven't caught me," she reminded him tartly. She took a sip of her coffee and stared up over the rim of the cup, her mind spinning with confused excitement. Six foot two and over two hundred pounds of lean, rock-solid masculinity standing there, water streaming off his body, taking up all the air in the room. He was almost too much for a girl to take. But then again, she was tougher than she looked.

"Can I please, please sit down?" His voice was warm and coaxing.

"No," she repeated.

The silence between them lengthened and grew heavy, charging itself with sultry, quivering heat. She licked her lips nervously, helpless to look away. She was locked in a clinch of breathless silence with him. The feeling was shockingly intimate.

His broad, sensual mouth curved knowingly, as if he knew just why she was shifting restlessly on the plastic booth. He knew that a hot, secret little ache of yearning was blossoming deep inside her body, and he was doing it to her deliberately, with his dark, laughing eyes, with his magnetic smile, with his raw male energy. God. This guy was more than just trouble. He was sexual dynamite.

Annie's breath stuttered in and out of her lungs. She forced herself to stop wiggling, and gave him a "don't-mess-with-me" stare, perfected on the tough streets of New York. "Look, Jacob. Whatever you want from me, you're not going to get, so don't waste your time."

His eyes gleamed with wry amusement. "Cruel Annie," he murmured. "Go ahead. Dash my hopes. Blow me off. I don't care. I'm still glad you're OK."

Her fingers tightened convulsively on the handle of her cup. It wobbled, and coffee slopped out onto her T-shirt. "I appreciate your concern," she snapped, dabbing at the stain with her napkin.

"I saw your tires," he commented. "You're lucky to be alive."

"My tires are none of your business," Annie said tightly. She tucked the extra saltines into her purse and slid out of the booth. She'd be lucky if she managed to pay for the gas to get her all the way to St. Honore, let alone buy new tires. "Thanks for sharing your opinion."

She shoved past him, and instantly realized that it was a mistake to have touched him, even slightly. Just brushing against his solid frame made her shiver with intimate awareness. He radiated warmth and power as he followed her stubbornly to the cash register.

"It's not an opinion, Annie," he persisted. "It's dangerous."

She ignored him. "A bowl of chili and coffee," she told the cashier.

He handed the cashier a twenty. "The lady's lunch is on me."

"No, it's not," she hissed. She tried to push down his proffered arm, but it was like swatting an oak branch. She held out her ten to the girl behind the register. The girl's pale blue eyes darted from one to the other of them, bewildered.

Jacob pushed down her arm, handed the girl his twenty. "I insist." His voice was gentle but implacable.

Annie fled the restaurant while the cashier was making change. The rain had stopped, and she splashed heedlessly through the puddles in the parking lot, obscurely panicked. He'd gone out in the rain to look for her, he was so glad she was OK, he'd fussed over her tires, he'd paid for her lunch, blah blah blah. The ploy was so transparent, but so damned seductive, it was embarrassing. Even though she didn't need any rescuing. Even though she knew exactly what he wanted from her in exchange. Men were so predictable.

What was unpredictable was her fluttering belly, her hot face, her scattered wits. She was raw, trembling, acutely aware of the quiet power that filled and defined the space around him, of the streamlined grace of his body and his thousand-watt grin. She cursed to herself as she fumbled for her keys. She had to rely on herself, and herself alone. She always had, ever since she was a kid. It was the one thing in her life that never changed, and she only came to grief when she let herself forget it. Fortunately, the world never let her forget it for very long.

Jacob's shadow blocked the window, knocking on the rain-spotted glass. She shoved the key into the ignition, hands shaking. He kept knocking, gentle but insistent. She rolled the window down a bare two inches, and he leaned close, taking everything in with one sweep of his keen dark eyes. She was suddenly embarrassed by her truck's dilapidated state. For her own limp, travel-worn appearance.

"Annie, listen." His voice had a hint of uncertainty for the first time. "If you really, truly want me to stop playing this game with you, I'll leave you be. Just say the word."

She wrenched her eyes away and stared out the windshield. *Tell him,* her sensible self urged. *He'll believe you if you say it now. You've got enough to worry about. Tell him to get lost.*

She looked up, opened her mouth to say it—and the challenge in his eyes robbed her of breath. She could read sensual invitation on his face as clearly as if he'd spoken aloud. It was a disorienting perception, as if the world had suddenly rent itself apart and revealed itself to be a dull, flat backdrop of painted canvas; and behind it, the glowing colors of the real horizon beckoned and allured.

Her heart seemed to stop for a long, breathless instant. She couldn't back down now. She was too intrigued. Besides, maybe she could teach him a thing or two, and wipe that smug, knowing look right off his gorgeous face. She'd never been able to resist a challenge in her life. It was one of her crowning defects.

Besides, all those miles of highway ahead would be such a dreary prospect without the Motorcycle Man's enlivening presence.

Oh, God. She was going to do it. She actually was. Her heart galloped madly in her chest as she turned the key in the ignition. She shot him a sidelong, provocative glance, let it melt into a tempting smile, and softened her voice to a husky contralto. "Figure it out for yourself, Jacob," she said, putting the truck in gear. She lurched forward, peeking into her rearview mirror.

A grin of delight had lit up his face like a torch, and she couldn't help smiling back, even though he was out of range and couldn't see her. She pulled out of the parking lot, beaming at the waterlogged landscape until her out-of-shape smile muscles ached in protest.

Annie had been so wound up all afternoon, she'd exhausted herself to calmness by the time she set up camp that evening. She made use of the campground shower, and then stood in front of the mirror for a long time, toothbrush in hand, studying her face. Trying to imagine how an outsider would see it. How Jacob might have seen it.

It was too pale. In the harsh, fluorescent light, her face

seemed tinged with blue. Her eyes were OK, big and gray, with a ring of indigo around the iris. Long lashes, dark at the root, gold at the tip. Thick dark eyebrows that needed some tweezing. Her lower lip was plumper than she would like. It gave her a sulky look, which she usually tried to offset by smiling a lot, though lately she hadn't had the energy. She looked tired. Washed out and wary. Not surprising, for a woman who was on the run from her wrecked life. It was depressing. She squeezed toothpaste onto the brush, telling herself to stop being foolish.

She was *not* hoping he would show up, she told herself as she fixed her dinner—freeze-dried chicken and rice soup—and opened a can of sliced peaches. Probably he'd lost interest. The gritty reality of Annie Simon, close up and personal, had popped the bubble of his road-sex fantasy. She didn't look like much of a prize in her jeans and shrunken T-shirt. Just a normal girl, with circles under her eyes, in need of a laundromat. She hadn't had either the time or the presence of mind to pack many clothes on that crazy morning when she'd seized her chance to finally get away from Philip. Just what she'd been able to shove into her backpack with trembling hands: some jeans, T-shirts, underwear. None of her nice, pretty stuff. And she hadn't worn makeup since the good old days back at Macy's, before Philip ruined that for her, too.

No, she'd seen the last of the sexy, mysterious Motorcycle Man. He was off in search of a perkier, livelier playmate. She visualized her much-loved and forever lost wardrobe with a sharp pang of regret. If she'd had her usual bag of tricks to work with, the story would have gone very differently. For Jacob she would definitely have opted for her scoop-neck pearl pink angora sweater, the cloud-soft kind that made men long to stroke it. She would have paired it with her wine-red silk wrap skirt, and her spike-heel lace-up boots. Beneath it all, her apricot stretch lace teddy, of course. A dab of cover-up under her eyes, a smidge of brown

liner and mascara, a slick of pink gloss on her lips. Her sexy
calla lily earrings, for luck. A dab of styling gel and a few
minutes with a blow dryer, and voilà, she could have made
him follow her to the ends of the earth. Men were so fickle.
But it was probably just as well. She fished out a peach slice
with a wistful sigh.

Suddenly the little hairs on the back of her neck prickled
to attention with a long, delicious shiver. She scanned the
forest around her, forcing herself not to leap to her feet.

"Hello, Annie," he said softly. He was a long, dense
shadow at the edge of the flickering light of her campfire.

She nodded politely. "Hello, Jacob." She managed to
sound cool, even though her heart was thudding. "I thought
I'd lost you."

His teeth flashed white in the gloom. "Not a chance."

She tugged her short T-shirt down over her belly, wishing
it didn't have a coffee stain. "Want some peaches?" She held
out the can.

He remained motionless, barely visible under the trees.
"No, thanks. I'm fine," he said politely. "I ate earlier."

She gave him a crooked, nervous little smile. "Why are
you lurking out there in the dark? Are you trying to freak me
out?"

"On the contrary, I'm trying not to. I won't come any
closer unless you invite me."

She laughed, surprised at his unexpected gallantry.
"You've been following me ever since Charlottesville. I didn't
invite you to do that."

"Philadelphia," he said simply.

Her jaw dropped. "Philadelphia?"

"You just didn't notice me until Charlottesville. Besides,
I couldn't help myself. Your beauty is an irresistible lure.
You're like one of those sirens in the old stories, enticing
love-struck mariners to their doom."

A terribly teenaged-sounding giggle burst out of her, and
the peach chunk slipped off her fork and plopped into the

syrup with a splash. "I've never lured anybody to his doom," she told him, dabbing at the splotch of syrup that had joined forces with the coffee stain on her shirt. "Still, it was a nice thing to say. Go ahead, Jacob, pull up a stump. Make yourself comfortable."

He glided silently closer, and she noticed that his hair was wet, combed smoothly back from his face. "Did you just take a shower?"

"Yeah, I washed up a bit," he said.

"Bet you thought you were going to get lucky, didn't you?"

He shrugged, and sank into a comfortable crouch across the fire from her. "A guy can hope."

She blushed, and stared fixedly into the fire.

"Your hair's wet, too," he observed in a soft voice.

"Yeah, well, don't flatter yourself," she snapped. "Some of us bathe for reasons other than intent to seduce." He laughed, unabashed, and her blush deepened. "Where did you first see me?" she demanded.

"At a restaurant off of I-95, right after Philadelphia," he told her.

"Philadelphia. That's wild," she murmured, trying vainly to subdue the foolish, flattered smile that kept taking control of her face.

"Yeah, I know," he agreed. "I was intrigued. A gorgeous, mysterious woman, traveling all alone, from who knows what to who knows where. I just got on my bike and followed you without thinking. Annie, the honey-blonde road siren. I'm hopelessly caught in your silken net. You've been dragging me in your wake across five states."

She covered her hot cheeks with her hands, loving the way his smile creased his lean face with sensual, deeply carved laugh lines. "I cannot believe I didn't notice you," she murmured.

He shrugged, studying her with intense curiosity. "You looked pretty distracted at the time," he said quietly.

"Yeah. I must have been." She had gone through Philadel-phia on the first dazed, delirious day of her journey. She wouldn't have noticed if an eighteen-wheeler had driven over her.

"Where are you headed, if you don't mind me asking?" he asked.

She hesitated. She hadn't told anyone about her destina-tion. She hadn't decided if it would be good luck or bad, but when she looked into his keen, dark eyes, she felt a surge of energy that could only be lucky. "I'm going to the Black Cat Casino in St. Honore, Louisiana," she said.

He looked thoughtful. "May I ask why?"

She put a possessive hand on the purse that sat beside her. "I have a stash of silver dollars. The last of the money I won there five years ago. That money helped me start a new life." Her voice shook, and faltered. "Now I need to start a new life all over again. I hope . . . that they'll help me a second time."

He prodded at the embers. "I wish you luck," he said in a careful, measured voice. "What's plan B?"

"None of your goddamn business," she flared, stung.

They were silent for a moment. "Don't be mad, Annie," he said gently. "Starting a new life is a hell of a lot to ask of a slot machine."

She snagged another peach chunk, but his calm words had robbed her of her appetite, and she let it plop back into the can with a dejected sigh. "There's no plan B." she admit-ted. "If it doesn't work out, I'll think of something when the time comes, like I always do."

"What are you running away from?"

Annie's jaw clenched. Thinking about Philip did not feel lucky. "I'd rather not talk about it," she said stiffly.

"Whatever."

There was a wealth of controlled curiosity behind the sin-gle quiet word. "I'm not on the run from the cops, or any-thing, if that's what you're wondering," she snapped.

"Relax, Annie," he soothed. "The thought never crossed my mind."

She shot him a derisive look. "How am I supposed to relax with you looking at me like that? You're a complete stranger, Jacob. All I know about you is that you want to have sex with me."

He watched her silently for a long moment, and she tugged her shirt down again, drawing his gaze to her belly. Under the weight of his eyes, that scant inch of exposed flesh seemed outrageously intimate. She covered it instinctively with her hand. His dark gaze dragged slowly up her body, lingering appreciatively at her breasts. She stared back, fascinated by the stark, elegant planes and angles of his face. The flames of the campfire flickered and danced hypnotically in his eyes.

"I want to be closer to you, Annie," he said softly. "Close enough so I can tell what kind of shampoo you used tonight. May I?"

Annie's lips trembled, and she clamped them together. The velvet-soft tone of his voice made her legs feel as if they wouldn't hold her if she stood, and an unfamiliar ache deep in her belly made her restless and anxious. His taut, muscular backside was beautifully showcased by his loose, crouching pose. She dragged her eyes away from it and pulled her mind back to his question. "Um, yes," she said, trying to sound casual. "And thank you for asking."

He rose to his feet with catlike grace, and walked slowly around the fire. He loomed over her for only a second or two, but the time dilated oddly as she stared at him from that odd perspective, her eyes skittering in nervous fascination up his long, muscular legs, over the bulge in front of his jeans, his flat belly and barrel chest. He sank down in front of her, studying her with grave concentration. He closed his eyes and took a deep breath, and a beatific smile spread across his face. "Lavender," he said softly. "Yum."

Annie's ears roared. His nearness affected her like the

deep, pervasive thundering of a huge waterfall, filling her senses and blotting out everything else. She stared, rapt, at the dramatic sweep of his black lashes, his sharp cheekbones, the seductive grooves that bracketed his lazy smile. "It's an aromatherapy shampoo," she explained in a small, breathless voice. "It's supposed to be, um, soothing."

He opened his eyes. "That's strange," he murmured in mock puzzlement. "I'm not soothed at all by the thought of steaming lavender-scented suds cascading over your pink, naked body. On the contrary."

An image of Jacob in the shower assailed her—that big, powerful body gleaming and naked, slippery with soap. Her head swam, and she swallowed hard and leaned forward, sniffing his damp hair. "Pert Plus, shampoo and conditioner in one," she guessed. "You're a no-nonsense sort of guy. Always on the move. No conditioning rinse, no styling gel, just wash, comb, and go. Right?"

His dark eyes held hers with quiet intensity. "That's true," he admitted. "I'm very high-energy. But I know how to slow down."

Annie clutched the can of peaches tightly to her chest with both hands, and looked down into the fire. "That's good," she said, almost inaudibly. "Going slow is very important."

They sat silently for a long moment. He put his big hand gently over hers, stilling its fine tremor. The whisper-soft contact sent a sweet, tingling flood of anticipation through every nerve in her body.

"I've changed my mind about the peaches," he said in a husky voice, tugging the can away from her. He speared a chunk, plucked it off the end of the fork and examined it, heedless of the syrup dripping voluptuously over his hand. He took a bite and closed his eyes for a long moment as he chewed and swallowed, then opened his eyes with a blissful smile. "Succulent," he commented softly. "Tender and soft and silky, dripping with sweet juices. Divine perfection in a can."

She stared, fascinated, as he slid the rest of the peach into his mouth with a growl of pleasure. "I've never looked at canned peaches in quite that way," she admitted.

He laughed softly. "You've got to look at things in just the right light before they'll give up their secrets." He snagged another piece between his thumb and forefinger, and admired it from all sides. "Under the enchantment of sweet Annie, these peaches are the manna of the gods. Come closer, Annie. Let me show you."

She gazed at him, flustered and nervous but irresistibly tempted by the burning invitation in his eyes. She leaned forward and opened her mouth to take a bite of the fruit. His other hand gently seized her shoulder, holding her still.

"Wait," he said in a low, admonishing voice. He leaned closer, surrounding her with his scent: shampoo and soap, crisp denim, damp leather. "First you have to concentrate. Yield to the enchantment. Let it lead you. There's no hurry."

Annie blinked, and gazed at the chunk of peach. She stared at his long fingers, wet and gleaming with sticky syrup, and she squirmed restlessly, her breath jerking in and out of her lungs. "OK, I'm concentrating," she said testily. "Now what?"

"Look at how beautiful it is," he suggested in a whisper, his warm fragrant breath tickling her ear. "How golden, and full of light. How juicy and plump. It's ready to give itself to you, to be absorbed into your body, to become part of you forever. Let your mouth get ready. Salivate. Savor the moment. Wallow in the sweet agony of anticipation."

The peach slid out of focus and became a shining golden glow in the foreground. His lean, dark face shifted into focus behind it, his eyes fixed intently on hers. "OK, I think I'm there," she told him, her voice low and shaky. "I'm pretty sure that I've, ah, yielded to the enchantment of the peach."

His teeth flashed in a swift, brilliant smile. "Good," he murmured. "Now open your mouth and close your eyes."

She closed her eyes and opened her mouth obediently, making a tiny gasping noise as the intensely sweet wedge of syrupy fruit nudged itself between her lips. She took a bite.

He was right. It was delicious, but she wasn't the one who had cast the spell that made it so. That was all Jacob's doing. The sweetness of the fruit shimmered on her tongue like trapped sunshine, and her body was hot, pulsing, dazzled. She opened her eyes, her defenses swept away, and stared into the endless depths of his black eyes.

Jacob's wild, potent magic tugged at her, opening up wild, verdant places deep inside her mind; places she'd never shared with anyone. A fey, fearless part of her took over, and she leaned forward, taking his wrist in her hand. She drew it toward her lips and took the last morsel of peach gently into her mouth, licking the peach syrup off his thumb and fore-finger with delicate little flicks of her tongue. She drew his fingertip into her mouth and swirled her tongue around it.

His eyes dilated, and his breath shuddered through his chest, harsh and audible. His face was suddenly tense, al-most grim, the teasing gleam in his eyes gone and the depth of his hunger unmasked.

Annie let go of his hand and shrank back, startled at her own boldness. Jacob looked down at his fingers as if they were not his own. "Does this mean that I can stay with you tonight?" he asked hoarsely.

A final spasm of doubt clutched her, warring with the ache of longing that he'd awakened, and making her uncer-tain if she could really live up to her silent promise of unbri-dled sensuality. And it was insane to make herself so vulnerable, all alone in the dark as she was. But if he'd wanted to hurt her or force her, he could have done so ten times over by now. And she'd been alone in the dark for a long time now, if she counted these last, bad months with Philip. What harm could there be in a lighthearted tryst?

"I've never fallen into bed with a stranger before," she whispered.

Jacob picked up a stick and stirred the coals with it, biding his time. "We're not strangers. I've been courting you for days."

She opened her mouth, and was utterly surprised when the simple, naked truth popped out. "I'm running away from my ex-boyfriend," she blurted. "I'm wrecked, Jacob. You're a really cute guy, and it's nothing personal, but I just got out of a bad situation, and chances are I'd disappoint you anyway."

He gave her a thoughtful frown. "I doubt that very much. Besides, just because your ex-boyfriend is a jerk, is that any reason to deny yourself great sex with a guy who asks nothing more of you but to worship at the shrine of your incredible beauty?"

That cracked her up. She forced herself to choke the giggles down when they threatened to melt into tears. "Mr. Modesty. What makes you so sure it would be great sex?"

A soft, amused smile crinkled up the lines around his eyes. "Listen to your heart, Annie."

The gentle words moved her. Something softened and shifted deep inside her chest, fanning slowly open like a crimson flower.

The fire crackled and popped, the coals glowed with shifting shades of red, like pulsing hearts. Jacob pushed back a lock of hair that was clinging to her cheek. "Let me please you tonight, Annie."

She gave a quick, jerky nod.

"Is that a yes?" His voice was satiny soft. "Let me hear you say it, so I can be sure."

A delicious shiver racked her, though she was far from cold. "Yes," she whispered.

Chapter Two

Jacob stirred the embers with his stick, shooting for an air of idle nonchalance, but the huge, goofy smile spreading across his face probably ruined the effect. The stick smoldered red-hot at the tip—not unlike the current state of his cock. Just in case there was a God, he sent up a prayer begging for enough self-control to not screw this up.

Annie folded her legs up against her chest and hugged them. "So?" she asked belligerently. "What are you going to do now?"

He studied the rigid set of her spine, the tremor in her hands. She was scared to death. The realization sent a rush of tenderness through him. "Nothing sudden," he said gently. "Nothing scary. Nothing rough."

She twisted her hands together. "Would you, um, like a toasted marshmallow?" Her voice was shaking.

Food was the last thing on his mind, but he smiled gently into her wide, anxious eyes. "Sure."

Annie leaped up and rummaged through a cardboard box on the picnic table, her brisk activity confirming the fact that she was not wearing a bra. Her high breasts jiggled and bounced, and his groin throbbed almost painfully at the thought of touching them, suckling them. He carved points onto the ends of two green sticks with his penknife and handed them to her as she settled down onto the ground again, a full two feet away from him. He grinned wickedly and sidled closer. Grinned and sidled again, and again, until she was giggling like a little girl at his foolishness.

She jabbed a marshmallow with a stick and handed it to him. "There you go. Enjoy my lavish hospitality."

He murmured his thanks, scooting the last few inches until his leg was touching hers. She didn't move away this time. She shot him a shy, sidelong look as they held their marshmallows over the coals.

"So, Jacob," she said with a businesslike air. "Where are you from?"

He turned his marshmallow, admiring the puffy golden underside. "Atlanta," he replied.

"And what brings you here?"

"You," he said simply.

"Oh, come on."

"It's true," he insisted. "I have no idea where I am. I've just been blindly following you. Like a lemming."

"Don't you have a life back in Atlanta?" she demanded. "What kind of person can just up and follow a stranger to hell and gone?"

He hesitated. The tedious tale of finally breaking off his tepid long-distance affair with Bridget, his decision to take a month's leave of absence from his architecture firm, none of it belonged in this magic circle of firelight. It was so worka-day, so rational, so boring. Looking into Annie's fey, smoky eyes, he was outside the confines of normal life, in a fantasy world where anything could happen. He thought of making up a new past for himself, but that didn't feel right either. He was abruptly excused from replying by grace of the fact that Annie's marshmallow burst into flames. She blew it out and pried the blackened marshmallow off the stick with a sigh.

"They're good that way," he said in a comforting tone. "I used to set them on fire on purpose when I was a kid."

"I like them toasty and golden, not charred," she confessed.

"Take mine," he said, offering it to her gallantly.

She looked at the perfectly browned marshmallow on the end of his stick, and smiled like a naughty little girl as she took it. She bit into it, and foaming white goo poured out like sweet lava. The sight of her little pink tongue eagerly lapping at it made his whole body tighten with excitement. He stuck the blackened marshmallow into his mouth and chewed it without tasting it.

The marshmallows were a stroke of luck, though, because the glistening, sugary strand clinging to her enticingly plump lower lip gave him just the hook he needed to get things started. He leaned over and delicately licked it off, drinking in her little gasp of surprise. His stick fell into the fire as he wound his hand into her damp, silky hair. Her trembling lips opened and he slid his tongue inside. She was delicious; a fresh, unique flavor, with sweet overtones of peaches and burnt sugar. Sexual hunger slammed through him, threatening his self-control. Every luscious detail of her got to him, tossing him off balance, and he needed balance. Something told him that the first time with the skittish, beautiful Annie needed to be just right. And he was shaking with raw lust, in no condition to give a peak sexual performance.

Annie's big gray eyes were wide with wonder. "You're as good at kissing as you are at sweet talk," she said, touching her flushed lower lip delicately with her fingertip. "It gives you an unfair advantage."

"The advantage, sweet Annie, is all yours," he said, kissing her nose. "The kisses, the sweet talk, it's all for your pleasure and delight."

She giggled, delighted. "Oh, you think you're so slick."

He took advantage of the lightness of the moment to grab her waist and lift her smoothly onto his lap. "Aren't I?"

She wiggled away from him, startled, but he held on tight, making gentle shushing sounds. "Relax," he soothed. "I just want to hold you."

She stopped struggling, though a tremor of nervous laughter shook her. "Yeah, right," she murmured. "I've heard that one before."

"I just bet you have," he said, nuzzling her neck. "You're so pretty, Annie. It's been driving me crazy. Eight hundred miles of pure torture."

She gave him a small, shy smile. "Oh, give me a break."

She was so soft, shifting her light, whispery weight back and forth across his instantaneous hard-on. A little too thin, he thought, running his hand over her back. She needed feeding up. Steak and potatoes, eggs and grits. He would see to it at the first opportunity.

He embraced her slender shoulders and pressed little, nuzzling kisses onto the velvety skin that emerged like a lily from the frayed neckline of her T-shirt. He wanted to taste every inch of that rose-tinted softness, the tender spot behind her ears, under her jaw, the shadowy hollow at the base of her throat, everything. She returned his kiss with a timid eagerness, and he drank in her sweetness, forcing himself to disregard the clawing need in his lower body. The trusting way she opened to him was inflaming him to a dangerous pitch. He slowed down, breathed deep. He wanted to give her a timeless, forever sort of kiss, slow and lazy. A kiss that coiled and uncoiled endlessly in the firelight's writhing shadows, no memory of when it began, no desire for it to ever end.

He rearranged Annie's quivering legs until she straddled him, her soft mound pressed against the hard bulge at the front of his crotch. He cupped her breasts with a sigh of pleasure. They were so soft and full, the hard little nipples tickling his palms. Her hands flew up and clutched at his, and he seized one of them and brought it to his lips, covering her knuckles with hot, ardent kisses. Her faded denim jacket smelled sharply of wood smoke in contrast to the perfumed sweetness of her hair. He wanted her naked so badly it frightened him.

A look of awe and discovery dawned in her heavy-lidded eyes as he gripped her hips and pressed his aching arousal against her. He urged her silently, with his hands, with his mouth, to yield to his pulsing rhythm. They floated together, his senses wide open, in a dreamy, timeless state in which he knew instinctively just how hard he had to press himself against her as his tongue plunged into her mouth, knew just how he needed to trace little designs on the palms of his hands with her nipples. He knew exactly what was necessary to prepare her, slowly and skillfully, for the demands he would make of her later, in her tent. When she was naked and completely open to him.

For now, there was no hurry, he reminded himself, biting back a groan. He'd promised. Admittedly, in the dreamy, half-drugged state he was in, he couldn't remember exactly what it was that he had promised, but ripping off her clothes and falling on her was not in the plan. He cupped her luscious ass lovingly in his hands, seconding the desperate little jerking movements she made. She was rubbing herself against him now, her breathing rapid, almost panicked. Suddenly she stiffened, arching her back like a bow stretched taut, and shuddered violently.

He caught her, keeping her from falling backward, and gathered her close. He cuddled her as she lolled against his chest, and greedily absorbed the delicate little aftershocks of her orgasm into his own body. "I think it's time to take this into the tent," he suggested gently.

Her eyes were languid and luminous. "I'm not sure if I can walk."

"I'll carry you." He shifted her off his lap and got up,

sweeping her easily into his arms. She looped her arm around his neck in a trusting gesture that made his heart turn over painfully. She was so soft and vulnerable. It made him feel fiercely protective; a primitive feeling that he deliberately did not allow himself to examine. Tonight was no time for psychological self-analysis. Tonight was all about Annie. Just Annie.

He set her down, allowing himself a fleeting moment of self-satisfaction for making her come before he even got her clothes off. Good work, that. Hadn't even stuck his hand under her shirt, though the effort might have taken years off his life.

Enough self-congratulation, he told himself. He crouched in front of her tent and unzipped it. He was still acutely aroused, and the night was young; there was plenty that could go wrong. But damned if he wasn't going to make her glad she'd let him stay. He would repay her trust many times over before the night was done.

Annie steadied herself against Jacob's solid shoulder. He gave her a reassuring grin and began to untie her shoes. She stared mutely at his bent head as he lifted her leg, prying off one of her battered high-tops. He cradled her bare, chilly foot in his warm hands and dropped a kiss on her instep, then set to work on the other shoe. He laid them under the rain canopy and held open the tent flap. "In you go," he said.

She crawled into the tent and sat cross-legged on her sleeping bag as Jacob unlaced his boots. He crawled into the tent and zipped the flap shut. He was huge in the tiny space, dominating it completely. Already his warmth was heating up the tent's chilly interior. And this powerful, completely unknown man was going to be on top of her. All over her. Inside of her. She hugged herself, shivering with delicious terror. She felt like a bird about to fling itself into the heart of a storm, a maelstrom of stabbing lightning and lashing rain.

She suppressed a twinge of panic. He'd been nothing but gentle with her so far. He'd made her laugh and relax. And come, oh, God, like she'd never come before.

She gathered her nerve and reached out in the dark. Her hand encountered his chest and she explored the dips and ridges of his thick muscles. His breath quickened as she brushed her fingers across his nipples. As a rule, she didn't get overwhelmed easily, but Jacob's sheer physical presence robbed her of words, leaving her shy and tongue-tied. Usually she was chock-full of smart-mouthed remarks, a trait that had gotten her into trouble all her life. Her favorite foster mother back in Payton had dubbed her "Scrappy." Philip's preferred endearment, toward the end, had been "you mouthy little bitch."

She shoved the memory away. *Don't think about Philip,* she reminded herself. *Don't let him ruin this for you, too.*

Jacob was feeling around, patting the floor of the tent. There was only a tarp, the nylon floor of the tent and a lightweight sleeping bag between them and the cold, hard ground. "Spartan," he commented.

"Sorry," she apologized hastily. "I know, it's awful. I had to leave in such a rush, and all I thought to grab was the sleeping bag. I've been regretting it every night."

"It's OK, Annie," he said, a hint of laughter in his voice. "You'll just have to be on top, that's all."

"I will?" She shifted restlessly at the thought of Jacob's strong body beneath her, bearing her up, warming her inside and out.

He skimmed his hands gently over her back and settled them at her waist, spanning it easily with his fingers. "Yeah," he murmured. "I must outweigh you by ninety pounds, if not more."

He pulled her onto his lap, and the contact of his hot body sent a shock of intense, melting pleasure through her. She snuggled against his chest, and part of her would have been eternally content to just stay there, listening to his deep, strong heartbeat. Another part of her was acutely aware of the bulge in his jeans that pressed insistently against her rear end, and the soft, yearning ache between her own thighs that answered it. She fought down the fluttery nervousness once again. Don't be a baby, don't be a tease, she told herself sternly. You invited the man into your tent, you've gotten him all hot and bothered, and besides, he seems like a really good guy. So get on with it, already.

She took a deep breath and shrugged out of her denim jacket. Her eyes had adjusted completely to the dim light that filtered into the tent, and she could see the hunger on his face as she peeled off her T-shirt. She tucked it into the corner and faced him, naked to the waist, her breasts sticking out in their usual perky, in-your-face sort of way. There. That had to be clear enough, she told herself. She'd bared her boobs. Now it was his move.

Jacob gave a rough sigh, and his big, hot hands circled her bare waist. Sweet, ticklish energy rippled along the surface of her skin as his hands slid up and cupped her breasts, exploring them with reverent tenderness. They felt oddly swollen, plump and acutely sensitive in his hands. He bent his dark head over her chest, and his hot, wet mouth dragged gently across her skin. Her chest heaved and she clutched him, astonished at the melting ripples of delicious sensation he pulled from her. He caught her nipple gently in his teeth, his tongue swirling with tender skill, and then pushed her onto her back and arched over her, his mouth waking up millions of beautiful nerve endings that had been sleeping all her life.

Jacob pushed her breasts tenderly together with his hands and buried his face in them, licking and suckling both in turn until she was a swirling vortex of sensation, out of control, arching and offering herself to him helplessly. Pleasure was shaking her apart, making her whimper and writhe. At some point, he had unbuttoned her jeans and insinuated his hand inside them, and she hadn't even noticed him doing it. He stroked her through her panties and found her damp and quivering. His finger circled her clitoris through the thin cotton cloth with delicate restraint, then slipped inside her panties.

He pushed his finger into her hot cleft and murmured softly in triumph to find her melting and soft, more than ready for anything he wanted from her. She couldn't stop the whimpering sounds she made as he coaxed her further open. She dug her fingers into his shoulders and spread her legs for him without protest.

"Let me taste you, Annie." His voice was raw with excitement.

Her body went rigid. "Jacob, I don't know how to say this, but . . ."

"But what?"

"But I can't do . . . that. It doesn't work for me," she confessed miserably. "It hurts too much."

"You mean oral sex?" His voice was incredulous.

"Yeah, I know it's really weird. It sounds so great in theory, but in practice . . ." Her voice trailed off as she tried to push away the memory of Philip and his hard, stabbing tongue. He always got so angry when she asked him to be gentle. Finally she'd learned to pretend to enjoy it, hoping he would get bored quickly. Which, praise God, he usually had.

"Your ex-boyfriend, did he—" Jacob cut himself off abruptly and shook his head. "It shouldn't hurt, Annie," he said gently.

She swallowed a sob. "I told you I'd probably disappoint you."

"Hush," he said, his voice low and angry. "Don't ever say that again." He leaned down and kissed her fiercely. "Do you trust me?"

She looked up into the shadowy pools of his eyes, and once again, the naked truth just popped right out. "Yes," she said wonderingly. God help her. She actually did.

"Then let me. Let me just try, and if it hurts even a tiny

bit, tell me and I'll stop instantly." Jacob's voice was low and coaxing.

Annie ran her hands appreciatively over the ridges and curves of his shoulders. "It's not like you have to do any more foreplay," she said timidly. "The peaches alone did the trick. The rest is just gravy."

He gently tugged her jeans and panties down. "Oh, Annie. That was only the overture," he said softly. "Lie back. Trust me."

"All right," she whispered, letting him push her down onto the sleeping bag. Jacob quickly stripped off his own clothes and positioned himself over her, a great solid mass of naked heat. She squeezed her eyes shut, bracing herself instinctively.

She was surprised to feel only a tender kiss, nudging her mouth open. He covered her with his body, not crushing her, but only keeping her exquisitely warm and sheltered. He coaxed her legs open, and his long finger penetrated her delicately, dipping into the sultry moisture pooled inside her hot, sensitive sheath. He spread it extravagantly around until her entire vulva was slick and soft, and gave her a soft, reassuring kiss before sliding down her body and settling himself between her trembling thighs. He nuzzled her navel, covering her abdomen with slow, dragging kisses that made her shiver and moan. He licked her thighs, her hipbones, sliding his tongue tenderly into all the valleys and curves of her hips. His hand brushed teasingly over her pubic hair, barely touching it, concentrating his attention on everything but the hot, aching core of sensation between her legs.

He caressed her slowly, tirelessly, with lazy, maddening thoroughness, until she was moving restlessly beneath his hands and mouth, ticklish and hot and frustrated. She began to burn for his touch to focus between her thighs. She lifted her hips, opening to him in silent, mindless pleading. He laughed softly, delighted, and then she felt the whisper of his warm breath on her inner thighs.

He put his mouth to her, hungry and passionate and incredibly gentle, sliding his tongue tenderly along the wet folds of her sex. She went wild, pushing herself against him, wantonly aroused by the sweet, melting sensations, the soft, lapping sound of his tongue. This was nothing like Philip. The unpleasant memory of her ex vanished and she lost herself in dazzled pleasure. And Jacob didn't get bored. He was insatiable; he seemed to want nothing more than to build her tension higher and push her up toward the crest. She sensed his fierce satisfaction as the wave crashed violently over her, pounding her under.

She floated back, boneless and utterly relaxed, and lay against his sheltering warmth for many long minutes. Slowly she became aware of Jacob's growing erection pressed against her belly. He didn't say a word, just stroked her shoulder and nuzzled her hair, but she could feel the rigidly contained hunger radiating from his body. She reached down timidly, and grasped his penis.

His arms tightened around her, her hand tightened around him, and he cried out in a low voice. "Gently," he murmured.

"Sorry, sorry," she said quickly. She petted him and then let her hand slide down the rock-hard length of it. Her hand curled around the hot flesh eagerly, testing his arousal, and she rolled up onto her elbow to inspect him better. "Do you want me to, um, return the favor?" she offered.

He propped his head up onto his arm. "Hmm?"

"You know. To go down on you," she explained bashfully.

He considered it, and then shook his head. "No."

She was utterly taken aback. "No?"

"I said I was going to worship at the altar of your beauty, and I meant what I said," he said. "This night is all about you, Annie."

She stared at him, suspicious. "Jacob, that's not normal."

"Probably not," he said with a short laugh. "The embarrassing truth is, I'm so turned on right now that if you so much as look at my cock cross-eyed, I'll explode all over you."

She started to giggle. "Cross-eyed?"

"For God's sake, leave a guy a shred of dignity," he muttered.

She reached down eagerly, and smoothed the silky drop of fluid on the tip of his penis around the swollen head, loving his harsh gasp of pleasure. "So do you want to make love, then?" she asked timidly.

"Oh, God, yes," he said raggedly, trembling under her hands.

She was moved, realizing how much effort he was expending to hold back and wait for her. She wrapped her arms around him and gave him a fierce hug. "I'm ready," she urged. "I want you, Jacob."

He rummaged through his jeans until he found a condom, and rolled it on swiftly. He lay down on his back, urging her up on top of him with barely controlled impatience. She reached down to caress his thick, rock-hard shaft with a pang of doubt. She hadn't had all that many lovers, and never a man of these dimensions. But there was no time to get nervous about it, because he was spreading her legs, guiding himself until he was lodged just inside her, caressing the moist lips of her vulva. He rubbed the tip of his penis against her cleft, and began to gently slide himself up and down the length of her hot, slick furrow in a slow, voluptuous rhythm. A shudder of startled pleasure unbalanced her, and she braced her hands against his chest.

"Do you like that?" he asked huskily.

"Oh, yes," she whispered.

He caressed her, teasing her with his hands, and her old self watched with mingled wonder and dismay as the new Annie undulated over him like some sort of wanton sex kitten. She closed her eyes and let him nudge her tenderly into another series of soft, shivering orgasms, linked like beads on a string into a glittering blur of pleasure, long and protracted and achingly sweet.

Finally, he gripped her hips tightly. "Now, Annie," he said, his voice pleading. "I can't wait anymore."

"Of course," she said soothingly. He prodded her, positioning himself, and began to push inside her, slowly and relentlessly. She gasped as the delicate muscles inside her resisted the blunt invasion.

He slowed down. "Relax, Annie," he said shakily.

She tried to relax, but he was so big and unyielding. Not even her first time had she felt so vulnerable. Jacob stopped, having shoved about half of his thick length into her. His grim silence and the steely tension vibrating in his arms attested to the effort he was expending to hold still. Enough, she thought. He'd given so much to her. She had to at least try to give this one thing to him.

She breathed deeply, concentrating on relaxing and yielding, and then tried to move, sliding up and down a tiny bit. She was surprised she could move at all, but Jacob's tender ministrations had made her incredibly slick and soft. Excitement rushed through her as the intense sensation began to slip into focus. She moved again, more boldly this time, clinging to him with every little muscle inside herself, and what had been a blunt, uncomfortable intrusion shifted seamlessly and became a stretched, sensual, utterly fulfilled feeling. She pushed herself down upon his heavy shaft with a shuddering sigh, hungry for more of him. He let out a hoarse cry, and that was it. She loved it. She was drunk on her power over him, she wanted to make him gasp and groan and shout. She slid all the way up the solid length of him, bathing him in her slick, sultry juices, and sank down again at the same moment that he gripped her hips and drove himself upward.

The incredibly deep penetration shocked a low cry out of her throat, and Jacob stopped. "Did I hurt you?" he asked urgently.

"No, no," she assured him, clutching his arms with trembling fingers. "Please, Jacob. Please, move, give me . . . let me feel it."

"Oh, yes," he muttered. His grip tightened, and he drew

himself out with lingering slowness, savoring the clinging caress of her secret flesh. He surged in again.

Annie's nails dug into the powerful muscles of his shoulders, each heavy thrust jerking a sob of terrified pleasure from her throat. She had never dreamed there was so much sensation deep within herself. The mouth of her womb pulsed with energy, every cell of her awake and luminous. She abandoned herself to the driving hunger of the powerful man beneath her, riding him higher and higher until agonizing pleasure jolted through her in rhythmic, shuddering waves. She collapsed on his chest, her hair flung across their faces. Jacob held her tightly, his hips jerking violently against her as he spent himself.

They lay there, wordless and trembling. Annie brushed her hair out of his face, wound it back behind her neck and kissed him, trying to silently convey her appreciation for his generosity. Jacob thrust his tongue into her mouth, and his penis swelled eagerly to fullness inside her. She wriggled voluptuously, savoring the sensation of his thick shaft embedded within her. A girl could get spoiled with one of those to play with every night. "Aren't you tired?" she asked, laughing softly.

"I've had this erection since Philadelphia," he said lazily. "It's going to take more than one orgasm to tire me out. But I challenge you to try." He dragged her possessively closer, his hips pulsing against her as his tongue greedily explored her mouth.

"I've never been able to resist a challenge in my life," she told him, her breath catching with excitement.

His laughter vibrated through them both, and she sighed and arched herself wider open to him as he slid his big, hard penis slowly in and out of her yielding body, loving the delicious fullness.

"The night's still young, sweet Annie," he said. "Go for it."

Chapter Three

His first thought when he woke was that the floor of the tent was unbelievably cold and hard. The second, as he opened his eyes, was that the sleeping bag had a threadbare flannel lining upon which could still be seen the dim figures of Santa Claus and his team of reindeer. And the third, which quickly became by far the most important, was the fact that the soft, naked woman in his arms was sneakily trying to slither out of the sleeping bag.

"Good morning, Annie," he said.

She twisted around, her eyes wide and frightened. His gaze dropped to her chest, which she unsuccessfully tried to cover with one arm while groping for her T-shirt. Her body was spectacular by daylight, what little, wiggling bits of her he could glimpse. Deep pink nipples poked impertinently over her arm, and his usual morning erection began to throb painfully. Down, boy, he told himself. After last night's marathon, Annie was going to think he was a sex maniac.

Which, come to think of it, was exactly how he felt.

"Hi," she said, in a strangled voice.

He tried to think of a way to make her smile, but his sleep

and sex-fogged brain wasn't up to the task at that hour. He plucked at a flannel reindeer, presumably Rudolph, though his outsized bulb of a nose had faded to a pale pink. "Seasonal sleeping bag?"

"It's mine from when I was a kid," she said. "I didn't want to take any stuff that Philip and I—" She stopped, swallowing visibly.

"Is that the asshole's name?" he murmured.

She pulled the T-shirt over her head, affording him a maddeningly brief glimpse of her stunning breasts. They jiggled as she tugged the shirt down over herself. He wanted to throw himself at her feet and beg like a dog for just one more peek. Dignity, he reminded himself. Dignity was key.

Her face emerged from the shirt, eyes narrowed. "Look, Jacob, I don't want to be rude, but I'd appreciate it if you'd get yourself together so I can fold my tent."

He watched calmly as she struggled into her panties and jeans. Her pale face was slowly turning a rosy pink. He grabbed his clothes, admiring her round, enticing ass as she scrambled out of the tent, and followed her out, stark naked. He stretched luxuriously and scratched his chest. Let her take a good long look at him and face reality.

She turned around, and squeaked in alarm. "Holy God, put that thing away!" she hissed.

He gave her a lazy grin and popped his shoulder blades. "You liked it well enough last night, sweetheart."

Just then, a portly matron in a pink jogging suit trotted down the path on her way to the bathroom. She looked over at them, gave a horrified squawk, and bolted back the way she came.

Annie's face was deep crimson. "You're going to get me arrested!"

Jacob gave her a "little ol me?" shrug, and looked down at his hugely erect cock as if noticing it for the first time. "Gee whiz, would you look at that. It's a tribute to your beauty, Annie."

"Put your pants on," Annie said furiously. "And don't you dare try to pull that Mr. Slick routine. That might work at night by the campfire, but not by the cold light of day."

Jacob grimaced as he folded his hard-on to the side and zipped his jeans over it. Ouch. "What would work, Annie?" he asked plaintively.

She lit up her camp stove, ignoring his question. "Would you like some instant oatmeal?" she asked in a brisk, let's-move-on sort of voice. "I've got maple sugar, country peach spice and regular."

He snorted. "After last night? Like hell. Let's get some real food."

Her back stiffened visibly. "I'm thrifty," she snapped.

"And I'm buying," he countered. "Let's go to that pancake place back on the highway. We'll get ham and eggs and grits. Orange juice and coffee and a big, buttery stack of pancakes. What do you say?"

She shot him an uncertain glance over her shoulder, looking tempted. Then her mouth tightened. "I'll stick to my oatmeal," she said stiffly. "I don't need any man to buy me breakfast."

He grabbed her shoulder, turning her to face him. "Hey, Annie. Hello. I'm not just 'any man.' I'm Jacob. Remember me? We met last night. Naked. In your tent. For hours. Does that ring a fucking bell?"

His voice came out harsher than he'd intended. She flinched away. "I'm sorry," she whispered. "This just . . . isn't what I expected."

He yanked on his sweatshirt. "What the hell were you expecting?"

"I don't know. I didn't even think about the next day. I thought that a one night stand was a . . . a no strings sort of thing."

He squinted. "Strings? What strings?"

She shook her head helplessly.

Comprehension dawned, and outrage followed swiftly in its wake. "You mean, you weren't expecting to have to deal with me in the morning? You thought I would just fuck you and then disappear?"

She looked miserably confused. "I don't know. I didn't think."

He shook his head, incredulous. "I've been chasing you for eight hundred miles. You think I've scratched my itch, and now I'm done?"

"But I thought that's how anonymous trysts with strange men were supposed to go!" she wailed. "According to the script you should've been gone before I even woke up. Just a . . . a bittersweet memory, like Zorro or something. Maybe a rose on my pillow, at most."

Jacob rubbed his aching lower back with a grimace. "You don't have any pillows, Annie," he muttered.

She looked so distressed that he decided it was time to try to make her smile. "Let's have a whole bunch of anonymous trysts, and let them run together into one long, indefinite tryst. What do you say?"

Annie's luscious lower lip trembled. "I just can't take this right now," she whispered. "I can't handle you, too, on top of everything."

Jacob stifled a sigh. Nice going, bonehead, he thought. He was just a barrel of laughs this morning. "Don't look at me like that, Annie," he said wearily. "I swear to God, I'm completely harmless."

That provoked a soggy little chuckle. "Hah. I can think of lots of words to describe you, Jacob, but 'harmless' is not one of them."

"And just exactly what have I harmed so far?" he demanded.

She stuck out her chin. "You're harmful to my peace of mind."

He made a disgusted sound as he shrugged into his jacket. "You didn't strike me as all that peaceful before."

* * *

He had a point, Annie conceded silently, but she would rather die than admit it to him. He leaned quietly against his bike, watching her as she bustled around dismantling her campsite. Not offering to help, which was fine with her, because she didn't need any help. None, zip, nada. Not from him, not from anybody. It was time to take charge.

But it was hard to feel in charge with Jacob's dark eyes following her around. God, he was gorgeous. This morning was the first good look she'd gotten of him naked. The lean, harmonious grace of his muscular body was heart-stopping. She started blushing again just thinking of the formidable erection he had just displayed to her. Incredible to think that all of that had been inside of her, over and over, all night long. A rush of liquid heat made her catch her breath and press her thighs together. She was even regretting the fact that she hadn't given him a blow job, which was odd because it had never been her specialty. But she actually wanted to take Jacob in her mouth, to run her tongue around the swollen crimson head of his penis. To rub her hands up and down that rigid shaft, make him groan and dig his fingers into her hair.

God, what was wrong with her? One minute she was giving herself a bracing pep talk, the next, she was staring into space, dreaming of Jacob's thick penis sliding in and out of her mouth. The man had her under a spell. She peeked at him. He was smiling, and the bulge in his jeans proved that he knew exactly what she was thinking. She had to get out of here, quick, before she started to beg him for it.

She packed her stuff haphazardly into Mildred, and turned back to him, digging her keys out of her pocket. What did people say in these situations? She hadn't a clue. She shook her head helplessly.

Jacob gave her a crooked little smile. "See you around, Annie."

"See you," she muttered, leaping into the pickup. She didn't let herself look back.

The ache started right about when she pulled onto the highway. It was nagging and painful, like a bad toothache, but in her belly. How rude, to just leave like that. She could have said something nicer, after that incredible night. Something sweeter. At least something polite.

She looked for him on the road all day. A couple of times she thought she saw a faraway motorcycle, but she couldn't be sure. She didn't stop for lunch, or to hike, just at a couple of rest stops to pee and stare blankly at the bare trees. She tried eating some saltines, but they wouldn't go into the cast-iron knot of her stomach.

She couldn't blame him for vanishing. In his place, she would have done the same, but now she would never have the chance to tell him how special and healing that night had been to her. All day she composed little speeches of all the things she wished she'd said to him. To hell with her pride. He was a really nice guy, and he deserved to know the truth—that he was sweet, and sexy, and fabulous in bed, and that he'd made her feel better than she'd ever felt in her life.

She found a campground at sunset, and set up her tent. Don't think about him any more, she told herself. Go about your business. Tarp, tent, pegs, poles. Rain canopy, sleeping bag, toiletries bag, camp stove. She rummaged through her supplies with a sigh. She didn't want the Middle Eastern Couscous Cup or Tia Rita's Black Bean Surprise. And she really, really didn't want any more of those goddamn canned peaches. Thank God the day was finished. Almost time to roll herself into a Santa cocoon and forget who she was in the oblivion of sleep.

"Hi, Annie," came a voice from the shadows behind her.

She whirled around. "Jacob?" She was so happy to see him that her heart swelled like a balloon. She smiled at him foolishly.

He stepped out of the shadows and placed the paper bag he was carrying on the picnic table.

"What have you got there?" she asked.

He looked wary. "Dinner," he said belligerently.

"Dinner?" Annie approached the table and sniffed. Mouthwatering smells were coming out of the bag. She pulled out a foam container and popped it open. Barbecued chicken. Oh, God. Her stomach yawned open joyfully.

"Yeah. So?" he said defensively. "Go ahead, Annie. Let me have it. Get it over with. Tell me what an asshole I am for buying you dinner."

Annie forced herself not to laugh at his martyred face. "Thank you," she said quietly. "It looks delicious. Let's eat before it gets cold."

He blinked, and visibly relaxed. "Really?"

"Really." She threw herself at him and hugged him hard. His strong arms circled her, and she hid her face against his chest, willing herself not to start bawling; she would just embarrass the poor guy.

She stepped back, giving him a shaky smile. Jacob grinned back, smoothing over the awkward moment by giving her a gentle kiss on her nose. "Let's eat, then," he suggested. "You hungry?"

"You have no idea," she said fervently.

They feasted on Jacob's bounty. Barbecued chicken, mashed potatoes with gravy, twice-baked cheese grits, collard greens and coleslaw and cornbread, and the crowning touch: two huge pieces of pie, chocolate pecan and pumpkin chiffon, swimming in whipped cream. It was so delicious it almost reduced her to tears again.

They finished the pie, and the process of licking various sticky bits of chocolate and pumpkin from each others' fingers segued into a sweet, clinging kiss. Jacob lifted his head reluctantly, dropping soft kisses on her upturned face like a sweet, hot rain. "Annie," he said in a soft, pleading voice. "I know I'm pushing my luck, but there's a really nice bed and breakfast in town. Four-poster beds, country quilts, private baths. Coffee and scones and orange juice in the morning."

Annie hid her face against him, trying not to show how tempted she was. How marvelous it would be to just creep under Jacob's big, strong wing and huddle there like a shivering, rain-drenched baby bird.

No. She was not a baby bird and she would not permit herself to act like one. She hesitated, choosing her words carefully. She didn't want to sound mouthy or mean. He didn't deserve it.

"Jacob, it's sweet of you, but I have to travel inside my own budget. If you want my company, then you're just going to have to—" She stopped herself abruptly. That was an ultimatum. Ultimatums sounded snotty and uppity. Be nice, Annie, she reminded herself. Think sweet. Make an effort.

She began again, in a halting voice. "You're welcome to stay with me . . . that is, you're more than welcome. I have to make do with my funky old tent, and I'm sorry it's so uncomfortable. But please stay with me." She closed her eyes, and added in a whisper, "I really, really want you to stay."

Jacob wrapped his arms around her fiercely. "You know damn well that I would sleep naked in the snow for a chance to make love to you again," he said roughly. "I just don't understand why we can't do it someplace warm and dry. But, whatever. At least our stomachs are full."

Annie rubbed her face against the velvety skin of his neck, weak with relief. "I'll do my best to distract you from how uncomfortable it is." She got up and tugged on his hand, drawing him toward the tent. "On your feet, Jacob. I've got plans for you tonight."

"Oh, yeah?" His voice was full of cautious speculation.

"Yeah." She kicked off her shoes and unzipped the tent flap. "Remember how you said that last night was all about me?"

She knelt and untied the laces of his boots. He stepped out of them obediently. "Yeah," he said. "Why?"

She looked up at him with a mysterious smile. "Guess who tonight is going to be all about?"

"Oh, God," he muttered as she dragged him into the tent.

She was different tonight, bold and fierce, shoving his jacket roughly off his shoulders.

"What's the rush?" he asked. "Are we late for something?"

"Cut the smart-ass remarks and get your clothes off, buddy," she snapped breathlessly. "I'm trying to make a point, here."

He wasn't about to argue with that. They stripped with feverish haste, desperate for the hot contact of skin and lips and hands. She ran her hands over his shoulders and arms with a murmur of approval, and yanked out the elastic band that held his hair, ruffling it into a wild mane. "I like you like this," she said. "I love your long hair."

"I grew it out just for you," he told her goofily, laughing as she buried her face in his neck and nipped it. She tugged his earlobe with her teeth and whispered, "Yesterday I asked if you wanted a blow job."

God forbid that she should think he didn't like them, he thought, with a flash of alarm. "Hey, just because I declined one yesterday doesn't mean that I don't—"

"Shut up, Jacob," she said in a low, purring voice.

He strained to read her expression in the dark. "Huh?"

"Tonight, I'm not asking you. Tonight, I'm telling you. Got it?"

"Oh," he said inanely.

"Lie down." She shoved him down imperiously until he was flat on his back, and knelt over him, the canopy of her hair brushing like a wide, whisper-soft kiss down the length of his torso. The hair between her legs tickled his navel as she straddled him, and the hot, moist kiss of her sex pressed intimately against his belly.

She leaned down, raining little kisses all over his face. He slid his hand behind her head and pulled her face down to his, but she made a fierce sound of protest, grabbed his wrists, and jerked them up above his head. He writhed luxuriously in her grasp, allowing her strong, slender hands to subdue him without protest. "I'm at your mercy," he said, with just a tiny tremor of laughter in his voice.

"You better believe it," she breathed into his ear. Her nails dug into his wrists as she thrust her tongue into his mouth.

He opened his mouth eagerly to her fierce, conquering kiss. It felt odd, being passive. It wasn't his usual role, but, hell, he would wear a pink tutu and hang upside down if that was what she wanted. And there was something very fine about having a beautiful, tough woman holding him prisoner, scrambling around on top of him, rubbing her fragrant, silky self against his aroused body.

She kissed him with an innocent aggressiveness that touched him almost as much as it turned him on, and then slid slowly down his body, letting her hair drag across his face and neck. She nibbled on his nipples while brushing her soft, downy bush gently back and forth across his stiff cock until he thought he was going to scream. She laughed, softly and mercilessly. She was doing it on purpose, just to torture him. It took every ounce of willpower he had not to flip her over on her back and ram himself inside her.

He almost wept with relief when she seized his dick, sliding her hands up and down with appreciative slowness. She measured him with a purring sound of delighted approval. "God, I wish there was more light in here," she murmured. "I want to see every detail."

"There's a flashlight in my saddlebags, on the bike," he gasped.

"And do you want to be the one to go get it?" She leaned down and swirled her tongue around the head of his cock, a wet, luscious vortex of sensation that rendered him breathless with delight. He let his head drop back onto the ground with a thud. "Next time," he moaned.

"I agree," she murmured. Then there was no more speech, just the soft, moist, delicious kissing and suckling sounds she made as she drew him into her mouth and out of his mind.

She was voracious and tender at the same time, swirling her tongue around erotically, licking up and down the whole length of him with voluptuous sweeps of her tongue until he was wet and slick. Then she grasped him, moving her slender hands up and down his shaft in a sensual rhythm along with her hot, suckling mouth. She cupped his balls tenderly in her hand. "There's so much of you, I don't know what to do with it all," she whispered seductively.

"You're doing fine," he assured her, his voice shaking. "If you did any better, I'd probably have a stroke."

She laughed and put her mouth to him again with tender eagerness, making his heart swell and throb almost as much as his cock, and then he forgot everything except for this stunning woman and this perfect, erotic moment. The universe was centered on Annie's hot mouth, her clever tongue, her gentle hands. The silky clutch and glide of her mouth against his exquisitely sensitive flesh was pushing him too close to the brink, and she made a soft, questioning murmur when he put his hands on either side of her face, slowing her down. "Don't make me come just yet," he begged. "It's too perfect."

"OK, OK," she whispered. She waited until his hands relaxed, and he stopped trembling, then began to move again with diabolical skill, patiently taking him to the brink and drawing back, again and again until he was thrashing his head from side to side, chest heaving, tangling his fingers into her hair.

She lifted her head. "After last night, it's only fair to make you come in my mouth, but I've got to have you inside me," she said in a soft, ragged voice. "I'm going crazy. I promise, the next time I'll—"

"It's fine, it's great. Whatever you want is fine, Annie,

anything. Make me come any damn way you please. Just . . .
do it *now*."

She clambered up over his body. "Do you have another . . . ?"

"Yeah, of course." He rummaged in the dark for his jeans
with a hand that shook uncontrollably. Annie took the condom from his hand, ripped it open and smoothed it over him
with bold, sensual strokes of her hand that shocked another
gasp of agonized pleasure out of him. He struggled into a
sitting position, pulling her toward him, arms trembling with
urgency. "Sit on me," he urged.

She crouched over him, reaching down and milking him
with strong, slow pulls from the base of his cock to the
swollen head. The rich sea smell of her arousal made him
drunk and dizzy. He slid his hand between her thighs, delving into the drenched, sultry depths of her cunt. Delicate little muscles tightened and fluttered around his bold invasion.
She let out a little sob and moved eagerly against his hand.
She was ready. More than ready. She was desperate, just like
he was.

She wrapped her arms around his neck and lowered herself over him with a shaky moan of anticipation. Jacob held
his breath and prayed for self-control as he guided his erection inside her moist opening. He prodded insistently until
they found the perfect angle, and they cried out together as
he shoved his whole thick, throbbing length inside her.

They clutched each other for a long moment as if they
were afraid of falling. The tight, clinging embrace of Annie's
shivering body was so exciting, he was about to come too
soon. He held her very still, willing the rising tension to ease
down once more. Just one more round, that was all he asked
of himself, and then he was going to have to let go.

Annie made an impatient sound, and rocked against him,
squeezing him with the delicate muscles inside her body.
She licked his neck, and he felt the sharp, teasing nip of her
teeth at his shoulder, and the last remnant of self-control fell

away. He slammed himself upward into her snug, hot sheath. Her arms tightened around his neck, her nipples pressed against his chest, her soft, pleading cries told him that she wanted him, that she needed what he could give her.

Every time he lost himself inside her, the pull got stronger, his need for her keener; but it was too late to pull back. Annie, sweet and searing, tart and prickly and utterly desirable; he was lost to her, a roiling mass of molten lava, and then a cataclysm of volcanic sweetness exploded through him.

He clutched her desperately, almost afraid of what was happening to him.

Jacob knew before he even opened his eyes that morning that it was going to be another bad scene. He'd been half awake, savoring the feel of her in his arms, wondering about his chances for some cuddling; maybe even another round of hot yummy sex to get the day started off right. He'd sensed the exact moment when she woke, figured out where she was, and went as rigid as a steel rail. Shit. He braced himself.

Sure enough, she started her now familiar I-don't-want-to-be-rude-but-get-the-hell-away-from-me morning wiggle. He resigned himself and let go, even though her sweet, rounded ass rubbing against his cock was having its predictable effect. She unzipped the bag with a sharp snap of her wrist. Cold air rushed in, shocking him and his hopeful privates brutally awake.

Annie clambered out and started digging for her underwear. He enjoyed the view, since it was clearly the only satisfaction he was going to get. Annie was definitely not the lazy morning sex type.

She shot him an uncertain glance. "Jacob, do you mind—"

"Getting the hell out of your sleeping bag and your tent?" he asked wearily. "Yes, I do mind. Since you've asked."

She had the grace to blush as she wiggled into her panties. "All I mean is, I really have to get on the road, and—"

"Yeah, you have that incredibly urgent appointment with a slot machine in Louisiana somewhere."

She made a furious little sound in her throat. "I never should have told you that," she hissed.

"Maybe not. What is it with you, Annie?" he demanded. "What's the formula? Every multiple orgasm earns me a snotty remark the next day? The better the sex, the bitchier you are in the morning?"

She whirled on him, her eyes snapping with fury. "Do not ever call me a bitch," she snarled. "*Ever.* Have you got that?"

He recoiled from her vehemence, drawing in a slow breath. "Whoa," he said quietly. "OK. I've got that. The B-word is totally off-limits. Bit by bit, by trial and error, I'm getting it, Annie."

"Sorry," she whispered, groping for her toiletries bag. She glanced up at him, and he leaned back on his elbows, flicking off the sleeping bag and blatantly displaying himself to her.

A tide of crimson swept over her pale face. "I'm going to take a shower," she said tightly. "When I get back, please be decent. I can't think straight when you're—when you're—"

"Stark naked and on fire for your touch? Sporting an enormous erection in your honor?" he offered.

"Smart-ass." She tried not to smile as she crawled out of the tent.

Jacob's eye fell on her purse as he was dressing, and he grabbed it without hesitation. He was sorry to do it behind her back, but there were things he needed to know, and she was too prickly this morning to ask direct questions. He rummaged through it. Sunglasses, Kleenex. Pepper-Gard defense spray. Wintergreen Lifesavers. A pack of saltines, battered to crumbs. A little velvet sack of silver dollars. A wallet.

He put it all back in except for the wallet, and thumbed through it with methodical precision. A New York driver's license, Staten Island address. Annie Simon. Now he had a surname. He dug deeper. A library card. A membership in a Blockbuster video club. No credit cards, no gas card, no bank card. He counted the cash in the billfold and cursed softly. No wonder she was driving on bald tires.

He put the wallet back in its place and poked around the rest of her stuff. A backpack of clothes. No winter coat, but she was headed for the deep South, so that could be considered superfluous. Food, however, could not. He rummaged through the box. Canned fruit, some freeze-dried instant soups. A bag of marshmallows. That was it.

It was making him angry.

He gathered up the foam containers from last night's feast, and shoved them violently into the dumpster, just as she came trotting back down the path, shivering. "Showers are cold," she said shortly.

"Thanks for the warning," he replied.

She hurried on without another word and began dismantling the tent with clumsy haste. He stared after her, tight-lipped. If he had any pride left, that would be his cue to leave.

He wouldn't let her see him follow her today. It was the only concession to pride he was capable of making after last night. The woman's ability with her tongue had brought him to his knees. She wasn't getting away from him now. No way.

Annie thumbed through the guidebook for Arkansas hot springs, looking for the page she had folded down. Helmslee Hot Springs. The guidebook promised secluded, undeveloped mineral pools in the streambed of a canyon. It had sounded like a soothing, healing sort of place. She had been making a point of finding beautiful places to hike and camp on this trip, so as soon as she set up her tent, she was heading straight for the trailhead. Maybe she could find some peace in a pool of hot mineral water, but at this point she doubted it.

She wouldn't be seeing Jacob again, after this morning's bravura performance as the knife-tongued hag from hell. Last night's lovemaking had blown her practically to bits. She couldn't handle these wild, seesawing emotions. They were scaring her to death.

"Hi, Annie."

She squeaked and spun around, dropping the guidebook. He stood at the edge of her campsite, holding two big plastic bags under his arms. His face was somber and guarded.

"I thought you'd gone for good," she said faintly.

"I'm not that easy to shake," he said calmly. "I lost you when I stopped at the sporting goods store in Carlson, but I picked you up again pretty fast. I've got an instinct for you now."

She gazed at the harsh planes of his handsome, unreadable face, feeling nervous and shy. "What's in the bags?" she asked hesitantly.

"A foam mattress, a lantern, and two down sleeping bags that zip together into one. Top of the line. Perfect for winter camping."

She stared at him, dumbfounded. "They must have cost you hundreds of dollars," she whispered.

He shrugged. "Don't worry about it."

She shook her head, tears welling into her eyes. "Jacob, I can't accept them."

He stared at the ground and let out a long, controlled sigh. His face was so patient and stubborn, she wanted to slap him, or kiss him, or just knock him down and jump on him. "How about an extended loan?" he asked in a long-suffering voice.

She shook her head, not trusting her voice.

"Fuck," he said in a low, vicious voice, flinging the bags to the ground. He stepped toward her, his eyes burning. She stumbled back, alarmed. "Would it kill you to accept just a tiny bit of help from me?"

She straightened up proudly. "I don't need any—"

"Yeah, right. You don't need any help from anybody. That antiquated piece of shit you're driving needs new tires and an oil change and God only knows what else. You've got nothing to eat that would keep more than a hamster alive. You've got next to no cash. No plastic. No bank card. No gas card. But you don't need any help. Oh, no. Not the indomitable Annie Simon. *Shit,* Annie!"

Her jaw dropped. "How do you know that I—"

"I looked through your goddamn wallet, that's how!" he spat out.

Fury flashed through her. "How dare you go through my stuff?"

"How can you travel like this?" he demanded. "You're walking a fucking tightrope, Annie! Where's your goddamn plastic?"

"Philip canceled all my plastic the last time I tried to leave him!" she yelled. "I'm not stupid, Jacob! Do you think I like this situation?"

Jacob drew in a sharp breath. "Did he hurt you?" he demanded.

She flinched. "None of your business."

He shook his head, his face rigid with frustration. "Christ, Annie. What about your family? Do they know where you are? Can they wire you money? For God's sake, tell me you've got some sort of safety net! Anything at all besides a fucking slot machine!"

His furious concern was reducing her to tears, pushing as it did at her most sensitive point. She had no sheltering family to call on. A series of foster parents in Payton, some better, some worse, and only one of whom she remembered fondly enough to send her a Christmas card. But no one she could ask for help. No one to catch her if she fell.

God, you'd think she would be used to it by now. She bolted past him, but he kept pace behind her. "Damn it, Annie! Listen to me!"

She whirled on him. "I can take care of myself, Jacob! And how dare you look through my stuff?"

He grabbed her arm. She yanked at it, but his grip was like iron. "I did it because I really care about you, Annie. So shoot me."

Her face crumpled, and tears starting oozing down, robbing her next words of any force she might have been able to invest them with. "I don't need to be rescued, Jacob," she choked out.

"Like hell you don't," he muttered.

It was too much. He was so beautiful and tough-looking, radiating protective energy like great waves of heat, and it was so incredibly sweet of him to care. All she wanted was to fling herself into his arms and say oh, yes, please save me, oh, my hero. She hated herself for being so tempted, for feeling so helpless. She wrenched her arm away and stumbled, catching herself on the trunk of a tree. She dashed her tears away roughly with the sleeve of her jacket.

"Listen, Jacob," she said in a low, trembling voice. "This trip is not about Jacob's red-hot affair with that weird chick he rescued on the road. This trip is about Annie Simon, alone and independent and free, finally getting her life back, in whatever way she can. Do you get that?"

He stared at her, his mouth compressed into a hard line. He gave a short, jerky nod.

"I'm going to hike up to the hot springs now. Please don't follow me. I want to be alone."

He nodded, his eyes bleak, and pulled on his helmet. "Whatever, Annie." He climbed onto his bike, fired up the engine and roared away without another word, leaving the bags he had brought behind him.

Her tear-blurred eyes followed his wavering image as he pulled out of the access road and onto the highway. Rain began to fall.

His gut roiled with anger. Calm down, chill out, demanded the cool, calculating part of his brain. If the damn woman doesn't know what's best for her, let her go it alone. She told you to fuck off in ten different ways, so fuck off already and get on with your life.

It was true, but every mile that passed, the pressure inside him mounted until it was almost unbearable. The whole situation was unbearable. He'd never lost it over a woman. He'd always liked them, enjoyed them, had his pick of them. He'd fully enjoyed that privilege, and been well aware of his good luck. And he had always prided himself on his detachment when it came to romance. He kept his head, didn't get swept away, didn't get trampled on. Ever.

It wasn't that he didn't have strong impulses and intense emotions. He did, and he recognized them and sometimes even acted on them, when he had decided that it was appropriate and in his best interests to do so. He, Jacob Kerr, the choice-maker, stood apart from those impulses and calmly ran the show.

Until he'd seen her shove her honey-blonde hair away from those haunted eyes, that sad, sexy mouth. Until his gaze had dropped to those soft, pointed tits that bobbed so enticingly beneath her T-shirt. Until the instant he'd seen that luscious ass, swaying like a round apple begging to be bitten, as she sashayed out of that fateful ladies' room.

And had subsequently gotten a brutal crash course in what it felt like to be dragged around by his cock.

He accelerated, in spite of the dangerous sheen of water on the dark asphalt. At the rate he'd been going, further exposure to Annie Simon would have reduced him to a slavering idiot. She'd done him a favor by sending him on his way, sparing what pathetically few brain cells still functioned in his head; from the feel of it, all his blood had migrated permanently south to his groin.

Discomfort weighed on him like a stone as the miles passed, making him weary and breathless. A bitter certainty began to grow in him as he negotiated the sweeping curves of the mountain road.

He had to go back. He couldn't leave her there by herself in the woods. She could scream and curse and carry on all she wanted; he just didn't have it in him. It was too fucking dangerous, and if she didn't understand that, well, that was just too bad. He was going to have to make her understand it, in whatever way he could think of; and by God, he could think of a few right off the bat.

He slowed to a stop and turned around, furious at her, at himself, at everything. An unfamiliar seething energy began to gather inside him, and he cursed long and hard and viciously into the whipping rain as he sped back toward Annie, spoiling for a fight.

Chapter Four

Annie sank deeper into the caressing warmth of the steaming mineral water, and watched rain patter into it with deepening melancholy. A stream cascaded to the left of her, and bare trees towered over her, their tops wreathed with fog. Billows of fallen leaves softened the bleakness of winter, their rich red and gold tones glowing in the pearly gray light of late afternoon. Tendrils of steam curled slowly up from the pool, giving it an eerie, mystical look.

The pool was deep and clear, lined with colored pebbles and glittering white sand, as hot as the most perfect bathtub. It was ringed by flat boulders of white stone, veined with fleshy, glittering pink streaks of quartz that gleamed in the rain. It was magical. A place to calm down, to ponder her future, to renew her faith in herself.

And all she could think about as she stared at the rain was the bleak, hurt look in Jacob's eyes.

Oh, get over yourself, she thought. She sank deeper into the water until her nose kissed the steaming surface. It was her own fault, and she knew it. Ever since she met the guy she'd been acting like a hysterical harpy. Predictably enough, he'd gotten sick of it and left. End of story. What point was there in beating a dead horse?

There was no point, but her restless mind was determined to torture itself. She couldn't stop imagining how perfect the hot spring would be if Jacob were in the pool with her, the whole lean, solid length and breadth of him pressed against her, the hunger in his beautiful dark eyes making her feel beautiful and cherished, utterly desirable. For the rest of her life she was going to dream of those two nights with him and probably wake up crying. A sob welled up in her throat, and she almost choked in her effort to force it back down.

A twig snapped in the bushes, and a thrill of fear shivered down her spine. She realized with an unpleasant jolt how vulnerable she was. It wasn't something she let herself think about very often; otherwise she would go stark raving paranoid and lose her nerve entirely.

The sound did not repeat, but her travel- and trouble-sharpened instincts sensed that she was being observed. The tiny little hairs behind her neck stirred, and the thought burst in her mind like fireworks. Jacob. He'd changed his mind and come back, in spite of everything. She dipped her face into the pool to conceal a crazy grin. He had disobeyed her dismissal, she thought, with a rush of feminine power. Bad boy. She would punish him for that later. Better yet, she would punish him right now. Let him watch her like a thief in the bushes and burn for her the way she burned for him. Let him beg for it.

She rose slowly, letting hot water cascade over her. Steaming rivulets snaked their sensual way down over the curves and valleys of her body. The water was hip deep, barely kissing the thatch of dark blonde hair between her thighs. She faced toward where she had heard the sound, arched her back and turned her face up to the rain, raising her arms high in a gesture of gratitude and acceptance. She folded them behind her head, thrusting her breasts forward in an aggressively sensual stance, and stretched luxuriously.

The water had made her so hot. Too hot. She was burning up.

Let him look his fill at her in the broad daylight, steam rising off her flushed, naked body. The thought of his eyes on her made her nipples tingle, and she cupped her breasts tenderly in her hands, flinging her head back to the pelting rain. She swayed, lifting her arms like a pagan goddess, dancing a sultry dance of sexual abandon. She scooped hot water over herself and watched the droplets beading on her heated skin, rolling down her body. She was a fey, sylvan creature, lost in her own sensual fantasy, wild and wanton and mysterious.

She sank down onto one of the broad, flat boulders at the pool's edge. The chill of the wet stone was a shock of pleasure to her overheated skin. She reclined against it, opening her eyes, her mouth, her arms to the sweet, cool rain, allowing the ravishing beauty and wild energy of nature to surround and embrace her. Sensual images flooded over her, and her hand trailed over her breasts, her belly, then lower.

She caressed her secret flesh with luxurious idleness until the memory of Jacob's passionate, skillful lovemaking seized her in its grip, playing through her mind like a vivid dream. Her breasts tingled and her sex grew flushed, swollen with liquid longing at the thought of his strong, beautiful body, his joyous grin, his infectious laughter. His big, gentle hands and ardent mouth, teaching her, coaxing her, urging her with infinite tenderness to undreamed-of realms of pleasure. The raindrops that struck her body had to be hissing off into pure steam, she thought, as she undulated against the wet stone. Her legs opened, and her fingers delved tenderly into her own sultry flesh, seeking that blissful, shivering sweet spot. Her hips moved in a subtle pulsing motion, her back arched, her breasts jutted out, pink and swollen. She caressed them too as she spread her thighs like a goddess opening herself to the embrace of a deity.

* * *

Jacob stared at her from behind the screen of bushes, transfixed. Part of him wanted to burst out of the trees and demand that she cover herself. A much stronger part wanted to fall on her and become the phantom lover that she was welcoming so rapturously into her body. He wondered with a stab of wild, irrational jealousy who she was thinking about as she parted her slender white thighs and caressed the deep pink glistening folds of her cunt, completely open to his sight as it had never been before in the darkness of her tent.

He bit down on his knuckles to keep from groaning, from screaming, and wondered how in the hell she managed not to hear his heart, thudding against his rib cage like a stallion kicking at its stall. She must know he was watching. She had to be putting on this show for his benefit. Otherwise he had to conclude that she was crazy to bare herself like that to the naked sky. Christ, anybody could be watching from the trees, just as he was watching. Anybody.

Possessive anger jolted through him, tugging at his reason. His cock was so hard, it hurt to move. He was primed to explode and make a mess inside his jeans. Wouldn't that be just the perfect final blow to his battered self-esteem, he thought with a flash of grim humor. Annie really knew how to take a man apart, piece by piece, until he didn't even recognize himself in the rubble.

He would wait, he told himself. He would hold back for just a few more moments, watching her lush, slender body glowing like a rose-tinted pearl as she writhed on the rain-washed slab of stone, as wide open as a sacrificial offering. He would let her finish her little pageant, and then he would burst out of these goddamn bushes and show her just exactly what kind of fire she was playing with.

Then he would drive himself inside her, deep and hard, and make her arch and writhe and open herself like that, just for him.

Then he would bathe himself in that glistening dew that

drenched the flushed, pouting folds of her cunt, that gleamed on her trembling fingers, tempting him, tantalizing him.

He watched her avidly, his breath sawing harshly in and out of his chest. Her hips jerked and she let out a shuddering cry, closing her thighs tightly around her hand as her face convulsed in ecstasy.

Suddenly, a loud crack and a rustling sound came out of the woods. Annie sprang up and slid swiftly back into the water with a startled gasp. There was the sound of bushes snapping back into place.

A bellow of primordial rage burst out of his throat. He crashed out of the bushes, ready to hunt down whoever had just seen the wanton display Annie had made of herself. And when he found the guy, he would convince him to forget every detail. Limb by broken, bloody limb.

Annie stood up in the water. "Jacob, I think it's just a—"

"Get the *hell* back down into that water!" His voice cracked like a whip. Annie sank instantly into the pool, her eyes huge and startled.

A doe leaped out of the bushes. She froze, and stared at him with enormous, fathomless dark eyes before she gathered herself and bounded away, feather-light and graceful. She disappeared into the trees on the opposite bank. The air slowly escaped from Jacob's lungs. He walked back to the pool, his fists still clenched. "What the hell did you think you were doing?" he demanded.

She looked up at him, her gray eyes mysterious and luminous. "You saw me," she murmured. "Exactly what it looked like I was doing."

Her cool, offhand tone enraged him still further. "Yeah. I saw you. So would anyone else who took a notion to hike up here today," he said, his voice shaking with fury.

Her lips tightened mutinously. "I knew it was you."

"How? How the hell could you be sure? Did you see me?"

She shrank away from the harshness in his voice. "I just knew," she repeated, in a small, stubborn voice.

He tried to stop his chest from heaving. "You knew," he repeated. "First you tell me to fuck off. Then you put on a sex show for me. What's your game, Annie? Are you trying to drive me out of my mind?"

She looked up sidewise and gave a small decisive nod.

That smug gesture was too much for him. He grabbed her upper arm and hauled her out of the water. She held herself proudly upright, not giving an inch. He stared down at her flushed, exquisite body, his heart thundering and his mind swamped with erotic images. He reached down and cupped her mound in his hand, thrusting his fingers inside her. She jerked and cried out, her chest heaving. Her cunt was slick and wet, silky soft from pleasuring herself. He slid his fingers slowly out of her tight sheath, then drove in again, deeper, rougher. "You play dangerous games, Annie," he muttered.

The seething darkness in his eyes finally registered. She licked her lips, her silky thighs clenching involuntarily around his hand. Her eyes dilated with alarm as she sensed his primitive instinct to subdue her with his body. His hand tightened on her arm, and she gasped.

He let go of her suddenly, in a spasm of self-disgust, and she stumbled back. "Get your clothes on," he rapped out.

"Jacob, I didn't mean to—"

"Not . . . one . . . word. Get your clothes on, or I'm going to fuck you right here. And I don't think you'd like it. I'm not feeling very generous."

The menace in his words finally appeared to sink in, because she scrambled to obey him. He forced himself to look away as she struggled into her damp clothes. He didn't trust himself in this state. He didn't even know himself.

He was on wild, uncharted ground.

Annie scrambled down the muddy path, clutching the towel over her chest to cover the nipples that were poking through her sodden shirt. She was acutely aware of his seething fury as he stalked silently behind her. It rolled off him in waves, it showed in his burning eyes and the grim set of his mouth. What on earth had she unleashed? She'd wanted to tease him, to make him laugh, to make his eyes light up with desire. By no means had she wanted to provoke a black rage.

God, she was sick to death of tiptoeing around men in black rages, she thought, with a burst of temper. She'd done more than her share of it in her lifetime. She whirled around to tell him so. "Jacob—"

He gave a short warning shake of his head. The look in his eyes made her turn tail and scurry on ahead of him, her heart in her mouth.

After an eternity of stumbling on her trembling legs, they finally arrived at the campground. The place was deserted; not another car or tent in sight. Rain streamed off the canopy over the tent. The sealed plastic bags Jacob had brought were beaded with rain. She was soaked to the skin, but too flushed and agitated to feel cold. Jacob's gleaming hair was plastered to his head. Raindrops slid down over the beautifully sculpted planes of his grim face.

Twilight was deepening. Charcoal gray clouds sat heavily on the hills above them, smothering the horizon in a thick, blurry fog that muffled the sound of the cars passing on the nearby highway. There was no other sound but the immense sigh and rustle of rain on the billows of fallen leaves.

Annie turned to face him, feeling very small and alone. "Stop glowering at me, Jacob."

"I can't. I'm fucking furious. You're jerking me around, Annie."

She shivered, feeling the cold for the first time. "I did it to please you," she whispered. "I'm sorry you didn't like it. I wanted—" She stopped. A hard knot was forming in her throat, blocking the words.

"You wanted what?" he prompted.

"To turn you on," she confessed in a tiny voice.

Instantly he was upon her, one hand pinioning her against his chest, the other twining itself deep into her tangled hair. "Yeah, well, it worked," he said roughly. "In case you were wondering." And his mouth covered hers in a hard, plundering kiss.

Always before his kisses had been exquisitely gentle, and she had loved his gentleness; it had set her sensuality free. But the savagery of this kiss unleashed something deeper, something dangerous and wild. She loved his fierce intensity, his controlled strength, his tongue plunging into her mouth, a possessive intrusion meant to subdue her, but it only inflamed her. She wanted to claw him, bite him, provoke him. The towel fell to the ground, and she grabbed a thick handful of his hair and kissed him back like a wild thing.

He pulled his mouth away with a suddenness that left her reeling. "Never play with me like that again, Annie."

She reached for him, dazed and aroused. "Jacob, I—"

His hands clamped painfully onto her shoulders. "Anyone who happened to be up there in that canyon could have seen you with your legs open and your hands on yourself."

She tried to twist out of his iron grip, but it was useless. "There was no one else!" she protested. "It was all for you!"

His hand moved swiftly, and buttons flew as he ripped open her shirt. "All for me," he muttered, staring at her breasts.

She displayed herself to him, feeling bold and reckless. "Did you like it, then, Jacob? Is the image burned into your memory?"

"Yeah, sweetheart," he said in a harsh, grating voice. "When my time comes and my life flashes before my eyes, that scene is going to get extra play time. Does that make you happy? Driving me nuts, messing with my mind, you find that really entertaining?"

"No!" she yelled, frustrated beyond endurance. "Christ,

Jacob, I'm sorry, already! I'm sorry for everything! I'm sorry for the hot spring, I'm sorry I was rude, I'm sorry I was ungracious when you tried to help me, I'm sorry six ways from Sunday! OK? Are you satisfied?"

"Not yet." His eyes glittered dangerously. "A lame-ass apology is not going to cut it."

She jerked her torn blouse together over her breasts. "So just what would cut it?" she demanded, her voice defiant.

He was silent. A gleam of speculation entered his eyes, and his gaze dropped, raking her body hungrily.

She took a step away from him, unnerved by the dark purpose in his eyes. "Oh, no," she whispered. "Not like that."

"Yes," he said, advancing on her. "Exactly like that."

"I don't want to," she said, wrapping her arms defensively around herself. "Not if you're angry."

He regarded her coldly for a long moment, and shrugged carelessly. "Whatever. I'm out of here, Annie. Have a nice life."

Rain dripped off the end of her nose as she watched him pull the cover off his bike. He flapped it vigorously to get the rain off and folded it with methodical precision, as if she no longer existed.

She wrestled with herself out of sheer habit, but she knew from the start that the battle was already lost. She couldn't let him go again. Not now. She would dissolve into the rain, evaporate into the mist, sink into the dead leaves as if she had never been. She couldn't face the night alone, no matter how much self-respect it might cost her.

Jacob put on his helmet, and panic clutched at her stomach. She stumbled forward as the engine roared to life. "Jacob," she called.

He cocked a questioning eyebrow, revving the engine. She tried to speak, but her throat was closed. She swallowed hard and tried again. "I'm really sorry," she called, over the sound of the motor.

Jacob cut the motor and waited, silent and impassive.

She took a deep breath, and slowly spread open her wet shirt, offering herself to him. "All right," she said in a tiny voice.

He pulled off his helmet and smoothed his tangled dark hair off his forehead, staring hungrily at her naked breasts. "All right, what?"

She closed her eyes, hoping he wasn't going to make her beg. "Don't leave me alone tonight. I'll . . . do whatever you want."

Jacob got off the bike without a word. He covered it and came toward her, his face implacable. If she'd hoped that her surrender would soften him, she had hoped in vain. A tiny muscle twitched in his jaw as he stared at her body, the only sign of emotion she could detect. Rain beaded on her pale breasts. He cupped them in his big hands, rolling the tight, puckered buds of her nipples between his fingers. He made a harsh, wordless sound deep in his throat and his hands grasped her shoulders, forcing her to her knees. Her face was level with the fierce bulge in his jeans. He wound her hair around his fingers and unbuckled his belt.

She gasped. "Here?"

"Right here."

"But anybody could just walk by—"

"You're just going to have to hope nobody walks by, if that bothers you." He tore open the buttons of his jeans, and his heavy, swollen penis sprang free. It was flushed a deep angry red, veins bulging on the stiff hard shaft.

"Jacob—"

"Suck me, Annie," he demanded, staring down into her eyes.

Hunger radiated from him, as powerful as a blast furnace. She stared up at him, considering the fierce challenge he was throwing out to her and sensing the subtle pleading in his fingers as they tightened in her hair, urging her to take him in her mouth. Her pride recoiled at his brutal power game, but still she craved his vigor and energy, understanding on a deep animal level that his was a heat that would not fizzle out, leaving her chilled and lonesome. At least this was for real. No matter how much he infuriated her, he was for real.

It was that silent understanding that seduced her at last, pulling her into his dark, seductive vortex. She brushed his hot, hard male flesh against her cool, rain-wet cheek and then grasped the pulsing shaft in both hands, savoring the sinuous energy that was uncoiling inside her. He was burning, his hard flesh warming her cold hands instantly. She stroked him, and his fist tightened in her hair.

"Don't tease, Annie," he warned. "I'm not in the mood."

"I know exactly how much you need this, Jacob," she said in a soft, taunting voice. "Don't even try to bully me."

"Oh yeah?" He covered her hands with his own and dragged them hard up and down the length of his penis, forcing her to pleasure him. "You said you were sorry, Annie. Show me how sorry you are. Suck me."

His mocking tone angered her. She twisted away, but her hair was trapped tightly in his powerful hand. She suddenly hated the submissive posture she was in. "You're poison mean, Jacob."

"I learned it from you, sweetheart," he said, as he thrust himself roughly into her mouth.

It wasn't like last night, when he'd lain back and gratefully appreciated the attention of her lips and tongue. This time he gripped her head and set the rhythm himself. She gave a choked cry of protest, and he slowed down. "Take more of me," he urged. "Come on, Annie."

Anger and confusion and a crazy burst of excitement; the volatile mix blazed through her body, making her impervious to the cool rain. Guided by his big hands, she found a way to give him the rhythm he wanted, relaxing instinctively and swallowing him whole. Even in this arrogant, masterful stance, he was desperate for her to lavish the sweet swirl and glide of her tongue on him. She pleasured him, loving the harsh gasps and groans that vibrated through the steely tension of his body. She was barely conscious of putting her hand between her legs and pressing her thighs together tightly, trying in vain to ease the pulsing agony of arousal that was driving her half mad.

She looked up, dazed, when he suddenly pulled her away from himself. He was still hugely erect and vibrating with excitement, but he tilted her head back, staring into her eyes with a look of discovery. "I'll be damned. Who would have thought," he murmured. "This vibe really works for you, Annie."

Annie shrank back at the predatory look on his face. She saw her hand between her thighs and snatched it away with a gasp, as if she'd let an enemy glimpse a secret weakness she hadn't even known she possessed. "Don't," she whispered.

"Don't what?"

"Don't look at me like that!" she cried out wildly. "Don't get any ideas. Tonight is . . . an unusual situation. The rules are different."

"What rules?" he asked softly. "There are no rules. It's just you and me, all alone."

She pulled away from his hand and scrambled to her feet, eyeing him warily and backing away. "You're scaring me, Jacob."

He followed her. "No, I'm not," he retorted, seizing her hand. "And even if I am, you're loving it." He forced it down and curled it around his swollen penis, trapping it inside his own big hand. His velvety skin was wet, from her mouth, from the rain, and her hand slid easily over his rock-hard shaft. He pushed her onto her knees again and grasped his penis, milking it roughly until a drop of gleaming moisture pearled at the tip. He urged her mouth closer to his hungry shaft. "Lick it off," he commanded. "Taste me."

Her body betrayed her even as her mind rebelled at his arrogant presumption. She opened her mouth and obeyed him, licking away the salty, silky drop of fluid. A shudder of unwilling excitement rocked her body. "Don't do this to me, Jacob," she whispered.

"I can't stop," he said in a rasping voice. "Not now that I know how much it turns you on." He pulled her up onto her feet and kissed her, his tongue thrusting into her mouth, his hands greedily cupping her breasts. "Whatever I want, right? Isn't that what you said?"

She stiffened. "Yes, but—"

"This is what I want, Annie. This is how it has to be tonight. *Look* at me, damn it." He jerked her face up to his, letting her glimpse for an instant the seething conflict in his eyes. He grabbed her arm, dragging her over to the picnic table and pushing her in front of him against it, reaching around from behind to deftly unbutton her jeans. He jerked her jeans and panties down over her hips until they were at her knees, baring her from the waist down and hobbling her at the same moment. She reached down to retrieve them, but he caught her hands behind her back and pressed her against the table, fitting himself against her so she could feel the hot brand of his penis against her cool, shivering backside. "Bend over," he ordered, his voice a husky rasp.

Her knees went weak. "Oh, for God's sake, Jacob," she whispered. "Can't we go in the tent?"

"Too dark," he muttered. "I want to see you, all spread out and open to me. Anything I wanted, Annie. You promised. Bend over."

She was frozen for a timeless, agonized instant, and then the dark tide of desire engulfed her and she bent over, arching her back and parting her legs for him as much as the wet jeans wrapped around her knees would allow. She was so aroused she wanted to claw at the rough wooden boards beneath her hands; the soft, sultry ache between her thighs pulsed and throbbed, and still he loomed behind her, a dark, burning presence, making her wait and wait and wait. Rain pelted down, running in little rivulets down the cleft of her bottom, trickling delicately over the moist, tender folds of her sex, now completely exposed to his sight. He made a harsh, incoherent sound. "God, Annie. You are perfect," he said, his voice a ragged groan.

His big hands fastened on her hips. She braced herself, expecting him to thrust himself inside her, but he sank down to his knees behind her, pinning her against the table. His hot breath fanned her thighs as he nuzzled her tenderly from behind. "I love this view of you," he said huskily. "I love all the colors and textures, the way those beautiful blonde ringlets get all dark and wet and glistening. I like how you're so cool and pale, like a pearl, here"—he caressed her trembling buttocks—"and so pink and crimson and hot in here." His tongue slid up and down the surface of her vulva and then dipped teasingly inside, licking and lapping ravenously at the moist, dewy folds and furrows of her sex. "I love it that you can't hide from me," he muttered, his tongue thrusting deeper, harder.

Annie squeezed her eyes shut, her knees rubbery and weak, gasping at the outrageous intimacy. His tongue teased with rapacious skill, thrusting deep and then flicking delicately across her swollen clitoris. She writhed against the rough, wet wood of the table, pushing herself back against his greedy mouth with a helpless, pleading moan.

"No, Annie," he said softly, holding her trembling hips still. "I'm not going to make you come like this. Tonight you'll wait until I'm inside you." He rose to his feet, his hands still cupping her backside, and leaned his scorching hot body against her. His breath heaved, and his erection prodded her buttocks. "You liked that, didn't you?" he asked, his voice husky and breathless. "You loved it."

"You never asked me what I wanted," she snapped. "Don't you project your teenage porno fantasies onto me, you macho jerk."

He laughed softly, and his hand slid between her legs, feathering across her hair and delving boldly inside her soft cleft, testing her silky moisture. "Tell me the truth," he demanded. "Your body already has, so you might as well." He thrust a long finger deep inside her, sliding slowly in and out, and she clenched his finger tightly inside the quivering muscles of her vagina. "You're so wet, Annie," he murmured. "You can't wait. You're aching for me to give it to you. Aren't you?"

She was stubbornly silent, not wanting to give him the satisfaction, but it was a losing battle and they both knew it. He lifted his hands for a moment, and she heard a little ripping sound. He tossed the condom wrapper on the table and his strong, skillful hands swiftly resumed their agonizing teasing. "Tell me how much you want it," he demanded. "Tell me how you want me inside you. I need to hear it."

She gave up the struggle. It was that or lose her mind completely. "I want you," she gasped out.

"How much?" He slid two fingers inside her, and moved his thumb around her clitoris in a slow, pulsing circle.

"Please, Jacob—"

"You're begging me? Is that what you're doing?" He finally touched her with just the tip of his penis, shallow thrusts that barely penetrated her slick, eager flesh. She pushed herself back to take more of him, but he evaded her. "Beg me," he demanded, rubbing himself in small, wet circles around the bud of her clitoris. "Come on, Annie. I need to hear it. I need to know how much you want me."

The harsh, hungry rasp of need in his words was the key she needed to unlock the maddening puzzle of pride and desire. As long as he was vulnerable to her, she could yield to him and endure her own vulnerability. Tears of frustration spilled out onto her cheeks. "OK, I'm begging," she said in a ragged voice. "Are you happy now?"

His strong fingers dug almost painfully into her hips. "Yes," he muttered as he shoved himself inside her.

The rhythm he set was swift and savage. Annie wanted to

kick off the clinging jeans that held her knees together, to spread her legs still wider, welcome him even deeper, but stopping was not a possibility, and soon even the vague impulse was swept from her mind. She stuck her hands in front of her face to protect it from being abraded by the rough table. Her body softened in quivering eagerness for him, welcoming his strength, craving the vigorous slide and plunge of his thick shaft. She had thought that their lovemaking in her tent had been passionate, but now she sensed that he had been leashing in nine-tenths of the passion that was his to give, hers to take. The sheer mass of him ramming into her from behind was violently arousing. Her doubts, fears, her anger and pride, all fragmented in the force of their joining, and the jagged shards spun in her mind, disconnected and brilliant. It was a kaleidoscope that pulsed and shimmered, pulling her toward a climax so intense she cried out loud, and lost consciousness.

When she came to, Jacob was collapsed on top of her, shivering in the aftermath of his own orgasm. He lifted himself off her with a harsh sigh, sliding slowly out of her body. She struggled upright and turned to face him. His face was as shocked and naked as she knew her own must be. She reached down with trembling fingers to pull up her jeans.

"Don't bother," Jacob said, yanking off his shirt. "Take your clothes off and leave them out here. They can't get any wetter. This rain's not going to stop."

The calm, practical observation grounded her a little. She tugged off her muddy shoes and peeled off her jeans and shirt, leaving them in a wet heap on the tarp. They stood there, stark naked in the rain, staring as if they were afraid of each other, both sharply aware of the heat that licked and curled between them, wholly unabated.

"Get into the tent," he said curtly.

She crawled inside. Rain pounded in a soft, constant roar on the plastic rain canopy, and she was grateful that she had set it up earlier. Her sleeping bag felt thin and clammy.

The zipper opened, and Jacob thrust in a dry, folded flannel shirt. "Dry yourself off with this. Your towel is buried in mud."

She was still rubbing herself with it when the zipper opened again. He shoved two big bundles into the opening and crawled in after them, closing the tent flap. She handed him the shirt. He dried himself briskly and flicked on his new lantern. It glowed a warm, rosy red.

His eyes were unreadable in the shadows. "Scoot over," he said.

She scooted, and watched him spread out the foam mattress.

"Jacob, I'm all muddy," she objected. "And they're brand-new."

"We need them," he said flatly, ripping the plastic on the sleeping bags open. He flung one on top of the other and zipped them closed. "I want to be on top."

She drew her knees up to her chest and hugged them. "You mean . . . you still want to . . ."

"Oh, yes. I still want to." He grabbed her hand and drew it to his lap, closing it around the hard, scorching flesh of his penis. "I'm not done, Annie. It's going to be a long night."

She pulled her hand away, unnerved by the remote tone in his voice. "Are you still mad?"

He regarded her with narrowed eyes. "Yes," he said coolly. "It's better than it was, but we've got a ways to go yet."

She shook her head. "I can't believe you have the energy to be angry after . . . after what just happened," she murmured.

He smiled, but it was not a smile that warmed her. "You'll be surprised what I have the energy for. Lie down on your back."

She hesitated. "Why does it have to be like this, Jacob?"

He shrugged, his shadowed face inscrutable. "I'll leave you alone, if that's what you want. Just say the word. But if you want me to stay, then deal with me."

She looked away from him, and he made a low, impatient sound in his throat. His hand hooked her chin and jerked her face around. "I'm not going to pretend for you," he said curtly. "Understood?"

She pulled away, her eyes locked with his, and nodded silently.

"Good. Lie down on your back," he repeated.

Annie scooted into the middle of the expanse of blue nylon and hesitantly lowered herself onto it. The fabric was cool and slippery against her skin, but the fluffy down was exquisitely soft and yielding. She lay back, looking up at him apprehensively.

Jacob studied her supine body for what seemed like an eternity before he reached out and put his hands on her knees, spreading her legs. He settled himself between them, holding her wide open and sliding his hands over the soft, sensitive skin of her inner thighs, staring hungrily down at her quivering, exposed flesh. She moved restlessly, but his hands tightened on her thighs, pinning her into place. He grabbed a condom from the box by the lantern, opened it and rolled it onto himself with a calm, purposeful air.

"I can't stand it when you're cold," she burst out.

His eyes flicked to her face. He splayed his warm hand on her belly. "I'm not cold," he said. "I've never felt so hot. I'm burning up." He pushed her thighs wide until she was folded back on herself, and slid his fingers inside her, finding her still moist and flushed from his last onslaught. He stared into her eyes as he mounted her, and she flinched as she felt the hard, blunt head of his penis nudging her open.

"That's not what I meant," she whispered, and then gave a sharp cry as he drove himself inside her, hard and deep.

Even though he had been inside her just moments before,

it was still a shocking intrusion, and she stiffened in automatic resistance. His steely strength pinned her down, and she realized that always before he had been gentle with her, careful not to overwhelm her with his strength and size and sheer physical presence.

He wasn't bothering to do so any longer. He shoved himself inside her until he was as deep as he could go. She felt breathless, ravaged and vulnerable, like a city that had been sacked. Panic flared inside her. This was all wrong, terribly wrong. She had miscalculated, she'd thought that she could take it, but she couldn't. It was unendurable, the helplessness, the remote, faraway look on his face. Anger exploded inside her, and she struck out at him, getting in a good, openhanded whack on his jaw before he caught her wrists.

"What the hell?" He bore down with even more of his weight, his eyes flashing with anger.

"I'm sick of your power games, you arrogant bastard," she hissed.

He pinned her wrists over her head and kissed her hard. "I'm not playing a game, Annie. This is absolutely for real."

She struggled beneath him. He responded with a heavy thrust that jerked a cry out of her throat, then another, and another. She shut her eyes tightly and trembled, wondering frantically how many more surrenders could she take, how far she could yield to his conquering energy and still be herself. How long it would be before this man looming over her plundered and claimed everything. She bit her lip to push away tears and forced herself to relax her trembling limbs. "Damn you, Jacob," she whispered. "Just don't hurt me."

His body went rigid. "I would *never* hurt you." His voice was sharp with anger. "How long is it going to take you to figure that out?"

"You're hurting me now!" she cried out wildly.

His chest heaved and he stared down at her with fierce

concentration, as if trying to read her mind. "You loved what I did to you," he insisted, his voice low and furious. "I felt how much you loved it. I felt you come. You couldn't hide it from me."

"That's not what I meant," she gasped out. Her body tightened around him eagerly as he thrust inside her once again.

"So what the hell do you mean?" His voice broke in frustration. "I feel it now, too. I feel how hot you are, how wet, how your body hugs me. I'm not hurting you, Annie. And you know that I won't. Ever."

He surged into her, and she squeezed her eyes shut as her hips jerked involuntarily.

"Look at me!" he demanded, and her eyes snapped open at the sharp command in his voice. "Say it, Annie. Let me hear you say that you've got nothing to fear from me."

She shook her head, knowing that he was wrong. He could hurt her. Oh, God, could he ever. He could break her heart into a thousand tiny pieces. That was the nameless terror that had been dogging her from the first moment he spoke to her. But with white-hot anger blazing in his eyes, she couldn't tell him that. Incomprehension lay between them, tangled and snarled, and she was frozen mute.

"Say it, Annie!" he demanded, his voice cracking with strain.

She cleared her throat. "I hope you appreciate the irony of trying to intimidate me into saying I'm not scared of you," she said softly.

He scowled. "This is no time for smart-ass remarks. Say it!"

She took as deep a breath as she could with Jacob's body pinning her down. "I know you would never mean to hurt me," she said quietly.

His eyes narrowed. "That's not what I wanted you to say."

"That's the best I can do," she told him.

A shudder went through him. He scooped her wet hair from beneath her neck, fanning it gently above her head. "Do you trust me?" he asked, his voice rough and urgent.

Her heart twisted painfully. "Yes," she said simply. In spite of everything, it was still true.

He hid his face against the wet hair coiled beside her cheek, and slowly let go of her wrists. "Put your arms around me," he ordered.

She did so without hesitation.

"Now your legs."

She wiggled beneath him, and he lifted himself up, letting her shift her hips until she was cradling him in a position of complete acceptance. He thrust himself deeply into her tight sheath until they were completely joined, and she wrapped her legs around him, clenching herself tightly around his solid warmth.

"That's better," he muttered.

She hid her face against his neck. "Yes, it is," she whispered.

He began to move, more gently this time, and groaned softly at the snug, gliding perfection of her welcoming body. He kissed her neck, lifted his head and said suddenly, "It was all a bluff, you know."

Her eyes snapped open. "What was a bluff?"

"All that stuff I said. About how I would just up and leave if you didn't yield to my dark desires."

She was speechless with surprise.

Jacob surged into her with melting tenderness, cradled her face in his hands and stared into her eyes. "I would never have left you alone tonight, Annie. Under any circumstances."

"Oh," she gasped, staring up at him. He was trying to tell her something, something incredibly important, but it was in code, and she was afraid to translate it wrong. "And I fell for it," she whispered.

"Yeah, you fell for it," he agreed, his lips twitching slightly.

The smile pissed her off. She stared up at him, eyes slitted. "You're a manipulative bastard, Jacob," she said in a low voice.

"Yeah, I know," he said in a wondering tone. "It's a whole new me."

Then he covered her mouth with his and there was no more space or air to examine hidden messages. There was nothing but his elemental force, driving her deeper and higher into herself. His anger had made her feel vulnerable, but his tenderness was even more perilous. It melted her barriers effortlessly, blurred her boundaries, left her utterly bare—a creature made of naked energy, pure emotion. Unrecognizable to herself.

There was no end to the layers he could strip off her soul.

Chapter Five

The rain had finally stopped, and dawn was near. Annie listened to the birds twittering, an ache of sweet exhaustion pervading her body, and tried to think of a way to extricate herself from Jacob's arms without waking him. It was a considerable challenge. His muscular arm was clasped around her waist; his hand splayed possessively across her belly and the tips of his long fingers tangled intimately into the hair between her legs. One long, sinewy leg was firmly wedged between her thighs. And he was so warm. It was hard to get up the nerve to break the seal and let cold air rush between them. She wiggled experimentally. Jacob sighed and pulled her tighter against him, fitting her backside against his belly. Nature called, however, so Annie gritted her teeth and flung back the warm, soft sleeping bag.

His arm clamped around her, as rigid as steel. "Where the hell do you think you're going?"

Her muscles jerked, and she schooled her face to calmness before twisting in his arms to look at him. "I have to pee," she said quietly.

He propped himself onto his elbow, frowning. "Don't go far."

"I won't," she promised, grabbing the only garment in the tent—the damp flannel shirt they had dried themselves with the evening before. She draped it over herself and crept out of the tent, teeth chattering.

The bathrooms were on the far side of the deserted campground, and the shirt only reached to mid-thigh, so she fished a pack of Kleenex out of the glove compartment in the pickup and headed straight into the forest. It was shadowy and fragrant, lambent with the subtle, pearly glow that preceded dawn. The world looked different. Everything inside her was shaken up, intensely alive.

She took care of her business behind a bush, and when she straightened up, she found herself looking into the eyes of a young male deer, no more than fifteen feet away. He gazed at her for a moment, apparently unafraid, and then bounded away with a casual grace that left her breathless. His beauty made her think of the doe at the pool the day before, which triggered an avalanche of images and feelings.

When Jacob had finally dozed off, holding her tightly against his chest, she had been unable to sleep. There was a quiet earthquake taking place inside her mind and her heart. Last night's shining seed of awareness had sprouted and grown over the night, and there was no longer any doubt. She was in love with him. It was a disaster, but it was too late for damage control. It had probably been too late from the first moment he kissed her.

"Annie?" Jacob's voice was sharp with impatience.

She jumped, startled out of her reverie. "I'm over here," she called back, hurrying back to the campsite.

It wasn't that she was afraid of him, she told herself stoutly, analyzing the jagged burst of adrenaline his voice had triggered. He was a force to be reckoned with, that was all; and after last night, she could hardly be blamed for taking him very seriously. And as shaken apart and fluttery as she felt, she didn't have the nerve to oppose him.

She found him in front of the tent, buttoning his jeans. His eyes snapped with annoyance. "You took long enough," he muttered.

"I saw another deer," she offered.

His eyes slid down, staring at her naked legs. She quivered as if his gaze were a licking tongue of heat against her skin. "That shirt is damp," he said. "Get into something warm."

Annie rummaged through the backpack in the cab of the truck and dug out the last of her clean clothes. A wrinkled cotton blouse, the faded jeans she had been reluctant to wear because they fit so tightly, her final pair of clean panties. She had to find a laundromat. Her clothes needed a wash, and so did she, after last night. Her thoughts flashed longingly to the hot mineral pool as she pulled on her clothes.

Jacob was wringing out their sodden clothes, draping them across the picnic table. "I need a bath," she said. "Want to go up to the pool?"

He looked thoughtful, then nodded.

The pool was crystal clear, ruffled by an occasional breeze and wreathed with tiny wisps of steam. Annie pulled off her clothes and tied her hair into a loose knot atop her head, careful not to look at Jacob as she climbed in and let the water close around her like a hot, tender caress. She watched Jacob as he stripped, wondering if he would be— yes, he was. Of course he was. Armed and ready, as always. The man was a veritable sex machine. It was ridiculous, after all they had been through together, that something so silly could still make her blush.

Jacob settled himself comfortably next to her. Annie leaned her head back against his arm and relaxed; as much as a girl could with a magnificent hard-on right at her elbow. They watched the clouds scudding across the sky, pushed by some high, faraway wind. Three stars still gleamed like solitary jewels against the deep, glowing blue. Over the rim of the canyon the sky was lightening.

Jacob's arm shifted, and when she looked up, he was staring at her shoulder. He moved to inspect her better, examining the marks of his fingers from when he had pulled her out of the pool the day before. There was a smaller, matching bruise on her other arm, and he made a soft, incoherent noise in his throat and kissed both of them; hot, tender kisses that made her throat swell and her eyes fill with startled tears.

His inspection continued down her arms, finding every little bruise and mark. The scrapes and scratches she'd gotten camping and gathering firewood, the little burn on her knuckle from her camp stove. Various and sundry mosquito bites. He urged her onto her feet and continued his search. There were little bruises on her hips from when he had held her at the picnic table, and she stroked his dark hair with a sigh of pleasure as he kissed and tongued them in sweet, silent apology. He set her on the edge of the pool, drew her legs out of the water one by one and covered them with kisses, finding every little hurt: the nick where she had cut herself shaving, the faded bruise from a briefcase that had banged her shin on the Staten Island Ferry almost two weeks ago, all the tiny, long-forgotten scars from her haphazard, misspent childhood back in Payton. He missed nothing. She would never have dreamed that the hollows of her ankles were an erogenous zone, or that there was so much exquisite sensation in her toes.

He stood up, his penis jutting out eagerly, and splashed steaming hot water from his cupped hands onto the flat rock at the water's edge. He gestured to it. "Lie down on the rock, the way you did yesterday."

Annie watched the water trickle down the lean, muscled contours of his body. "You're giving lots of orders," she said, but the words were robbed of their tartness by the way her breath hitched in her lungs.

Jacob grabbed her by the waist and lifted her easily. Her backside made a little slapping noise as he deposited her on the wet stone. "Pretty please," he said in a steely voice.

He trapped her eyes in his; he trapped the very air in her lungs, and she wondered frantically how he did it. With a touch, a kiss, with the timbre of his voice, he reduced her to quivering mush. He made her want to fling open every door, give him everything she had to give. His power was terrifying, but still she lay back on the tilted rock, breathless with excitement, and spread her legs for him without being asked.

He ran his hands hungrily over her wet, steaming body until they closed over her vulva. She reached down, trapping his hands. "I'm sore from last night," she murmured, with a flash of uncertainty.

"I'll be gentle," he assured her, coaxing her thighs wider.

And he was gentle, exquisitely gentle, but something had changed, and it took many delirious, writhing moments before she could identify it. When he first seduced her, he had coaxed, persuaded, courted her. Now he was claiming her. She felt the arrogant, possessive authority with which he handled her body, but she was in no position to protest as his tongue swirled sensuously, teasing and laving her, flicking tenderly across her clitoris. He held her trembling body still with masterful strength, and she let her head fall back, staring into the sky. The clouds had turned a startling, wild-rose pink, the world was a wild contrast of dark and light, heat and cold, and her body was at the center of it all, moving helplessly against the wild magic of his sensual mouth. She sobbed with the unbearable perfection of it as he pushed her gently over the crest, just as the last, faint burning star in the sky was swallowed up by the pale blue of morning.

He gathered her into his arms and lowered her body gently back down into the water, cradling her in his strong arms until the tremors melted away. She clung to him for a long time, her face hidden against his neck, before venturing to look up.

He shifted her body to face him. "Tell me something, Annie."

"What?" she asked, wrapping her arms around his neck.

"Your ex. Did he hurt you?"

She stiffened. The tone in his voice put her feminine instincts on full alert. "Why do you want to know?"

"Just answer the question."

He stared into her eyes, and the truth tumbled right out, as it always did when he demanded it. "Nothing really too awful," she said, a little too quickly. "Just . . . ugly. He called me names a lot. And he, um, he got me fired from my job."

"I see." He waited patiently for her to continue.

Annie took a deep breath, and pushed on. "Then it started to escalate. Pushing and shoving, wild threats. He slapped me once. That was when I decided not to hang around and see how bad it could get."

He studied her face, as if trying to read between her words.

"It's all over now, Jacob," she insisted in a forceful voice.

Jacob splashed his face and smoothed back his hair. "If he hurt you, I'm ripping him to pieces," he said with appalling calmness.

"No way," she gasped. "Let him be. I don't want anything to do with him. Case closed, page turned, game over. Got it, Jacob?"

He tucked a damp lock of her hair gently behind her ear and smiled mercilessly. "Let's get going," he said in a matter-of-fact voice.

She stared at him in blank dismay. "Jacob, please don't—"

Water sloshed and cascaded down his powerful body as he stood up. "Come on, Annie. Get a move on. I'm hungry."

Annie scurried down the path, so agitated that her legs trembled and her mind spun in helpless, trapped little circles. She couldn't wait to get on the road and have some privacy. She needed distance from Jacob's intense, brooding presence so she could calm down, get the events of the last two days sorted out in her mind.

She packed her stuff at triple speed at the campsite, and regarded the soggy tent with dismay. "If I pack it now, it'll mildew," she told him. "It has to dry. Go on ahead if you want breakfast."

Jacob snorted in disgust and began dismantling her tent himself. He flung pegs and rods into a careless pile and bundled the sodden fabric carelessly into one of the plastic sacks he had brought the night before. "You won't be using this again," he informed her.

Her jaw dropped. "What the hell are you doing? That's my tent!"

"You want a tent, fine," he said coolly. "We'll stop at the first mall we see and I'll buy you a decent one. But for now, we're staying in motels. I'm sick of the cold and damp." He stalked toward the pickup.

She scrambled after him, panicked. "Jacob, you can't just—"

"And the Santa sack has got to go." He plucked it, one-handed, out of the pickup.

"No way!" she squawked, lunging for it.

He lifted it out of her reach. "Does it have sentimental value?"

"Not particularly, but it's the only—"

"Then it's history." He shoved it into the plastic bag along with her tent, and headed toward the dumpster down the road with long, purposeful strides. He flung the bag inside with a vicious flick of his wrist and gave her a steely, intimidating stare. "And don't even think about fishing them out."

He marched back to the campsite. Annie watched, dumbfounded, as he calmly proceeded to unlatch Mildred's tailgate and tilt the nose of his motorcycle up onto it. He braced himself, lifting the heavy machine into the truck bed without apparent difficulty, and glanced back at her with a "what-are-you-going-to-do-about-it?" look on his face.

She stumbled toward him, her heart fluttering like a trapped bird. "Jacob, I . . . we've had a misunderstanding. I never said that I—"

He slammed the tailgate shut with a resounding clang. "You still don't get it, do you?"

She shook her head mutely.

"We're traveling together," he said curtly.

She stared at him, rooted to the ground. "We are?"

"Like hell am I letting you out of my sight again."

She stared at him, frozen like a statue with her mouth agape. He grabbed her by the shoulders, all the potent force of his will blazing out of his eyes. "Look, Annie. You want to go to this casino and play your lucky dollars, fine. Well go. But we'll go *my* way." He reached down, plucked Mildred's keys neatly out of her jacket pocket and jerked his head toward the passenger side. "Get in. We need breakfast."

Annie climbed numbly into the truck. Jacob started up Mildred's engine, frowning at the rusty cough. "This thing needs help," he said. "I'll take a look at it after breakfast."

His words gave her a flash of wild, irrational panic. If he stuck his hands under Mildred's hood and won her over too, that would be the final blow. Her last ally, seduced away from her. Jacob had seized the upper hand, and she hadn't the slightest clue how to wrest it back from him. She felt like one of Bo-Peep's fluffy little sheep. Baa-a-a. Meek little woman with her big bad Alpha male. Look at her, sitting in the passenger side of her own vehicle, as docile as you please. He had her completely cowed.

It was not to be endured.

Breakfast helped a little, but not as much as he had hoped. Even after a four-egg Western omelet and a double stack of pancakes, Jacob was still in a jagged, dangerous mood. He'd been in its grip for the past twenty-four hours, and it wasn't getting any better.

Worse yet, sex didn't dissipate it. On the contrary. He clenched his jaw and watched the service station guy pour in the second quart of oil. They had a full tank of gas and four new tires, and he'd met Annie's attempts to pay with a glare so menacing she had shrunk back against the door, her eyes huge. Nice going, he told himself. Now she was scared of him, and he didn't blame her. He was scared of himself.

He yanked the Arkansas and Louisiana maps out of the door pocket and buried his face in them, trying to plot out the quickest route to St. Honore, but he couldn't concentrate worth a damn. He'd shocked her speechless when he ditched the tent and Santa sack. And maybe hijacking her pickup had been a little over the top, he thought guiltily. But he was sick of playing games. It was time for her to face reality. Besides, it wasn't like he could choose what he said and did. Jacob the sexually obsessed macho lunatic was acting out, while Jacob the cool, rational choice-maker watched, aghast.

They were grimly silent on the road. He stared at the highway with eyes that burned and stung, examining the strange new shape of the world now that Annie was in it. There were too many doors in his mind flung open all at once, too many crazy, unfamiliar emotions crowding out. For the first time in his life, he didn't know what strings to pull. The world had never seemed so dangerous and wild.

He pulled off the highway onto a strip mall of fast food restaurants, motels and car dealerships. "Lunch," he said shortly.

She gave him a cautious little nod.

He parked in front of a Lone Star Steakhouse and killed the engine. He couldn't stand her guarded silence for another second. He would rather she scream and yell, give him something to grapple with.

"Annie," he said in a rough, hoarse voice. "Come here." He held out his hand, willing her silently to take it. She stared at it, biting her luscious lower lip, and he wondered frantically what was going on behind those smoke-colored eyes. They were veiled from him by the dark sweep of her lashes, by that rich curtain of honey-blonde hair.

Then she reached out, her slender fingers twined with his and she scooted tentatively closer to him on the seat. Dizzying relief surged through him, and she gasped in surprise as he dragged her across the seat and onto his lap. He slid his fingers into her hair and kissed her ravenously. He couldn't get enough of her sweet taste, the plump, trembling softness of her mouth, the way she blushed when she was excited. She was rosy pink right now, cuddling on his lap. She slid her hand beneath his jacket and splayed it against his chest as she kissed him back with timid eagerness.

He yanked her blouse out of her jeans and thrust his hand inside, cupping her breast. He rolled her taut little nipple between his fingers and kneaded the soft, luscious roundness hungrily in his hand.

She stiffened and tore her mouth away from his. "Not here!"

"Why not?" He was drunk with her flavor, her scent, her silky texture. She was like a drug, and he was strung out, wild for her. He barely noticed her struggles as he unbuttoned her jeans and thrust his hand down inside her panties, sliding his finger unerringly into her hot cleft, down where she was so slick and sweet and marvelous. He would caress her, slowly and patiently, waiting until she was slippery and hot, until he felt the beautiful little pulses of her first orgasm clutching rhythmically around his finger, and then, when she was shivering and desperate, he would peel off those skin-tight fuck-me jeans she was wearing. He would spread her beautiful white thighs wide open and ram himself into her hot, quivering body, give her everything he had—

"No! Jacob, damn it!"

She was clawing at his wrist, wriggling on top of his raging hard-on. He forced himself to focus on her words. "What?"

"Have you gone nuts? We're in the parking lot of a family restaurant!" she said furiously.

He glanced out the window, dazed. "Oh. I forgot," he muttered.

"Forgot! Hah! I do not want the worthy citizens of Bernhard, Arkansas, to actively participate in my sex life, so get your greedy paws off me, you sex-crazed maniac!" She seized his wrist with both hands and yanked it out of her jeans, glaring at him as she buttoned them up.

He deliberately licked the fingers he had thrust into her panties, savoring the sweet, rich flavor that lingered there, and turned the key in the ignition. "We're checking into a motel," he said. "Right now."

She looked bewildered. "I thought you were hungry—"

"Yeah, and you're lunch," he muttered, putting the pickup in gear. He laid his foot on the gas and the pickup leaped eagerly forward, toward the budget motel down the road.

As soon as the door lock flashed green, he propelled her into the room and slammed the door shut. He flung his jacket on the floor and shoved her against the wall. "Those jeans drive me crazy," he growled, sliding his hands hungrily all over her hips.

"They're too small," she said shakily. "They shrank in the wash."

"They're perfect," he insisted. He wrenched open the buttons of her jeans and fell to his knees, dragging them down around her ankles.

She clutched his shoulders for balance, staring down at his dark head, his thick hair straggling wildly out of its elastic band. He pressed his face against her mound, breathing in her fragrance with deep, hungry breaths, and put his hand between her legs, forcing them apart. He leaned forward and thrust his tongue into her cleft, swirling it tenderly around and around the flushed delicate bud of her clitoris, sucking on it with slow, devastating skill until her knees sagged and she started to slide down the wall. He reached up his arms to brace her, and his tongue plunged deeper, lapping up the heated juices that pooled between her legs. "Jacob, you're obsessed," she gasped.

His teeth flashed in a swift, feral grin. "Yeah," he agreed, prying off her shoes. He yanked her jeans off her ankles. She heard the sound of ripping fabric and her panties sailed after them. She backed away, unbuttoning her blouse as he stripped off his clothes; with that wild look in his eyes, it was clearly up to her to salvage what was left of her wardrobe. He seized her and bore her down beneath him onto the bed, his hands everywhere, as if he were trying to learn her by heart.

Her body clenched. He was too heavy and hot and desperate, and she was jittery and wild, her nerves on edge. "No," she protested, pushing at him, but it was like pushing a mountain.

"What?" His chest was heaving, but he froze in place, waiting.

"It's too much," she said shakily. "It's freaking me out. I need you to be—" She searched for words, but they eluded her.

"What?" His voice was a grating rasp of frustration.

"I don't know. Slower. Softer. You're scaring me."

He rolled off her onto his back, still panting, and clapped his hand over his eyes. "Shit. *Shit,*" he said, his voice furious.

His long, muscular frame vibrated with tension, his furiously erect crimson penis rose stiffly all the way to his navel. A tangle of conflicting emotions bewildered her: fear at his raw hunger barely held in check, pity for his evident distress, all mixed with a secret female satisfaction at her own power that she could drive him to such a state. She edged closer to him. "I didn't say you had to stop completely," she said. "I just wanted you to calm down a little." She petted the hair that lay flat and silky against his hard belly, leaned down and gently swirled her tongue around the swollen head of his penis.

He jerked up onto his elbows with a muttered curse. "God, Annie," he groaned. "This is supposed to calm me down?"

She cradled his balls tenderly in her hand, licking him from the base to the tip of his shaft with one long, wet, luxurious swipe of her tongue. "Do you like that?"

"Don't ask stupid questions," he said furiously. "I'm not in control of myself. Bear that in mind if you provoke me."

The low tremor in his voice made her want to soothe him. She crawled on top of him impulsively and pressed her mouth to his in a soft, yielding kiss. "That's just a risk I'm going to have to take," she said. "I trust you, remember?"

His eyes never left hers as he groped on the floor for his jeans. He ripped open the condom and smoothed it swiftly over himself. "Maybe you shouldn't," he said. "Roll over."

She stared at him blankly. He made an impatient sound, and flipped her over himself, and she found herself suddenly on her stomach, the mattress bouncing beneath her as he splayed his hands over her backside and pressed her down onto the bed. He kissed and tongued the little twin dimples at the base of her spine, and his strong hands shoved her thighs wide open.

She pressed her face into the rumpled sheets, lifting herself for him in a fevered agony of anticipation, far beyond any teasing or game playing. He thrust his fingers inside her, spreading her silky juices all around until she was slippery and soft and ready. She let out a low moan as his penis slid slowly into her tight sheath, stretching her wide. She was sore and oversensitive from the last night's endless hours of intense lovemaking, but too aroused to care. She arched her backside up to him in eager, silent invitation.

He drove himself all the way inside her with a hoarse

shout, crushing her onto the bed with his big, hot body and claiming her completely, and she finally began to understand what his harsh warning had meant.

She clutched handfuls of the sheet, trembling in confusion. Panic was mixing crazily with excitement as he drove his thick shaft in and out of her in a deep, savage rhythm that bordered on violence; but she knew instinctively that he was too skillful a lover to hurt her. It was his very skill that was so dangerous, his intense, seductive power that battered down her defenses, demanding that she yield herself up. She could lose herself to him, and be utterly possessed.

Their struggle took place on a plane of consciousness she had never known existed, with a clashing explosion of energy that shook her mind, scorched her body, turned her inside out. She yelled at him in raw, incoherent anger, thrashing beneath the plunging, rhythmic invasion of his body, but her struggles only inflamed them both further. He would not be denied; she felt it in the way he held her, the way he arched his long, powerful body over hers and drove himself into her. The desperate tension in her muscles sharpened the edge of the climax bearing down on her to an unbearable pitch, wrenching a wailing cry of pleasure from her throat. She felt his triumph in every cell of her body as she convulsed around him.

He began again almost immediately, rolling her onto her side. He folded her leg up, toying mercilessly with her shivering, unresisting body, relishing the sight of her, heavy-eyed and flushed and panting.

Then he mounted her again, his passionate desire unabated. Annie's body responded helplessly, her sheath supple and slick as he took her from every angle, in every position. He moved and lifted and turned her to suit his pleasure as if she were a doll. He made her come again and again, with his hands and his mouth and his insatiable penis, but when he came close to his own orgasm he stopped, his body rigid. He held her crushed and breathless beneath him—and began again.

"Enough," she begged him. "Please."

"Not yet," he said, his voice a harsh gasp. "I warned you, Annie."

For this round, she was flat on her back, spread-eagled and writhing beneath his pumping body. She reached up and grabbed a handful of his hair, yanking down hard. He gasped, startled. "Damn it, Jacob," she said furiously. "Are you doing this to punish me?"

"God, no." He deftly unsnarled his hair from her fingers and pinned her hands behind her head. "I'm doing it because I love watching you come. I love when you clench up and squeeze my cock inside you, when you make those sexy sounds, when your face gets all rosy red. I just cannot . . . get . . . enough of it." He punctuated each word with a sensual thrust. "Come with me now, Annie," he urged. "Together. Right now. Let's fly together."

"No," she whispered, shaking her head, sure that it was part of his sorcerous plan to bind her to him utterly. She thrashed on the rumpled bed as he thrust his tongue into her mouth and ground his hips against hers. He insisted, using the innate skill of his body, changing the angle so that his hard shaft stroked relentlessly against her most sensitive point. He demanded, compelled, dragged her inexorably over the brink with him, and they fell through dark and light together, fused into a single pulsing wave of rapture.

When she came back to herself, she was weeping. Jacob rolled onto his side and gathered her close. At first she just lay there sobbing in his arms, but as consciousness crept back, her anger slowly ignited. How dare he presume to comfort her when he was the arrogant bastard who had reduced her to this ravished, unglued state. He was still inside her, wedged so deeply that she could feel his heartbeat pulsing against her womb. She lashed out at him, but he jerked away from the blow.

He swelled again to full arousal within her as she struggled, and she was suddenly exhausted. She went limp, sobs tearing at her chest. "Don't, Jacob," she whispered. "Leave me be. I can't take any more."

Jacob stared down at her, a tiny muscle pulsing in his jaw. His face convulsed, as if in pain, and he withdrew from her body. He sat on the edge of the bed and hunched over, putting his face in his hands. Annie curled up on the bed until the sobs subsided, and took deep, shuddering breaths, willing herself to calm down. Jacob's muscular back was rigid and trembling. The room was utterly silent.

Jacob removed the condom without looking at her. He disposed of it and pulled on his jeans, his face an impenetrable mask. "Get dressed," he said curtly. "We're getting something to eat."

Annie forced herself to sit up, draping her hair over her breasts, and watched him silently as he laced up his boots. "Would you bring me back a sandwich?" she asked, unable to control the tremor in her voice. "I'd like to take a bath."

He frowned as he shrugged on his shirt, his face dubious.

"I could really use some privacy," she said softly. "Please, Jacob."

He walked slowly to the bed and pushed back the hair that veiled her face from him. He cradled her cheek and tilted her face up. "Do not leave this room," he said slowly.

She shook her head.

He caressed her cheek with his fingertip, and stepped back, obviously reluctant. He plucked his wallet out of his jacket, and left.

And she could finally breathe.

Theoretically. If she breathed too deep, the tears would start again. If she held her breath, she would pass out. She compromised with short, strangled little gasps and stared at the horrendous motel art—some sort of obscenely bright-colored mallard duck. She put her hands over her eyes to block it out, and tried to pull herself together.

She had to grab onto the last, ragged, fluttering shred of her independent will and run, far and fast. She couldn't let herself be taken over, swept away. For God's sake, the man had just fucked her practically senseless, and she still wanted him. She doubled over with a strangled laugh and pressed her face against her knees.

After three short days with Jacob, the whole Philip story, which had seemed so apocalyptic, was blotted practically out of her mind. The memory now had a tinny sense of distance, like a scary but more or less insignificant movie she had seen somewhere, a long time ago.

She dragged herself upright. Minutes were ticking away, and this might be her last chance. She had to haul ass or she would lose her nerve. One more assault on her defenses like the last one, and she would crumble—and become the body-and-soul property of a man about whom she knew practically nothing.

She had read somewhere that one of the quickest ways to make a person feel helpless was to take away their clothes. Conversely, putting them back on ought to give her a shot of instant backbone. She got up and rooted around in search of her underwear. She longed for a shower, but didn't dare take the time. She found her panties, the crotch ripped out and hanging in pathetic shreds. Whatever. Going without underwear never killed a girl yet. She would find a K-Mart. Buy panties.

She yanked on her jeans, starting to shake. Half of her was terrified he would burst into the room, sandwich in hand, and bend her to his will again. The other half was silently begging him to get back quick, before she did something irreversible.

But he didn't come back. And she knew what she had to do.

Her gaze swept the room. Mildred's keys. Crucial detail. She pocketed them. Purse. Likewise. She grabbed it.

Then her eyes lit on Jacob's jacket, and an idea sprang to her mind. She reached gingerly into the pocket and fished out the keys to his bike. She would hide them in the motel safe. Let him think she had taken them. It would give her the edge she needed without grounding him completely, or weighing on her conscience.

It was time to go, but her damned stupid leaden feet wouldn't move. She grabbed the pen on the desk and scrawled on a sheet of motel stationery.

Jacob, I'm so sorry. I have to go because I need to . . .

She wadded it up and threw it into the trash basket, and grabbed another.

Jacob, I can't let my life be taken over again . . .

She stopped, wadded, threw.

On the third sheet of paper, she watched, appalled, as her hand wrote,

I love you.

Tears started flooding down, and she flung the incriminating shred of paper at the trash basket, despising the little hiccupping sounds that were jerking out of her throat. She wrote

Sorry.

in a big childish scrawl, and laid it on the rumpled bed. On impulse, she dug into her purse and pulled out the sack of lucky dollars. She pulled one out and held the chilly coin until it had absorbed the heat of her hand, silently wishing him luck. All the luck and love in the world. She dropped it on top of the note, and fled.

She blew her nose repeatedly, practicing a cheerful expression in the elevator. She dinged the front desk bell until she got the attention of a plump blonde girl whose name tag read "Tammi."

"Tammi, would you do me a favor? My boyfriend left the keys to his motorcycle in the room. He asked me to leave them in the motel safe if I had to go out. Would that be OK?"

Tammi looked doubtful. "Couldn't you just leave 'em in the room? I mean, it's not like they're jewels, right?"

Annie gave her a woman-to-woman smile. "It's his beloved bike," she confided. "You know how men are. He's paranoid. Humor us."

Tammi giggled. "I sure do know what you mean, ma'am. I'll just call the manager and have him put 'em right in there for ya."

"Thanks so much, Tammi," Annie said, bolting out the door.

With the help of a couple of burly guys who were passing by, she got the motorcycle out of the truck, though it cost the two of them far more effort than it had cost Jacob to lift it by himself. She was wild-eyed, nervous, sure that he would appear at any moment. He didn't.

She pulled onto the road, and all the accumulated tension from the past few days slammed down on her at once. She knew she shouldn't drive while she was sobbing, her eyes constantly filling and refilling with tears, but she didn't dare pull over to cry herself out. She just blinked hard, wiped her nose on her sleeve, and tried not to drive off the road.

Chapter Six

"For God's sake, all I asked for was a turkey club, a burger, fries, a beer and a Coke. I didn't order a six course meal," Jacob barked to the Lone Star Steakhouse hostess. "It's already been more than a half an hour!"

The hostess's cherry-red mouth tightened. "It'll be right out, sir."

"That's what you said the last four times," he grumbled, sinking back down onto the bench. He was as agitated as hell, his boot pounding a staccato rhythm on the floor. He covered his eyes with his hand, horrified at himself. He had never tried to intimidate a woman with his size and strength before. He had never needed to, but the resistance he sensed in Annie goaded him to keep pushing her, to break down her defenses. He couldn't seem to stop. It was like a bad dream. At this rate, he was going to end up in a padded cell.

He would bring back her lunch and throw himself on her mercy. Apologize for being such a controlling asshole. He couldn't handle the stress of wondering if she would still be there every time he turned around. He might try asking nicely if she would please stay with him, instead of pounding his chest like a gorilla. If he knew she wouldn't bolt, maybe he could calm down.

"Here's your order, sir."

He took the bag, muttering a distracted thanks, and burst through the restaurant doors. He started through the parking lot at a brisk walk, which quickly transformed into a lope, then to a dead run. The more excess nervous energy he got rid of now, the better his chances of not fucking up with Annie.

The thought hit him just as he was shoving the key card into the back door of the motel. It froze him into place for a good fifteen seconds.

He shoved open the door and took the stairs. He needed at least four flights of stairs to process this revolutionary concept. Annie, cuddled up with him on his couch, watching videos and eating popcorn. He wondered if she would like how he had rebuilt his condo. Whatever. He could rebuild it to suit her if she didn't. Annie in a beautiful evening gown, looking gorgeous on his arm at the annual New Year's gala charity ball. Annie meeting his parents. That slowed him down for a moment. Dad was no problem; one look at those big gray eyes and the old man would be eating right out of her hand. Mama would be tougher, but Annie could win her over, he thought optimistically. He would just buy Annie a pastel linen suit and some little pearl earrings, and she could take care of the rest.

By the time he got to the top of the last flight of stairs, he was already planning the guest list. It was so simple, so obvious, so perfect. Why the hell hadn't he thought of this before? He could have been in bed right now, cuddling his fascinating, sexy fiancée. He fished the key card out of his pocket, hoping she would still be in the tub.

He felt her absence like a blow when the door swung open. He forced himself to look around and check the bathroom, even though he knew it was too late. He looked out the front window. The motorcycle sat where her pickup had been. The bag of food fell to the floor.

He should have known better than to turn his back on her. Jacob grabbed the silver dollar off the bed and stared down at the single word scrawled across the sheet of motel stationery, clutching the coin so tightly that it bit into his palm. Then he spotted the crumpled sheet of paper on the floor, and lunged for it. He smoothed out the wrinkles and read *"I love you."*

His knees gave way and he landed hard on the bed.

He wanted to howl like a wolf and trash the room, but there was no time to indulge himself. If he didn't catch up with her by the time she reached the Black Cat, he might never find her. He yanked his jacket from the floor and shrugged it on, thanking God for automatic checkout. He dug in the pocket for his keys. His body froze.

He dug in the other pocket. The inside pockets. He turned the pockets inside out. He checked every horizontal surface in the room, sweeping brochures, menus, stationery, cable guides, all onto the floor.

Then he punched the wall so hard that the surreal duck picture slid down the wall behind the TV. The crash and tinkle of breaking glass and the blood on his knuckles did not make him feel any better.

Christmas Eve at the Black Cat Casino was rowdy and crazed, ablaze with colored Christmas lights. Annie felt as drab as a field mouse as she fingered her little sack of silver dollars and stared at what she was almost certain was her lucky slot machine. She had never felt so unlucky in her life. She had a gaping hole inside her and her luck was leaking out of it, swirling like a whirlpool in a bathtub drain. She could feel the miserable little swirling sensation deep in her gut.

Of course, that feeling could be the result of not eating or sleeping. She'd just driven endlessly, stopping to doze now and then at rest stops until a state trooper knocked on her window, reminding her that she wasn't in a campground and it was time to move along.

Buck up, she told herself. You made it. You're here. But still she stared at the machine, a sick, sinking fear in her belly. Not that she might lose her money; that was the least of her worries. Her fear was that she'd made a terrible mistake back in Bernhard, Arkansas. She'd torn her heart out of her body and left it in a budget-motel room. And she didn't even know his last name. She'd burned her bridges utterly.

Well, that was Annie Simon for you. If there was one thing she was spectacularly good at, it was burning bridges. In her current luckless state, she'd be smarter to just take her silver dollars and buy herself a sandwich and a cheap room for the night.

Stubborn pride stiffened her backbone. She couldn't give up now. She'd come too far, given up too much. She had to at least try.

She let out her breath in a long sigh, held her lucky dollars in both hands and closed her eyes. Concentrate, she told herself. Think lucky thoughts. New beginnings. Sunrises. The Milky Way. Colored balloons rising into a clear blue sky. Ice cream.

But Jacob's face was burned into her memory. His huge, out-of-control grin lighting him up like a Christmas tree. It was impossible to think of anything else. It hurt her heart to think of him.

She opened the bag and began to play, sliding in coin after coin and yanking down the handle. She lost, lost, won eleven dollars. Lost six times in a row, won three dollars. Lost, lost, lost, won two. Lost, lost, lost, in a long string. The dollars drained away with that same miserable, swirling, bathroom drain feeling.

Finally she was holding the last coin. She slipped it into the slot with fatalistic calm. Lost.

Well. That was that. She stared at the machine with blank, numb relief. Now she knew. No more surprises. Down to ground zero.

It was time to head to the ladies' room, to wash her face and comb her hair. Eleven o'clock on Christmas Eve in a casino wasn't the ideal time or place for job hunting, but she had nothing better to do. She squared her shoulders, turned.

Her heart skipped a beat, and started to gallop.

Jacob stood there, his hair loose and windblown, his face haggard and unshaven. A silver dollar gleamed in his outstretched hand. "You've got one more coin to play, Annie," he said quietly.

She drank in the sight of his pale, weary, incredibly beautiful face. "I gave that dollar to you," she whispered. For luck."

He shook his head. "I want more than that from you."

"What do you want?" she forced out.

His eyes burned into hers with piercing intensity for a moment, and then a brief, tired smile flashed on his face, softening his harsh expression. "Everything," he admitted.

She tried to laugh, but it came out like a sob. "You think big."

"You better believe it," he said, reaching for her.

She was losing herself in his eyes, and she couldn't fight it anymore. Her eyes filled with tears as his lips met hers with a kiss of reverent, hushed gentleness, as if she were precious, sacred, adored.

"I love you, Annie," he whispered. His arms tightened and he hugged her so tightly that she could barely breathe.

The colored lights began to dip and spin around her. She wound her arms around his big solid frame and hung on. "You do?"

"Yes," he whispered, his voice muffled against her hair. "Don't run away from me again. I need you."

"Oh, God, I need you too," she choked out. "I love you, Jacob."

His arms tightened. "Then you'll marry me?"

She blinked, astonished. "Marry you?"

His voice was urgent. "I only acted like a lunatic because I'm madly in love with you, and you made me chase you all over hell's half acre. Promise to marry me, and I swear to God I'll calm right down."

"Marry you?" she repeated stupidly.

Jacob's face tightened in dismay. "Don't tell me I'm scaring you away again. I'm so tired of chasing you, Annie. You're wearing me out."

She soothed the anxious line in his brow with her fingertip, and slid her hand down to caress his scratchy, beautifully formed jaw. "It would take a lot to wear you out, Jacob," she observed.

He closed his eyes and leaned his forehead against hers. "Maybe so," he said quietly. "But I'd rather save my energy for other things."

Her heart swelled with tenderness at the exhaustion in his voice. She couldn't fight the feeling any longer, and besides, this had to be right because it felt incredibly, marvelously lucky. She rose up on tiptoe and pulled his head down to meet her kiss. "I won't run away."

His eyes flashed. "Promise?"

"I promise."

"So will you marry me, then?"

She laughed, delighted. "Well, maybe you could tell me a bit about yourself. Like, what's your last name?"

"Kerr. I'm an architect. Very respectable. Nice family, no prison record," he said swiftly. "Now will you marry me?"

Her jaw dropped. "Architect?"

A big man with a red nose prodded Annie's shoulder. "Hey, you guys gonna use this machine, or what?" he brayed in a boozy voice.

Jacob grinned and held out the silver dollar. "So? Are you going to play?"

"I've already won," she said, happy tears trembling on

her eyelashes. "But I guess I might as well. This won't take long," she assured the red-nosed man with a smile. She inserted the coin into the slot and hauled down on the handle.

Jackpot. Bells dinged and people cheered. Shining silver dollars clattered out in a thick, liquid-looking stream. Annie leaped into Jacob's arms, and wrapped her legs gleefully around his waist.

"Tonight, the motel's on me," she crowed. "And the champagne, too!"

Jacob buried his face against her neck and held her close, his body trembling. "Deal," he said.

Later, cuddled together in the sagging bed in the first roadside motel they found, Annie stretched and rested her head on his broad, warm chest. "I would never have pegged you as an architect," she said in a wondering voice. "That long hair of yours."

He gave her a guilty smile. "I thought it would ruin my bad-ass, biker dude image if I let on that I know how to iron a dress shirt."

She laughed and reached for her glass, taking a lazy sip of champagne. "I thought you were going to ask me to be your biker babe, and ride off into the sunset with you on the back of your hog."

He wrapped one of her curls around his finger and stroked it against his cheek. "Would you have gone for it?"

"I think you could convince me to do just about anything," she said with absolute seriousness.

"I still haven't convinced you to marry me," he grumbled.

She rested her chin on her crossed arms. "Give me more details, Jacob," she teased. "Like, what's the name of the firm where you work?"

He snorted. "Are you going to call and check my references?"

"Spit it out, Kerr," she said in a steely voice.

He rolled his eyes. "It's called Kerr and Associates," he muttered.

Annie's eyes widened. She was silent for a long moment. "As in . . . Jacob Kerr and his associates?" she said hesitantly.

"Yeah," he snapped.

"Ah," she murmured. "And . . . what do you and your associates build?"

He shrugged. "Various things. Stadiums, office buildings, airports."

"Airports?" She disentangled herself and sat up. "Don't tell me you're a young urban professional with a closet full of Armani suits and ties."

His eyes narrowed. "Are you going to hold it against me?"

She scrambled off the bed, flushed with outrage. "You lied to me!"

"Not really," he muttered defensively. "I just never got around to telling you about myself. You weren't all that forthcoming, either."

But Annie was on a roll. "You snake! You stalk me, and pursue me, and seduce me, and mess with my mind, and bend me to your will, and now I find out that you . . . that you build *airports*!"

His face was abjectly contrite. "I'm so sorry. Really."

"And after all that, you have the nerve to ask me to marry you?"

He reached out a long arm and yanked her back down on top of him. "I'm begging you, then." His voice was rough with intensity.

She scrambled off his hard body and slid off the bed. He followed with catlike swiftness.

"That's enough of that strong-arm stuff," she warned him, backing hastily away. "I won't stand for it. You be nice, Jacob."

He stopped dead in his tracks, his eyes wary. "I'm sorry," he said carefully. He waited, naked and beautiful, his arms at his sides and his fists clenched. The silence between them was thick with emotion, with words unsaid and questions unanswered. The air hummed with it.

Oh, enough, already. Her mind was made up, and there was no reason to keep torturing him.

Well, then again . . . maybe just a tiny bit.

She crossed her arms over her breasts and widened her stance aggressively. "I'm afraid a lame-ass apology is just not going to cut it."

A wary smile played about the corners of his sensual mouth. "Just what would cut it?"

She put her hands up on his muscular shoulders, and shoved down hard. A comprehending grin of delight split his face, and he folded promptly to his knees. "Your wish is my command, Empress Annie," he said softly, nuzzling her belly.

"It damn well better be," she said breathlessly. "Start apologizing, buddy, and you better make it good, because your ass is mine tonight."

He looked up, laughter crinkling up the gorgeous laugh lines around his eyes. "Do you mean that literally?"

Annie smiled down at him, sweetly, cruelly. "That's for me to know and for you to wonder about, loverboy," she purred.

He shook with laughter. He didn't look as scared as he ought to be, she thought, trying not to giggle. A ruthless dominatrix did not giggle. But there was too much emotion bottled up inside them both. It fizzed out like champagne bubbles, and they laughed until their laughter melted into something deeper, more wrenching. Jacob's shoulders shook, and Annie cradled his dark head against her belly. She sank down to her knees and wrapped her arms around his neck. "Of course I'll marry you, you big idiot," she whispered.

His arms encircled her, squeezing her breathless. "You mean it?"

She pried his damp face away from her shoulder. "You still need convincing?"

He nodded, his face somber. "You better believe it."

She cradled his face in her hands and kissed him tenderly. "I never could resist a challenge," she said.

MELTDOWN

Chapter One

Jane hugged her lunch booty to her chest as she stepped out of the elevator. A mocha frappuccino, chicken and pesto on a baguette, a fresh fruit cup, and just one tiny, perfect precious jewel of a dark chocolate champagne truffle rattling around all on its lonesome in a white paper bag. She silently repeated the resolution of the day to herself; no more skipping lunch because of her frenetic boss Charlene's crisis management style. From now on she was going to take at least a few minutes to eat, and she would chew each bite properly, too, like a civilized human being. It wasn't so much to ask, considering how she busted her buns for this place.

Mona, the receptionist, held out a thick sheaf of pink message slips and rolled her eyes expressively as Jane walked by the front desk. "Charlene couldn't find you. She's freaking out. Where'd you go?"

"I have to eat." Her voice sounded guilty and defensive to her own ears, so Jane took a calming breath and smiled at Mona as she took the messages. She was in control. Dignified. And now she was going to sit down to eat lunch at her desk, as was her God-given right and privilege.

Erica, one of her coworkers, grabbed Jane's arm as she passed her cubicle. The frappuccino listed dangerously to the side. Jane barely managed to catch it in time.

"There she is, the woman of a thousand voices! Sylvie and I are fishing for marketing managers, but we've hit a wall. Would you make some of your magic calls for us, Jane?" Erica pleaded. "Pretty please? Be the spoiled southern belle. I love that character."

"Oh, no, be the English dowager duchess," Sylvia begged. "She's my favorite. That snooty old bitch always gets results."

"No floor show until after I've eaten my lunch, you guys," Jane said firmly. "Then I'll be anybody you want me to be. I promise. OK?" She marched onward to her office, avoiding Erica's and Sylvia's imploring puppy dog eyes. She was such a hopeless sucker for guilt.

The whole headhunting firm took shameless advantage of Jane's well-honed theater skills. She could impersonate anyone, fooling the most suspicious receptionists or secretaries when it came to ferreting out the names and titles of her prey. And once they had identified the most likely executives, she and her colleagues then did their best to lure them away and place them elsewhere. For a nice, fat commission.

She was good at it. Scarily good. But first, lunch. Everyone deserved to eat, and a hardworking headhunter was no exception.

She had just settled in at her desk and raised her sandwich to her lips when Charlene burst into her office. "Jane! Finally! Where on earth were you? What's the status of the Brighton account?"

Jane put down her sandwich with a sigh. "You gave me that file forty minutes ago, Charlene. I've barely had time to read it, let alone—"

"Turn up the heat on this one, Jane!" Charlene gestured

frantically. "Everything else goes to the back burner. Brighton Group just lost their general manager to Corinthian Hotels and Resorts. I want you to find a hot candidate, soon! Al Brighton just called me, and the man practically had a stroke on the phone. I want to throw him a bone. Like, now!"

"Yes, I know," Jane said patiently. "I read the file. I understand the situation, and I was just compiling a list of their main competitors. I'll start making the calls as soon as I finish eating my—"

"Start with Crowne Royale Group. Their management team rocks. Everything they touch turns to gold. And I've got the number right here. I looked it up for you. Am I a peach of a boss, or what? Go on. Call 'em."

Jane cast a longing look at her melting frappuccino. "Of course I will, as soon as I—"

"I need your killer instincts on this, Jane. Brighton will fork out two hundred thousand a year for a kick-ass general manager, and if you get lucky, Pierce and I will renegotiate your contract. Twenty-five percent of each commission, starting with this one. You do the math. And we can even sweeten the pot by tossing in a nice, fat contribution to that youth theater group of yours, hmm? Never let it be said that Grayson and Clint don't support the arts."

Dollar signs flashed in Jane's mind. The headhunting firm took fifteen percent of the first year salary of each candidate she placed. Twenty-five percent of that sum would be hers. $7,500. If her bosses kicked in a donation on top of that— oh, boy. She would almost have a budget for the fall project for her theater troupe of at-risk neighborhood kids, the MeanStreets Playhouse. Rehearsal space, sets, props, lights, costumes, none of it came cheap. She and the other Playhouse founders were always scrambling for funding.

The Playhouse was the only thing in her life that she really gave a damn about. Being able to personally guarantee the kids' fall project . . . oh, it was tempting. Even more tempting than a melting frappuccino.

Jane exhaled slowly. "I need a strategy." She could feel her voice harden as she slipped into work mode. "I'll be a writer. I want to write a fawning feature article on their hotel, so I need a tour from the GM."

Charlene grinned in toothy triumph. "Go on. Call 'em up. I love watching our prim little Jane morph into a ruthless shark."

Jane dialed. "Crowne Royale Group," a young woman responded.

Her acting skills clicked into high gear. "My name is Jane King. I'm from *Europa Air Inflight Magazine,*" she lied smoothly. "I'm writing a series of articles on luxury accommodations, and I hope to feature Crowne Royale Group. I'd like to organize a preliminary tour so I can get an idea how I want to proceed. Is your general manager available?"

"Um, actually, he's in a meeting right now," the girl said. "One sec while I check his schedule . . . oh, wait. How about today at three?"

Jane blinked. It was already almost two-thirty. It was never this easy. "Uh, that'll be fine," she said. "And I'll be meeting with . . . ?"

"The GM's name is Gary Finley," the girl told her.

Charlene beamed as Jane scribbled down directions. "Well? Don't just sit there! It has to be destiny! Freshen up your war paint!"

"Right, boss."

Jane's dutiful smile faded as soon as the door clicked shut. She sincerely liked her flamboyant, high-maintenance employer, but she had no energy to spare for drama right now. She fished her makeup bag out of the desk, set up the mirror and stared into it with critical eyes.

Yikes. Fluorescent lights would make even a Hollywood diva look like death warmed over, she reminded herself. She'd been tossing awake, staring at the ceiling every night, and it had started to show.

She should be feeling pleased with herself. She was the

best headhunter in the firm. She'd dragged in a lot of revenue for Grayson & Clint. Problem was, she was sick of the intrigue, the power games.

It had started out innocently enough. Her budding theater career had gone straight down the toilet four years ago in the wake of her disastrous affair with Dylan. She'd needed money, and a distraction. This job had provided both. She'd been edgy, angry, in the mood to jerk people around. Headhunting the way she did it was an outlet for her thwarted acting skills, and a way to crawl out of the hole that Dylan had put her in. She'd never meant it to be permanent.

She wasn't angry and edgy anymore. She was tired and lonely, and her personal life was a flinty wasteland, but hey. One problem at a time. It was a longish cab ride to the Crowne Royale Group's executive offices. No time to mope, or to eat lunch, either. She had to pop into a phone booth and emerge as the headhunter from hell.

She pulled off her glasses, and popped in her contacts. She dug out some hairpins and proceeded to twist and tuck until she had a smooth French roll. She liked the smidgen of extra height, the Gwyneth Paltrow air of restrained elegance. The brown skirt and nipped-in blazer were fine. Shimmering mocha lipstick, translucent powder to soften the freckles, a sweep of mascara, and her face was in order. She slipped her feet into the pumps that added three inches to her well-rounded five-foot-three frame, and watch out, world. She was good to go.

The job ahead of her was simple: to inveigle herself cleverly into Gary Finley's office without compromising his current job. If he looked promising, she would then persuade him that he would be better off working for Brighton Group than for Crowne Royale. Too bad she hadn't worn a low cut blouse, but no biggie. Her boobs commanded respect even when she was buttoned up to the neck. So, unfortunately, did the breadth of her hips, but it was better to accentuate the positive, right?

It was well worth jerking around a few overpaid hotel executives if it let her fund the MeanStreets kids' fall project. So what if she lied through her teeth to get past the receptionist? Big fat deal. She was a good actress, not a bad person. Maybe she should've become a spy, and used her talents for deception in the service of her country. She gazed into the mirror, affecting the steely poise of a Hollywood superspy.

"The name's Duvall," she said coolly. "Jane Duvall."

She snorted at her own goofiness, but hey. If she had to lie like a dog to make her living, she should at least try to have some fun at it.

The executive office of Crowne Royale Group was located in a side wing of the Kingsbridge Crowne Hotel. It was a former nineteenth-century timber baron's mansion in the Queen Anne district, and had been fully restored to its original splendor. Jane looked around the reception area, grudgingly impressed. Sixteen-foot ceilings. Sumptuous furniture, the kind you sink into with a grateful sigh, but need a crane to get yourself out of. Antique area rugs. Sunshine blazed through the windows, rare for a Seattle afternoon even in the summer. It lit up the rich tones of the dark, gleaming parquet. The minimalist arrangement of blush pink orchids on the receptionist's desk probably cost hundreds of dollars by itself. The place practically dripped money. Ripe for the plunder.

The only jarring note was the girl behind the desk. She was strikingly pretty, with liquid dark eyes, but her gleaming dark hair was twisted up into strange, spiky knobs over her ears. Hair sticks were stuck through, decorated with bobbing beads on springs that looked for all the world like insect antennae. Her lush mouth was painted a bright, frosty purple.

"May I help you?" the girl asked politely.

"I'm here to see Gary Finley," Jane said. "I'm Jane King."

The receptionist's grin showed off a mouth full of braces. "Oh! The writer from the magazine, right?"

Ah, excellent. Jane smiled. An ingenuous receptionist was a hard-bitten headhunter's dream. "Yes. I had an appointment with—"

"With Gary, I know. I have some bad news. We had an emergency at one of the restaurants. Gary had to run off and fix it."

Jane sighed inwardly. I see. Can I reschedule?"

A thoughtful frown tugged the receptionist's brows together. "I have a better idea," she said, her dark gaze oddly intent upon Jane's face. "I'll just have you meet with Mac. He used to be GM. He's been everything around here, from busboy on up. Who better than Mac?"

A prickle of tension ran up Jane's back. "And who is Mac?"

"Our CEO, Michael MacNamara," the receptionist said proudly. "He knows everything there is to know about this place, believe me."

It was clear from the girl's expression that Jane should be pleased and honored. It took all of Jane's iron self-control not to look aghast. The last person she wanted to chat up was the guy she was plotting to steal a key employee from. "Oh, I don't want to bother your CEO—"

"No bother! It'll do him good to remember where he came from. He gets too big for his britches sometimes." The receptionist stood, revealing a very bare and enviably flat midriff. "Come with me. I'll just put you in his office until I have a chance to tell him about you."

"Oh, no, really!" Jane said desperately. "I'd rather reschedule—"

"Don't worry! Mac is great. You'll like him. Follow me." The girl's antennae bobbed jauntily as she strode down the corridor.

Jane followed, running rapidly through her options. She could cut her losses and bolt, or she could bluff this out in the hopes of contacting Finley later. Charlene would be very unhappy if she blew this before she'd even made contact. Damn.

Oh, whatever. For the MeanStreets kids, she could spin out this charade for a few extra minutes. She was a trained actress, after all.

Wow, that purple leather miniskirt was fearless. The girl was like something out of a rock video superimposed onto an ad for luxury real estate. "Amazing hair ornaments," Jane commented.

The receptionist grinned over her shoulder. "You like them? I bought them on my lunch break. Mac's gonna have kittens."

This CEO had some problems getting respect from his subordinates, if this girl was any indication. She was awfully likeable, though, and certainly beautiful. Maybe she traded on her looks.

The girl flung open the door to a large office and gestured Jane in with a flourish. "Make yourself comfortable. Mac will be along any second. I'm Robin, by the way. Can I bring you some coffee or tea?"

"No, thank you." Jane was charmed at Robin's friendliness in spite of her awkward predicament.

Out of force of habit, she scrounged a piece of company letterhead out of the printer. She was tapping names and titles into her Palm Pilot when she heard the commotion. A furious, rumbling bass. Robin's light alto responding, protesting. The noise grew steadily closer.

". . . enough of your garbage, Robin." The words were spat out like bullets. "I'm sick of you testing my patience. Get those damn things out of your hair."

"I'm just expressing my individuality, Mac—"

"Individuality, my ass. You knew that Danny and I had a three-thirty with Carlisle and Young, and still you schedule me to babysit a magazine columnist? That's a job for Gary!"

"But Gary's not here! The sous chef at the Copley was

having a nervous breakdown, and Gary had to go deal with it!"

"So why didn't you schedule her to come in on another day? Use your brain, for God's sake!"

Oh, dear. She'd landed smack in the middle of an internal power struggle. If there were a back door handy, she would slither out of it and to hell with Gary Finley. But there was no back door.

The voices were getting louder. Jane braced herself.

"I never claimed to be a secretary, Mac. I'm just trying to help. If you don't like how I manage your schedule, maybe you should fire me." Robin's voice was supremely unrepentant. "Go ahead. Make my day."

"Goddamn it, Robin—" The door was slapped open so hard, it crashed against the wall. Jane flinched back.

He filled the door frame. Utterly filled it. Her indrawn breath stopped in her lungs and just hung there, motionless.

He was amazing. It wasn't the perfect word, but it was the first one that stuck to him. Gorgeous was too frivolous. Handsome was too bland. His face was square and raw-boned, with hollows beneath broad, jutting cheekbones. His gleaming dark hair was clipped severely short. Straight black brows, penetrating gray eyes. His features fit together so perfectly. The blunt jaw, the hooked nose, the sculpted perfection of his sensual lips. The raw force of will stamped all over his face.

She couldn't look down and examine the rest of him, because her eyes were locked with his. She got a vague sense of big, broad. Tall. Well dressed, but his clothing was subordinate to him, and therefore unnoticeable. All she really saw were those eyes. Fierce and bright. Preternaturally aware, like a timber wolf on the prowl.

His eyes moved over her body. She became very conscious of how much smaller she was. Of the bulk of his big body, blocking her exit. Her blazer felt too tight, her skirt too short. Her clothes too . . . hot.

"Hello," he said simply.

She opened her mouth, but the dry squeak that came out was audible only inside her own head. She felt so intensely female. The lace of her bra rasped against her taut nipples. Her belly pressed against the satin lining of her skirt. Her panties felt too snug.

His lips looked velvety, sensual. Merciless.

She clamped her thighs around the rush of sexual awareness—if that was what this was. She wasn't sure. This feeling had no precedent.

He appeared to have forgotten his dispute with Robin. Antennae boinged as the girl shoved him aside and poked her head around his massive shoulder. Her eyes were wide with delighted curiosity.

"Ms. King, this is Michael MacNamara," she announced. "We call him Mac. I swear, he's not usually like this. He's usually much more smooth and civilized. I bring out the worst in him. He's my big brother, you see. We have issues. But he's a really good guy."

"Ah. I understand," Jane murmured.

Robin stabbed the man's broad chest with her finger. "Be nice to her, Mac. This isn't her fault, so be mad at me, not at her."

His eyes flicked down. "Don't worry. I'm plenty mad at you." He whipped the hair sticks out of her hair. Robin squawked in outrage as knobs of gleaming hair unraveled over her face. "Get lost, shrimp," he said. "I want to talk to Ms. King in private. I promise I'll be nice to her."

"Give those back!" Robin lunged for her hair sticks, but her brother evaded her flailing arms with ease. She gave Jane a dark look. "Don't let him bully you like he does me!"

Jane blinked at her. "I, ah, can't imagine why he would."

"And watch out if he tries to sweet-talk you! First he lays on the charm, and then poof, it's the thumbscrews and the sodium pentothal!"

"Robin, you're losing it." MacNamara's voice was rigidly calm. "Remember our conversation about professionalism?"

"Screw professionalism! Give those back!"

He swept his arm backward, nudging his sister gently out the door. "We'll discuss the dress code later. Cover the phones, please."

He slammed the door and flicked the door lock shut.

The sound of the lock click sent a tingle of primitive feminine wariness through her. He froze, his hand lingering over the knob. "Sorry," he said. "It's just a reflex. I do it when I need privacy." He opened the lock with a deliberate flick of his finger. "Didn't mean to make you nervous."

"That's OK." His perceptiveness made her more nervous still.

He tossed Robin's hair sticks onto his desk. "I apologize for the circus act. My sister's going through her rebellious stage."

"Maybe you should fire her," Jane blurted. "She wants it so badly."

It was the first thing that popped into her mind, and judging from the sudden chill in his eyes, it had been the wrong thing to say.

"Thank you for sharing your opinion," he said.

She winced. "Sorry. Forget I said that." She fidgeted under his cool regard for a long, tense moment.

He relented, and a brilliant grin transformed his face, carving deep dimples into his cheeks that flanked the sexy grooves around his mouth. As if he needed dimples, on top of everything else. "Never mind," he said. "Let's try this again. Please call me Mac." He held out his hand.

Jane extended her own. She was speechless again, and he was patiently waiting for a reply. Her fingers were swallowed by his huge hand. He didn't shake it, just held it, in a warm, implacable grip.

"And you are Jane King," he prompted. "The magazine writer."

His words jolted her. Where was she going to find the presence of mind to lie to this man when she could barely speak at all? He lifted her hand, and pressed his smiling lips gently against the hollow between her first two knuckles.

The softness of his lips, the heat of his breath against the back of her hand, unleashed a storm of emotion inside her, like a flock of startled birds taking off, a fluttering rush of wings beating all at once.

It shocked tears into her eyes. She had to tell him . . . what? Her mind was blank. She wrenched her gaze away. This was silly. So a sexy guy was ogling her. Big freaking deal. She should ogle him right back. She was a ruthless headhunter who used men and tossed them away.

Except that this man didn't look particularly . . . tossable.

He stroked her palm with his fingertip. She glanced furtively down at his left hand. No ring. "I've intruded on a busy afternoon," she said.

"Not at all," he said. "This has been the best moment in my day. So far, anyway." His fingers tightened around hers.

It felt so natural to drift ever so slightly deeper into the warm, buzzing force field that surrounded him. "But your schedule—"

"There's nothing I'd like better than to show you around the hotel," he said smoothly. "I'm proud of this place. I live for this stuff."

"And your three-thirty meeting?" She glanced at her watch. "What can we do with only twenty minutes?"

He pressed his lips tenderly against her hand. "A lot, if we focus." His voice was a low, seductive rumble, caressing every nerve. "I'm very focused, Jane. May I call you Jane?"

"Ah . . . yes. Of course." This was the most overt sexual come-on she'd ever gotten, and she was actually considering—was she?

Yes, she was. Oh, God, she really was. She dragged a stuttering breath into her lungs. This had never happened to her, an impulse so strong, so shocking, but why the hell not? She was single, independent, adult. What was the harm in taking what his eyes were offering? She *chose* her response, she reminded herself. Big girls made choices. They reached out, and took what they wanted. Why not her?

"So? Let's get to it, then." He opened the door, and seized her elbow. The contact sent a shiver up her arm. He had a fresh, herbal smell. She wanted to rub her cheek against his shirt. Gulp him in.

He led her away from the reception area. "We'll use the back staircase," he said, in answer to her questioning glance. "I don't want to engage with Robin. That would be a poor use of our precious"—he checked his watch—"nineteen minutes and thirty-nine seconds."

His big, warm hand settled possessively at the small of her back. Faraway thunder rolled in her mind as he led her up the narrow staircase. Were there rules governing these situations? Conventions? She didn't have a clue, and their silence was so . . . eloquent. With each moment that passed, she might be tacitly agreeing to any wild, erotic thing that he might want from her. Her head swam with sensual images. She stumbled. He steadied her, his arm circling her waist.

"Careful," he said softly. "I've got you."

Oh, didn't he just. He swept her past the second floor landing with a gentle, decisive push of his hand. "The espresso bar, hair salon, tourist office and fitness center can wait, for now. I want to show you the luxury bedroom suites. They're our big selling point." His low voice brushed over her skin like silk. His hand pushed her gently onward.

She was so excited, she could hardly breathe.

He stopped in front of a door. "Each of the luxury suites has a theme," he told her as he unlocked it. "This is the Baron's Suite."

He opened the door. She took a deep breath, and then walked in.

* * *

Mac left the door carefully ajar as he followed her into the room. He flipped on the light and circled around so he could catch her reaction. Bringing her up here was a low-down, dirty trick, but all was fair in love and war, and he felt perfectly justified in a preemptive strike. The Baron's Suite was calculated to make a woman weak in the knees, and judging from the startled delight on her face, it was working.

"This room is a reproduction of a bedroom from an eighteenth century baron's palazzo near Naples," he told her. "The bed is a reproduction of a bed that the baron commissioned for his mistress. This suite is the Kingsbridge Crowne's answer to a honeymoon suite."

"I see. It's, um, remarkable." She drifted closer to the immense bed. The massive gilded headboard writhed with cupids, nymphs and satyrs. Upon first glance, it was just a busy swirl of golden baroque eye candy, but upon closer inspection . . . yes, she was catching on, moving closer. Mac sidled around so he could peek at her face as she realized just exactly what that chubby little shepherdess was doing to that goat-footed boy to justify his blissful smile. What all of the cavorting nymphs and satyrs were doing—in every conceivable position and combination.

She drew in a startled breath and clapped her hand over her mouth. For a second, he was afraid he'd shocked her, but the sparkling glance she darted at him reassured him. She wasn't a prude. God, she was pretty when she blushed. "Let me show you the bathroom," he said.

She followed him through the sumptuous room, taking it in with wide, dreamy eyes. Mac felt as if he'd been split in two. One of him was giving a courtesy tour to a fellow professional, and the other watched Jane like a hawk, just in case his wildest dreams should come true. He wasn't making any rash assumptions, no matter how many smoldering glances she cast at him. She had to give him a clear, unmistakable sign.

And he would gracefully take it from there.

He flung open the bathroom door. "We decided to sacrifice historical realism in favor of luxury. The baron and his mistress would have appreciated modern plumbing. But we used marble quarried from a place near Naples, to stay in the spirit of the palazzo."

He watched her look around at the huge, sunken bath, almost big enough to swim in. The Italian marble was pink tinted and fleshy and sensual. Gold-toned fixtures gleamed. The fantasy rose up; the tub full of steaming scented water. Jane stepping in, her bare bottom rosy from the heat. Smiling over her shoulder at him in sultry invitation.

"Wow. It's bigger than my living room," Jane said.

He stared at her flushed, delicate profile. Her hairdo hinted at thick red waves, rolled up tight and pinned into stern submission. Calculated to tease a guy who loved a challenge. Her body was perfect: trim, but lush, like a juicy peach. Something inside him had stood right up and said *gimme that.* He wanted to peel those clothes off her and then let those satyrs and nymphs look down and learn a thing or two.

She turned back to him. "It's beautiful."

He jerked his gaze away from her tits just in time to smile innocently into her wide, indigo eyes. "This place really lends itself to a lavish pictorial color spread," he said. "What photographer do you use?"

Her eyes flicked away from his. "Oh, I, um . . . I work with a few different people, actually. I haven't decided yet."

"I could make some recommendations for you," he offered.

"Thanks, but I'm covered," she murmured. She brushed past him out of the bathroom, and he sensed her tension in the faint, glancing touch. She was vibrating at a very high frequency, he could feel it humming in the air, but he still wasn't sure what she wanted him to do.

He didn't dare guess. This was way too important.

He followed her into the bedroom and found her trans-fixed by the painting of Leda and the Swan. In this render-ing, Leda was a plump naked maiden with long dark curls. She reclined on a canopied bed heaped with crimson and gold pillows, and her bare skin glowed like a pearl against the shadowy draperies. The swan was poised between her parted thighs, wings spread wide. From the naughty twinkle in the swan's black eye and the voluptuous flush of surrender upon Leda's face, it was clear that a very good time was about to be had by all.

Jane put her hand over her mouth. Her eyes gleamed with suppressed laughter. "There's no safe place to rest your eyes in here."

"This was painted by Manfredi Cozzoli," he said. "An un-known Sicilian painter, early ninteenth century. I picked up his Zeus and Europa at the same auction. Cozzoli was heavy into mythical subjects."

"Europa?" She frowned, puzzled. "Which one was she?"

"Zeus changed himself into a bull to seduce her," he ex-plained.

She choked on a giggle and looked away swiftly. "Good heavens."

"Yeah, it was a little much," he admitted. "We decided that Leda was our best bet."

"It's, ah, certainly not your standard hotel art," she ven-tured.

"There's nothing standard about our hotels," Mac said. "Each one is unique. We want every guest to feel"—he kissed her hand, felt her delicate bones, her soft skin against his lips—"caressed by luxury."

Oh, Lord, did that cheesy line really come out of his mouth? He must be getting desperate. He forced himself to let go of her hand. He hoped he wasn't blushing, but his face felt suspiciously hot.

Jane looked at Leda and the swan. She looked at the nymphs and satyrs. She looked back at him. His heart began to race.

She walked to the door, shoved it closed, and turned the key in the lock.

Chapter Two

It wasn't wishful thinking; this was really, truly happening. She felt delirious, lost in a feverish dream. Her heart thudded against her rib cage as if it wanted to get out. And now that the door was shut, she had to turn around and face him. She had to . . . to *do* something with him. She caught a glimpse of herself in a lavish, gilt-edged mirror. Pale, heart-shaped splotch of a face, eyes wide with terrified excitement.

His warm hand came to rest on her shoulder. She turned and looked up. His clear gray eyes asked a question that her entire body longed to answer. That was when she realized why her throat felt closed. She didn't want to lie to him. Even a passive lie felt wrong. She couldn't care less about Brighton Group. This was more important. She'd never felt so alive, poised on the brink of something miraculous.

But if she told him the truth now, the miracle bubble would burst and the moment would be lost. It would be all business: explanations, apologies, a hasty and embarrassed retreat with her tail between her legs. A sharp lecture from her boss to look forward to.

She couldn't risk it. If it came down to a choice between fantasy or nothing, she'd go with the fantasy. For as long as she could.

She reached out and rested her palm against his chest. He jerked as if she'd burned him. The smooth white field of fabric looked as cool and pure as snow, but beneath it, he was all hard, resilient muscle and vital male heat. His rib cage rose and fell. His heart thudded rapidly against her hand. He was so tall, she was going to fall over backward.

He must have read her mind, because he cupped the nape of her neck with a low murmur, slid his other arm around her waist and pressed her against his hard body.

It had been so long since she'd embraced anyone, other than brief social hugs. The intimate contact was a soothing, stimulating rush of pleasure. She drank it in with a tiny moan. "Mac, what are we doing?"

"Isn't it obvious?" His hot breath fanned her cheek, her ear.

His mouth covered hers. His lips were as velvety soft as she had imagined. She knew the pros and cons of teeth and tongue, open versus closed, and all the gradations in between. She had her preferences, like everyone else, but this feeling was entirely outside her experience.

The warm, seeking pressure of his mouth called to every buried yearning in her heart. His faint beard stubble rasped across her jaw. Flames raced through her body like beacon fires over a dark landscape, stirring desires she'd never felt. Warmth unfurled in her chest, her belly, between her legs. Colors exploded, swirling behind her eyes.

His kiss grew bolder, coaxing her wider open. He tasted hot and deep and wonderful, with a hint of coffee in the background. His breath was sweet against her face. She flung her head back, gasping for air.

"Your lips are so soft." She blurted the words out before she had time to wonder if it was a stupid thing to say.

He laughed softly against her mouth and kissed her again.

His fingers tightened on her hair, and his mouth demanded more.

She flung her head into his hands and opened to the bold thrust of his tongue. Her mouth danced with his, exploring him with eager abandon. She was suspended in space, a chaos of seething heat.

A thread of panic uncoiled inside her. This shaky, falling apart feeling was not what she'd expected. She'd certainly never felt this way with Dylan, or anyone else. "Mac? I feel—I feel like I'm—"

"I know," he murmured. "All yours, angel. Don't worry."

She pulled away from him, flustered, and stumbled back with her hand clamped over her swollen mouth. Her heel caught in the carpet. Mac dove to catch her, and they toppled together onto a soft, brocade-covered sofa.

Mac lifted his weight swiftly off her body. "Damn. Sorry about that. Are you OK? Did you hurt yourself?"

She started to shake with silent, hysterical laughter. "I'm fine, thanks," she said. "Just . . . falling to pieces, that's all."

He dropped to his knees in front of her, resting his big, warm hands on her knees as he gazed searchingly into her face. She would never have dreamed that knees could feel so much, drinking in his heat, tingling with pleasure.

"You sure you're OK?" he asked hesitantly. "You look like you're about to cry."

She shook her head. "I never cry," she told him.

They stared at each other. He reached up and gently pushed back a lock of hair that was trailing over her cheek. She leaned closer, until she could feel his warm breath. His magnetism tugged something deep inside her—a slow, inevitable pull, an aching hunger for his scent, his heat, his vital essence. Her arms slid around his neck as his lips caressed the side of her face. He smoothed her tight, straight skirt up so that he could move between her parted thighs and slide his arms around her waist. The closer he got, the closer she wanted him.

His weight shifted, and he hoisted her up so she was lying on the couch. He bent over her, his lips moving over her face with sweet, seeking gentleness. She was floating, clinging desperately, barely noticing the buttons on her shirt giving way, one after the other, tiny little silent pops, the pressure of her blouse releasing over her breasts.

And oh, God, he was all over her now, so big and hard and heavy. This was happening so fast. Her body was going nuts. She vibrated beneath him. Her skirt was shoved up to her waist and Mac lay between her splayed legs, giving her all his strength and heat to push against. She wanted all of it. Needed it.

Need? She couldn't afford to need this man. She knew nothing about him. She tried to stop her hips from pressing eagerly up against the hard bulge at his crotch. She couldn't stop. She could barely move beneath his weight, and every breathless, heaving wiggle deepened the pleasure, sharpened the throbbing tension.

Mac's mouth moved over hers, caressing and exploring, drawing out sweetness and giving it back in equal measure. She turned her face away to gather her wits, but he caught her face in his hands and jerked it back, covering her mouth again with a low growl of command. He stroked the sheer fabric of her thigh-high stockings, all the way up until he reached bare skin. "Your stockings drive me crazy," he said roughly.

She clutched his shirt, crumpling the fabric in her fists as her hips tightened, squeezing him. She arched, taut as a bow about to release—oh, God, no. No. This was insane. All alone in a hotel room with a total stranger. She would fall apart. Never find her way back.

She wrenched her face away again. "Mac? Please—"

"I know," he soothed. "I feel it, too. I'll take care of you. Relax."

Her panic swelled to a frenzy. What had she done? She'd had no idea the stakes would be this high. She was gambling with coin she could not afford to lose. She'd met this man twenty minutes ago, and these emotions were stronger than anything she'd ever felt. If he took what she'd offered him and then buttoned up his pants, thanks, that was fun, have a nice life . . . what was your name, again? It would be no more than she deserved, but she would be destroyed. She didn't do casual sex. She'd wanted it, yes. Ached for it. She'd thought she could handle it, and it had taken this inside-out feeling to realize how thin the veneer of her self-control really was. How vulnerable she was beneath it.

Suddenly she could move. Cool air moved over her damp face and her bosom. It rushed into her shuddering lungs. Mac was up on his knees, unbuckling his belt, yanking his shirt out of his pants. His face was flushed, his eyes fierce and hot and focused upon hers.

She struggled up onto her elbows. "Mac, please stop."

He went still, hands frozen on his shirt buttons. His shirt gaped over his broad, muscular chest. An arrow of dark hair disappeared into low-slung briefs, and she wrenched her gaze away—too late. She'd already seen what was poking out of those briefs, long and thick and hard against his flat belly. Whew. Formidable.

"What?" he said, incredulous.

She was shaking so hard, she collapsed onto her back again. Her breath rasped audibly between parted lips. "I can't just, ah . . . do it."

He stared down at her. "I thought this was what you wanted."

She pressed her hands against his chest, but instead of cotton, her hands found hot, naked skin. She tried to snatch her hands back, but Mac trapped them against his chest. His muscles shifted beneath his skin with each breath. His heart throbbed, quick and hard against her palm. "I know it looks that way," she faltered.

"Looks?" His chest jerked beneath her hands in a soundless laugh.

She bit her lip. "I'm sorry. I know I came on to you, and when you kissed me, I lost my head. But it's too much. I just met you, what, twenty minutes ago? I can't just . . . have sex with you, out of nowhere."

"Jane." His voice was flat. "This didn't feel like nowhere to me."

She squeezed her eyes shut. "Sorry. Really. I'm so sorry, Mac."

The silence was so long, she finally opened her eyes and peeked. He was staring at her body. Taut nipples poking through the lace of her bra, skirt crumpled around her waist, legs sprawled wide. Face hot.

He released her hands, and sighed raggedly. "I can hardly be blamed for getting the wrong idea."

Her face flamed hotter. "I know. I'm sorry." She attempted to button her blouse. A lost cause if ever there was one, lying flat on her back. She couldn't make a single button connect over her breasts.

He lifted himself off and stood, closing his fly. He ran his hand over his reddened face. "I'm the one who should be sorry. I read your signals wrong. I don't force myself on women. It's not what gets me off."

"Of course not!" She struggled to sit up. "It's not your fault! I was very misleading, and I'm the one who should be sorry. Not you. Really."

"Then, kiss me again," he demanded.

Her eyes dropped. She buttoned her blouse with shaking fingers. "I don't think that would be a very good idea," she whispered.

He lifted her chin, forcing her to look at him. "I won't open my pants. I won't force you in any way. Just kiss me again, like you kissed me before." He sank down next to her on the chaise. "Please."

She shrank back. "Mac—"

"Please. Just a kiss. I'll fall to pieces if you don't."

His stark tone silenced her. His face was taut, his hands

clenched into huge fists. She wasn't the only one shaking apart. She was moved. Her emotions felt so clear and bright. The impulse to soothe and reassure him was irresistible. She knew how it felt to fall to pieces.

She leaned closer, and brushed her lips against his grim mouth.

The erotic promise implicit in that tentative kiss made Mac shudder. Every sensation was magnified, amplified. The press of her soft lips, the rush of her breath. The shapes and contours of her mouth, the pouting swell of the lower lip, the sculpted curves of the upper, the borderline where the matte velvet of her lips gave way to the moist, satiny secrets of her inner mouth. The flirtatious flick of her tongue.

She pulled back, gazed at him as she pulled her full bottom lip between her white teeth. She'd chewed the lipstick away, and the natural, hot blush pink showed through.

He clenched his hands into fists and stared into her wondering eyes, willing her to sway forward and do it again before he keeled over and died. He'd never seen eyes like that: storm-at-sea blue. With her pupils dilated, the color faded to indigo, then black. Bottomless lake eyes, against cloud-pale skin, framed by autumn-leaves-on-fire hair.

Yeah, a boner of these proportions could turn the most pragmatic man into a fucking poet. "Please." His voice rasped. "Again."

Her lips moved over his, brushing like a warm breeze, then pressing their yielding sweetness more fully, opening to him.

He'd never read a woman so wrong before. He should have figured it out as soon as he touched her. He'd expected the bold enthusiasm of a woman who knew exactly what she wanted, but she hadn't been like that at all. She'd been like a fourteen-year-old getting her first kiss. Shaking like a leaf. Vulnerable. Yeah, that was the word he was groping for. She kissed him again, more boldly. The tip of her tongue ventured shyly inside, brushing his. He inhaled her sweet breath, electrified.

This felt so fragile and tenuous, like she might dissolve into a puff of smoke if he made a wrong move. Vulnerable. The word hovered around the edges of his mind as she stretched him out on the rack of this agonizing kiss. Vulnerable implied risk. Responsibility. Unknown quantities that had no place in a bout of anonymous sex. Her tongue flicked against his, and he opened for her with a sigh. She gasped against his mouth when his fingers clamped around her arms.

She rose up onto her knees and steadied herself by clutching his shoulders. Her fingernails dug into the fabric of his shirt like small claws. A flush of arousal painted her face, her lush bosom. She was primed. He could push her right over the edge with a puff of breath. He could take her right now and make her love it.

Some deep, wordless instinct held him back.

She explored his mouth, nibbling and licking, her breath a warm cloud against his face. "I love your smell," she whispered shyly.

"It's just my shower gel," he told her. "I don't do cologne."

"Mmm. Nice." She sniffed. "Tangy. Pine needles in the summer."

He grinned like a fool. So he wasn't the only one waxing poetic. "Want to take a shower with me?" he offered. "I'll share."

He was emboldened by her soft giggle. He slid his hands around the back of her legs, stroking her sleek thighs. He hesitated when he got to the lace border at the top of the stocking, lingering in a sweet agony of anticipation as she tortured him with those moist, smooching kisses. She tasted so sweet and fresh. Lemon drops and mint and springtime.

He let out his breath in a harsh sigh as his fingers strayed into forbidden territory—a humid bower of silk and flower-petal softness. A tiny bit higher, and his fingertips were touching lace. Damp stretch lace, over soft, springy ringlets. Very damp. She was more than ready.

He dug his fingers into the wavy hair that was tumbling down at the nape of her neck and seized full control of the kiss. He wanted to strip that lace away, spread her wide open and explore all those secret female folds with his hungry mouth.

She wrenched her face away. "Mac, you said just a kiss!"

"I'm sorry," was all he could manage. He bore her down beneath him onto the sofa and traced the crevice of her labia with his fingertip. She was shivering and taut in his unrelenting grasp, but she was so close. It was killing him. He had to finish it. He had to make her come.

She clamped his hand tight between her quivering thighs so that only the tips of his fingers reached her mound. Fine. Fingertips would do the job. He flicked his tongue against hers as he moved his fingers in small, teasing circles, found the tight protuberance of her clit, caressed it. That wild squirming was going to feel incredible when he was embedded in her hot depths. Plunging and sliding.

Fucking her was going to be so good. She was small, but strong, with those big soft breasts barely contained by the lacy bra. Lithe, vibrant, well built. She wouldn't break beneath his big body when he wanted to be on top, but just to be on the safe side, he'd put her astride for the first few times. Just to let her get used to his size.

He thrust his tongue into her mouth as he imagined her riding him, the swell of her hips gripped in his hands, rosy tits bouncing and swaying. She would take him in, whimpering with pleasure as he pulled her down and filled her up with his stiff, aching cock. Then the moist cling, the quivering tug as he lifted her up again, sleek and skintight as a leather glove. The fantasy almost made him come in his pants.

She writhed beneath him, as if she were afraid of the climax he was driving her towards, but he couldn't relent. He wanted this edge—every possible advantage, all the points he could garner. He wanted to back her into a corner, claim her for his own.

He caressed, insisted, until she stiffened in his arms and let out a sobbing wail. Her orgasm throbbed against his fingertips, jolted through her body and echoed through his own. He hadn't even gotten her panties off yet. This was going to be the hottest sex he'd ever had.

He nuzzled the side of her face, and waited for the verdict. She panted, eyes squeezed shut. She was afraid to look at him, he realized. He pulled her face gently around. Her bones felt so sharp and delicate beneath the velvet soft skin of her face.

"Hey," he prompted. "Hey. Jane? Everything OK?"

Her eyes fluttered open, and she struggled up onto the edge of the sofa. He followed, pressing his thigh to hers. He didn't want her to shiver outside the influence of his body's warmth as the sweat dried and the doubts started.

Her skirt was riding up, stockings rolling down. Her garter had come loose. A stipple of reddish freckles was strewn across the tops of her thighs. He stroked his hand over them, lingering over the downy softness of her skin. She snatched his hand, blocked it.

"You told me just the kiss," she accused him.

His fingers splayed over her warm flesh, digging boldly into her thigh. "You liked the orgasm, too," he said.

"That's not the point," she said softly.

They stared at each other for a long moment, wordless.

The heavy knock on the door made them jump as if they'd both been struck. Mac swore under his breath. "Who is it?"

"Mac? What the hell is going on in there?"

Mac buried his face in his hands and groaned. His brother, Danny. Chief financial officer of Crowne Royale Group Hotels. A good brother, if a difficult one. A good guy, too, when he wasn't being an uptight son of a bitch, which admittedly wasn't often. Mac was convinced that Danny just needed to get well and truly laid. This was not going to be pleasant.

Jane leaped up. He reached for her, but she evaded his hand.

"I'll be out in a minute," he called out.

"What do you mean, a minute?" Danny demanded.

Tension radiating from Jane's small, curvy body. She tried to attach the garter to the stocking, but her frantic fingers couldn't manage it. She squeaked and batted at his head when he sank to his knees in front of her. "Relax. Let me fix this for you," he soothed.

"Christ, Mac! Carlisle and Young have been waiting in my office for over fifteen minutes, and Robin says you've waltzed off to give a tour to a cute magazine writer? Are you out of your goddamn mind?"

"Shut up and give us a minute," he snapped. The shadowy mysteries beneath Jane's skirt deserved his undivided attention. He snagged the fluttering garter and inhaled deep, hungry breaths of her heady female sexual smell as he hooked the garter to the stocking.

Then she got down onto her knees to look under the sofa for her shoes, and he almost forgot his predicament just admiring her ass.

The force of Danny's disapproval radiated right through the door, but Mac ignored it with the stoic fortitude forged from years of practice. Danny was unbearable when he was in one of his controlling, self-righteous snits. Ignoring him had always been the best policy.

Jane had finally struggled into her shoes. He helped her to her feet and cast around for a new excuse to touch her. "Your blouse is misbuttoned," he said. "Let me fix it."

She quivered as he reached for her, but she didn't pull away. He was rewarded for his boldness by a delicious last peek at her lace-covered tits before fastening her up again.

He let the backs of his knuckles brush up against the under-side of her breast, flicking delicately over her taut nipples. "Have dinner with me," he said.

Her indigo eyes flicked away from his. Damn. He'd come on too strong. He'd overwhelmed her, and now she was bolting. She could disappear from his life as quickly as she had appeared.

"Mac," she said stiffly. "I, uh, have to tell you some-thing—"

"I never gave you a tour," he broke in. "I'll take you to the Copley Crowne for dinner, and give you a tour afterward. Please."

Her nose wrinkled in a cute grin. "You mean, like this tour?"

He straightened her collar. "A real one," he promised rashly. "Any kind you want. You call the shots. No tricks, no traps. I'll be so good."

"Um . . . but, Mac? I, ah . . ." She looked like she was gearing up to tell him something he didn't want to hear.

He headed her off instinctively. "I have to see you again, Jane."

"But I have to tell you something," she insisted. "I'm not really—"

"Say you'll have dinner with me," he persisted. "Just say yes."

"Stop interrupting!" she said tartly. "You never let me fin-ish!"

He stepped back, and let his hands drop to his sides. "Sorry. It's a bad habit of mine. Say whatever you need to say." He braced himself.

She took a deep breath, and tried again. "I'm not really—"

"Mac!" Danny thumped the door. "It's been six minutes. Shall I tell Carlisle and Young you're too busy indulging your animal instincts to discuss their possible investment in our hotels? Just say the word."

"Take a pill, Danny," Mac snarled back.

"Just wondering"—Danny banged until the door rattled—"if you're planning on coming out of that room some time in this century."

The moment was irretrievably lost. Jane was buttoning the blazer beneath the awe-inspiring shelf of her bosom, her face hidden by waves of fiery hair. "I'll just, ah, get out of your way." Her voice was unsteady.

"Please." He seized her arm. "Don't run away. Whatever you need to tell me, you can tell me at dinner. OK?"

She hesitated for so long, he was horribly certain that she was going to blow him off. Then she nodded, and he could breathe again.

He grabbed his phone and punched up the address function. "I'll pick you up at eight. Where do you live?"

She backed away and scooped up her purse from where it had fallen during their tempest of kissing and groping. "Oh, don't worry. I'll just meet you at the restaurant."

She was side-stepping him, leaving her options open. He hated it. "At least your number?" he pleaded. "Your E-mail? Jesus, anything?"

Danny pounded on the door again. "Damn it, Mac!"

Mac stalked to the door, unlocked it and flung it wide. "You're going to pay for this, Danny."

His brother's dark eyes were narrow slits of fury. "I already have. Crowne Royale Group has paid for it, too. I don't think Carlisle and Young have much of a sense of humor about this kind of thing."

Mac glanced back at Jane. Her face was snowy pale, but for the splotches of embarrassment on her high, delicate cheekbones. "Excuse me," she murmured. She pushed past him, out into the corridor.

Danny's glacial gaze swept over her. "This is the writer?"

"This is Jane King," Mac supplied, when Jane seemed incapable of replying. "Jane, this is my brother, Danny Mac-Namara."

Danny's eyes took in the tousled hair, the crumpled skirt, the lipstick kissed away from her mouth. "I'm going to be very curious to read whatever article you end up writing, miss."

The biting sarcasm in his brother's voice made her flinch. Mac's hands clenched. "Do not be rude to her, Danny. Or I will flatten you."

Danny's dark eyes locked onto his. Not many could go nose to nose with Mac, but his brother was six three, just like him. Danny was thinner, though. Whipcord lean. His dark, intense face was a sharper, narrower version of his brother's, and he wore his black hair long, smoothed back into a perfect, gleaming ponytail which still somehow managed to look classy and perfect with his Armani suits. Go figure.

"I'm not as easy to flatten as I used to be," Danny said evenly. "But whatever, man. Go for it."

Jane tugged on Mac's arm. "It's OK, Mac. Just go about your business. I'm gone." She scurried towards the main staircase.

"Meet me at the fountain in the Copley Crowne rose garden!" he called after her. "Eight-thirty! You know how to find it?"

"I'll figure it out." She cast a wan smile back over her shoulder and disappeared around the corner. Her heels clattered unsteadily down the stairs. He hoped she was holding on tight to the banister.

He turned back to Danny. "Thanks, bro. You scared her away. But of course, that's your specialty."

"Do I need to send somebody up to change the sheets?" Danny bit the words out.

Mac smiled thinly. "That won't be necessary, thanks to you."

Danny snorted as they strode towards the back staircase. "I would consider it a real professional courtesy if you would seduce your women on your own time, and in your own condo."

"Jealous? Been a while, hasn't it, Friar Danny?"

"Grow up. I've been stalling those guys while you—" Danny's gaze flicked down Mac's body. He let out a grunt of disgust. "Go to the john and think about the Wicked Witch of the West. You are not presentable."

Mac surveyed the bulge in his trousers with a casual shrug. "It's on the decline. You should've sent Robin in to distract them. She could've juggled paperweights. Pulled quarters out of their ears."

"Yeah, with her belly button hanging out. That would do wonders for our business credibility," Danny muttered. "You think this is all just a game for your personal entertainment, don't you?"

"What if I do?" Mac had never been able to resist a chance to bait his brother. "If it's a game, I always win. It's the results that count. You're the one who takes it all too god-damn seriously. Relax, already."

"What was my crime?" Danny asked the ceiling. "Why do I always get to be the humorless prick in our surreal family dramas?"

"Lighten up," Mac advised. "I'm not as much of a slut as you think I am. Just because I don't keep my dick in the freezer like you—"

"Ahem. Excuse me?"

They jerked to a halt. A chubby man in a gray suit was poking his head out of the conference room. His eyes bulged with anger. "What a volatile place this is," he said. "Have we come at an unfortunate time?"

"Not at all, Mr. Carlisle," Danny's voice was as smooth as ice cream. "I was just retrieving Mac from his, ah, meeting. It ran late."

"I can well imagine." Carlisle's eyes flicked over Mac with unfriendly sharpness before his head popped back in the door.

Mac punched up his friend Henry's number as he dove for the men's room. "Yo, Mac. What's up?" Henry greeted him.

"Hey, Henry. You still seeing that woman Charlotte?"

"Yeah. Why?"

"She still on the staff of *Europa Air Inflight Magazine?*"

"She sells ad space for them, yeah. Want to advertise?"

"I think we already do, actually," Mac said. "I met a woman who writes for them. I was wondering if you would ask Charlotte to, ah . . ."

"Tell you all the dirty details of this woman's life behind her back? Sneaky, underhanded bastard. You ought to be ashamed of yourself."

"Will you or won't you?" Mac demanded.

"What's this chick's name?"

"Jane King."

"King. Got it. I'm in the middle of something now, but I'm seeing Charlotte for dinner. I'll ask her then, and call you back. How's that?"

"Sooner is better than later," Mac told him.

Henry snorted. "You never change, buddy. Talk to you tonight."

"Later." He hung up, his mind circling uneasily around whatever Jane had been trying to tell him. *I'm not really . . .* Not really what? Maybe something unpalatable, like "I'm not really interested in having dinner," or "I'm not really looking to get involved right now."

Or something really bad, like "I'm not really available." But there had been no ring on that tiny, slender hand. He'd checked, first thing. Oval nails, buffed to a high sheen, pink and shell-like and kissable.

And her response had been real. Raw, honest. No faking that.

So, unfortunately, was his own, just from thinking about that orgasm fluttering against his fingertips, and he'd only just gotten his dick back down to socially acceptable proportions. Damn.

He tried to think about the Wicked Witch, but she kept morphing into Jane. Green skin, black pointy hat, hooked nose, striped stockings, they just weren't as compelling as damp stretch lace strained to its utmost over lush feminine curves, an errant garter dangling over her soft white thigh. Rippling red hair. Storm-at-sea eyes.

He was fried. He wanted Henry to call back right now to assure him that she was single, eligible and relatively sane. He had to be careful. She was skittish and shy. He would court her slowly, seduce her gently, but he was still going to book a suite at the Copley tonight.

A good guy could hope.

Chapter Three

She had the situation under control. She'd come here in her own car, to a crowded public place. She had no intention of getting into trouble. She wasn't even going to peek over that cliff at the churning, heaving water, let alone fling herself over the brink. No way. Not her.

She'd been saying that to herself all afternoon. She hadn't even gone back to work. She'd been too rattled, and the only solution for that, of course, was emergency mall therapy— which had resulted in the purchase of an evening dress and matching shoes, neither of which she could afford. To say nothing of the outrageously sexy lingerie.

And once she had the perfect outfit, well, damn. It seemed a terrible shame to stand him up. A tragic waste of time and money.

But she had no intention, absolutely none, of jumping him.

So why the condoms in your purse?

No good comeback for that one. There was nothing wrong with keeping her bases, ah, covered. So to speak.

She pulled up, killed the engine and rested her hot forehead against the steering column. She had to cool down, get a grip. She didn't dare sweat in this dress. She'd spent way too much money for it.

Think Gwyneth Paltrow, she told herself. Cool, calm, collected. She was a strong, capable person. She'd proved Dylan wrong, and she had the professional accomplishments to show for it. It took rock-steady self-control to channel the MeanStreets kids' volcanic energy into art. That meltdown in the Baron's Suite was just a temporary aberration.

And oh, what an aberration it was. Lips locked, writhing, panties soaked, thighs clenched around his hand. She was sweating again.

Compose yourself, Jane. Nobody likes an embarrassing scene.

Jane laughed silently. *Thank you, Mother, for sharing.* Her mother had always been repelled by strong emotions. How shocked Mother would be to see her now, tarted up in a sexy dress. Firmly in the grip of unruly, embarrassing emotions. Terror, embarrassment, lust. Hope.

The hope scared her most of all. It left her wide open.

The Copley Crowne was a turn-of-the-century mansion, frilly with turrets and towers and various other architectural ribbons and lace, but the total effect was one of cheerful exuberance rather than fussiness. She'd looked the place up on the Internet, and found that the Copley Crowne had a famous chef, a five star rating and gushing reviews from famous food critics. Too bad she was too nervous to eat.

She smoothed down her skirt. The bias cut silk clung to her damp hands. She owed her entire next paycheck to Mastercard, but it was worth it. The dark blue dress skimmed her hips and flared out in a luscious frill over her ankles. Spaghetti straps had forced her to buy a black bustier, which shoved up her boobs and created a provocative valley of cleavage. She couldn't actually breathe in the thing, but what the hell. With Mac, she never breathed anyway. Oxygen was overrated.

She'd shaved and plucked and painted herself like a harem slave about to be led to the sultan's couch. She wondered if Mac would look at her with that intense, focused heat in his eyes when he saw her.

Come now, he probably looks at all women that way. Don't read so much into it. Don't be silly and needy and credulous.

Back off, she told the snotty voice in her head. She was on shaky ground as it was. She should never have agreed to a date without telling Mac what she was up to. It wasn't like it was such a dreadful secret, after all. She wasn't hurting anyone, or doing anything illegal. Still, it put her at a terrible disadvantage. She couldn't take the stress.

She would tell him the truth straight off. Then he could decide if he still wanted to invest the time and energy in having dinner with her.

He might be angry, and conclude that she was more trouble than she was worth. Maybe he would be right. Dylan had put her off men for years. Four years, to be precise. No wonder she was climbing the walls.

She kicked that thought back into the dusty corner where it belonged. Thinking about Dylan was a big no-no. She wouldn't sacrifice one more crumb of her attention to that freaking vampire. She'd regained control over her life from him at great cost. She was hanging on to it with a death grip. She marched towards the graceful, welcoming beauty of the Copley Crowne as if going to face a firing squad.

The hostess directed her towards French doors that opened out onto a magnificent garden. A rose-scented breeze lifted her hair, ruffling the dark foliage around her. It misted her face with cool spray from the fountain. Her skirt fluttered around her legs, a caress of moving silk. Trellises draped with climbing roses shaded shadowy nooks. Paths wound through the bushes, all of them making their way towards the central fountain. The marble fountain glowed a pale pink in the deepening twilight.

The noise and bustle of the restaurant was sealed away behind a wall of glass on the opposite side of the garden, creating an oasis of fragrant calm. A few people strolled along the aisles. There were roses of all kinds and colors: white, pink, peach, yellow, crimson—from tight-furled buds to lush, full-blown extravagance. They seemed to float against the dark green leaves. Petals carpeted the walkway like confetti.

Sensual music throbbed in the air. A classical guitarist was sitting in one of the rose arbors, playing Spanish gypsy music.

Mac stepped out of the shadows. He liked the dress. His eyes devoured her. She was out of her element, out of her league, out of her mind. She really, *really* needed to breathe, but it just wasn't an option. He walked towards her. Her legs were rooted to the ground.

He was so graceful and perfectly proportioned, despite his height and solid, heavy musculature. Loose-limbed, sinuous like a big hunting cat. A white linen shirt set off his dark skin, draping elegantly from those wide, powerful shoulders. He oozed potent masculine charisma.

He stopped a couple feet away, no doubt to savor the buzz of anticipation before gobbling her up in a single bite. His eyes dragged over her from head to toe. "Storm-at-sea blue," he said.

She was bewildered. "What?"

"Your dress. It's the color of your eyes. The color of a stormy sea."

Oh, he was smooth. She was so flattered, her toes curled up. "Thank you, but they're, um, just dark bluish-gray."

He reached out, his finger tracing the line of her jaw. "You will learn to accept compliments from me before the night is over."

The soft words sounded like a promise—or perhaps a veiled threat. She couldn't quite tell which. "Ah, we'll see," she said dubiously.

"I'm glad to see you," he said. "I wasn't sure you'd show."

"Why wouldn't I?" Like she hadn't been asking herself that same question all afternoon.

"You wouldn't give me your address. You were keeping your options open."

"Oh. I didn't mean to make you feel like I was—*mmph!*"

The swift, possessive kiss took her by surprise. He was so vibrant and strong, bending her over backward, pressing her against his body. His faint beard shadow rasped her cheek.

She blinked up at him, dazed, when he lifted his head. "You take a lot for granted," she blurted.

He shook his head. "The dress is a statement. I'm just responding to it. You make a move, I make a countermove. Cause and effect. It's a natural law, like gravity. Simple, elementary physics."

She swallowed back her giggles before she could start to sound hysterical. "I must've been absent that day in science class."

He dragged her higher against his long body until she practically dangled in midair, her tiptoes barely touching the ground. "Did you see the way the men looked at you when you walked out here?"

"I didn't see any other men," she admitted. "I was looking for you."

She glanced down. Yikes. From this vantage point, he could see her areolas, peeking right over the edge of the bustier.

"Well, I saw the way they looked at you," he said. "A man has to stake his claim when his woman is dressed like that."

His woman? Whoa. "Mac, I—"

This time the kiss was slower, sweeter. Pure seduction, drawing her into a timeless haze of longing. She softened against him like melting caramel, eyelids heavy, knees quivering. The kiss lightened to a teasing suction at her lower lip, a tender flick of his tongue against hers, a rain of hot, soft kisses against her throat. Shivers raced over her skin as he nibbled her earlobe. "Our table's ready," he murmured.

She realized, with a start, that her arms were wrapped around his neck. "Oh. Ah, yes," she stammered. "Of course."

He wound her arm through his, and she drifted along in his wake, giddy and dazzled. The sweet talk, the soft guitar, the sensual, over-the-top luxury was all just a thin veil over the primal truth between them. She felt it in every cell of her body. He was luring her into position, and when he had her there . . . God. Explicit images assailed her. Herself, naked and helpless, spread out beneath his powerful body. Writhing with pleasure. She wanted him so badly, and it scared her.

Why, oh why was she like this? Why such endless conflict, such tiresome drama about sex? Always a life-or-death production. Always such a big deal. Why couldn't she just relax and indulge herself? What was wrong with her? She was a goddamn freak of nature.

An opened bottle of wine had been left on the table to breathe. Mac poured the wine and lifted his glass. She lifted her own. The stem of her glass wobbled after the crystalline *ting* of contact. She gathered her nerve. It was ridiculous to continue this pointless charade just because she dreaded looking silly for letting it go on so long in the first place. She took a deep breath. Opened her mouth. "Mac, I have to—"

"Good evening!" said a familiar alto voice. "Well, well, well! What have we here? Isn't it lucky that Gary was gone this afternoon?"

Jane looked up into Robin's smiling eyes. She looked very different in the sleek black pants and crisp white blouse of the restaurant waitstaff. Her hair was slicked back into a tight bun.

"Christ." Mac closed his eyes. "No. Tell me this isn't happening."

Dimples very similar to Mac's deepened at the corners of Robin's expressive mouth. "One of the waiters had a family emergency, and Gary asked me if I would cover for him," she explained. "Remember Lecture Number Six Eighty-seven, about being willing to pitch in? Well, I'm pitching in." She laid a basket of fresh bread on the table and cut them a deep, theatrical bow. "You should be proud of me. So eager to lend a hand."

"How did you know I was coming here?" Mac demanded. "Did Danny tell you? That's it. I'm flattening him. He's history."

"Mac!" Robin looked wounded. "Danny and I would never intrude on your private life!" She winked at Jane. "I wouldn't dare. I'm so cowed. If Mac gets into heaven, which I have begun to seriously doubt, St. Peter will take one look at him and put him to work as a bouncer."

Wine sloshed in the glasses as Mac's hand hit the table. "Robin—"

"He'll be the mean-looking, musclebound guy with the mirror sunglasses and the walkie-talkie, checking ID's at the Pearly Gates."

The words that popped out of Jane's mouth surprised her. "You don't strike me as cowed, Robin. On the contrary."

There was a startled silence, but Robin recovered quickly. "Well, that's only because I'm as tough as nails. Lucky for me, because—"

"Get lost, Robin." Mac's voice was calm. "Switch tables with one of the other waiters. Do not bug us. Or else."

"Certainly not. Wouldn't dream of it. I'll send Maurice to take your order. Be good, Mac." Robin flashed her braces at Jane. "Watch out for him. He's nothing but trouble. Enjoy your meal." She spun around and weaved gracefully away between the tables.

Mac was eyeing her thoughtfully when she turned back to him. "Thanks for sticking up for me," he said. "Sorry about the interruption. I thought we'd be safe here, but I was wrong."

Jane thought of the strained politeness that had characterized her interactions with her own family. "She teases you because she trusts you. She's not afraid of you. Be grateful. It's a compliment."

He snorted. "If that's a compliment, I'd hate to see an insult. My brother's no joke, either. We fight like cats and dogs. You got siblings?"

"No. I'm an only child," she told him. "An unfortunate accident late in my mother's life."

"Hardly unfortunate. You look like you turned out fine."

She shrugged. "My mother was unamused," she said dryly. "You're lucky to have brothers and sisters."

He lifted a dubious eyebrow. "Sometimes I wonder. Robin scares me to death. Danny and I raised her on our own, so we've got the worry and responsibility of parents, but none of the respect or the clout."

She was intrigued. "What happened to your—"

"Out of the picture when Robin was a baby," he said curtly.

"Oh," she murmured. "How old were you when—"

"Thirteen. Danny was eleven, Robin was one."

She itched for more, but the brusque way he was cutting off her questions discouraged further probing. "It looks like you did a fine job."

"We'll see." He rolled his eyes. "Now she wants to be a clown."

Jane smiled. "She certainly is high-spirited."

"Oh, no. I'm not speaking figuratively. I mean that literally. As in Bozo the Clown." He sounded aggrieved. "She wants to go to clown college. Wear a red plastic nose. Make kids laugh for a living."

She was taken aback by the stony disapproval in his voice. "What's wrong with that?" she asked hesitantly.

He looked incredulous. "It's ridiculous, that's what's wrong with it. Danny and I busted our asses to give her career opportunities in the hotel industry, and what does she want? A red plastic nose. She'll be juggling eighty dollar bottles of wine before her shift is over."

She couldn't stifle her laughter, despite his glowering face. "Face it," she told him. "She's a dreamer."

"She's young and rebellious, and she doesn't know what's good for her. She'll come around. Everybody has to accept reality sometime."

Ouch. Time to get going on her own reality check, before she lost her nerve. "Heaven help your own kids when you have them," she said.

An odd silence fell. "Well," he said slowly. "At least no kid of mine is ever going to have to wonder whether or not I give a damn."

Jane's eyes dropped. "There's, ah, something to be said for that." She took as deep a breath as the bustier would allow, which wasn't saying much, and pressed on. "Mac, there's something I have to—"

"So she showed up, after all. You get points for nerve, Ms. King."

They looked up. Danny loomed over them, white teeth flashing in his lean, dark face. His hair fell loose and gleaming over the shoulders of his elegant jacket. A discreet diamond stud winked in his ear. It was unreal. The whole family was drop-dead gorgeous. All three of them.

Mac stared up at his brother. "So what's your excuse?"

Danny shrugged. I wanted to check on Robin. You know, just to make sure she didn't decide to do her shift wearing her bra outside her shirt. With Robin, it pays to be vigilant." He glanced at Jane, and a charming grin lit up his chiseled features. "I also wanted to apologize, for being rude to you this afternoon. Forgive me."

Jane blinked at him, bewildered. "Oh. Ah, thanks for the thought, but I didn't notice any rudeness."

I did," Mac said wryly. "Rule number one, Jane. Watch out for Danny when he's smiling. That's when he's at his most dangerous. Danny, what do you want from us?"

"Nothing." Devilish amusement gleamed in Danny's eyes. "You're doing your ogre act, bro. Try to be suave, like me, while you're having dinner with a beautiful redhead. May I call you Jane?"

"You may not," Mac said. "Stop sucking up to my date. I don't appreciate being tortured by my family while I'm trying to enjoy a private, quiet evening with my lady friend."

Danny's mouth twitched. "You'd have more luck with your quiet, private evening if you stayed the hell away from your own restaurants."

"Tell me about it. I would have, but I promised her a tour."

"Oh!" Danny laughed. "Like this afternoon's tour? Yowza!"

Mac's eyes narrowed. "Stop ogling her cleavage and go find your own date, Danny. Good-bye."

Danny seized Jane's hand and kissed it, his eyes fixed on his brother's face. A delighted grin spread slowly over his face. "You're certainly territorial tonight," he observed. "Enjoy your evening."

Jane looked at her hand as he strode away, flustered. She looked at Mac's face, and stuck the just-kissed hand swiftly under the table.

I suppose I should be grateful that my brother busts my balls, too?" Mac asked. "Just another compliment, huh?"

She knew he was being ironic, but the words popped out anyway. "Yes, actually. It is. He's not trying to hurt you. He's just curious. You guys play rough, all three of you, but there are rules."

"Rules, my ass. He thinks he's so slick."

"Complain all you want," Jane said. "I envy you. I can't imagine what it would be like to have someone in my family interested enough in my private life to pester me in a restaurant."

Mac rolled his eyes. "Robin says we form an unholy trinity. Like Kirk, Spock and McCoy from the really old *Star Trek*."

Jane laughed out loud. "And I bet you're Kirk, right?"

"I don't look like Kirk, so how do you figure? Is it the masterful way that I use my phaser?"

"I haven't seen any phaser action yet," she said demurely.

"I figured you for Kirk because he always grabs the girls and kisses them."

Mac reached across the table and took her hand. "Why waste time?"

She stared at his long fingers. "Do you do that in every episode?" she asked timidly. "Grab the girl, I mean?"

"I've grabbed my share," he admitted. "But I've gotten more discriminating with time. Lots of episodes go by these days with no girl-grabbing. But I'm hoping to make up for lost time. Real soon."

A cell phone rang. Mac pulled it out of his pocket and checked the display. "Would you excuse me while I answer this?" he asked. "I've been expecting this call all day. I promise I'll be quick."

"Feel free." She stared at the perfect rose that adorned the table, trying not to listen to his low conversation and failing utterly.

"Hey, Henry. Did you talk to . . . yeah? And? . . . Yeah, that's the name . . . Oh. Wow. That's really weird. No, can't talk right now. Uh-huh . . . yeah, I will. Thanks, anyway. Thank Charlotte for me, too. Later."

He clipped the phone shut and stared at her for a long moment.

"Bad news?" she asked timidly.

"You could say that," he said. "But I'm handling it."

The silence lengthened. The frequency between them had changed somehow. The teasing warmth in his eyes had disappeared. He looked tense and cautious.

He reached for her hand, turned it over, and splayed her fingers wide, as if to read her palm. "So tell me about yourself," he said quietly. "What's it like to work at *Europa Inflight*? Tell me your deep, dark secrets, Jane."

That was an opening to confess if she'd ever heard one, but she had wanted to broach the subject herself, of her own free will. She most certainly did not want to be put on the defensive and have her embarrassing confession interrogated out of her. "It's, ah, a little early for deep, dark secrets, isn't it?" she hedged.

He tilted an eyebrow. "Let's start with simple biographical data," he suggested. "I'll make it easy for you. Ever see those info sheets about centerfold models that you find in men's magazines?"

She shook her head.

His thumb stroked her palm with hypnotic slowness. "Of course you haven't. Along with the naked pictures, we get the vital stats. Like, for instance, Kaia Marie, twenty-three years old, Libra, 38-24-36, born in Anyplace, U.S.A., graduated from U. of Wherever. Loves: kittens and open-minded people. Hates: broccoli and bigots. Want me to go first?"

He waited for her short, nervous nod. "OK," he said. "Michael MacNamara, thirty-six years old, Sagittarius. Born in Las Vegas. Six foot three, two hundred ten pounds, graduated from U. of Washington. Loves: winning. Hates: . . . liars." He lifted her hand, and kissed it. "There's nothing I hate more. Your turn, angel."

Her stomach fluttered anxiously. "You're making me a little nervous," she said. "Can't we, ah, savor the mystery a little longer?"

He studied her face for a long moment. "OK. Fine. If that's the way you want it, there's no need to waste time playing games."

She felt like an actress who'd been handed the wrong script. "What on earth are you talking about?"

"Never mind." He shoved his chair back. "Come with me."

"But . . . dinner?"

He grabbed her arm and pulled her to her feet. "We'll have it sent up to the room."

Jane barely managed to snag her purse before he slid his arm around her waist and swept her out of the dining room. She scurried to keep up with his long strides as they hastened across the rose garden.

She'd been aroused all day at the thought of having sex

with Mac, but his quiet, purposeful urgency made her nervous, and she'd been plenty nervous to begin with. Another dim back staircase, another dark corridor, another portentous silence broken only by the scrambling click of her heels, her panting breath. "Mac," she protested. "Slow down."

He swung around, lifting her off her feet so that she straddled his muscular thighs. He pinned her against the wall, and his mouth claimed hers in a kiss of pure sensual possession. She opened to the bold thrust of his tongue, too busy kissing him back to be intimidated.

Oh, yes. Here it was again, that feeling that she'd glimpsed in the Baron's Suite. It was real. She hadn't been dreaming. It wasn't wishful thinking. Every muscle in her body was wildly alive, every inch of her skin screaming for his touch. She wrapped her arms around his neck with a low, throaty moan.

"Why slow down?" He nuzzled her neck until her insides went soft, liquid and quivering. "Let's get on with what we started this afternoon. We can do it right here, in the corridor if you want, or we can take to the room. Ladies' choice, sweetheart."

"In the *corridor*?" Her heavy-lidded eyes popped open. "Are you crazy?"

"Nah. Just out-of-my-mind horny." He hauled her skirt up and stared down at her gartered hose, her skimpy black lace panties. "Oh, man. Look at you. To hell with the room. I vote for right here."

He trapped her breathless protest against another delicious, marauding kiss. She forgot what she had been trying to say. It lost all its importance when he slid his finger beneath the damp lace of her panties. She gasped against his mouth as he teased it along the plump, slick folds of her labia. He flicked it over her clitoris, swirling with slow, wicked skill, and thrust his finger slowly inside her with a ragged sigh. "Oh, God. Jane. You're so hot," he muttered. "You're incredible."

Her mouth was full of his thrusting tongue, his finger was shoved inside her body. Pinned against the wall of a corridor lined with doors that could open at any second, and she actually didn't care. She couldn't stop clenching around his caressing hand, couldn't stop making rough mewling sounds. He caressed a marvelous spot inside her that made her squirm and whimper out loud.

"Here?" His voice was utterly confident. "Now?"

It took a second to remember what he was talking about. "No!"

"The room, then." He let her slide down his leg. When her tiptoes hit the carpet runner, he seized her arm, and they practically sprinted together to the end of the corridor. It was something she would never have dreamed of doing in four-inch heels, but she practically floated on his strong, steely arm. Her feet barely touched the floor.

Mac groped in his pocket for a key, unlocked the door and swept her into the room. The door swung shut with a slam that rattled her overstimulated nerves. She backed away into the dark, panting. She was about to explode with excitement.

Just enough fading twilight sifted in the sheer curtains to make out a sofa, wingback chairs, the sitting room of a bedroom suite. That was all she saw before he shoved her against the wall. His hands were all over her, sliding over her silk-covered curves, under her hair, over her back looking for a zipper, but there wasn't one. This was a dress she had to shimmy out of, but things were hurtling forward far too fast for any seductive shimmying. She reached down for the hem of her skirt and jerked it up over her thighs, to give him a hint.

He laughed and shoved it higher, fumbling for her panties. He ripped out the gusset, and she was bare to his tender, probing fingers. His breath was hot against her throat. He smelled so good. She was so sensitive to his caressing hand, she jerked and shuddered in his grasp. She grabbed his shoulders to steady herself, and a framed picture bumped her shoulder and slid to the floor. Glass crashed and tinkled.

"Damn." He lifted her higher, letting her feet dangle. "Hold tight to my neck. Lift your feet up off the floor and watch out for that glass."

He set her down in the middle of the room and started to unbutton his shirt. She backed away into the dark unknown on rubbery ankles. She was trembling on the brink of a blinding revelation that could transform her completely. Turn her world on its head.

He advanced on her, unbuttoning his cuffs. He shrugged the shirt off and let it drop. The powerful muscles of his shoulders and arms and chest gleamed in the faint light. He was lean, hard, perfect. An arrow of dark hair disappeared into his waistband, where his hands were busy unbuckling his belt. He herded her through a door. He picked her up with shocking ease and tossed her backward into a dark nowhere.

She landed, bouncing on a big four-poster bed and struggled up onto her elbows. "Whoa! Hold on, Mac! Take a deep breath, and chill. This is very intense. I hardly know you."

"I tried to get to know you," he said. "You said you wanted to savor the mystery. So here's your chance, Jane. Savor it." He bent over and pried off his shoes. They thudded off into the darkness.

His cool tone stung her, and she scrambled up until she sat on the edge of the bed, just as he stepped out of his pants and briefs. He stood before her, his magnificent body stark naked.

She forced her mouth to close. Forced herself to inhale. Tried to remember what she'd planned to say to him. It was gone, beyond recall.

She tried not to stare, but it was impossible. His penis jutted out before him, thick and long and heavy.

"Scared, Jane?" he asked softly. "Want to run away again, like you did this afternoon? Please, don't. I could please you. If you let me."

She tried to swallow. Her throat was too dry. "Can't we just . . . ah, lighten up? Take this a little slower?"

He shook his head. "No. I can't." His voice was stark. "Sorry. It's just not going to be like that. Not tonight."

They stared at each other's faces through the shadows. Mac reached out for her hand, and drew it slowly towards himself, his eyes fixed on hers as if silently daring her to pull away.

She didn't. He wrapped her fingers around his penis. Her hand jerked like a drop of water sputtering on a griddle, the sensation was so startling. So hot and hard and solid. So velvety smooth.

He stroked her hand slowly over his hard flesh, more roughly than she would have dared to touch him on her own. "This is how it is," he said. "This is how I am tonight. Take me or leave me, Jane."

"But I—"

"Touch me." His low voice was ragged with intensity. "Squeeze, with your hands. Please."

She was electrified, intensely aroused by the thick, blunt head of his penis, the broad stalk, the suede-soft skin, the raised, throbbing tracery of veins. His heart pumped against her hand. She wondered how he would react if she sank down and pressed her tongue against him. So much of him, thick and taut and swollen to bursting.

Wow. She wasn't sure he would even fit into her mouth.

His fist tightened, swirling her fist, spreading the fluid until his penis was slick with it. He pumped her hand slowly up and down his length. "Do you want me?" His voice was a hypnotic whisper.

She leaned her forehead against the damp skin of his chest. That liquid that lubricated him was magic stuff, more slippery than any oil. The force of his desire made her tremble and sweat. It was so raw, so visceral—the urgent pressure of his big hands wrapped around hers, the hard, stabbing thrust of his thick shaft into the slick recesses of her clenched hand. "Yes, I definitely do want you, but this is too—"

"Shhh." He bent down and slid his tongue seductively along her swollen, trembling lower lip. "Yes, or no. There is no middle ground."

"But I—"

"If you want it, I'll give it to you. My way. I can't make nice and be a good boy tonight. You have to just trust me."

She pressed her face against his chest, tasted the salt tang of his skin against her open mouth, felt the pulsing heat of his penis clutched in her hand. She sank her teeth into the muscle of his shoulder, hard enough to make him gasp. He was so beautiful and compelling, and the only way she could have him was to give herself over to him completely. It wasn't fair of him to drive her into a corner, but she had to have him.

"Yes," she whispered.

"Say please." His triumphant tone made her grateful for the darkness to hide her blush. He waited. "Say it, Jane. Set me free."

She hesitated for one last second, pressed her face against his neck, and whispered it into his ear like a guilty secret. *"Please."*

Chapter Four

Things moved swiftly after that. He rolled on the condom and knocked her back onto the bed. So this was how it would be. Straight-up Neanderthal. Fine with her. She was in no mood to be teased.

He climbed on top of her, surrounding her with his heat. He made her feel small, but not fragile. She felt lithe and strong, like a wild animal. She reached around his big body, stroking the thick muscles of his back, his shoulders. His smell was woodsy, herbal—the sweetness of soap, the sharpness of salt. She buried her nose in his sweat-dampened hair and tried to wind her fingers through it. It slipped right through them, too slick and glossy and short to get any grip.

He tossed her skirt up and shoved her legs wide. He wasn't even going to undress her. Fine. Their tryst in the Baron's Suite was foreplay and then some. She'd been clenching her legs around a damp throb of arousal all day, now. Enough agony, already.

His body vibrated with a low rumble of approval when he brushed his fingertip over her mound and slid it between the slick folds of her labia. "Oh, wow. You do want me."

She ran her hands over his big shoulders. "All day, I've been like this," she admitted. "I had to change my panties twice."

"Tell me about it. I've had this hard-on all afternoon," he told her. "And my problem is bigger than yours."

"Oh, much," she murmured.

He laughed as he thrust his tongue into her mouth, and slid his fingers tenderly around her clitoris, spreading the slick moisture. He thrust his tongue into her mouth with the same seductive, pulsing rhythm as his hand. She was too aroused to be embarrassed at the soft, liquid sounds his fingers made as he caressed her. He pushed the thick head of his penis against her, moistening himself.

The blunt pressure made her stiffen up with alarm.

He was big. Bigger than anyone she'd ever been with, and it had been a very long time. And she'd never quite gotten the knack of just relaxing and letting this happen. She always tensed up, tried too hard.

He went still, and kissed her face gently. "Relax. I won't hurt you. "

She tried not to brace herself, but it was an involuntary reflex.

She waited, but nothing happened. He lodged the tip of himself inside her, barely clasped in her moist folds, and there he stayed, motionless.

Finally she opened her eyes. He held her gaze intently as he slid his penis along her labia, a gentle, caressing slide. He lowered his head to her mouth and echoed the same light stroke with his tongue along the sensitive inner part of her lip. Slow, seductive and delicious.

He was waiting for her to tell him to go on. She hadn't expected patience, or sensitivity. Particularly since he hadn't promised it.

Something softened and relaxed inside her. She lifted her face to him and arched herself open. He had demanded her blind trust, and in some quiet, instinctive way, he had earned it.

A rough sigh shuddered out of him. He rocked against her, tiny, teasing thrusts until the head of his penis was firmly wedged inside her, and then he slowly pushed himself inside. The pressure tightened into a wonderful, burning ache. She was distended around his thick shaft, the nerves in that sensitive place shocked to full awareness at the heavy intrusion of his body. Her sheath clung to him, quivering and stretched.

"My God, you're tight," he muttered. "You feel amazing."

She couldn't reply. Her throat was vibrating too hard.

He shoved himself all the way inside, and withdrew himself, with maddening deliberation. It was getting easier to accommodate him. She was slicker with each stroke. She was starting to sense his rhythm and cautiously enjoy his thick, hot, sliding presence inside her when he flexed his hips and thrust himself deeper.

The intensity of the sensation made her gasp.

He froze. "Damn. I'm sorry." Mac trapped her face between his hands and kissed her gently. "I'm really sorry," he repeated. "I'm just so turned on. I didn't mean to do that so hard. It got away from me."

Her heart thudded so hard it seemed to fill her chest and leave no room for her lungs. She could not acknowledge his apology, or tell him it was all right, or that it wasn't. She was overwhelmed.

"Hey. Jane?"

His pleading tone pulled her into focus, and she dragged in a shallow breath and kissed him back. "It's OK," she said. "I'm fine."

"You sure?"

"Fine. It just, um, surprised me. You're touching a place that I don't think has ever been touched. In there, I mean." She patted his face.

Mac's big chest vibrated with silent laughter. He rested his hot, damp forehead against hers for a moment, panting.

Then curved himself over her body, and began. Slowly and carefully at first, but his movements became deeper and harder as her body softened to accept him—and then demand him.

Jane had always imagined that if she ever got it right, that good sex would feel sweet. Pleasant. Nice. *Hah*. The gliding intrusion of his penis, his sleek, hot, beautiful body pinning her down, melding with hers, it was marvelous, terrifying tension that ratcheted higher and higher. Anything but nice. Each time he thrust inside her, she wanted more, she wanted *now*, she didn't even know what she wanted, but if he didn't give it to her she was going to scream and claw and bite him for it. It was thunder, lightning, lashing rain. Her body tingled—fingers, toes, face. Her hair practically stood on end. Her chest ached like she wanted to weep. Her hips bucked up to meet him, hands sliding over sweat-slicked skin, nails digging into his muscles. He angled himself so that every stroke of his thick shaft caressed the hot glow inside her sheath, sliding heavily over and over it. Churning her into a frenzy.

The bed squeaked in the dark room. There was no sound but the slapping of flesh on flesh, panting gasps she was helpless to control. His thrusts were rough and deep, driving her exactly where she needed to go, just not fast enough, damn it. She wanted everything he had. *Now.*

She clenched her arms and legs around him at every ramming stroke. It was wild, earthy, crazy, perfect. She yelled at him, shoved and slapped furiously at his chest because she knew he would trap her hands over her head, bear down harder, thrust deeper. Give her all the ballast she needed to push off and launch herself into glittering space.

She almost dragged him along with her when she exploded. He used every trick he knew to hold it back. He sucked in his breath, clenched the muscles around his cock, balanced on the head of a pin inside his head as he chanted the silent mantra: *not yet not yet not yet.*

He wasn't going to be winning any prizes for finesse tonight, but Jane seemed to like it raw and uncomplicated. She was white-hot, stunning. Perfect, but for the small detail that she was a scheming liar and a con artist. But for the fact he was hurt and disappointed. He'd been fighting his anger, ever since Henry's call. And being more turned on than he'd ever been in his life didn't help matters any.

Aftershocks fluttered through her lush, delicate body. He waited until she relaxed and lay still beneath him, limp and soft and panting.

She made a low, startled sound as he folded her legs wide and started right back in on her. She probably needed a break. Too bad. He didn't mean to come for a while yet. He had one shot at this before he confronted her with the truth, and he would make it last.

"I'm not done," he told her.

She stared up into his face, and gave him a nod, wiggling beneath him for more freedom of movement. He adjusted his stroke so that it didn't rub her oversensitized clit. She might be trying to scam him, but she was still small and delicate. He didn't want to hurt her. On the contrary. He wanted her to remember this night for the rest of her life.

He reached out to flip on the bedside lamp. Jane blinked, startled. He needed light to brand every detail of her onto his memory—even if they gave him sweat-soaked fevered dreams for the rest of his life. Her stockings were shredded, which must be his doing although he didn't remember it. He liked the effect, the slutty contrast to her fine-textured white skin. The scent of her tight, slick little cunt made his head swim.

She still had those spiky blue sandals on. The panties he'd ripped open were sheer black lace. Her dress was crumpled around her waist. Her breath was shallow, her fathomless eyes blue-black, wide with wonder. The moist folds of her cunt peeked out of the nest of reddish ringlets. He pulled out and surged back in, savoring the snug kiss of her inner lips, distended around his cock. "I knew it," he muttered.

"Knew what?"

"That red hair of yours is for real." *If nothing else.*

He unbuckled her fragile sandals and flung them behind him. He gripped her ankles and opened her wider. She sighed and undulated beneath him as she took in his slow, lazy thrusts. She loved it like this, with him looming over her. She got off on being dominated, which suited him fine. They were perfect for each other.

The fleeting thought made his stomach tighten. He tried to block it. This was a one-shot deal. Stupid to blow it by getting emotional. He dragged his mind back to the sexy details of her body. "I love your underwear," he told her.

Her laugher was so open and shaky and sweet, it rattled him. "It sure doesn't look that way. You tore them to shreds. I bought them just for you, Mac, and they weren't cheap."

"Oh, yeah?" He pressed her thighs wider. "I'm honored. It was a good investment. I'll make sure it was worth your while."

"You're hard on underwear, Mac. You ruined my stockings this afternoon, too," she told him.

"Sorry about that." He braced her feet against his shoulders, folding her completely in on herself. The angle allowed him to penetrate her even more deeply. Her mouth opened in a soundless gasp as he shoved himself inside her, to the limit. She squeezed her eyes shut. Tears squeezed out between her sooty lashes and flashed down her face.

The tears alarmed him. "You OK?" he demanded.

A short, jerky nod was his only answer, and it didn't satisfy him. "You like it?" he persisted. What a bonehead, bleating for reassurance from a professional liar. "You want more?"

Yes. Her trembling lips made the shape of the word, but no sound came out. Her eyes opened, glittering and overflowing. She nodded.

Vulnerable. Just like this afternoon. It made him frantic and confused. Everything about this was perfect. The way she took him in, like they were one mind, one body. Like he knew her by heart.

Turning on the light had been a big mistake.

He wrenched her low-cut bodice down. Her plump breasts had overflowed the confines of the black lace corset. Her nipples were tight, flushed raspberry red. His breath rushed out of his lungs. Those tits deserved hours of foreplay on their own sweet merits, but he couldn't stop now. Not if someone put a gun to his head. He had to cram a lifetime of sex into one, single, explosive lay.

He pressed his hand to her heaving bosom, between her breasts, over her heart, felt the rapid, wild throb of her pulse against his palm.

She reached up, pressed her own hand against his heart. Her dark blue eyes accepted him, made room for him. All of him, even his anger, even his darkness. Oh, man. Oh, no. The look in her eyes was more than he could take. He had to finish this. *Now.*

He shut his eyes, opened the gates and hurled himself into the orgasm which had been gathering momentum all day. Pounding black waves of agonized pleasure rolled over him and blotted him out.

Oblivion was short-lived. His gut ached as soon as he drifted back to full awareness. He pulled himself out of her clinging body. She reached to touch his face. He jerked away. He climbed off the bed and took off the condom, avoiding her gaze. He was drenched and shivering.

"Mac?"

He turned his back and headed for the bathroom without a reply.

He cleaned up, and stared into the mirror with bleak eyes. The orgasm had actually made him feel worse, amazingly. He'd planned to make this last all night, but he hadn't expected to feel this bad.

He didn't have the heart to string it out for a second go at her, no matter how sexy she was. Best to wrap it up, put on his clothes and get out of here. Maybe get drunk someplace that was walking distance from his condo. It wasn't his thing, but tonight was a special case.

What irony. He of all people should be proof against a con artist's smooth, lying charm. Those liar's tricks were mother's milk to him.

She'd suckered him, with those stormy blue eyes. Vulnerable, his ass. He'd been eating out of her hand, dreaming about matching his-'n-hers terry cloth bathrobes, all the way up to Henry's phone call. He'd never met anyone better than his own daddy until today.

Time to find out what she was mixed up in. He cursed into the mirror. He hated the look in his own eyes. Hadn't seen it for decades.

Get the fuck on with it, he told himself. He shoved open the door.

Jane was curled up on the edge of the bed, arms wrapped around her knees. "What's wrong?" she demanded.

He could tell by the look on her face that his feelings were showing. He'd never been able to hide them worth a damn. That was Danny's gift, not his. "How about you tell me?" he challenged her.

She was the picture of innocent bewilderment. "You're angry. Why? What happened? What did I do?"

He crossed his arms over his chest and reminded himself to play it cool. "Do you have something to tell me, Jane?"

Her hand crept up to cover her mouth. "Oh, dear."

He let out a long, measured breath, stared at her, and let

several seconds tick by. "You don't work for *Europa In-flight*," he said flatly.

Jane squeezed her eyes shut and shook her head. "Ah, no. Actually . . . I'm an executive recruiter."

He was completely lost. "Come again?"

"A headhunter." She hid her face with her hands. "I was looking for a candidate for a general manager. I was scheduled to meet Gary Finley. Posing as a writer was just a ploy to get past the receptionist." She peeked out between her fingers. "I certainly never meant to meet the CEO. Robin stuck me in your office, and . . ." Her voice trailed off.

He was dumbfounded. Headhunter? *That* was her horrible secret? Holy shit. His mood shot towards the stratosphere, but he didn't dare relax just yet. "Prove it," he demanded.

She slid off the bed and padded into the other room.

"Watch out for that broken glass," he called after her.

"Yes, thank you." She came back rummaging through her purse. She found her wallet, fished out a card and held it out to him. Gingerly. The way one might hold out a chunk of meat to a starving predator.

He took it from her shaking hand, and stared at it. *Jane Duvall, Executive Recruiter Grayson & Clint.* "I'm calling your boss," he told her.

"Please do," she said. "I'll give you her home number. You might get me fired, but that's fine. At this point, I think I would be grateful."

He kept staring at the card, as if he could squeeze reassurance out of it. He was starting to feel like an idiot, but that was no big deal. It wasn't the first time he'd lost his cool and done something stupid.

"Who needs a general manager?" he asked.

She hesitated for a moment. "Brighton Group," she admitted.

"No shit. So Rick Geddes finally told that constipated old man where to get off. I'm glad he finally found his balls."

"So you know the Brighton people, then?" she asked hesitantly.

"I don't give a rat's ass about the Brighton people," he said. "All I want to know is why you lied to me."

She sank down onto the edge of the bed again and twisted handfuls of her skirt into her hands. "At first, I just didn't want to blow my cover, but then . . ." She looked miserable. "I meant to tell you as soon as we got to the Baron's Suite this afternoon, but then . . ."

Her hesitation was driving him nuts. "But then what? Why didn't you? Do you enjoy playing games?"

She slapped her hands down against the mattress. "No! I do not! I didn't tell you because you were coming on to me, and I liked it!"

He turned that over in his mind a few times, but he couldn't make it fit. "Uh, Jane? Hello? I would've wanted to go to bed with you no matter what you do for a living. You have to do better than that."

She crossed her arms over her middle. She wouldn't meet his eyes. "I didn't want to break the spell," she whispered.

"Spell?" He squinted at her. "What spell? This is way too deep for me, babe. Help me thrash through it."

She threw up her hands. "It was like magic, this afternoon," she said desperately. "I'd never felt anything like it. I got swept away."

He gestured impatiently for her to go on. "Yeah? So? Magic, swept away, that's cool, that all works for me. And your point is?"

She made a sharp growling sound that Robin sometimes made when she was frustrated at him for not comprehending some insanely complicated girl thing. "If I'd told you I was a headhunter, everything would've changed. I would've spent that time apologizing and explaining and being uncomfortable, instead of . . . you know. Kissing you madly."

"Ah. I see," he said cautiously. "Uh . . . that sounds really weird and convoluted to me, but whatever. I guess I'll buy it."

"I tried to tell you this afternoon, and your brother interrupted," she said heatedly. "I tried again, tonight, and your sister popped up. Then whoops, your brother again. I swear, it was like a bad joke. Then you got that phone call, and—oh. It was the phone call, wasn't it? You changed, right then. You turned into a . . . a conquering barbarian!"

"Barbarian?" He tried not to grin. "Yeah, it was the phone call. I know a woman who works at Europa. She knows everybody on staff. She'd never heard of a Jane King contributing anything to them."

"I see," she whispered.

"I figured you must be a con artist, running some sort of scam. I meant to play you along, find out what your game was."

Her eyes widened, horrified. "Running a scam? You thought I was a *criminal*? Good God! Then why did you bring me up here?"

He shrugged. "I wanted to fuck you anyway."

She flinched back. "Ouch!"

"Yeah, that's how I felt when I found out Jane King didn't exist," he said. "But I figured the ugly scene could wait until I'd nailed you."

Her face went white. "How could you do that? You are ice-cold."

"Actually, I feel like I'm running a fever," he told her.

She slid off the bed and backed away. "Oh, no. Don't you look at me like that. Don't even think about touching me again. I can't believe you thought I was a thief and you still wanted to . . . to . . ."

"To fuck your brains out? Welcome to reality, babe. The little head doesn't always agree with the big head. Compromises have to be made."

A hot buzz of sexual tension still shimmered between

them. Sex hadn't dissipated it at all. Jane lifted her chin. "I don't use language like that, under any circumstances," she said. "And I don't compromise."

"You will," he said slowly. "If you want something, you will, Jane. And maybe I'm rude and nasty, but you still want me."

"No." She shook her head warily. "No, Mac, I don't. I've changed my mind. This has gotten too weird for me."

"It's not my fault it got weird," he said. "I'm not the one who told the lies." He lunged for her before she could back away farther, and hooked his fingers through the thin straps of her dress. "Can you believe I still haven't seen you naked? And after all this drama, too."

She pulled back, batting at his hands. "No way. You're not going to see me naked. This is my cue to go."

He caught her around the waist, and she kicked and flailed in his grasp as he dropped down onto the bed, pulling her onto his lap. "I think you got your cues mixed up," he told her.

She struggled furiously. "Hold it right there, buddy—"

"Jane," he said. "I like that name. I'm glad it wasn't fake. Short and sweet. A no-bullshit name. Where do you think you're going, Jane?"

"Home," she snapped. "You can't keep me here."

"Sure I can," he said calmly. "Watch me."

Being trapped against Mac's hot, naked body, his thick arms clamped hard around her waist, was not soothing. To say the least of it.

His arms were like steel. She twisted around to glare into his face, and the hot, purposeful glow in his eyes made her stomach flutter. Predator eyes. He pressed his lips against her shoulder. His hot breath caressed her skin, and she felt it everywhere.

"You're scaring me," she said. "Don't do this, Mac."

"Don't be scared," he soothed. "I won't hurt you. Or force you."

"Then let . . . me . . . *go!*"

Her struggles didn't budge him. "Don't wimp out on me, Jane. We're going to get through this. All the way to the other side."

"I am not wimping out!"

"Then stop flopping like a fish on a hook and talk to me! I won't let you go, so don't waste your strength. You're going to need it."

She stiffened. "It's comments like that, that really make me nervous."

He let out an impatient grunt. "Cut the ravished maiden routine. I know you liked what I did to you. I felt it. Every detail."

"That's not the point," she snapped. "Besides, why even bother to make me come if you thought I was out to screw you over?"

He grinned, and nibbled delicately on her shoulder. "I wanted it to be memorable for you. I wanted to make you scream with pleasure."

"Don't hold your breath," she said stiffly. "I'm not the screaming type. Even if I were staying the night with you. Which I am *not*."

"You don't even know what type you are," he said. "You're figuring it out right now, as you go along. Right?"

Her sharp reply faltered. How the hell did he do that? He made her feel as if all of her secret needs and guilty fantasies were wide open to him, written on her forehead. He could maneuver her so effortlessly.

His lips curved in a triumphant smile. "Stay with me tonight," he urged. "You'll find out exactly what you like, sweet Jane. Don't be afraid. Or ashamed. I'll help you. I was born for this."

"You are arrogant," she informed him.

"I'll show you arrogant, sweetheart. I've only had you once, but I bet I know more about what makes you hot than you do yourself."

"Oh, please," she sputtered. "That's just ridiculous."

"Oh, yeah? Look me straight in the eye and tell me you didn't love it. Just the way I gave it to you.'"

His boasting infuriated her, but she was tuned to his frequency, now. She saw beneath his words to the steely tension of his body. The rough timbre of his voice betrayed his vulnerability. He wasn't quite as confident as he pretended to be, and that observation calmed her down.

"I loved what you did to me in bed," she admitted. "But I hated it afterward, when you pulled away and wouldn't look at me. It was like being slapped in the face. I'm still jittery from that."

He looked puzzled. "I'm not angry anymore," he pointed out.

She shoved at his arms. "Maybe you're not, but now I am!"

He scooped her legs around until she sat sideways on his lap. "One thing I might as well get straight with you, being as how you're a headhunter and all," he said. "Leroy Crowne, the owner of these hotels? He's my uncle. These hotels are successful because Danny and I worked our asses off to make them that way. Having been my uncle's employee since I was sixteen, I know how to treat employees, and how not to. I know what keeps them loyal. Put your arm around my neck."

She draped her arm tentatively across his hot, muscular shoulders. His arm tightened around her waist, cuddling her closer. "I pay Gary Finley very well," he continued. "I doubt he could be tempted to screw me over, particularly not for a humorless old fart like Brighton. But I invite you to try it. Call him. I'll give you his cell phone number."

She licked her lips. "No, thank you," she said carefully. "I haven't the slightest interest in calling Gary Finley right now."

"Good. I'm glad to hear that."

They stared at each other silently for a long moment.

"So here we are, then," he said. "No con artists, no scams, no business agenda, no fake names. No bullshit of any kind. Just a man and a woman naked in bed."

"I'm not naked." She meant the words to sound defiant, but her husky murmur sounded almost inviting.

"Yeah, and I'm going to fix that problem right now."

He grabbed the straps of her gown and pulled her down to kiss her again. Jane put her hand over his mouth and chin and shoved.

"Hold it right there," she said. "Don't you strong-arm me. Just because you're not mad anymore does not mean anything goes!"

He kissed the palm of her hand until she snatched it away. "I just want to feast my eyes on your beauty," he coaxed. "Take it off, Jane."

She felt silly, but she couldn't bear to take off the dress. She already felt so vulnerable. It was ridiculous, after having had such intense sex with him, but the thin silk of her dress felt like the last fragile barrier she had left over her dignity and self-control.

"Come on, Jane," he wheedled. "You'll like being naked with me."

"Sorry. No. Right now, I need my space," she whispered.

"You need more than that." He cupped her breast, and her nipple tightened. "You've got plenty of space in your life already. Too much."

His comment was so dead on the mark that angry humiliation reddened her face. Her loneliness and longing was her own private business. "You do not know me," she hissed. "And I do not *need* this."

"I do," he said baldly. "I'm dying for it. I would do anything to get some more. I'm not ashamed to admit it, so why should you be?"

"I'm not ashamed!"

"Then why do you run away, and lose your nerve, and tell lies, and put on fake names?" His voice was soft and relentless.

"I did it for my job!" She jerked her face away. "Leave me alone!"

"No." He tossed her onto the bed. "I don't want to leave you alone. And you don't want me to, either." He slid down the length of her body, tossing her skirt up over her waist. "You don't need to pretend with me, Jane. I don't know why you ever thought you needed to."

She caught his face in both her hands. "What makes you think I'm so unsatisfied?" she demanded. "How do you know I don't have a whole stable full of lovers? One for every damn day of the week!"

He pressed a lingering kiss against her inner thigh, and tenderly licked her groin. "I know it from the way you act when I fuck you."

She shoved at his face. "My God, you are crude!"

He trapped her hands and held them still. "Sorry. Can't help it. I can't explain how I know, but you don't open up easily. And you haven't done this in a long time. It's true, right?"

She couldn't look into those bright, piercing eyes and lie at the same time. She nodded reluctantly.

A triumphant grin split his face. "Of course not. You're too shy and uptight to go after what you want. You need a rude, crude barbarian like me to storm the gates. Am I right?"

"Don't get any ideas, MacNamara."

"Too late. I've got more than ideas. At this point, they've already solidified into plans. Shy Jane." He shoved her thighs wide and stared down between them. "Oh, man, look at you. Juicy and hot. I'm going to have to take you lingerie shopping, but the stuff turns me on even more when it's ripped to shreds. Is that kinky?"

Her body vibrated at the sight of his face poised over her

mound, his hot breath fanning her most secret flesh. "Very kinky. Mac, don't."

"Yum. Why not?" He rubbed his face against her inner thigh.

She said the first thing that popped into her mind. "Because I must taste like latex."

"Not when I'm through with you, you won't."

Chapter Five

She flinched at the first touch of his mouth. The sensation was unbearably sweet, so electric that she arched right off the bed, but his big hands held her wide open no matter how she writhed. His mouth fastened onto her, suckling and lapping like he could never be satiated.

He shoved her legs high, fluttering his tongue delicately across her clitoris, then sliding with voluptuous deliberation along her inner folds. He plunged his tongue deep inside her, licking her greedily.

The sensation was unspeakably, deliciously intimate. He trapped her splayed thighs flat against the bed as she bucked and writhed. She absorbed his rumbling laughter into her body, her shivering tension rising higher and higher to an agonizing crest.

It broke, and washed over her, sweetly, endlessly.

When she finally managed to open her eyes, he was staring at her, fascinated, his head pillowed on her thigh. "You taste so good, Jane," he said. "I could eat you forever and never get tired."

She tried to laugh, but her muscles didn't remember how.

She wanted to tug him up so she could embrace him, but her limp fingers found no purchase against his hard, thick shoulders.

Mac slid up her body and pressed his face to her breasts while he thrust two of his fingers deep inside her sheath.

She stiffened with shock. "Enough," she pleaded. "Let me rest."

"You don't have to do a thing. Just lie there and gasp and come."

"Damn it, Mac—"

"Shhh." His fingers slid deeper, pressing in tender circles inside her. "When I'm going down on you, I concentrate on your clit. But I don't want to neglect this place right here . . . right? Isn't this the spot?"

She answered with a whimper of shocked delight. It almost hurt, but a deep, diffuse pleasure was building inside her, spreading out in concentric rings, getting deeper, wider, sweeter. She closed her thighs around his hand, clenching and pumping.

"That's good." He crooned his approval. "That's beautiful, Jane. Move against my hand. Show me how much you like it." He tugged the cups of her bustier down. He tugged at her nipple with light, teasing suction, then swirled his hot, wet tongue lavishly over her breasts while his thumb circled the taut nub of her clitoris. She arched, thrust herself against his hand. He drove it deeper, muttering rough encouragement until she was carried away on yet another long, shuddering wave.

She was dimly aware of him climbing off the bed, moving around the room. She let her head fall to the side. Her eyes fluttered open. He stood by the bed, his enormous erection bobbing inches from her face.

He smoothed a condom over himself. Her embarrassment was gone. It was the most natural thing in the world to wrap her fingers around his thick shaft, and stroke him. He hissed with pleasure and turned her so she faced him, her legs dangling over the bed.

She struggled up onto her elbows, moving in slow motion. She lifted her legs, pulled her skirt up, and mutely offered herself to him.

He dragged her hips down to the edge of the bed and piled pillows behind her, propping her up. He dragged her hand down, wrapping it around his penis. "Put me inside you, Jane. Show me you want me."

She was so startled, she almost laughed. "It's a little late to try to be politically correct now, isn't it?"

"I don't give a damn about politically correct. I just want to be sure we're on exactly the same page."

"Don't worry. We are," she assured him. "I want you."

"Put my cock inside you." His voice had the edge of command.

She gripped him with a trembling hand, pressing the thick head of his shaft against her drenched folds until it nudged her open.

He seized her hands, and placed them on his hips. "Pull me in."

She shook her head. "Don't play games with—"

"Just *do* it."

Her eyes widened at his harsh tone. She gripped his hips, pulled. Both of them groaned as he slid slowly, heavily inside her.

Their eyes locked. "All of me," he said softly. "You can take me."

She embraced him even more deeply, and gasped at the aching intensity of his hard flesh pressed deep against her womb. She wrapped her legs around his waist. "Satisfied?"

"Almost," he said. "Now ask me to fuck you."

She almost screamed in frustration. "Damn it, Mac! Why are you doing this? I'm ready! Go for it! What more do you want from me?"

"Everything you've got. Ask me, Jane." His voice grated, his fingers dug into her waist. His eyes were glittering, relentless.

"OK, fine," she yelled. "Please, Mac. I'm asking. Are you happy now? Have I abased myself enough to suit you?"

"Use the words I used. The exact words."

This strange drama had the feeling of a ceremonial ritual. She opened her mouth, and closed it again in consternation. "I can't," she said helplessly." I just can't do that. It's not in me."

"You have to," he said. "I want to hear you let go and say that nasty, naughty, dirty *f* word. That would really rock my world, Jane."

"It would be completely artificial," she said. "I would feel stupid."

"We'll never know until you try it, will we?" He teased her clitoris with his fingertip, and slid the head of his penis ever so slightly deeper, teasing. Rocking. Making her frantic.

"You evil, controlling bastard. This isn't fair!"

"I'm sorry you feel that way," he said. "Ask me to fuck you, Jane."

His voice was implacable. She was so furious, she pounded her fists against his chest and tried to squirm away from him. He trapped her hands, pinning them down. "Do it!" he snarled.

She stared into his blazing eyes. "Please fuck me," she forced out.

He drove inside her. An intense orgasm tore through her almost instantly, she was so primed. Mac waited and watched the pleasure shudder through her before he began to thrust. She lifted herself for more, crying out with savage joy at every hard, driving stroke.

"You see, Jane? Now I can give you what you need, and you can't say I muscled you into it. You don't want polite." His eyes were bright with triumph. "Polite would bore you. You're such a wild woman."

She swatted him on the shoulder for his smug arrogance and braced her feet against his hard, sweaty chest. "You talk too much, MacNamara. Shut up and do your duty."

He let out a harsh shout of laughter and obliged her with a deep, sensual grind, a maddening friction that drove them up and over the top together, into a long, soaring fall through nowhere.

She lay on top of him, drifting in a timeless haze. Even half awake, she was conscious of Mac's vibrant, thrumming energy beneath her. She floated into a sensual dream where he was her boat, and she was adrift upon him in a rippling blue ocean of endless pleasure.

"Hey. Jane. You awake?" he asked softly.

She pressed a kiss to his hot, salty chest in reply.

His arms tightened around her. "You still mad at me?"

She nuzzled him. "For what? Manipulating me with sex? Not at the moment. For taking me for an unscrupulous con artist? Hmm. If I think about it for a minute, I will be."

"Better keep you from thinking, then." His fingers slid down and tangled into her damp pubic hair.

She wrenched his hand back up to her belly. "No way! I am wiped out! If you touch me there again, I'll go right through the roof."

"How am I going to make you forgive me?" he asked plaintively.

She giggled and struggled as he tried to fondle her. "I forgive you, I forgive you! No orgasm required. I'm too tired to be mad, anyhow."

He rolled her over and kissed her deeply. "Actually, it's lucky things went this way," he said. "We cut through a lot of red tape."

"Oh, please," she scoffed. "Exchanging polite conversation over dinner is your idea of red tape? What a typical guy thing to say."

He looked aggrieved. "Don't be sarcastic. I'm serious."

"So am I." She pulled herself out of his arms and sat up. "What would you have done differently if you hadn't taken me for a criminal?"

He rolled onto his back and folded his muscular arms behind his head. "Well, I would have taken things slower. I would have been witty and charming. I would have tried to make you laugh. Tried to impress you with how hip and cultured I am."

She thought about it. "That sounds like fun."

"I would have tried to get to know you better before I took you to bed, so you wouldn't think I was a superficial, oversexed animal."

She giggled. "God forbid."

"But I don't have to pretend anymore. My cover's blown. You already know I'm a superficial oversexed animal. I can't fall any lower. What freedom. It thrills me." His hand slid under her skirt.

She slapped his hand away. "Watch it, MacNamara! I am resting!"

He gave her a lazy grin and stretched, making his big, lovely body ripple and flex. "I would have been gentle and careful when I took you to bed," he went on. "I would've tried to get you to relax and trust me."

"That sounds nice, too," she said primly. "Nothing wrong with that scenario at all, Mac."

He reached for her hand and massaged it between his thumb and forefinger. "No, there's not. But I would never have known that you like it wild and rough. Because you would never have told me. Right?"

She stiffened. This turn in the conversation startled her.

"I bet you didn't even know it yourself. It's a first for you, right?" His words vibrated through her body like a plucked string.

"I would never have known that you go for it really raw,

just like me," he went on. "Think of all that precious time I would have wasted, trying to be a good boy so as not to offend you."

She felt like the fingers of a powerful, invisible hand were closing around her. "There's nothing wrong with gentleness," she whispered.

"Nope," he said lightly. "Gentleness is great. So is nice, polite sex. It's a lot better than no sex at all. But sex like this . . ." He shook his head. "Unbelievable. You clawed me when you came, you know that?"

Her eyes widened in shock. "I did *what?*"

"Oh, yeah." He looked triumphant. "Big time."

"Let me see!" she demanded.

He rolled over obligingly. She clapped her hand over her mouth. Angry red weals raked his back, and she didn't even remember doing it.

"I'm so sorry," she said faintly. "I've never—"

"Good. I'm glad you never. I'm proud of them, Jane. I bet you've never slapped a man and yelled at him to fuck you harder, have you?"

She slipped off the bed and stood, unnerved and aroused by his provocative questions. "I'm not comfortable with this conversation, or your choice of language," she said. "Please don't talk to me that way."

"I'm not interested in making you comfortable. I'm a lot more interested in making you come. I'm on the right track." He inhaled deeply, and his feral grin stood her hairs on end. "I can smell it."

"You're being rude again." She took a step back. "Don't."

Mac's hand shot out, his fingers clamping over her wrist. His posture on the bed was the picture of lazy relaxation, but his hand around her wrist was like a steel manacle. "You think that's rude? I'll show you rude. Lift up your skirt, Jane."

"Mac, please. For God's sake," she protested.

He jerked her towards him, dragging handfuls of her skirt up, and pulled her until his face was pressed against her pubic hair, his warm breath tickling her. "Hold still, Jane. I was rude and bad, and you're a prissy ice goddess. Let me beg your forgiveness—with my tongue."

His long, strong tongue delved into her cleft. The hot, luscious swirl of bliss made her knees shake beneath her. He suckled her clitoris until she was clutching his head, knees shaking violently.

"Can you come on your feet, or will you fall?" he asked.

"I don't know." Her voice was breathless. "I've never—"

"Good. Another first. I like that. Come here. Climb up on the bed."

The fingers of that invisible hand tightened around her again, despite the wild pleasure of his touch. She wrenched out of his grip with a burst of desperate strength and stumbled backward. "No!"

"I just want to please you." His muscles rippled like a big, sinuous cat as he sat up. "Come here, Jane. You know I won't hurt you."

She stood up as straight as she could. "You're cutting through too much red tape, Mac. It's too much, too soon. It isn't right."

His eyes narrowed. "It would upset you so much to sit on my face?"

She jerked back. "God! That is so—"

"Rude. Yeah, that's me." He slid off the bed and stood. His naked body towered over hers. Fiercely erect. The man was insatiable.

"I'm serious." She struggled to make her voice steadier. "If you'd gone through all the dull bureaucratic channels of getting to know me, there would be ground beneath our feet. This way, it's . . . too intense."

He crossed his arms over his chest. "Let me get this straight, Jane," he said slowly. "The bottom line is, if I want to give you another screaming orgasm, I've got to get to know you first? *Now?*"

She steadied herself on the dresser as she tried to stare him down. "Oh, you poor baby," she snapped. "What a terrible chore."

He shrugged. "You're trying to lock the barn door after the horse is gone. What's the point, Jane? Just let go."

"No, I would say this is more along the lines of going out to look for the horse so you can put it back in the barn where it belongs."

He pondered this with calculating eyes. "Excuse me if I get gritty and practical, but how quickly does this process have to take place? Is there an exchange rate? A point system? Like, for oral sex, we exchange childhood reminiscences, but for full-penetration sex, we have to get down and dirty and tell the first time we ever did it in the—"

"You're being deliberately crass and rude!" she snapped.

He threw up his hands in mock helplessness. "Babe. This is me, uncut and uncensored. You'll get to know me quicker if I don't pretend."

He had a point, but she still felt outmaneuvered. "You're overdoing it, though," she said tightly. "As always."

"Ah," he murmured. I see how this works. You don't want to hear anything that makes you uncomfortable. This is another game for you to hide behind, like your fake names and your lies, right? You run away from the truth whenever it scares you."

She shook her head. "No. That's not what this is about."

"If you want to know me, you've got to deal with the real me," he said. "And I want the real you. Not just what you feel comfortable with. Otherwise, there's no sense to it. Are you ready for that, Jane?"

He'd turned the tables, put her right back on the defensive, but she was the one who had started this, and she had to see it through.

She stuck out her chin. "I'm ready."

They stared at each other. Mac gestured towards the bed. "Come on back to bed, then," he said. "I won't jump on you."

She walked past him, and slowly reclined on the bed. Mac stretched out his long, gorgeous naked body next to hers. "So? Let's get started," he said. "Go for it."

She stared into his bright eyes, intimidated. "Where am I supposed to start?"

He slanted her an ironic glance. "This was your idea, angel. Tell me everything about yourself."

"Everything is pretty broad. Let's establish a jumping off point."

He skimmed his hand over the curve of her thigh. "Start with the naked centerfold model vital stats."

It was as good a starting point as any. She thought for a moment to recall the format. "Let's see. Jane Duvall, twenty-eight years old. Pisces. Five three, a hundred and thirty pounds. Born in San Diego, graduated from UCLA. Likes: . . . that's tough. There's a lot that I like."

"Pick a random one," he suggested, when she hesitated too long.

"Violets," she began. "Shakespeare. Fine dark Italian chocolate."

"You were suppose to pick one," he reminded her. "Two, max."

"Oh, I'm just warming up," she told him. "Raw honey in the comb. Flowering cactus. Silk. Rainbows. Antique perfume bottles."

"You can't get a one-word answer out of a woman," he grumbled.

"You expect me to decide between silk, rainbows and chocolate?"

"Let's just move on," he said in a long-suffering voice. "Hates?"

She felt his warm hand against her skin. In the course of petting her thigh, Mac had pulled her skirt up over her legs. She yanked it down. "Stop that. Let's see, hates . . ." Her euphoria evaporated as she thought about it. "Meanness," she said. "Spite. Back-stabbing."

He propped himself up onto his elbow, frowning. "I didn't mean for this to be a downer," he said. "Don't take it so seriously, Jane."

She snorted. "That's the story of my life. Your turn, Mac."

"We need a system," he said thoughtfully. "This is like a get-to-know-you party game. Truth or Dare, or Psychiatrist. Or strip poker."

"No strip anything, please," she said hastily. "How about childhood dreams? Tell me what you wanted to be when you grew up." It was as neutral and nonsexual a topic as she could think of.

"Astronaut," Mac said without hesitation. "I wanted to walk on the moon, be the first man on Mars, and wear a bubble on my head."

Jane laughed out loud. "So what stopped you?"

"Physics." He grimaced. "My brain wasn't wired that way. I saw the Indiana Jones movies and figured being an archaeologist would be better. Less math, more adventure. Then my snotty little brother told me I would spend the rest of my life dusting off pottery shards with a toothbrush. Trust Danny to take the bloom off of a dream. In the meantime, when I wasn't keeping Robin from running off cliffs, I was working like a bastard for my uncle. I was good at it, I studied business and hotel management, one thing led to another, and here I am."

"Very nice," she said. "Well done, Mac. This is exactly the kind of conversation we should have had over dinner."

"You liked it?" He surged up onto his elbow. "What's it worth? How many points did I earn towards another bout of hot, grinding—"

She shoved at his chest, knocking him onto his back. "Hold it right there, buddy!"

He blinked up at her in exaggerated innocence. "Huh? What?"

"This is not a game!" she protested. "You do not win points!"

He looked genuinely puzzled. "But everything's a game, Jane. It all comes down to winning in the end."

"You're wrong. This is about trust and communication!"

"Yeah. The direct advantage of which is that they lead straight towards another bout of hot, grinding, pounding—"

"Stop!" she snapped. "You are deliberately driving me nuts! Trust and communication are their own reward, you . . . you animal!"

He shrugged. "It all depends on your priorities, babe."

The sparkle in his eyes made her suspicious. "You're just teasing me, right?"

He gave her an evil grin. "Which answer earns me more points?"

She seized the pillow and swatted him with it. "You are hopeless!"

Mac yanked the pillow away and pulled her into the crook of his shoulder. "Relax. This hug is an affectionate gesture meant to facilitate trust and communication. OK, let's have it. Your childhood dreams."

Her heart galloped madly at the contact with his hot, smooth skin. It was hard to think. I wanted to be an actress," she confessed.

"No kidding," he said. "Like, Hollywood?"

"No, a stage actress. I liked the classic stuff. Shakespeare, Ibsen, Moliére. It started in high school. My folks . . . well, they're older. They never wanted children. I had a very quiet childhood. It was important to never bother them. No scenes allowed."

He nodded for her to go on, his eyes intent upon her face.

"So my sophomore year in high school, I was stage manager for the school musical. We were doing *Li'l Abner,* and the girl who was playing the femme fatale broke her arm the day before dress rehearsal. I was the only one without a part who fit into the costume."

"Femme fatale?" He grinned. "I can see it. Yum."

"It was just a bit part, but all the sudden, I found myself in a tight slinky dress, walking out on the stage as Appassionata Von Climax."

He shook with startled laughter. "You're kidding!"

"Nope. Cross my heart. Anyway, it was a revelation. Some switch flipped on inside me. I projected this sexy energy. It was magic. The guy who played the lead asked me to the prom, of all things."

"You don't say."

"Don't laugh," she said. "He was one of the popular boys, I was a nobody, and his girlfriend was playing Daisy Mae to his Li'l Abner. It was a huge scandal. I almost got lynched in the girl's locker room."

"I'm sorry for your trauma," he said meekly.

"I just bet you are. The problem was, once I took off the outfit and wiped off the makeup, the magic disappeared. I went to the prom, but I was so shy, I couldn't think of anything to say to the guy, so it fizzled out fast. But that's how it started. I was bitten by the theater bug. What a relief, to let it all explode out of me in a big, loud voice."

He waited for more. "You studied theater in college?" he prodded.

She nodded. "It was great. I got cast as Juliet once, and it was like *Li'l Abner* all over again. Romeo fell for me—during the run of the show, that is. Then I was Kate in *The Taming of the Shrew*, and Petruchio got a mad crush on me—for the duration of the show."

"And after the show closed?"

She laughed uncomfortably, and wondered what had possessed her to volunteer such embarrassing details to him. "They lost that loving feeling. On stage, I sparkle, but off-stage I'm pretty stiff and shy."

"Not with me, you're not," Mac said, with clear satisfaction.

"I never even got a chance to be stiff and shy with you!"

He stuck his finger into her neckline and tugged it. "You see the advantages of cutting through that pesky red tape?"

She slapped his hand away. "Down, boy! You haven't earned anywhere near enough points yet to take those kind of liberties."

"Arf, arf," he said. "So why didn't you become an actress?"

She hesitated for a little too long. "It didn't work out," she said lightly. "It's a tough business. I had to pay the rent somehow."

"You're holding something back," he murmured. "I can feel it."

She pulled herself out of his arms. No way was she telling him about Dylan. Talk about downers. "That's the story. Take it or leave it."

"Let's see. What can I make of this?" His voice was low, musing. "You blocked your emotions and only let them out on stage. Interesting. You like playing roles. You love control, almost as much as you love losing it. Complicated, challenging. I like mysterious women. You play at intimacy, but you're afraid of the real thing. Right?"

She forced herself to laugh, although his analysis made her want to squirm. "Are you psychoanalyzing me, Mac?"

"Hell, no," he said readily. "Real men don't do that." He stared at her, narrow-eyed. "You're not on stage now, Jane. And feel this." He took her hand and slid it down to his hot, rigid penis. "I haven't lost interest for a nanosecond. I'm the one who's stiff. Not you."

She giggled. "You must've broken the spell I was under."

He looked pleased with himself. "Prince Charming, huh?"

"Hah!" She wrenched her hand away. "Prince Un-Charming is more like it. Once you get me alone, the charm goes right out the window. You could try a little harder. This is a first date, after all."

He yanked her back down so that she lay half across his

broad chest. "This isn't a first date conversation. I don't know if I've ever had a conversation with such a high reality quotient, let alone on a first date. It's not first date sex, either. It's more like thank-God-we-were-saved-from-the-river-of-boiling-lava sex."

"I might have known we'd get right back to sex," she grumbled. "You're obsessed, Mac."

"No, just focused. And really tired of this goddamn dress." He seized her skirt. "We've had sex twice. I've gone down on you twice. We've even had a deep, meaningful conversation. I'm being as charming as I know how to be, and I still haven't seen you naked."

She tugged her skirt back out of his grasp. "Mac—"

"Don't fight me, Jane. If you don't take the dress off right now, I'm going to rip it off you."

Their eyes locked. "I . . . I paid way too much for this damn dress," she sputtered. "So don't even think about—"

"So strip, if you like the dress," he cut in. "Otherwise it's going to be sacrificed upon the altar of my immoderate lust."

She scrambled off the bed. "Do not order me. I don't like that tone in your voice."

His eyes flashed. "Maybe not, but it works for you. I've got you figured out, Jane. If we'd had nice, polite sex, you might have been able to keep me at arm's length, like you're trying to do right now. But we didn't, babe. You know you can't control me. That's why I turn you on."

She wanted to scream with frustration. "I'm not trying to control you, damn it! I'm trying to communicate with you!"

He shook his head. "Wrong again. You hide behind words. I have to look deeper than just words if I want to unlock my shy, complicated Jane. For you, words are the wall, babe. Not the key."

"You're pretty damn sneaky with words yourself."

A slow, merciless smile spread across his hard face. "I try."

Jane covered her trembling mouth with her hands. "I'm

not in the mood to spar with you, Mac. I told you intimate details about myself, and now you're turning them on me. It's not fair."

He stood up and stroked her upper arms. His hands left a tingling shiver in their wake. "Life is never fair," he said. "That's how the game is played, Jane. Find your opponent's weak point—and exploit it."

She gave him a sharp, angry push which barely budged him. "So I'm your opponent, then? All you want is to vanquish me?"

He lifted her hair off her shoulders and bent to kiss her throat. "Sure, if being vanquished turns you on. That's what I want. Whatever makes you hot. I'll hunt it down . . . and I'll pin it right to the wall."

The savage intensity of his voice made her tremble. She turned her hot face away from his demanding kiss. Mac jerked it right back around. "That turns you on, doesn't it, Jane?" he crooned. "Admit it."

It did. His dominating power turned her inside out. He'd broken the spell that bound her, not with a chaste fairy-tale kiss, but with his wild desire, with his unflinching honesty. Her Prince Un-Charming.

He'd wakened not just her passion, but everything that had been crushing it down—stones of petrified anger and sadness. But a paradox was at the heart of his sexy power games—something treacherous and painful. She didn't dare give in to him. He would run right over her.

She took a slow, calming breath, and gathered her power as if she were about to step on stage. "Back off, Mac." She said it in a clear, strong voice, designed to carry to the very back row.

His eyes widened. He let go, took a step back and lifted his hands in mock surrender. "Yes, ma'am."

She studied him. So far, so good. "Even if your macho posturing did turn me on—and I'm not saying that it does—

I won't just lie there whimpering and conquered," she said. "You need a sharp lesson."

"Oh, yeah? Going to spank me, Jane?" he taunted. "Hand-cuffs?"

"I don't need props," she said coolly. "I'm learning from an expert. I just have to find your weak point . . . and exploit it."

He frowned. "What's the use of that?"

"Ah, I see," she mocked. "It's OK for me to be vulnerable, but not for you, hmm? Heaven forbid that the big, bad hunter—"

"You like to lose control, and I like to make you lose it," he said impatiently. "Why mess with that? I just want to give you pleasure."

"And you want to run the whole show," she said.

"Sure, I do. Why not? I'm good at it," he said. "Trust me, Jane."

"So you can exploit my weak point?"

"No!" he snarled. "So I can please you, goddamn it!"

She tried to look down her nose at him. A neat trick, since he was a foot taller than she. "Maybe it would please me to vanquish you, Mac."

The tension humming between them got thicker every second.

Mac folded his arms, and shrugged. "OK, Jane. Let's see how long you can keep this up. Vanquish me if you can. Do it quick, though, because I'm going to rip that dress right off if you don't make a move."

His challenge rang in the air. Her mind raced. He didn't look like he had any weak points. How on earth was she going to dominate him?

"Scared, huh?" he taunted. "What would Appassionata do?"

Ah. Of course. She had the answer to her dilemma, and Mac had handed it right to her. A smile curved her lips. "Appassionata would eat you alive, Mac," she said softly. "It's dangerous to invoke her."

"Anything to get things going," he grumbled.

She shoved his chest, driving him across the room towards the chair. "Sit." She knocked him back, a sharp, imperious gesture.

He was so startled, he actually obeyed her and fell back heavily into the chair. An excellent beginning. Beyond her wildest hopes.

"Don't move until I say so," she said. "Or else. Understand?"

He nodded, his eyes quietly watchful.

"Now watch, Mac." She began to strip.

Chapter Six

The change that came over her was unnerving. He couldn't pin it down exactly; maybe it was the wild glow in her eyes. The shape of her lips changed, her posture, the tilt of her eyebrows. She was someone else, confident and armored, completely closed to him. Then she began to shimmy the dress down over her tits, and all coherent thought fled.

The dress dragged the lace cups of her bustier down along with it. He almost whimpered when the fabric snagged on her taut nipples. It stretched, strained . . . and finally popped over. Her breasts were bare, propped up on the shelf of the provocative black lace corset.

There was another moment of delicious suspense when he wasn't sure she was going to get it all the way over the rich swell of her hips. Her tits jiggled, her hips swayed as she worked it steadily down. It slid to the floor, and she kicked it aside and struck a pose for him. Leg lifted, foot arched, arms over her head. She tossed her hair, swiveled her hips. She turned her back to him and bent over, back arched.

His breath stuck in his lungs as if it had turned solid. He

gaped at the rounded globes of her ass, the shadowy glimpse of her cunt.

She reached down, unhooked the garters from the lace-trimmed stockings. He could barely make out her face beneath the swirling red curtain of her hair as she reached behind herself to unhook the corset.

He reached for her. "Hey, let me help you with that."

"Get down." Her voice stung him like a slap in the face. "If I want something from you, I'll ask for it."

He fell back into the chair, shocked into total stillness. Whoa. She was dead serious about this, but he didn't have time to feel weird about it, because right then the corset fell to the floor, and the world stopped.

The graceful totality of her naked torso stole his breath. Her skin was so luminously pale, marked with the scratchy lace. He stared at the swells and hollows and delicate curves. Her breasts were abundant, the taut nipples high, the rich undercurve perfect to lick and nuzzle.

He reached for her. She shoved him back into the chair, hard enough to make him grunt. "Bad boy," she said. "Slow learner, hmm?"

He panted up at her, his cock as hard as a railroad spike. "What the hell's the matter with you, Jane? What are you doing?"

"Looking for your weak points," she told him. "Suffer . . . baby."

"What do you care about my weak points?" he demanded. "What good are they to you? It's my strong points that can serve you."

She scooped her hair up over her head and let it tumble back down in a witchy tangle to veil her mysterious eyes. "Hush, Mac. You think too much." She lifted one graceful, arched foot, and placed it on the arm of his chair, giving him a ringside view of the folds of her cunt pouting out of the curly red thatch. "Pull my stockings down," she commanded. "With your teeth."

He leaned forward, irresistibly drawn to the hot, damp nest of woman-scented hair. She kicked him back into the chair, her foot pressing hard against his chest. "The stocking, Mac," she repeated.

He tried not to pant as he seized her stocking in his teeth. This was strange, not his usual vibe, but any opportunity to rub his cheek against her skin was fine with him. He pulled the stocking free. Tiny pink toes, toenails painted frosty silver. He wanted to suckle each one.

She patted his face. "Good boy. Now the other one."

She turned and lifted the other leg for him to service. If he leaned forward, he could just bury his face in her juicy, delicious—

"No." She slid her fingers through his hair and jerked his head back, hard. "Focus, Mac."

He dragged the other stocking down. He realized, to his dismay, that he was trembling. She lifted her foot so he could pull the stocking free, and ruffled his hair, as if praising a dog that had retrieved a stick.

"Very good." She widened her stance. "Now my panties."

He took the elastic between his teeth and pressed his face against the silky, yielding warmth of her belly. Incoherent anger gripped him. She knew damn well this servile love-slave routine came hard to him. She wanted to see how far she could push him before he snapped.

Problem was, he wasn't sure himself. The one thing he was sure of was that he wanted to know Jane Duvall. He wanted to learn her by heart. He wanted the keys, the codes, the goddamn operating manual.

That was the only reason he was playing along. If she needed so badly to be in control, he would grit his teeth and see how much he could take—to a point. He buried his face in her pubic hair, thrust his tongue deep into that hot, slick furrow. She made a startled sound and seized his face in both hands as if to push him away. She didn't.

She let him worship her for several silent, trembling minutes, until her knees started to buckle. She stumbled back, dazed. Staring down into his face. He wiped his mouth. He was unable to hide his triumph. Her eyes focused, and her chin lifted. "The panties, Mac," she said. "And don't take liberties." Her body shook, but her voice held firm.

What the hell. He was secure in his sexuality. He could indulge a woman if she wanted to play the dominatrix bitch, as long as they both knew damn good and well who was boss. It cost him nothing.

But something very weird was happening—this burning in his chest, the ache in his gut. He couldn't stop shaking. He hated the mysterious, impenetrable look on her face. It made him feel lonely and desolate. It messed with his head. She could take him apart. She didn't need whips or chains. She did it with her eyes.

He dragged the panties down. She was finally naked, thank God. Never in his life had he struggled so hard to get a woman's clothes off.

"Now, sit." She sank to her knees beside him and seized his cock. Her bold grip made him gasp and jerk. "Don't be afraid," she purred. "You've been very good, Mac, and now you're going to be rewarded."

She grasped his cock firmly, licked the tight, swollen head, and sucked him deep into her mouth. Oh, God, she was good. Passionate, voracious, skillful. She sucked him deep, sliding her tongue along his length, flicking it across the most sensitive spots with teasing, fluttering strokes. Her strong, slender hands followed the slippery path of her mouth, gripping and stroking him. It was shivering agony, the tight, dragging suction as she drew him out of her mouth, the luscious glide as she took him back in again. Deep and yielding and wonderful.

She took her time, and she didn't get tired. She drew his cock into her mouth deeper than he'd imagined possible, and then peeked up at him through her lashes. A wicked smile gleamed in her eyes as she watched his reaction to the clutch of her moist pink lips, the lash of her tongue. He shuddered and groaned, all his attention narrowed down to her swirling, suckling mouth. Just when he thought it couldn't possibly get better, she cupped his balls, caressing them with her fingertips, and pressed that sensitive spot beneath them.

He fought back the orgasm that was about to flatten him, and Jane lifted her head, sensing it. "Don't even think about coming yet," she said. "I have other plans for you. Understood?"

He nodded, and then shook his head, confused. Yes, he understood. No, he wouldn't come. Yes, no, whatever. Anything she said, anything she wanted. Anything at all. Just more. Just *now*.

"Where are your condoms?" she demanded.

"Box in the bathroom," he managed to say.

Off she went, to the bathroom. Mac hoped whatever she had in mind involved fucking him, hard and soon. Otherwise he was going to be in urgent need of medical help. She posed in the bathroom door like a Venus, all voluptuous curves and creamy paleness and rippling hair.

She advanced on him, smiling, and knelt down, smoothing the condom over his cock. She stood up, backlit by the bathroom light. Her hair was a fiery halo. Her face was wreathed in mysterious shadows.

"Scoot down in the chair, so I can straddle you," she commanded.

He trembled in pathetic eagerness to do her bidding. Her hand cupped his chin, jerking his face up. "Look at me, Mac."

He looked. She stood astride him, eyes in shadow, hair lit from behind like a corona of flames. Terrifying and gorgeous and pitiless.

He loved it and hated it. She'd stripped him of all the power and self-control he'd worked so hard to gain. He was an ignorant, vulnerable boy again, and she was a cruel, unfathomable goddess with the power to bestow life or death. He burned with need. He was prostrated with fear, terrified of disappointing her, failing her in some way.

"Ask me to fuck you," she said. "And say please."

He opened his mouth, but the words stuck in his throat. He swallowed, and tried again. "Please fuck me," he said.

She smiled, caressing his cheek, and guided his cock, nudging it between her legs. She lodged it in the tender opening of her body, and sank down with a moan, shoving him deep inside herself. The muscles in her cunt fluttered around him. It was too good. It was killing him.

He was terrified to move, he was so close to orgasm, and he would die of shame if he lost control of himself now. Jane sensed his dilemma. She waited, motionless, until he opened his eyes and gave her a nod.

Then she started to ride him. It was perfect, it was heaven, it was hell. He was miserable. Her body rose and fell against his in an urgent rocking slide. Her skin had a pearly sheen of moisture. She was so goddamn beautiful. This erotic bitch goddess was wildly sexy, but he hated the look on her face. He missed that sweet, open look, the soft vulnerability. He wanted it back. He wanted his sweet Jane.

She pried one of his hands off her hips and pressed it against her mound. "Touch me," she said shakily. "Make me come, Mac."

Hell, yes. That was his ticket out of this bizarre sexual torture. He bucked beneath her and caressed her clit. His hard, stabbing strokes from below were just what she needed to detonate the explosion. She arched back, cried out and came violently, clenching him inside her.

He fought his own orgasm back. He couldn't climax with her now. It would make her victory too complete. He had his limits, and he'd reached them. She'd had her fun. He was done.

"Come back to me now," he said. "I've had enough."

She lifted her head. Her hair clung to his sweat-dampened

skin. Her eyes gleamed with laughter. "Who asked you if you'd had enough?"

His fingers dug into her waist. "Do not fuck with my head, Jane."

Her eyes widened, and she fluttered her lashes. "Such intensity. You think one spectacular orgasm gives you the right to run my world?"

"Come off it," he demanded. "The dominatrix routine is a flaming turn-on, but I've had enough of it. I can't take it anymore."

A mocking smile played about her lips. "Oh, no? Well, then. Here we have it. This must be the weak point I'm supposed to exploit."

He shook her. "Cut out the man-eating bitch act and talk to me!"

"Talk?" Her light laughter grated on him. "I thought it was only girls who ruined sex with talk. And just when I'm moving in for the kill."

"Don't push me, goddamn it." His voice shook. "I'm warning you."

"And give up my advantage?" She touched his face, and he jerked away from the caress. "No, Mac. That's not the way the world works. You told me so yourself."

That was it. Something exploded inside him. He slid off the chair to his knees, carrying her down to the floor beneath him.

She must have seen something in his face that scared her, because her eyes went big, and she pulled away, scrambling out of his grip with the swiftness of panic. She rolled over and tried to crawl away.

He seized her ankles. She flailed and struggled, but he flung himself on top of her, pinning her down on her stomach.

Even better. This position suited him just fine.

She twisted around to look at him. "Mac, I—"

"Be quiet," he snarled. "Everything you say makes me angrier, so just *shut up*."

He slid his arm beneath her hips, dragging her up onto her knees. He knocked her legs apart and drove his cock inside her.

She cried out, and pitched forward onto her forearms. He was possessed, shaking with strain as he held her down and pounded his body into hers. Sharp gasps jerked out of her at each heavy stroke. His cock gleamed with her slick, hot moisture. He knew it was too rough, but he couldn't ease off. Not many of his lovers had been able to take his whole length. Neither had Jane, at first. He was used to holding back, but he wasn't now. She was made for him. He could plunge to the hilt.

She was *his*. He let out a guttural shout as triumph and dark fury prodded him over the edge and into a blinding, explosive release.

He lifted himself off when he drifted back, so weak he could barely move. He collapsed onto his back and covered his face with his hand.

His gut ached. The formula to this man-woman thing was beyond his understanding. Love could be given and taken away. No warning, no explanation, no apologies. He accepted that fact, even profited from it. He'd given and taken it as it pleased him, when it was convenient, when he was in the mood. He'd left it behind without a second thought.

He'd never wanted to keep a woman under lock and key. To force her to love him. Ironic. If there was one thing he'd known since he was a kid, it was that love couldn't be forced. There was no commanding it, no controlling it. It did what it goddamn well pleased.

He should ask if she was OK. He should be solicitous and apologetic. Fuck it. It was beyond him.

"Mac?" she asked cautiously.

At least she could talk. He was the destroyed, humiliated one.

"Mac, please say something," she urged.

He turned his face away. "What do you want me to say? You were looking for my weak point. Looks like you found it. I hope you liked it. I hope you had a great time. Because that'll make one of us."

He measured the silence by his own pounding heartbeat.

"Do you want me to go?" Her voice was soft and timid.

"No!" His hand flashed out, clamping around her wrist.

Jane slid the condom off his cock, and tugged gently at her wrist until he released it. She got up and went quietly to the bathroom.

He was limp, motionless, exactly as she left him, when she came back. She knelt down and started to pet his damp chest. "I'm sorry, Mac. I shouldn't have done that. I didn't mean to hurt you."

The irony of it made him laugh. "Uh . . . I think that's my line."

She shook her head. "No. The minute you weren't having fun anymore, I should have given in. I don't know why I didn't. I had something to prove, I guess. You, ah, sort of challenged me to a duel."

"Don't remind me." He shivered. "You were just getting back at me for being a controlling dickhead. I guess I deserved it."

"No. You didn't," she said. "You pushed me hard, but you never went too far. I went too far."

He made a sharp, angry gesture of negation. "Forget it. Please."

"No," she persisted. "It was cruel, and I'm sorry."

Her apology shamed him, made him feel even more vulnerable. "Let it go, for Christ's sake," he growled. "I don't want to think about it."

Her hair coiled in silken loops on his face and chest as she bent to kiss him. "All right," she said softly.

"You're OK, right?" he asked. "I didn't hurt you, did I?"

She hesitated. "No biggie. My knees are stinging from the carpet, and I might have a bruise or two. But I'm fine."

He reached up and ran his hands over her body. "Damn. Where?"

"Don't worry." She put her mouth to his ear. "Actually, it really excited me," she whispered. "But that's a deep, dark secret, so don't you dare throw it back in my face."

"Hell, no," he said fervently. "I've learned my lesson."

The real Jane was back. He could finally breathe. He closed his eyes. Her soft kisses were soothing, like warm raindrops. They eased the burning in his chest, made the clenched knot in his belly relax.

His stomach rumbled. "I'm hungry," he said. It sounded so prosaic, after the thunder and lightning and crazy sex, but there it was.

"So am I," Jane said. "You made me skip dinner. You were in such a tearing hurry to plunder the fortress."

He peered into her face, and cautiously concluded that she was teasing him. "Plundering fortresses is hungry work. I'll order up some dinner. How about you go run a bath?"

"Dinner?" She glanced at the bedside clock, and back at him, amazed. "You can get dinner sent up at this hour?"

His chest jerked in a derisive laugh. "I run this place."

"Ah." Her eyes widened. "The lord of the manor is back, I see."

"He was never gone," he said shortly.

"Oops! Excuse me, Your Exalted Masterfulness. I'll just trip obediently off to the bathroom to do your bidding now—"

"No more," he barked. "I have had enough."

He instantly regretted his tone, but she just covered her mouth with her hand, eyes sparkling. "Sorry. I'm so bad. Didn't mean to push."

She left the door wide open as she set the bath running. That was a good sign. So was the fact that she . . . wow. She was humming.

He'd been so sure he'd fucked up beyond redemption, but she was still here. Humming, for God's sake. Go figure.

He grabbed the phone and dialed the kitchen. "This is Michael MacNamara," he said to the guy who picked up. "Send a bottle of Dom Perignon up to room twenty-eight. Put together a cold dinner for two, whatever's good tonight. Lots of it. Knock loudly and leave the cart outside the door. But I want the champagne right now, so grab it, and run. Got it?"

"Yes, sir. Right away, sir," the kid assured him.

He hung up the phone and stared at the open door. Steam wafted out the door in curling streamers. The tub was big enough for two. She was singing now. She had a pretty voice, husky and rich and soft.

Damn, he was confused. He would never understand how this stuff worked, but he wasn't stupid enough to waste time worrying about it while a beautiful naked woman waited for him in the bathtub.

Jane hummed the refrain to the sappy old show tune as she sank into the steaming water. It stung as it covered her sore spots, the deep ache between her legs. The world was shimmering with possibilities. She felt so alive. Poised on the edge of disaster. Like a dream where she was flying and knew she might fall, but flying was worth the risk.

Mac appeared in the doorway, a bottle of champagne in his hand. She gave him an encouraging smile, and admired his spectacular naked body as he walked in and held out a champagne flute. She caressed his muscular flanks, and the weight of his dangling penis and testicles, heavy against their thick nest of springy dark hair.

She accepted the champagne. "You're beautiful, Mac."

He grunted, lifting a heavy brow. "Thanks," he said doubtfully.

She sipped the icy cold, frothing champagne. It stung against her throat. A bold impulse struck her. "Would you do something for me?"

"Uh, what, exactly?"

His narrow-eyed caution made her giggle. "Turn around," she said. I want to look at you from behind."

He frowned. "No funny stuff."

She laughed out loud. "No! I just want to admire your, um . . ."

"My ass," he supplied. He shrugged, and turned around, widening his stance. "There it is. In all its glory."

Oh, dear. It wasn't fair, it wasn't right. His body was superb. Powerful shoulders, his muscles lean and graceful, not at all like the swollen bulk of steroid-popping body builders. His back narrowed to a lean waist, a tight butt, thickly muscled thighs, ropy calves. Even his ankles and feet were beautiful. Masculine perfection personified. She wanted to grab him, assure herself that he was real.

The throbbing ache between her legs reminded her that he was very real indeed. She put the champagne down and rose up onto her knees. He jerked as she put her hands on his hips. "Don't worry," she soothed. "Your body is so perfect, Mac. I just want to touch it."

"That's what I'm supposed to say to you," he complained.

"Move closer to the tub, please." He hesitated, and she tugged at his resistant body. "'What's wrong?" she teased. "Am I so scary?"

He allowed himself to be pulled closer. "Yeah," he admitted. "You are pretty damn scary, Jane. It feels strange, to have my back to you."

"No funny stuff, I promise," she assured him.

She stroked the curve of his spine, the smooth, resilient dips and curves of his flanks. She pressed her lips against the dimples over his buttocks, the tuft of hair at the small of his back. He smelled of sex. He tasted hot and salty. She slid her hand into the heat between his thighs. Her fingertips brushed the warm, velvety skin of his scrotum.

He stiffened, shuddered. "Oh, Jesus. Don't get me going."

She deepened the caress, nuzzling his back. "Do you like that?"

"Yeah." He turned around, his erection bobbing in her face. "See?"

She fell back into the tub, startled. "Good God! You're insatiable!"

"I know. This isn't normal. I feel like we're just getting started."

She ran her fingertip over his erection. "How long are you?"

Mac laughed. "You mean, my cock? I've never measured it."

She flicked water at him. "That is a big fat lie! No way have you never measured that thing!"

"It's true. Running for a ruler is the last thing I think about when I'm hard. I'm more interested in measuring, say, these." He knelt, slid his hands into the water and cupped her breasts. He stroked his hands tenderly around her ribs, her waist. "Thirty-four-D," he said. "Dress size, ten."

She stretched and purred at his touch. "Bingo. You're good."

"I know. Measure me if you want, Jane." He pulled her hand out of the water and wrapped it around his penis. "I thought we were taking a time-out, but if you want to get right back to it, that's fine."

"I'm not ready to have sex again," she admitted. "I didn't know you'd be so quick to, um . . . that is, I didn't mean to lead you on."

He looked like he was trying not to grin. "Yeah, you said that this afternoon. After kissing me senseless and coming all over my hand."

"It's your own fault, for having such a tempting body," she said primly. "The bath is very nice. Want to join me?"

"Hell, yes." He refilled their champagne glasses and climbed in.

She curled up to make space. She felt wild and free, almost drunk. Their dynamic had changed. Mac seemed less arrogant, almost wary of her, and she felt more confident and relaxed with him. Maybe it was perverse, but if it worked, it worked. She was being more honest with him than she'd ever been. Saying what popped into her head, not thinking it to death for fear it would get her into trouble. It felt fabulous.

His big body displaced a huge amount of water. It sloshed perilously near the rim. He arranged her legs so they floated on either side of his knees. His indefatigable erection lay high against his belly. He slanted her a crooked smile. "I knew it was too soon to seduce you again, but I had to try," he said. "Nothing ventured, nothing gained."

She laughed. "That's what I tell my kids all the time."

"Kids? You have kids?"

She giggled at his startled expression. "Not my biological children, silly. The kids in my theater troupe. The MeanStreets Players."

"MeanStreets?" His face turned thoughtful. "Robin mentioned them a while back. There was a buzz about a Shakespeare production using a bunch of local gang delinquents. It got good reviews."

"That was us," she said proudly. "Except they're not delinquents. They're the MeanStreets Players, and they rule. A few years ago, I got asked to direct a skit with some at-risk teenagers at the youth center where I volunteered. It went so well, we decided to keep on with it. We're doing *A Midsummer Night's Dream* this fall. In fact, my boss promised to help fund our fall show if I bagged your GM."

His eyebrows twitched. "Oh. So by thwarting you, I'm destroying the dreams of underprivileged urban kids? As usual, I'm the bad guy."

"Hardly," she scoffed. "I don't need your stupid old GM. There's more than one fish in the sea. We'll fund that show somehow."

"I'm sure you will," he said. "You're a force to be reck-oned with, Jane Duvall. Those kids are lucky."

"Theater saved me when I was young," she said simply. "It gave me a place to dream. Every kid should have a place to dream, whether it's sports, music, whatever. I just want to give that back to those kids."

"That's great. I salute you for it." He lifted his glass to her.

The warmth of his smile was like a physical caress. She took a gulp of champagne and beamed back. She felt giddy and fearless. "Your turn, Mac," she announced.

"For what?" he said suspiciously.

She nudged his hard belly with her foot. He pulled it to his mouth, and she giggled and squirmed as he suckled her toes. "Stop that! Our party game, Mac. You know things about me that I've never told anyone. Your turn. Tell me one of your deep, dark secrets."

He shrugged. "I don't have any deep, dark secrets. I suck at secrets. Can't keep one to save my life. Danny is the se-crets man."

She rolled her eyes. "Don't be difficult, Mac."

"It's true," he protested. "I swear. I'm a what-you-see-is-what-you-get kind of guy. A real simple creature, when you get right down to it."

"Yeah, right," she scoffed. "We can pick a tame, easy topic if you're feeling nervous. How about hobbies? I just told you mine."

"Hobbies?" He laughed derisively. "I've never had time for hobbies. I was always either working or dealing with Robin."

"Forget hobbies, then. Tell me how is it that you got left with a baby sister to raise," she suggested. "I've been itching to know."

His eyes slid away from hers. "I don't want to talk about that."

She drew designs on his chest with her foot and waited.

Mac sighed, drained his glass and set it down on the shelf. "I'll give you the short version," he said grimly. "If you insist."

The silence was marked by the hollow plop of water from the faucet. Mac's eyes were far away. "Any version is fine," she prompted.

"My daddy was a con man," he said, in a halting voice. "He drifted around the country, swindling people. He was in Olympia running a real-estate scam when he met my mom. When he had to run from the law, he persuaded her to run with him."

"Oh." She blinked, and forced her gaping mouth to close. "That must have been, uh, hard," she ventured timidly. "On your mother."

"Don't waste any sympathy on her. She worked with him when he needed a partner. So did I, sometimes, but mostly he used Danny. Danny was sneakier than I was. A better actor. My daddy used to say that Danny had the makings of a good grifter, but not me. I was hopeless. I wear my heart on my sleeve. Like I said, I suck at secrets."

"I, ah, see."

"So the short version of this saga is, when I was thirteen, somebody from my daddy's past caught up with him—with a baseball bat. The guy was still very pissed for having been ripped off, even years later. Daddy died ten days later in the hospital. Internal bleeding."

"I'm sorry," she whispered.

He didn't acknowledge her words. "My mother fell apart," he said. "We went to stay with my uncle Leroy. But when she got out of the hospital, she never came to get us. She just couldn't deal, I guess."

Her heart twisted in sympathy. "You never saw her again?"

He shook his head.

"And your uncle Leroy? Did he, um . . . was he—"

"No." He dismissed his uncle with a gesture. "He was an

older man. He gave us a roof over our heads. School. Work, when we were old enough. That was as much as he could do. I did the rest myself."

She studied his tight face for a long, careful moment before she risked the next question. "Do you even know where she is?"

"Leroy kept tabs on her. She ended up in Texas. Married again, had a couple more kids. I don't know the details. Don't want to know."

"So that would explain why you assumed I was a—"

"Yeah," he said curtly.

"And why you were so upset about it," she finished softly.

"That's right. Liars and swindlers make me violently angry. Anyhow, I made excuses for her for as long as I could. I waited for her like a faithful dog. Finally I realized that I was on my own with Danny and Robin. For good. That was the worst day of my childhood."

The silence that followed his words had real, physical weight.

Jane fished around the water for his foot, and propped it up onto her knee. She lathered her hands with the lavender scented soap, and massaged his feet. "You never forgave her, did you?"

He looked incredulous. "Why the hell should I?"

"Not for her sake," she said. "For yours. To drain the poison."

"I don't feel any need to forgive her, for my sake or anybody else's. She ran away from her baby girl. I crossed her off my list."

The stony anger in his voice made her hands falter for a moment.

"She screwed me over but good." He pulled his foot away, let it slop into the tub. The water sloshed and heaved around their chins.

Jane stared at his brooding face. There was nothing simple about Michael MacNamara, no matter what he said to the contrary. He was a tangle of contradictions. Calculating and spontaneous. Tender and rock hard. Angry, competitive, sensual, with a fierce sense of honor and responsibility. Raunchy and shocking in bed. Complicated. Passionate.

She would never be done figuring him out.

His eyes met hers, shadowed with old pain. "So, Jane? Satisfied? Any other dirty secrets I need to reveal before I can fuck you again?"

She decided to push her luck. "Yes, actually," she said. "Why do you call yourself Mac? Michael's a perfectly good name."

He dropped his head back against the bathtub with a sharp sigh. "Michael was my daddy's name. It's bad enough that I'm a dead ringer for him physically. Robin and Danny take after my mom, but I'm pure MacNamara. A surname is as much as I can stand to share with him."

She decided that it would be prudent to lighten the mood, by brute force, if necessary. Mac was quite a handful when he was badly upset. "You could get your name legally changed," she suggested.

"Jesus," he muttered. "How about we get the subject of this conversation legally changed?"

"It's just a suggestion," she protested. "Let's pick out a brand new name for you. Alfred? Bartholomew? Or how about Cedric?"

She was encouraged by the reluctant smile that tugged at his mouth. "Try it out," she urged. "Oh, Cedric, touch me like that again. Please, Cedric. Oh God, Cedric, yes. Has a nice ring to it, doesn't it?"

He lunged for her. Water sloshed over the edge as he dragged her up over his body. "You just don't know when to shut up, babe."

"Actually, I've always suffered from the opposite problem," she admitted. "You do something strange to me. It's only with you that I can't shut up. I just feel compelled to torture you, for some reason."

"Wow. Lucky me," he said sourly. I feel so unique."

She kissed the tip of his nose. "How about Raymond? Or Murray? Or Hubert? Oh, Hubert. Please, Hubert—do it again, Hubert—"

"Shhh." He slid his fingers into her hair and covered her mouth as he maneuvered her into the position he wanted, astride him. He slid her sensitive labia slowly, sensually, up and down the length of his penis.

A loud knock sounded on the door. She jerked, startled. "What?"

"It's the food," he grumbled. "The kid's timing sucks."

She scrambled to her feet, conscious of his eyes on her body. His eyes dragged over her. "Turn," he said. I want to look at your ass."

Well, it was only fair. He'd been a good sport, and so should she. She undid the knot on top of her head, letting her hair tumble down. She slowly turned around. "No funny stuff," she warned him.

It felt strange, to have her back to him. The water heaved around her legs as his hot, wet hands seized her hips, stroked the curve of her waist. He pressed kisses down her spine while he stroked her backside. The sensitive skin of her bottom went wild in tingling, ticklish delight.

"You have the most gorgeous ass," he said. "I love this view." His teeth grazed tenderly along the curve of her buttock.

She trembled at the bold caress. "Ah . . . biting my butt definitely falls under the heading of funny stuff, Mac. Stop that."

"I can't help it. You're perfect," he protested. "I want to open you up, like a peach. Find all the sweet, delicious juice hidden—right here."

He slid his finger inside her sheath, and she almost fell.

He steadied her, and rose to his feet, curving his body over hers. "Bend over. Brace your arms against the wall. I'll hold you."

She was so tempted, but she was so giddy, from hunger and hot water and champagne. She couldn't let him sweep her away. Not yet.

"No, Mac. Time out. Feed me, and we'll see." She waited, breathless, to see if he would do as she asked.

It was like holding a wild beast at bay, with her will-power alone.

Chapter Seven

Mac lifted his hands from her body. Breath rushed into her lungs.

She stepped out of the bathtub onto quivering legs without looking at him. He placed a terry cloth robe over her shoulders.

"Dry off," he said. "I'll go out and get the dinner cart."

When she emerged from the bathroom, Mac was laying platters of food onto a tablecloth that he had spread out on the carpet.

"I figured we'd do this picnic style," he said. "All right with you?"

"Sure." She stared down at the sumptuous feast, open-mouthed.

There was a platter of roasted glazed ham, one of rare roast beef, one of smoked salmon. Caesar salad, frilly greens with grilled swordfish strips strewn across them. There was fresh bread, herbed butter, a platter of grilled vegetables. Puff pastries filled with artichoke hearts and cheese, pasta salad dressed with goat cheese, sausage, sun-dried tomatoes and Greek olives. A bowl of black-red cherries. A glass bowl filled with trifle: sponge cake layered with berries and Bavarian cream. She almost fainted. Her abandoned lunch was still sitting on her desk at work. She hadn't eaten since her breakfast bran flakes.

"Did they know there's only two of us?" she asked faintly.

"They knew that I was one of us," he said. "More champagne?"

They dove in, and Jane quickly concluded that the food critics were right. Every bite was savory perfection. When they finally began to slow down, Mac loaded his plate up with sliced ham and stretched out on his side. "Let's get on with the party game," he said. "Your turn."

She dug into a plateful of savory, tender swordfish and greens. "The database is vast," she said. "I need a key word to begin my search."

He tossed up a cherry, caught it in his mouth, and gave her a crafty grin. "Tell me about the very worst day of your childhood."

She winced. "Oh, God, Mac."

"Don't even try." His face was implacable. "You made me do it."

She covered her face with her hand. "But it'll make me feel like I'm trying to make you feel sorry for me. I hate that."

"Did you feel sorry for me when I told you my worst day?"

"Not exactly. I felt compassion, but you weren't looking for pity."

"Well, neither are you. Just tell me. No matter how gut-wrenching it is, I won't pity you. I'll just say, jeez, is that all? I can top that with one hand tied behind my back. Then we can do a fucked-up childhood one-upmanship competition. That's always fun."

She giggled so hard she started to cough. "OK." She popped an artichoke pastry in her mouth and washed it down with a fortifying gulp of champagne. "But my childhood didn't have any traumas that they make made-for-TV movies about. It's hard to pick out a particular—"

"Stop waffling." He forked some more roast beef onto his plate. "There's got to be a worst day. Just pick one."

She dragged her eyes away from his stunning nudity with some effort. "Here goes. When I was eleven, my uncle came to visit us. He—"

"Oh, Christ, no." He jerked up onto his elbow, so suddenly that he almost knocked over his champagne. "Don't tell me."

She was startled. "What? You're the one who wanted this!"

He covered his face with his hand. "Uncle-come-to-visit stories. They can get really weird."

Comprehension dawned. "Oh! No, no, no! It's not that kind of story." She petted his arm. "Relax. My uncle is a very decent man. The nicest, kindest person in my whole family."

"Thank God." His hand dropped. He gave her a sheepish smile. "I'm sorry. I shouldn't have reacted like that. But the thought of anybody hurting a little girl like that . . . it's like an electric shock."

She stroked his bare, muscular leg. "You can relax," she soothed him. "I don't have any stories like that to tell."

"Lucky for your uncle. If you had, I would have to hunt him down and take him apart. Chunk by bloody chunk."

His vehemence startled her. "Do you want to hear this, Mac?" she asked gently. "We can change the subject if it's too upsetting for you."

"Just get it over with." He sat up and wrapped his arms around his knees, scowling. He looked like he was bracing himself for a blow.

"Uh, OK," she began cautiously. "So this sweet, innocent uncle of mine gets the bright idea to give me a chocolate

Labrador puppy for my birthday. I had him for a week, the whole time my uncle was visiting. He was the cutest puppy that ever existed. His name was Brownie."

"Aw, shit," he muttered. He clapped his hand over his eyes again. "I see where this is going."

"I warned you," she said. "You promised, Mac. No pity."

"Of course not." He crossed his arms over his chest and squeezed his eyes shut. "So? What happened to the damn puppy? Did he die in a heroic leap off the roof after saving you from a burning building? Go ahead. Tear my heart out of my chest and stomp on it."

"My uncle left," she said simply. "My mother took the puppy to the pound. He made too much of a mess, she said. But the truth was, I think he was just too happy for her. All that jumping and wagging and licking. She was horrified by emotional excess."

She waited. Mac was glaring into the remains of the pasta salad as if they had offended him deeply. He would not meet her eyes.

"So?" she prompted gently. "There it is. I was so heart-broken, I thought I was going to die. But I lived to tell the tale."

He rubbed his jaw, and swallowed hard. "Icy-hearted *bitch*."

The raw fury in his voice jolted her. "You said no pity."

"I don't pity you," he snarled. "I'm pissed. Which is different."

He looked like he wanted to hit something. "Mac? I'm OK now," she reminded him. "It was a really long time ago. Seventeen years."

"It's one thing to say no from the get-go," he fumed. "Sometimes you have to. But to let a little kid get all attached, to let a whole goddamn week go by, and then take the dog away? Jesus, that's cold!"

Tenderness for him bloomed in her chest. "You know what, Mac?" Her voice was soft with wonder. "You're a great big softie."

His jaw dropped. "Me? Hah!"

"Yeah, you. You can't fool me. You try to come off like a bossy, arrogant hard-ass, but you're all soft and squishy inside."

He looked alarmed. "Not me. Check me out, Jane." He let his thigh drop to the ground and revealed the thick jut of his erection. "Hard as a rock. And just as pitiless."

"Of course," she said. "A classic macho defense mechanism. You're so predictable, Mac. Put you on the spot, and you steer us right back towards sex. Safe and familiar ground."

He shook his head. "No. Sex with you is not safe and familiar. It's way out there. Places I've never, ever been."

She started to smile. He was sensitive and tenderhearted, no matter how he tried to deny it. She wanted to give him all the sweetness and gentleness he craved. To feed his hunger, and her own.

She took the bowl of trifle and two dessert spoons, and scooted over until their knees touched. She shrugged her robe off and scooped up a spoonful of sponge cake layered with custard and cream and syrupy berries. It quivered on the end of the spoon.

"You try so hard to be Mr. Macho, but you're just like this dessert, Mac." She closed her lips around the spoon and moaned with agonized pleasure. "Sweet. Tender. Full of cream." She scooped up another spoonful and held it out. "Here. Try some."

This damn party game of hers was dangerous. The more he knew about her, the more he wanted to know. The more possessive and raw he felt. And now she was hand-feeding him manna of the gods, a voluptuous, naked nymph of paradise. He was a goner.

He took the spoonful she offered and scooped up another one for her so they could have simultaneous sugar orgasms.

That touched off a dance—feeding spoonfuls of dessert to each other with lazy, sticky, nibbling kisses flavored with berries and cream between each bite. A glob of custard fell onto his chest. Jane hastened to lick it off.

"Jane?" He couldn't control his shaking, pleading tone.

She kissed the burning heat of his cheekbone. Her damp hair was cool against his fever-hot face. "Hmm?"

"Go down on me again," he begged. "But no weird games this time. I'm not in the mood for kinky stuff. I just want my sweet Jane."

She leaned her forehead against his. "You have to be sweet, too," she said. "Sweet like cream custard. No scoring points, or nailing me to the wall, or storming the fortress. No chest pounding of any kind."

"Deal. I'll be an éclair, a cream puff, a tiramisu. Anything."

He shoved platters aside to make room, and she curled up in front of him and pillowed her head on his thigh. She began to play with his cock with her soft, cool hands, stroking him with tender eagerness.

When she took him in her mouth, it was so sweet it brought a hot lump to his throat. He dug his fingers into her hair and tried not to whimper. He'd always loved blow jobs, not just because they felt so damn good, but because of the way they made him feel about himself. Pumped up. Powerful, like a prince, or a god receiving his due of worship.

But this was completely different. He felt helpless, vulnerable. No ego inflation, no prince, no god. Just a man, shaking with emotion, desperate for her tenderness. *Her love.* He shoved the thought back down to the depths from which it had arisen, but the damage was done.

He curled around her, moving his trembling hands over her body, mapping every inch he could touch: the freckles, the milky paleness, the faint blue tracery of veins beneath delicate, flower-petal softness. Lush curves, delicate bones, strong, lithe muscles. A miracle of nature, holding him with all her strength, pleasuring him with all her skill. She pulled his cock into her mouth with long, lazy, caressing strokes.

He put his hand between her thighs. She was hot and drenched, quivering around his thrusting fingers. Going down on him turned her on, just like burying his face between her thighs did it for him.

He rearranged their bodies so he could stretch out alongside her and spread her legs. She shuddered and moaned as he thrust his tongue hungrily into her slit, lapping up the warm, sweet flavor of her lube. He'd never cared much for the sixty-nine position before. He preferred either to relax and receive his pleasure, or to exert himself to give it with single-minded precision. He'd never seen the point in doing both at once, clumsy and distracted and half-assed.

But there was nothing clumsy or half-assed about surging with her on wave after wave of pleasure. With every luxurious stroke of their tongues, he blended more wholly with her. His pleasure and hers were a single moving, sighing, melting swirl. Over and over he came to the shuddering brink. Every time he dragged himself back, unwilling to let it end, until her pleasure finally burst and throbbed against his mouth.

He drank it in, then turned around and mounted her damp, spread-eagled body. He forced himself inside her just in time to feel the end of her long orgasm pulse through her. He was already plunging and sliding in a liquid agony of bliss before he realized that there was a reason why his cock felt so amazingly, deliciously, *unusually* good.

He'd forgotten the condom.

She remembered at the same moment. Her eyes popped open. They froze, clenched around each other. Both unwilling to stop.

"Uh, Mac?" she whispered, wide-eyed.

"I'm sorry," he pleaded. "I should be safe. I never do this without a condom. I've never just lost it, and forgotten. I swear to you."

She cradled his face. "I believe you. Me neither. I haven't done this in years, and I was always safe. But I'm not on the pill. So, ah . . ."

He rested his damp forehead against hers. He should pull out and suit up with latex like a responsible male of the third millennium, but his body wouldn't obey him. It kept surging, in waves that just got higher, stronger, rocking him farther and farther from the shores of sanity or good sense. "I won't come inside you," he promised, but he was in no condition to promise anything of the kind. The normal Mac could have, but not this madman. "I can't stop. It's too perfect."

Her stormy eyes were endlessly deep and gentle. "Yes," she said. "It's too wonderful to stop."

He was speechless at her trust. She deserved compliments, love words, poetry, but he was helpless to provide them. She put her arms around his neck and moved herself against him with sinuous grace.

She was so soft, so strong, giving herself to him with a generosity that humbled him. They surged and danced, heaving against each other, giving and taking, following the shining path together towards the bright perfection that beckoned them. He barely managed to pull out before he exploded and spurted his hot seed across her trembling body.

Some time later, Jane extricated herself from the damp knot of their bodies, and stumbled to the bathroom. She shut herself inside. The sink ran. The water stopped. Silence. He sat up. Waited some more.

More silence. Too damn much silence.

He got up, knees still shaking, and knocked on the door. "Jane?"

"I'm OK." Her muffled voice through the door sounded strange.

He waited some more. "What does OK mean?" he demanded.

She didn't answer. Fear yawned in his belly. She was slipping away from him, and he didn't know why, and there wasn't a goddamn thing he could do to stop her. There fucking never was.

His knocking turned into banging. "Jane! Open the door!"

"Just give me a minute." Her voice sounded even stranger.

"I'm coming in," he warned her. "Stand back."

"I'm fine, Mac. Please don't—oh, God!"

His blow to the door ripped the brass hook-and-eye lock out of the door frame. Jane stood in front of the mirror, hands clamped over her mouth. Her eyes were wide and startled, her face shiny with tears.

He was horrified. "What did I do? Jesus! What's wrong?"

"It's not you," she quavered.

"Then what?" His voice cracked like a whip. "Tell me!"

She flinched. "Don't worry."

"Don't worry? How the fuck am I not supposed to worry? Jane, just tell me what's wrong! Let me fix it!"

"You can't fix it!" She shoved past him into the bedroom. "I'm sorry! I never cry. I don't know why I'm crying now. There's no reason for it. I swear to God, if I could stop, I would!" She scooped up her dress from the floor, and turned it right side out.

That was a bad sign, very bad. He wrenched the dress out of her hands and flung it away. "Forget it, Jane," he said. "No way."

She hugged herself and backed away, still sniffling. "I can't handle the barbarian routine now," she warned him. "Don't, Mac!"

"I'm not letting you run out on me." He tossed her onto the bed, and climbed on top of her. "I'm going to hold you till you sleep."

"You can't do this!" She struggled wildly beneath his

weight. "I can't sleep! How the hell do you expect me to sleep like this?"

"So I'll hold you while you don't sleep. If you want to cry, cry. Tears don't scare me. You running out on me, that's what scares me."

He tucked Jane between himself and the wall and wound his leg between hers, braiding them together. She was going nowhere unless he said so. He waited patiently, hoping she would initiate the conversation. Even spitting insults were preferable to this tense silence.

He decided to take the initiative. "You asleep?" he whispered.

She jerked her head. "Hah," she muttered. "Dream on."

"You're not crying anymore," he said. "Maybe you should."

"I can't do it on command." Her voice was sharp.

"Oh." He nuzzled her fragrant hair. "You want to talk about it?"

"Now I'm the one who wants to get the conversation legally changed," she grumbled. "You're like a pit bull, Mac-Namara."

"I just don't want to screw up again." He kept his voice neutral.

Her body shook, with laughter or silent tears. "It's not your fault."

"How so? How not? Tell me, for Christ's sake."

She sighed. "For various reasons too tedious to recount, I get freaked out when I lose control," she said. "Something about you makes me lose it, and it seems to be getting worse. Like an earthquake."

"Oh." He pondered her words. "Yikes."

"It's not . . . your . . . *fault,*" she repeated, emphasizing every word.

"Yeah. I'll comfort myself with that the next time you're cowering inside a locked bathroom."

"I was not cowering!" she shot back. "And it didn't help

to have you rip the lock out of the door and muscle me around like a caveman!"

"So shoot me," he said. "I was scared."

The silence began to feel ominous again. Mac gathered his nerve. "If you can't sleep, let's do a round of our party game," he suggested.

"Oh, get real," she snapped.

"I think we should." He kissed her neck soothingly. "You still haven't told me why you didn't become an actress."

Her body went rigid. "It's your turn. I went last with the heartrending puppy story, remember?"

"I will never forget the puppy story, unfortunately," he said wryly. "But I already told you about my blighted dreams to be an astronaut and an archaeologist. So I skip my turn. Back to you, Jane."

The heavy quality of her hesitation rang his alarm bells. They'd been circling around this moment all night, spiraling closer and closer.

"This won't calm me down," she said. "It's not a nice story."

"You have to tell me now, or I'll die of curiosity," he told her.

She stared up at the ceiling for so long, he started to twitch. "My senior year in college, there was a guy on the faculty of the theater department," she said finally. "Dylan. Charismatic, talented, conceited."

His muscles contracted. "I hate the dickhead's guts already."

"Good. Be my guest," she said. "So I got involved with Dylan. I was so flattered that he wanted shy little me. How lucky, to be molded by someone so experienced, I thought. And at the very beginning of my career, too. Oh, thrillsville."

A sound came out of him that could only be described as a growl.

"Mac? Can you deal?" she asked. "Do you want me to stop?"

"I'm not that fragile, goddamn it," he snapped.

She sighed. "Dylan was an egomaniac. He had to be at the center of attention at all times. And he didn't want me to find theater work. That would have diverted my attention from its proper place—squarely focused on him. When I figured this out, I tried to leave him. He freaked out . . . and then he cut me off."

"Come again?"

"He had me blackballed," she explained. "He was very connected. He knew all the directors and producers in the business. He spread it around that I was mentally unstable, that I used drugs, you name it. Suddenly, I was uncastable. No more summer stock, no more student films, no more nothing. I got rejected from the grad schools I applied to, even the ones that had been courting me. Nobody wanted to take a chance on me after he was done. My reputation was trashed."

Mac's world turned bloodred. "What's this guy's last name?"

She looked over at him with a wary frown. "Why do you ask?"

"Just curious."

"Curious is how you'll stay, buddy," she said. "Dylan loves attention. Even negative attention. What he truly hates is to be ignored. So please. Ignore him, for God's sake."

"He wouldn't love my attention," Mac said. "I guarantee it."

There was a short, nervous pause from her. "Be that as it may, I would prefer it if you let it go," she said tightly. "It's old news."

"It wouldn't be that hard to find out who he is," he mused. "Some time on the Internet, a few cross-referenced facts—"

She jerked up onto her elbow. "Don't, Mac!"

"OK, OK. Calm down," he soothed. He tugged her back against the warmth of his body. "So how did you get loose of this prick?"

She buried her face against his chest. "When I figured out what had happened, I ran." Her voice was muffled. "I didn't have anyplace to go, so I ran home. The ultimate mistake in a long series of mistakes."

He petted her hair. "And why was that a mistake?"

She shook her head. "Dylan had been calling my mother for weeks, working on her. Telling her how messed up and hysterical I was. She didn't believe my story. She took his part."

He went rigid with outrage. "Shit! No way! Your *mom*?"

"To be fair, I must have seemed unbalanced, with all my wild stories about being sabotaged. My mother thought studying theater was a sign of insanity already. This was just one more confirmation for her."

"So she sold you out." His voice was harsh. "Like with the puppy."

"She lectured me for giving him so much trouble," she said wearily. "Advised me to be grateful to have such a patient man. Then she called him. He came to pick me up. They had a prior agreement."

She fell silent. The suspense made him want to scream and pound his feet on the bed. "And?" he prompted. "So? What happened?"

"At that point, I was almost convinced they were right," she whispered. "I was a mess. Dylan and my mom had a good time analyzing me. Two rational adults clucking their tongues and shaking their heads, and one freaked-out girl who couldn't stop crying. Dylan took me back with him to L.A." She paused for a moment. "It took me a week to work up the nerve to run again."

He could tell from her voice that she wasn't going to talk about that week, now or ever. Just as well. Imagining it was bad enough.

He cuddled her to his chest, sick with anger. "Where did you go?"

"I came here, to Seattle," she said. "I camped out on a

friend's couch. I waited tables, temped. I discovered head-hunting. It was a pretty tough time, but I suppose I should be grateful to him."

That comment threw him. "How so?"

"If it hadn't been for him, I would never have founded the MeanStreets Players. I was a pretty good actress, if I do say so myself, but I think I'm a better director. And I love the artistic control."

He stroked her back. "Now that's what I call a good attitude."

"I had to think of it that way, or I'd have gone nuts." She was silent for a moment. "I haven't seen my mother for four years now."

Mac snorted. "Hah. That's nothing. I haven't seen my mom for, let's see, almost twenty-four years. I've got you so beat."

He was relieved to hear her giggle. "OK," she said. "You win, Mac."

"No pity," he said.

She shook her head. "None."

"Your mother's a heinous bitch, though."

"That's enough," Jane snapped. "She's not a cruel person. Just misguided. She truly thought she was trying to help me."

"Whatever." He snapped off the light, organized their limbs in a braided tangle, and wound a lock of her hair around his fingers, to be on the safe side. No way was he letting go of her now.

You're so intense, Jane. Pull yourself together. No one wants to deal with an emotional black hole. It's embarrassing for everyone.

A square of moonlight crept slowly down the wall. Jane watched it with eyes that burned and stung. She'd spent five years trying to prove Dylan wrong. Mac had swept that work away in one wild night.

It had been a huge mistake to tell Mac about Dylan. It woke up all the frustration, the anger, the confusion, the shame. Dylan had used her own emotions against her, and he'd been diabolically clever about it. He'd provoke her into a frenzy, then manipulate her into discrediting herself. The more she fought him, the crazier she'd looked, and the more he'd played up his martyr act. Her only solution had been to develop an artificial calm, as deep and thick and cold as a glacier.

And Mac had shattered that calm to smithereens.

She couldn't face what was underneath. She was a mess. A black hole, like Dylan used to say. Look at her, sobbing uncontrollably after sex, spilling her guts about all her past traumas. A total basket case.

She wondered why Mac was hanging on to her so tightly. Maybe he felt sorry for her. Maybe he felt responsible. His body felt so good. She loved the weight of his muscular leg thrust between hers, his thick arm wrapped around her waist. She wished she could just relax into his solid warmth, but she kept seeing tomorrow morning's scene.

Stark reality, revealed by the pitiless light of day. The discomfort in Mac's eyes as he searched for a polite way to tell her he didn't want to deal with her emotional baggage, her intensity, her "issues."

It would be unbearable. She felt like she had no skin as it was. She started, very slowly, to shimmy out of the tightly wound cocoon he'd made around her with his body. Her hair was caught fast. She reached up to free it, and found his hand snarled in it.

She squeaked as he grabbed her wrist. "I knew it," he said.

His quiet voice made her freeze. "Knew what?"

"That you were going to try the vanishing act. I fucking *knew* it.

Her heart thudded as if she'd been caught doing something bad. "That's why you grabbed my hair? That's creepy, Mac."

"You're not running away." The bed shifted, and Mac climbed on top of her, pressing her facedown into the tangled sheets. He shoved her legs apart. She pressed her face against the sheets and gasped silently as he penetrated her in one deep, relentless shove. She was wet and soft, but very sore, and his invasion was so complete.

"Close your legs," he commanded.

She was confused. "What?"

He straddled her thighs with his own and pushed her legs together, settling his weight against her bottom. He rocked against her, wedging himself still deeper between her tightly clamped thighs.

She felt breathless, trapped. She could barely move. She struggled, and he responded by clamping her wrists together and trapping them against the pillow in front of her face. "Mac? I—"

"Shh." He slid his hand beneath her, in front of her hips, and slid two fingers into her slick folds, catching her clitoris between them. The deliberate friction against that swollen bud and the deep penetration of his body from behind kindled a glow of delicious excitement inside her.

She strained against the calculated weight of his body, his ruthless grip on her wrists, but with every stroke she became hotter, softer, more liquid around him. Tears of frustration burned in her eyes. His penis pressed against the mouth of her womb. "Squeeze your thighs around my fingers. Around my cock." His voice was soft, but there was a cold, sharp bite of anger to it that she felt throughout her body. "You'll like what happens. Harder. Good, like that. You like that?"

"Let me up, Mac." She tugged at her wrists. "This is not OK."

"Yeah, that would explain why your clit is practically vibrating between my fingers. You hug my cock. All of it. You like me inside you." He swiveled his hips with slow, sure skill. "You want me." He seized her earlobe between his teeth, bit it, and suckled it to soothe the sting. "Or else I wouldn't be doing this to you. I'm not stupid."

"I never said that you were," she protested. She tightened, clenching around him instinctively. "You don't have to hold me down."

"Oh, no?" He thrust into her, hard enough to make her gasp. "You plot to steal from me. You start out the evening by lying to me. You finish it up by trying to run from me. Yeah, you really inspire confidence, sweetheart. I'm not letting go of you for a goddamn second."

"I wasn't running," she lied. "You were pulling my hair. I was just trying to get comfortable—oh, God, Mac. Please."

"Please, what? Please, harder? Deeper? Why run, Jane? Because you're embarrassed? Because you cry when you come? Big fucking deal. Cry all you want. I love to see you come apart when I get you off."

She shook her head. His furious, insatiable sexuality was melting her down, making her crazy, desperate. "I don't want to come apart."

"Too bad. I don't care," he said. "I love it when you sob and writhe and clench yourself around my cock. I know that you need me."

"Mac—"

"I need you to need me, Jane." He ground his hips against her, stoking the pleasure to a searing blaze. "Don't run away."

She moaned, writhed beneath him. "I wasn't!"

"Don't lie. The more you hide, the more I see. Don't lie, Jane."

She shook her head frantically. "I won't."

"And don't you dare disappear on me, goddamn it."

"No," she sobbed. "No, I won't."

"Promise me!" His hips heaved and pounded, driving her relentlessly towards wild, seething chaos. "Promise it!"

"I promise," she gasped. "Don't make me fall to pieces, Mac."

"I have to." His rough voice shook. "Let me make you come, Jane. Let me have that much. Come for me. Give it to me."

She pleaded, but neither one of them could stop. They were both long past the point of no return. The harder she struggled, the bigger the feeling that swelled inside her—a crescendo of emotion.

She loved him. That was the realization she'd been fighting against all day. She'd known him for twelve hours, and she was madly in love with him. He had the power to break her heart to pieces, and she'd never felt more vulnerable and fragile in her life.

The world exploded. She lost herself in chaos. Throbbing darkness swelled up and sucked her under.

Dawn lightened the window to deep grayish blue. Mac held Jane's soft body tightly against his. His cock was still stone-hard and aching, clamoring for its own reward, but he'd wrestled the orgasm down.

Unfortunately, his hard-on wasn't so readily commanded. It throbbed hopefully against Jane's round, sexy ass. Clueless, as always.

He was miles from sleep. Wired, wound up, horrified at himself. Pinning her down and fucking her after she tried to run, whoa. Thousands of years of human evolution, wiped out in the blink of an eye. He'd never forced a woman, even in play. Never wanted to. Something about Jane drove him nuts, made him desperate. Sure, she'd been hot for him, but that meant nothing. The body didn't always agree with the mind. He, of all people, should know that.

If she didn't want him, he couldn't hold her. The harder he tried to pin her down, the more it would tear him up when she left.

And knowing that didn't help worth a damn.

He pulled away from her, and sensed the subtle tension

that came over her body. She was awake. The air felt chilly after her heat.

She stirred behind him, sat up. He swung his legs over the bed and waited, hunched over, for the axe to fall.

It wasn't in his nature to wait. He wasn't a patient man, never had been. He was restless and edgy, wound up tight as a coiled spring, and he'd never been able to bear the weight and chill of silence.

He turned around. She was so pale, her eyes huge and shadowed with smudged mascara. She looked fragile, and very nervous. Probably wondering if he was going to leap on her like a slavering wolf.

Either she wanted him or she didn't, he told himself. Either she could handle him, or she couldn't. He'd fucked up. He shouldn't have tried to hang on to her last night, but what was done was done. Period.

She reached out her hand, but changed her mind at the last minute. Her hand fell short and landed on the sheet. "Are you all right?"

"You keep stealing my lines," he said grimly.

"It's not a line." Her eyes flicked down to his unflagging erection.

"Sorry about that," he said. "Pay it no mind."

"Nothing to be sorry about." Her voice was wary.

His body's blunt, humiliating betrayal made him furious. His hope and hunger, naked to her. "I wouldn't want to embarrass you," he said. "I'm trying to play it cool. Too much jumping and wagging and licking will get me taken to the pound for sure."

Her face contracted. "Oh. Ouch, Mac. That was unnecessary."

Smooth move, asshole. Being gentler wouldn't hurt his cause.

A lock of tangled hair had fallen over her eyes. He reached towards her to smooth it back. She flinched away.

He snatched back his hand as if he'd burned it. He was

screwed. She was afraid of him, and he had no one to blame for it but himself.

The silence between them got heavier. The fear lying on his belly got colder, sharper, until it transformed itself into hard anger.

"Mac, I, um . . . do you want me to . . ." Her voice trailed off to a frightened thread of sound. He couldn't stand it. "Do you, ah, want—"

"Whatever," he burst out. "Do whatever the hell you want. I'm not going to tie you to the fucking bed, Jane. I'm taking a shower."

He stalked to the bathroom and slammed the door shut before she could see his face crumple.

He had to let go. He couldn't force her to love him. To wake up with him every morning and go to bed with him every night until they were old and toothless and doddering. Love did as it goddamn well pleased, every time. He knew that. He'd always known it. This was no surprise to him. He got under the shower. Turned the dial to ice-cold.

But tears still came out hot, even with icy water pelting down.

The bathroom door was so blank and mute, and yet so terribly eloquent. It whispered things she didn't want to hear. Wasn't this what she got for falling wildly in love with a man after one sweaty night? Besides, how could she have been so stupid as to hope he would still want her in spite of everything? He knew too goddamn much.

He couldn't even bear to look at her. This was worse than the discomfort and embarrassment she'd been afraid of. The suppressed violence in his voice sounded as if he almost . . . hated her.

Do whatever the hell you want. I'm not going to tie you to the fucking bed. She slipped off the bed and went to the bathroom door. She leaned her hot forehead against the wood, listened to the water hiss.

There was no lock on the door. He'd torn it off last night. So? What was the plan? Climb into the shower, beg him to love her? Maybe she could drop to her knees, all desperate and submissive, and give him a supplicating blow job. That would be right in character.

She'd summoned that image to punish herself for being so stupid, but it backfired on her, sparking a flush of feverish lust. Miserable as she was, it weakened her knees, it curled her toes to think of it: the hot water pounding down on them, his muscular legs planted in that wide, aggressive stance, his big hands holding her head, his fingers tangled in her wet hair as she pulled as much of his thick, hot penis into her mouth as she could take without choking on him.

She was stupid, crazed, undone. Her legs shook, from violent emotion, lack of sleep, too much sex. He could tie her to the bed if he wanted. Her body went nuts for him, no matter what he did. Gentle and sweet, rough and wild, it didn't matter, as long as it was Mac. Everything her mother and Dylan had said about her was true. The grain of the dark wood swam before her eyes. He wielded such power over her. She'd given it to him freely, and she had no idea how to get it back. She felt as fragile and transparent as blown glass.

He didn't want her. The only thing to do was run. Quick. Salvage what was left of her dignity before she started to snivel and beg.

She looked around for her dress. There it was, a crumpled tangle under the bed. She was lucky it was in one piece. The bustier with all its hooks and eyes would take too long, the panties and stockings were completely trashed. Her fingers trembled so hard, she could barely tug the dress over her body. She snatched her purse, tiptoed out the door.

She was blocks away from the Copley Crowne, running like a stumbling lunatic through the misty dawn before she noticed that she was barefoot, and only because she stubbed her toe on a sidewalk crack and pitched forward, scraping the skin off her hands and her knees.

She was sobbing like a child by the time she reached her car.

Chapter Eight

"One thousand forty-eight dollars and eighty-one cents is the grand total of the damage to the room." Danny flung the manila folder on Mac's desk and gave his brother his patented dark, brooding look.

"I'll write out a check," Mac growled.

"And there are the complaints. Robin and I are used to your tantrums, but the guests and the cleaning staff aren't. I don't think Rosaria even wants her job back after seeing you naked on the rampage in the hotel corridor. Jesus, Mac. The poor woman has high blood pressure to begin with. She can't stop crossing herself, they tell me."

"Leave me alone, Danny."

"Word is out that the colorful, eccentric CEO of Crowne Royale Group needs his thorazine dosage adjusted," Danny informed him. "You've always been high-strung, but smashing a roomful of antique furniture is over the top, Mac. Even for you."

"I'll write the fucking check," Mac repeated grimly. "Then go."

Danny had that look on his face, as if he were puzzled

and alarmed to find himself related to such a strange, exotic beast. Mac was familiar with that look. What he wasn't used to was the shadow of anxiety in his brother's eyes. The hard, worried line of Danny's mouth.

Not that Danny would ever admit to such feelings, thank God. Mac wouldn't know what the hell to do with him if he did.

"You've run through more women than I can count, but I've never seen you like this," Danny said fretfully. "You're not eating, you're even more rude than usual, you look like shit. Get a grip. There are thousands of women out there, throwing their goddamn phone numbers at you by the truckload. This writer chick is not worth it!"

"She's a headhunter, not a writer. She was going after Gary."

"Yeah, you told me." Danny's voice was suspiciously gentle. "We're lucky she never got her claws into him. If this is what she did to you, she would've made hamburger out of poor Gary."

Mac surged to his feet, and Danny skittered back warily, his reflexes honed by a lifetime of brotherly wrangling. "Take the check, apologize to the staff and leave me the hell alone," Mac snarled.

Danny stalked out and slammed the door. Mac was one of the few people on earth who could goad him into doing that. Usually he enjoyed the challenge, and savored his little victories. Today, he couldn't care less.

The door opened just as he sank back down into his chair. Only one other person would dare come into his office without knocking.

Mac didn't look up when he felt her cool hand on the back of his neck.

"Hey, you," Robin said gently.

"Don't be hurt, but I need to be alone," he said. "Get lost, shrimp."

As usual, his little sister ignored his command. "This is

awful," she said. "I feel really bad, because it's partly my fault."

He grunted suspiciously. "How do you figure that?"

She dropped a kiss on top of his head. "I knew I should have rescheduled her to meet with Gary, but I decided I wanted you to meet her. I know you go for the sweet, luscious type with big, pillowy ta-tas."

He buried his face in his hands. "Oh, Christ, Robin. Why?"

"It seemed like a good idea at the time," she protested. "She was cute, and she looked smart, too. You need a challenge. You bore easily."

"A challenge she was," he mumbled. "No question about that."

"So why are you moping?" Robin demanded. "It's not like you. When you go after something, you always get it. You're like a pit bull."

He flinched to hear the exact words that Jane had used. "News flash, shrimp. She ran out on me. Which is a pretty big fucking clue that I'm not perfect for her, get it? I'm too much. Over the top.

Robin perched on his desk. "I see. Well, you do take some getting used to. But you're worth the effort. When you bother to exert yourself."

"Gee, thanks. What a sweet, loyal baby sister."

"Sweeter than you deserve," Robin said crisply. "So did you?"

"Did I what?" he snarled.

"Exert yourself, silly."

"Hell, yes!"

Robin looked superior. "I don't mean sexually, you big pig."

"Don't talk about sex, damn it. You're too young."

Robin rolled her eyes. "What I meant is, did you exert yourself to be charming? You know, compliments? Sweet talk? Making her feel cherished and special? Standard, romantic stuff like that?" She stared searchingly into his face and her dark eyes widened in dismay. "Oh, Mac. You've got that look on your face. You didn't. You big idiot."

That final, ugly scene with Jane flashed through his mind, in all its painful detail. "It wasn't like that," he hedged. "It's complicated."

"Then the ball's in your court," Robin snapped. "And you don't need my sympathy. You need a swift kick in the butt. Stand up and turn around, Mac. Good thing I wore my pointy shoes today."

He sprang to his feet. Robin stumbled back. "She's the one who ran out on me!" he bellowed.

Robin stuck out her lower lip like a belligerent toddler. "Only because you were rude and horrendous, I bet."

"Get lost, Robin. For the last time. Or else."

"Or else what, big brother? So she ran out on you. Big deal. You're notorious for never staying the night with your conquests. You're practically an urban myth. Michael Mac-Namara, sexual superhero. He uses up a whole box of condoms, and poof, he's gone by dawn."

"Stop talking about sex!" he roared. "You're pissing me off!"

Robin was undaunted. "You know what your problem is? You're used to winning, and you sulk like a big baby when you lose. But love isn't a game. Seduction, maybe, yes. But love, no. It's not like closing a deal, or winning a tennis match, or getting the last word, Mac."

"What the hell do you know about love or seduction?" he demanded. "You're just a kid. Go play clown. Stop lecturing me."

Robin started to reply. She stopped herself, and pressed her lips together. "I'm not a kid anymore," she said tightly. "But you'll never accept that, so why do I waste my breath?"

She stalked out. His door was slammed, for the second time in five minutes. He was on a roll. The whole world was pissed at him.

Robin was right about his sexual track record. He never invited women to his condo, or slept a whole night with his lovers. It was a big waste of time, he'd always thought. Sleep he could get in the privacy of his own bed at home. If he was in bed with a naked woman, why sleep? There were better things to do. Hours of them.

But he'd slept with Jane. Tried to, at least. He wanted to sleep with her on his own big bed, snuggled under his comforter. He wanted to pull the covers up over her sweet body to keep her warm. Cuddle her all night. Make breakfast for her in the morning.

Why was he torturing himself? It never stopped. This feeling sucked. He hated it. He'd tried everything, and he couldn't shake it.

He collapsed forward onto the desk, rested his head on folded arms and tried to think it through, but reason had never been his default setting. He'd always had more luck with action, impulse, instinct. Reason came hard to him, especially with that feeling roiling in his gut. A sickening, sinking feeling, horribly similar to fear.

He'd distanced himself from the world by making everything into a game, but Jane had unmasked him. He was hunched over an ugly, unhealed wound. He'd distracted himself from it all his life by pumping up his ego, trying to be smarter, faster, better.

Now look at him, flat on his face, stomped to a pulp beneath Jane's ridiculous sandals. Which were currently locked in his desk like Cinderella's glass slipper.

How pathetic. Reduced to fondling a woman's shoes in secret.

Prince Un-Charming. The details of that night were etched on his mind. Every rude, mean thing he'd said and done to her. His courtship strategy had been the emotional equivalent of running her over with a tank. Hardly a way to convince a woman that he was husband material.

Whoa. He lifted his head. His heart sped up and started to

thud anxiously against his ribs. Yeah, that crazy thought had originated in his own thick, hard head. No point in playing dumb. One night, and he was convinced. Life would be flat and stale without her. He wanted that zing, the vibrant push and pull. He wanted to shock her, make her laugh, drive her wild with pleasure. Make her open up like a flower.

Something in him stopped struggling, relaxed into its proper place with a sigh of dumb relief. The odds were against him, but he had to try. She'd already ripped his heart right out of his chest. He might as well do something useful and flashy with it, like fling it at her feet.

The idea exploded in his head like fireworks. Oh, man. Of course. He was so brilliant, he blew his own mind. He knew what she longed for, what she valued. He could start racking up points right away. He would put his most aggressive pit bull tendencies right to work on it.

Project Prince Charming was under way.

He grabbed the phone, dialed the Crowne Royal Group program director. "Hi, Louise? It's Mac . . . good, thanks, and you? . . . great, great . . . I have a question about our corporate contributions to the arts this year. I've decided to take a more active interest in our . . . yeah, I know . . . well, there's this local youth theater group that's doing great things, and I was just wondering what we could do for them . . ."

"Mr. Mysterious strikes again! Here's another one!" Mona called out to the office at large. The receptionist bustled into Jane's office and laid the box on her desk. "God, this is fun. Hurry, Jane. Open it."

Four more of her female colleagues instantly crowded into the room. "Get a move on!" Maria demanded. "Need some scissors?"

Jane stared at the box and put her hands over her hot cheeks. The diabolical, seductive bastard. She ripped open the box and peeled away layers of tissue paper. A collective gasp of delight went up.

It was an antique perfume bottle. Iridescent rainbow tints shimmered on its surface. No card, no note. Just a silent message, like a kiss on the back of the neck. The confident caress of a man who didn't have to ask. He knew what she liked. No need for words.

"Oh, Lord." Erica sighed. She took it reverently out of Jane's hands and held it up to the light. "A Kessler. Original. Beautiful. Circa 1870. Would fetch, oh, say, nine hundred bucks on eBay, minimum."

Jane winced. "It's a gift," she muttered. "Don't be crass."

"Crass, my ass," Erica said. "For God's sake. Say yes, or at least give us this guy's phone number so we can have a crack at him."

Jane hid her face in her hands. "I can't take much more of this."

"Good." Her boss's crisp voice rang out from the doorway. "I can't, either. The suspense is cutting into our corporate productivity. Give in, or the man won't have enough money left to buy you a decent ring."

Jane's spine straightened. She plucked the bottle out of Erica's hand, swaddled it in tissue paper and stuck it in her purse. "I'm cutting out early today," she said. "Bye-bye, ladies. Have a good one."

Charlene glanced pointedly at the wall clock. "At three-twelve?"

"Fire me if you like, Charlene," Jane said. "I need some time to myself. I'm feeling a bit crowded."

Shocked silence followed her words. Her colleagues tiptoed out, eyes frozen wide. The door clicked shut. Jane and Charlene stared at each other across the desk.

"You've developed quite a little attitude, Jane," her boss said.

"It's about time, wouldn't you say?" Jane kicked off her

pumps, and slipped into her walking shoes. "Haven't you always told me I should find out where I put my spine?"

"Well, yes," Charlene admitted reluctantly. "But did you have to find your spine during office hours?"

"You'll live." Jane shrugged on her suit jacket. "Or not."

"I don't want to fire you," Charlene fretted. "You're good at this."

"In that case, I would like to draw your attention to the fact that we still haven't renegotiated my contract. Twenty-five percent of each commission I bring in would be more than fair, at this point."

"Don't push me." Charlene fluttered her hand. "Off with you. I'll talk with Pierce about your contract. He'll be reluctant, but—"

"I'm worth it. Pierce knows it, too. And if he doesn't, he'll learn."

"Out! Enough! You're unbearable when you're like this. Go call that poor man and put him out of his misery. Heartless hussy-pants."

"I'm holding you to your promise," Jane said. "Talk to Pierce."

"Out! Shameless opportunist. You try my patience! Out!"

Jane pretended not to notice the covert glances as she walked out of the office. Over a week had passed since that wild night, and her skin was still thinner. Her glacial shield was utterly gone.

She was dancing a whole different dance with the world. Sounds were louder, smells stronger, colors brighter, lines sharper. And the tears were ridiculous. Even dog food commercials made her cry.

She got angry faster, too. She spoke her mind without thinking. She didn't even care if Charlene fired her. She didn't love this job. She wouldn't starve. She could always temp, or wait tables. She felt fearless, reckless. Strange. Her priorities were so clear, they shone.

She'd lost her cool—and she didn't miss it. Not one tiny bit.

And Mac's silent, devastating courtship was weaving a thread of bright suspense through her days, a teasing tug that kept her constantly off balance. It had started with the bunch of violets, breathing out whiffs of elusive sweetness. The next day, a gold foil box of flowers molded in exquisite detail out of the finest dark Italian chocolate. The next day, a silk scarf, the exact color of the dress she'd worn to meet him. Storm-at-sea blue.

A chunk of glowing honeycomb in a wax-paper lined white box, dripping and golden like trapped liquid sunshine. A miniature cactus with one luminous pink blossom floating out to the side, a gossamer dream of a flower. It faded away in two hours, leaving only a dry violet thread. The messenger who had delivered it had been sweating for fear of damaging it. He'd had to calm down in the conference room with an iced coffee, patting his shiny brow with a tissue.

Each day a lovely surprise. A leather-bound volume of *Romeo and Juliet,* dated 1714, in near-perfect condition. Erica had gotten onto the Internet and priced that item, too. The sum had made Jane sink into a chair and put her head between her knees. Better not to know.

Then it had been a faceted crystal window ornament. Mac was working his way steadily through her centerfold model's list of likes—and he'd dreamed up a way to give her rainbows.

Rainbows, for crying out loud. It was pure psychological warfare.

Every gift was a message designed to bypass her head and zing straight on to her heart. She would never have dreamed that such a volatile man could be possessed of such seductive delicacy. It brought back all the marvels of their night together. The shocking intimacy, the almost unbearable pleasure. The honesty, the tenderness, the passion.

But she was so vulnerable to his overwhelming personality. His brutal last words were still ringing in her head. She was wide open to him. She couldn't shield herself to Mac as she had with Dylan. Mac was too intelligent, too powerful, too crafty at slipping past her barriers. He knew her too well, after only one night. He could hurt her so easily.

He wanted her, but she didn't dare speculate why he'd changed his mind. She was confused. So tempted and allured, as if by the haunting whistle of enchanted pipes, luring her to sensual doom in the hall of the mountain king. So seductive. Almost worth the risk. Almost.

She swallowed over an aching lump in her throat as she watched the city go by. Her loneliness had sharpened, taking on a poignant edge. The silence of solitude was more profound. Harder to bear than before.

The message light was blinking when she got home, but she headed to the bedroom to change first. She placed the perfume bottle carefully on her vanity next to the chocolates and the cactus. She opened the gold foil box and yielded to her new after-work ritual, which involved struggling not to take out a chocolate flower.

The struggle lasted about three seconds today.

She broke off the outer petals of a chocolate rose, placing them on her tongue. She would *not* chew, she told herself. She would savor the chocolate bliss turning liquid on her tongue for her whole shower.

Afterward, she dried off and tugged on sweatpants and a skimpy white tank top—one of the reinforced kind that were theoretically designed to hold your bosom in place even without the benefit of a bra. In her case, the tank top made a valiant and commendable effort, and if it fell short of its goal, who was ever going to know? She lived alone.

That fleeting thought depressed her even more. She stared at herself in the mirror and bounced up and down on the balls of her feet. She caught herself wondering if Mac would appreciate the Jell-O jiggle.

The ache of longing that brought on made her stuff the rest of the chocolate rose into her mouth for instant comfort. She sucked on it as she trotted barefoot down the stairs to listen to her messages.

She punched the message button. "Jane, this is Patti," said the stage manager of the MeanStreets Players. "The most incredible thing just happened! I tried you at work, but they said you'd gone home. I hope you're not sick, but if you are, this news will cure you! Call me!"

She dialed Patti's number. "Hey, Patti, it's me. What's up?"

"We got a corporate contribution!" Patti crowed. "A big, whopping mother of a donation! We're set for the fall show! We're in fat city!"

Jane's backside connected hard with the kitchen chair. "We what?" she squeaked. "How? From who?"

"Crowne Royale Group Hotels, whoever the hell they are! I never even knew they existed!"

"Mac," Jane whispered. "Oh, my God. Mac funded our show."

"Who? No, honey, you're not making sense. The program director is a woman named Louise Reardon, and she says . . ." Patti's words flowed out in a high-pitched, unbroken stream, but Jane could no longer follow them. She clutched the phone to her ear, bent over a keen ache in her belly. Mac had funded her show. No one had ever stirred themselves to help her. No one had ever given her a gift so valuable.

". . . Jane? Hey! Jane, you still there?"

She dragged her attention back to Patti. "Sorry. I'm in a daze. This is incredible news. Patti. I've got to go. I'll call you back, OK?"

"OK, fine! Till later, then."

Jane placed the phone in the cradle and stared out the kitchen window. Beams of golden afternoon summer sunshine slanted in, split into lazily spinning rainbows by the crystal that hung in the window.

Rainbows, everywhere. Mac's gift to her. Flashes of extravagant, sensual beauty. She was surrounded by them, on all sides.

She pressed her hands against her wet eyes and started to laugh. It was so Mac, this careless, flagrant generosity. He was nothing like Dylan. He was passionate, complicated, difficult, but he was also kind and gentle and immensely tenderhearted. He was pulling strings behind her back, like Dylan, but while Dylan had done it to punish and control her, Mac pulled his strings to make her dreams come true.

He was a magnificent sweetheart. Her heart had known the truth from the start, but she hadn't dared to listen to it. She'd been too busy trying to keep her heart safe from him. A pointless exercise if ever there was one. Her heart would never be safe from Michael MacNamara.

She grabbed the phone and dialed. "Crowne Royale Group Hotels," said an older woman. Not Robin.

"May I speak with Michael MacNamara, please?"

"I'm sorry, he's out of the office. May I take a message?"

The doorbell rang at that moment. "I'll, uh, call back, thanks," she said. She hung up, went to the front door and peeked out the spy-hole.

No one appeared to be standing on the porch. Her heart thumped heavily as she unfastened the deadbolt and opened the door.

A high-pitched whimper pulled her attention down. A loose-woven covered basket sat on the porch. She crouched and flipped open the lid.

A puppy poked its fuzzy head out. It whined and licked her hand with a tiny pink tongue. A chocolate lab puppy. Its small body vibrated with emotion, its dark eyes woeful with fear and tremulous hope.

She lifted the squirming animal out of the basket and settled it into the crook of her arm. She rubbed its plump, naked pink belly. A male puppy, she noticed. He wiggled, practically bursting with love.

Her heart swelled till it felt like it would explode. She rubbed her face against him and breathed in that odd, sharp smell that only puppy fur had. Woo hah, crying again. Big deal. She had Kleenex in her pocket, she had industrial strength waterproof mascara. She was set.

She walked down the porch steps and out onto the sidewalk. The pavement was hot against her bare feet. She cuddled the puppy and looked around, realizing that she didn't even know what car he drove. Their party game had never gotten around to such mundane details.

She walked out into the middle of the quiet residential street, and turned like the dancing ballerina in a jewel box, eternally spinning to a tinkling, romantic tune. The pop of a car door jerked her gaze around.

Oh, please. She might have guessed that he would drive a black Jag. Bold, sexy, eye-catching, extravagant. So very Mac.

He got out of his car. His physical reality was like a blow to the center of her chest. God, he was beautiful. Even taller and broader than she remembered. He was wearing jeans and a snug white T-shirt that did nothing to conceal the muscular perfection of his body. His face looked hard and wary. Leaner. A quarter inch beard shadowed his face.

He walked towards her, and stopped a few feet away, his eyes wary. "I'm not stalking you," he said, in a low, careful voice.

She cuddled and soothed the trembling puppy as she feasted her eyes on him. "Of course not. I would never have thought that you were."

"I'm only here at your house because I thought it might be awkward to have a puppy delivered to your workplace."

"Very thoughtful. I loved your presents, by the way. Thank you."

"You're welcome." He shrugged. "You, uh, never called me. So I did kind of wonder. If you liked them, I mean."

She hid her smile against the puppy's fuzzy head. "You never left a note," she pointed out.

"I was trying to be restrained," he said wryly. "For a little change of pace, you know?"

"You act more like a fairy godmother than a stalker," she said.

"Oh, great," he said sourly. "What a turn-on. Bippity boppity boo."

She started to laugh. "You know that movie?"

"I raised a little girl." His voice was long-suffering. "Believe me. I know my Disney. Better than I ever wanted to."

The puppy tried to crawl up onto her shoulder, and she gently rearranged his wriggling body. "Fairy godfather, then?" she teased.

"That's problematic, too," he said gruffly. "Makes me sound like some bad-ass Mafioso, about to make you an offer you can't refuse."

"Are you?" she asked.

His mouth hardened. "You can always refuse, Jane," he said. "Always. And I'll respect that. I promise. You get what I'm saying?"

Her eyes filled up. She blinked the tears away and nodded. "Thank you for getting us the donation," she whispered.

"You don't have to thank me." His voice was tense. "I'm not trying to buy you, or anything sick like that. I just wanted you to have it."

"Try not to be so twitchy and defensive, Mac," she suggested. "Just take a deep breath . . . and try. It's going to be OK."

"Oh yeah? Easy for you to say. I'm the one who's out on a limb. I'm the one who scared you away. I don't want to fuck this up, but I—"

"You won't," she said simply.

He closed his mouth. His throat bobbed. "I won't?"

She took a careful step closer. "I only left because I thought you didn't want me," she confessed.

He shut his eyes. "I felt bad," he said tightly. "For losing control, and pushing you around like I did. I thought you wouldn't want me. That's why I, uh, took that shower. To give you an out. So you could cut and run, if you didn't want to deal with me."

She bit her lip. "Oh, Mac," she whispered.

"You ran," he said. "I wasn't surprised. I didn't blame you, but I can't stop thinking about you, Jane. I'm sorry about what happened. I want another chance. Please."

She couldn't get any words over the lump in her throat, so she went up on her tiptoes, and kissed him gently on the mouth.

He accepted her kiss, but did not return it. His body was rigid. "I'm not like that asshole who trashed your life," he said.

"I know," she said. "I'm so convinced." She swayed forward, caught a whiff of the sweet-smelling detergent his clothes had been washed in. She strained for the warmer scent of his skin and hair and breath. She had so much to say, she didn't know where to start.

"Don't torture me." His voice sounded strangled. "Say something."

She touched his chest. "Do you want to come into my—"

"Yes. Please."

He followed her into her house and looked around, fascinated. "Weird, that I know so much about you but I've never seen your place."

"I know. I felt that way when I was looking for your car," she told him. "We crammed a six-month affair into one night."

"Yeah." He peered at the photos on her wall. "Emotional overload. No wonder we had a meltdown."

She put the puppy down, and he rolled onto his back, presenting his quivering belly hopefully. She crouched down to pet him. "He's the cutest puppy that I've ever seen," she crooned. "Absolutely adorable."

Mac turned, a frown tugging his brows together. "I know it's a risk, a gift like that, which is another reason I wanted to give him to you in person. I can take him back, if you don't have time for a—"

"No power on earth could take this puppy from me." Her voice rang with authority. "This puppy is *mine*. Body and soul."

Mac's big shoulders visibly relaxed. "So he's an OK gift, then?"

"He's a spectacular gift," she said firmly. "Inspired."

A cautious grin woke his mischievous dimples. "I picked out the most jumpy, wiggly, waggy, emotional puppy in the whole litter for you."

She let out a watery giggle. "You know me so well."

"So have I succeeded in my campaign of tricking you into thinking I'm a deep, sensitive guy?" he demanded.

She folded her arms beneath her bosom as she pondered her reply. She noticed his eyes drift down to her chest. She deliberately hiked her boobs up a couple of inches. "Face it, Mac," she said. "You *are* a deep, sensitive guy. A total sweet-heart. A complete honey."

"Yeah, right," he said. "And that is the most provocative article of clothing that I have ever seen in my life."

The air crackled with the heat that arced between them. "Here you go again," she said. "Turning the conversation to sex when I tell you you're sensitive and sweet. You're so pre-dictable."

"I didn't say a word about sex. I was talking about your tank top."

She waved an impatient hand at him. "Don't even try. I am so on to you, Mac. Whenever things get sticky—"

"You think this is sticky?" he cut in. "I'll show you sticky, angel."

The silence grew even heavier, more sexually charged. Mac blew out a sharp breath. "Damn. I didn't mean to do that."

"Do what?"

"Come on to you, before I even get things straightened

out. Keep looking at me like that, and I'm going to nail you right here in your foyer, up against the wall."

She pulled in a quick, startled breath, and steadied herself against the wall. "Let's straighten things out quickly, then, shall we? Go on, Mac. The clock's ticking. The foyer wall is waiting."

He started to grin. "Oh, man. I am so in for it."

"And speaking of sticky, I've got some chocolate flowers we could put to creative use. This deep, sweet, sensitive guy I know sent them to me. And when we run out of those, I've got some raw honey we could lick off each other's, ah, tender spots. It's got a flavor that just explodes in your mouth—like some other things that I could think of."

"Whoa. Slow down, sweetheart." He held up his hands, his eyes feverishly bright. "Let's get this straightened out first. I've been thinking up some new questions for our party game, and I want to try them out." He seized her upper arms and tugged her towards him. "Like, for instance, where do you want to spend your honeymoon?"

Her eyes widened. "Oh, Mac."

He tilted her chin up and kissed her with exquisite gentleness. "Do you want a big wedding, or a small one? Do you want kids? How many? Do you want to start trying now, or would you rather wait? Do you squeeze your toothpaste from the top, or the bottom?"

Her body was turning rosy pink, a deep glow starting in the center of her being and radiating out like the sunrise. "I've never thought about the honeymoon, so I'll pass on that one for now," she said. "Small wedding. Two to three kids. I'd love to start now, but I would wait if you wanted to. And I squeeze from the bottom. I hate waste."

The silence had the breathless suspense of a diver about to leap off the board. Mac leaned his forehead gently against hers. "Uh-oh," he said. "Trouble ahead. I'm a spendthrift, wasteful top squeezer. A sucker for instant gratification, as you know."

She swayed against him, giggling helplessly. "Oh, dear. What a dilemma. What are we going to do?"

"Separate toothpaste tubes," he said promptly. "Problem solved."

"Thank goodness," she murmured.

His smile faded, and he gazed at her with searching, shadowed eyes. "You know what I'm like," he said. "In bed, and out. I'm a very aggressive person. Always will be. I take up a lot of space."

"I love the kind of person you are," she said.

"I tend to act before I think," he went on, as if rushing to get the worst out. "I like to be the center of attention, but I'm not pathological about it. I get angry easily. I've been known to say stupid things that get me into trouble, but it never lasts. I know how to apologize. And I'll treat you like a goddess, Jane. You don't ever have to be afraid of me."

She shook her head. "Oh, I'm not. I can handle you, Mac-Namara. And I will. Very skillfully. Using some of my sandalwood bath oil, so my hands can slip and slide all over that big, thick—"

"Hold it right there, babe. Let me do this right. Here I am, trying to do the right thing, and you . . . is this all just about sex for you?"

She laughed at his outraged tone. "Are you accusing me of being superficial and oversexed?"

"Actually, I'm just trying to figure out if I'm dreaming," he said.

She reached down to his crotch, cupped him, and squeezed. "You're awake, Mac," she said throatily.

"Uh . . . yeah." He shuddered, groaned. "You've convinced me. OK, Jane. I've sounded you out, and it looks promising. I'd better get this over with while I can still talk. So, ah . . . here goes nothing." Mac swallowed hard, and sank down onto one knee. "Jane Duvall, I love you. Please don't laugh at me. I know this is trite, but I wanted to stick with the classic Prince Charming schtick—"

"It works," she whispered. "Don't stop. It's fine. Really."

His face lit up with pure joy. "Marry me, Jane." He seized her hand and kissed it. "Be my bride. I'll love you till I die."

His beautiful face wavered and swam. She brushed the tears away. "I'm a great big crybaby," she warned. "In case that bugs you."

"I don't care. I think I even like it. Is that kinky? Marry me, Jane."

"And I've got a pretty hot temper myself," she said. "I almost got myself fired today. And even if your conquering barbarian routine turns me on in bed, get this, Mac. I will not take any crap from you. Ever."

His eyes widened. "Whoa! Strict Jane! Marry me quick, babe. I can't wait to be put in my place by a gorgeous redhead every night." He embraced her hips, nuzzled her belly and looked up through fluttering lashes. "Just don't be too cruel to me," he pleaded. "You know how sensitive I am. Be gentle with my tender feelings."

She cradled his face, laughing through her tears. "We've only spent a total of maybe twelve hours together. It's, uh, kind of quick."

"I knew in the first ten seconds," he said simply. He pulled a little velvet box out of his pocket, snapped it open and held it out to her. Her jaw dropped, her voice snagged in her throat.

It was a stunning, square-cut sapphire, flanked with diamonds.

"It's that storm-at-sea color," he said hesitantly. "I love that color on you. If it's too old-fashioned for you, we could reset the stones—"

"It's perfect. I've never seen anything more perfect." She sank to her knees and wound her arms around his neck. "I love you, Mac. I would love to marry you. I would love to spend my life with you."

Mac unwrapped her arms so that he could slip the ring on her finger. His arms circled her, pulled her tight against him.

He dropped light, sweet kisses against her face, and his hands moved over her with anxious care, as if he were afraid she might break. His caution made her want to cry with tenderness for him, but she was starved for raw passion. Time enough for gentleness later.

"Hey." She pulled away, and shoved him down onto the floor on his back. "It's been over a week, buddy, and I'm not made out of glass!"

"What's that supposed to mean?" he said belligerently.

"It means you don't have to be so damn careful. You've proved that you're capable. It's gone onto your record. You've racked up more than enough sensitivity points for a bout of hot, grinding, unbridled sex." She straddled him, whipped off the tank top and shook her bare boobs in his delighted face. "So get to it, Mac. Satisfy my carnal lust."

The puppy chose that moment to join the romp. He jumped onto Mac's chest and licked everything his tongue came in contact with, which in short order became Mac's face. Mac lifted the squirming animal into the air with a sigh. "This isn't going to work."

"What about the wall in my foyer?" she asked.

He laid the puppy to the side, shaking with silent laughter. "I, um, thought that might be a bit too raw for your delicate sensibilities."

The puppy yipped excitedly and scampered away into her kitchen, tiny toenails clicking and skittering against the linoleum.

"Wrong." She clambered off him, rose to her feet, and shoved her sweatpants down. "There's nothing delicate about my sensibilities."

They came together in a tender fumbling haste. She clawed off his T-shirt, unbuckled his belt. They shoved his jeans down so that his magnificent erection sprang out, swaying heavily in front of him.

He fished a condom out of his jeans and sheathed himself in latex, too quickly for her liking. She'd wanted to run her hands over that hot, velvety club of male power and pleasure, but Mac was running the show with his usual high-handed style. No biggie. She knew she would get her chance to whip him into line. The struggle would be endless fun. Enough push and pull and laughter to last a lifetime.

He shoved her against the wall. The wild look in his eye made her chest tighten with excitement. He scooped his arm beneath her knee and jerked her leg up high, stroking his finger down her tender cleft.

"You're so wet and soft. You drive me crazy. I love you, Jane."

"I love you, too," she said shakily. "Please, Mac. Now."

He pushed himself inside her, shoving deep until his hips pressed against hers, until she was utterly filled. He scooped up her other leg and began the deep, plunging invasion that she craved. He rode her deep and hard, pinning her against the wall with the strength of his powerful body. She sobbed with pleasure at each heavy thrust.

"The wild beast is unleashed, baby. And you've got nobody to blame but yourself," he panted.

"Give me everything you've got, MacNamara," she said.

And with a groan of pure bliss, he did.

TOUCH ME

Chapter One

Tomorrow at four, tomorrow at four. Jonah's appointment was tomorrow at four. The thought looped through Tess Langley's mind with the annoying persistence of a commercial jingle, the only difference being the jangling, feverish edge to the tune.

Mrs. Vailstock had canceled, leaving her a blessed free hour, so there was no need to rush as she ticked off the points on her checklist: heating pad, fresh sheets, adjust the massage table for her next client, blankets, towels. She rummaged through the tape box until she found the whale songs, and lit a pink Love Dreams candle. Irene's favorites.

The busier she kept herself, the less liable she was to start mooning over Jonah Markham's storm gray eyes, his sensual lips, his unimaginably perfect body. Or writhing over the effect he had upon her. He left her tongue-tied, practically blithering. Thank God the service she provided for him didn't require her to speak much.

It wasn't just that he was gorgeous and built. Sports massage was one of her specialties, and she had many pro athlete clients with incredible bodies. Kneading their muscles was interesting from an aesthetic point of view, but had never thrown her into a tizzy of speechless lust before. No, Jonah Markham was special. Whenever she touched him, something magical happened. A tingling rush of enhanced sensory awareness, as if someone had slipped an aphrodisiac into her mug of organic green tea. For heaven's sake, he wasn't even due in today. It was stupid and unprofessional to fixate on a client. Particularly not a guy who ought to have "trouble" tattooed on his forehead. It had taken all her courage to get where she was right now, and would take another quantum leap to get where she wanted to go. What she did *not* need in her life was an arrogant, brooding, drop-dead gorgeous sex god who probably went through women the way he went through socks.

Concentrate, she told herself. She was so tired, and Irene Huppert was coming in at six, the compulsive talker with sciatica. Yay, hurray. She squirted grape seed oil into a bottle and personalized it with lemongrass and lavender essential oils, her mind racing. A guy like him could never be interested in her, at least not for long, and really, it was just as well, she told herself desperately. She didn't even have the energy to keep a cat, let alone invest in the care and feeding of a hungry male ego. And Jonah Markham was bound to have . . . a big one. So to speak.

So why couldn't she stop thinking about him?

Because he asked you out last week, airhead, whispered the little devil on her shoulder. Wonder of wonders. And the week before, and the week before that. At the beginning of his session, he'd turned his close-cropped dark head, and fixed his gaze upon her face like a hot gray tractor beam. "You married?"

Her mouth flapped uselessly for a moment. "Uh, no."

He didn't even blink. "Boyfriend?"

She fully intended to roll out her well-rehearsed, friendly-but-not-too-friendly "I'm not available" routine. It jammed, and all that escaped her was a strangled little "No." He gave a short, satisfied nod, and laid his head down, closing his eyes. At which point, she had seen the claw marks on his shoulders. Long and red and angry looking.

She'd stared in horrified fascination for almost a minute before she'd finally worked up the nerve to begin, very carefully. Those gouges had to hurt. Finally, she'd just shut her eyes to block them out.

As always, she'd been swept away by the spell of touching him, which left her woefully unprepared when she lifted her hands off his body, still soaring on a thunderous rush of unfamiliar endorphins, and heard, "Will you have dinner with me?"

She had to be dreaming. Hallucinating. She was speechless, rattled, blushing . . . and so incredibly tempted. Even if she ended up getting used and tossed away, she was willing to bet that being used by Jonah Markham would be one hell of a memorable experience.

So would the tossing away part, unfortunately.

She let out the trapped air in her lungs. "No," she said quietly.

His dark brows snapped together. "Why not?"

She fished around for a good brush-off, polite and yet forceful. Nothing floated to the surface of her brain but the raw, uncensored truth. *Because you've obviously just had wild crazy sex with a woman who's way more responsive and uninhibited in bed than I am.*

"I'm sorry, Mr. Markham, but we've run overtime, and Mr. Stillman is waiting." Her words sounded lame and flat. A pitiable evasion.

She was convinced that she would never see him again, but the next week he was back, right on time. And at the end of his massage, he asked the same question. The claw marks had faded away, but her memory of them had not. She refused again. Last week, he was back again, with dogged persistence in his eyes. Same question, same answer, same long, searching look that probed her motives, challenged her fears. She wondered if he would ask again tomorrow.

Which must mean, God help her, that she was actually beginning to consider it. She'd been depressed for days after seeing those claw marks, but she'd also lain awake nights wondering what exactly he'd done to that woman to make her react like that. Which led to a whole host of other fantasies, as uncontrollable as they were inappropriate.

Like, what might happen if she just bent over one day and kissed the supple, velvety skin at the curve of his neck, right where his hair was razored off in a sleek line. His neck was so thick and strong. Tense, badly in need of soothing, stroking.

The neck-kissing impulse was sparked by not just lust, but something that felt almost like tenderness. The alarming thought made her squirm. Tenderness? She didn't even know the guy. How pathetic and absurd to project her lonesome, love-starved fancies onto him. But the back of his neck still called to her. So deliciously . . . kissable.

He had surrendered the rigid armature of his muscles to her with such perfect trust, she had been startled and moved. Such a thing occurred more often with dancers, or practitioners of massage, yoga, or other bodywork. People who were used to exploring other dimensions of sensory awareness, who were accustomed to profound relaxation and trance states. It never happened with men like him. High-powered, cutthroat businessmen without a fanciful bone in their bodies. Men who never let down their guard, or dared to be vulnerable.

Vulnerable, my butt, she told herself. The only vulnerable one around here was Tess Langley, starry-eyed idiot, and the only thing she should allow herself to obsess about was saving up the money to open her studio. She didn't have the looks, the legs, or the wardrobe to be part of that guy's harem. She knew better than to try to be something she was not. Been there, done that, crashed and burned to a blackened hulk. From here on out, it was no-frills, no makeup, sensible shoes, what-you-see-is-what-you-get Tess.

She repeated that sobering resolution to herself, forcing herself to picture the kind of woman Jonah Markham usually dated. Tall and leggy, not like her shrimpy five foot two. Gym-toned, hard-bodied, not round and over-full in the chest and rear. Perfectly dressed and styled, like she'd tried so hard to be for Larry. All that effort. All in vain.

Forget it. Just say no. She knew how this movie would end. He would take what he could get and bore very quickly—but not quickly enough. Not before the damage was done. She'd just barely succeeded in piecing herself back together after the Larry debacle, and here she was, contemplating hurling all that carefully reconstructed self-esteem right through the plate glass window that was Jonah Markham.

Bet he's good in bed . . . The red-clad devil waggled her pitchfork as she chirped that thought into Tess's ear. *Good like Larry wasn't. Good like you've never imagined. Looks like he's had loads of practice.*

She was startled out of that disturbing but highly stimulating line of thought by a commotion up front. Lacey, the receptionist, was yelling. Someone was shouting back. A deep, resonant male voice.

Dear God. It was him. But he was Thursday, not Wednesday. This wasn't possible. She wasn't constitutionally capable of confusing that particular appointment. She hustled out of the back rooms, and sure enough, there he was, glaring down at Lacey over the receptionist's counter. His eyes flicked up to her, like chips of gray ice.

"What's wrong?" Tess demanded. "Did I make a mistake in the scheduling?" They both started to talk at once. Tess clapped. The explosive sound cut them off into a startled silence.

"People are getting massages! Keep your voices down! What is going on?" She jerked her chin at Lacey. "You first."

Lacey flounced her hair with her usual self-importance.

"Mr. Markham wants an emergency appointment! I explained to him that you're booked up, and he can wait till six if he wants Elsa, and he—"

"All I asked was if it would be possible to reschedule another one of your clients today," Jonah broke in icily. "Offer a free massage to whoever you reschedule, and I'll pay for it. Hell, offer them two."

"But she's *booked,* I already *told* you, and it's not our *policy* to—"

"Stop, Lacey!" Tess held up her hand and studied his face.

He looked tense and strained, his eyes hollow, his mouth white about the lips. He was hanging on by a thread. She knew that feeling all too well. She wished she knew him well enough to ask what was wrong.

Jonah let out a long, controlled sigh. "At the end of the day?" There was a tight, pleading edge to his voice. "After your last client?"

"No way am I staying late to lock up after you!" Lacey piped up. "And no way would Jeanette let a therapist stay in the center all alone with a client! I'll just call Jeanette right now, and she can deal with—"

"No," Tess said quietly. "Don't call Jeanette."

She knew how that would play. Jeanette would come thundering out of the back office. She would throw her weight around until Jonah was completely affronted. He would storm off and never come back.

She couldn't bear the thought of it.

Besides, she wanted to comfort him, soothe him, pet him until he felt better. Until the tension melted out of his face and body, until he purred with bliss. She was a pushover, a softie, a blithering idiot, but she was nudging Lacey out of the way and dialing Irene's number.

Lacey's painted eyes grew wide with outrage. "You're actually going to let him get away with bullying me?"

Tess waved her down. "Hello? Irene? It's Tess, at the

Multnomah Massage Center, and I . . . yes, I'm so glad I caught you at home. I just wanted to . . ." It took two minutes of false tries to trample on Irene's prattling monologue. "Irene, please let me finish. I've had an emergency . . . nothing terrible, but would you be kind enough to let me reschedule you for tomorrow at four? Oh, thanks . . . no. Chloe isn't the one who's going to be looking at that stenciling every day. You are. Tell me about it tomorrow, OK? Bye." She hung up, and shot a quick, guilty look at Lacey.

"That is, like, so totally unprofessional," Lacey hissed. "Jeanette is gonna have kittens when she finds out."

"Jeanette can fire me if she likes," Tess said, with forced bravado. She turned to Jonah. "You—" she sternly indicated a seat, "—wait quietly while I prepare the room. And Lacey, please pretend he's not there. No more yelling or rudeness. Is that clear?"

Lacey flipped her hair and pouted. Jonah sat and lifted his big shoulders in a meek little "who, me?" shrug.

The room was ready, but she went down her checklist, just to calm herself. She adjusted the table. Lavender and lemongrass weren't right for Jonah. She filled a bottle with almond oil, and added some sandalwood oil and just a touch of coriander. Her heart had to slow down before she marched out there, all calm and businesslike, and—

"You ready?"

She spun around and dropped the oil. "You scared me!"

"Sorry." He scooped up the bottle that was rolling toward him. "The receptionist from hell was making personal phone calls, so I—"

"Lacey is not a receptionist from hell." Tess snatched the oil out of his hand. "She is a very good receptionist. When treated nicely."

"I was perfectly nice," he growled. "I even offered her a big tip. What's with the candle?"

She remembered the hot pink, embarrassingly phallic candle, with "Love Dreams" scripted on it in pale, glowing wax. She lunged to blow it out. "Um . . . nothing. It was for Irene. My six o'clock."

"You could've left it burning." His deep voice made the fine hairs prickle on her neck. "I like love dreams as much as the next guy."

The room seemed breathlessly warm. "Go ahead and get ready," Tess murmured, sidling past him. "I'll be back in a few minutes."

When she stole back into the room a few minutes later, he was laid out between the sheets. No claw marks today, thank goodness.

She put oil on her hands, and smoothed them over his back, tracing ropy knots of tension with her fingers. He hissed in pain, his muscles twitching. "You're very tense," she said. "Did you get a chance to do those stretching exercises I recommended last week?"

"Too busy. Crazy week."

"Try to make the time," she urged. "They really will help."

"You're always scolding me." He twisted around, and his gaze swept over her as if that hideous white dress that Jeanette mandated was actually sexy. "But that's OK. I kind of like it."

She gaped at him. "I do not scold!"

"Next you'll tell me I'm a very bad boy and need to be punished. I'm already laid out on the table, ass-up. Go ahead. Smack me one."

Tess drew in a shaky breath. Suggestive comments were wildly inappropriate in the context of a therapeutic massage. She would be within her rights to stop the session.

It was the very last thing she wanted to do.

She cast around for the perfect response in their gentle game of deflect and evade. Something to keep him at arm's length, and yet not threaten their delicate equilibrium. She didn't want to drive him away. She desperately needed something sparkling and effervescent in her life, even if it were just a faraway fantasy. Life without weekly doses of Jonah would be intolerably drab and savorless.

She placed her hand between his shoulder blades and pushed him gently down. "I think you've had a very stressful day," she said softly. "And we are both going to forget that you just said that."

He was quiet as she spread oil across the quivering muscles in his shoulders with broad, circular strokes. "Sorry," he muttered.

"Shhh," she whispered.

It took longer than usual for him to calm down, but eventually the door between them opened up like Aladdin's cave. Everything she'd ever learned in massage school or technique workshops melted away, along with every other conscious thought. His body was a vast landscape for her to wander through, following pure instinct, raw feeling. Horizon upon horizon, wild and exotic and unknown.

She wanted to map them all.

Her voice floated to him from so far away that the words had no meaning. All he caught was the caressing tone in her husky alto voice. He had to hold the words in a containing cell in his blissed-out mind until he woke up enough to process the data.

He fished the words out of the containing cell when the fog cleared. It was just what she always said. *"Take a few minutes to come back before you get dressed. I'll be out front."*

How could such an innocuous statement sound so sexy? He swung his legs down from the table, sat up, and dropped his face into his hands. Massive boner, of course, but he was used to that by now.

He rubbed his face, and bit by bit, the painful details of his monumentally horrible day floated back to him. The early morning call about the heart attack. Granddad with an oxygen mask and tubes stuck in him, sniping at him from his hospital bed, telling him to get lost. His cousins John and Steve, staring at him from across the room with blatant loathing. And as if that wasn't enough, the apocalyptic scene in the restaurant with Cynthia three weeks ago had to come floating back, too. He'd have been better off not remembering.

Too bad he couldn't maintain the floating high that Tess's massages gave him, but he would have to abuse controlled substances to maintain that kind of buzz. Not his scene. He was doomed to keep both feet flat on the concrete. A chip off old Granddad's block.

The up side, of course, was that if the old bastard had enough energy to kick Jonah's ass out of his hospital room, then he must not be ready to die yet. Even if Granddad wouldn't speak to him or forgive him, he was still roaring like a steam engine, making noise, dominating his world. He allowed himself to be comforted by that.

He put his watch back on. She'd massaged him for almost an hour and a half. Yeah, she liked him for sure. He grinned as he pulled on his clothes, remembering how tense and awkward he'd been the first time he'd walked into the place. He'd only done it because his office staff had gotten together and bought him a six-massage package at the Multnomah Massage Center, and though they'd laughed it off as a gag gift, it was a pretty damn costly gag gift. It had gotten his attention, conscious as he was of exactly how much he paid them all. Besides, Eileen, his assistant, had seen to it that he got the real message, which was *"Dude, you are losing it, and you need to chill. Right now."*

Then his doctor told him that the headaches were due to muscle tension and the stomachaches were from the painkillers he took for the headaches. Yo, bozo. You're creating the perfect conditions for an ulcer.

Fine. Message received; everybody could stop beating the dead horse, already. He would get some freaking massages.

Then Tess had walked into the waiting room and called

out his name. Shaken his hand with her small, capable-looking hand. Looked him over with those big, tilted gold-green eyes. Asked him brisk, businesslike questions about his medical history, his headaches, his back pain. What a turn-on. Who'd have thought.

She was so pretty, in a subtle and yet luscious sort of way. With those generous tits, tightly constrained in the white dress that was clearly designed to discourage sensual thoughts while utterly failing to do so. Her Jennifer Lopez-esque ass, which he checked out thoroughly as he followed her into the back room. A few massages from that bodacious little number suddenly seemed like a very good idea.

It had taken him the entire first session just to get used to the concept of someone touching him for any reason other than to make him hot. Hah. Tell that to his cock. It had no clue.

Truth was, just lusting after his massage therapist wouldn't have been such a big deal. So what? He would just keep his boxers on and stay rigorously face down. It was what happened during the massages that blew his mind. She put her hands on him and *zing,* the world turned upside down. Since Granddad's business troubles, and the subsequent series of heart attacks, Jonah's stomach had been in knots, his lungs tight and constricted, his mind racing day and night. But when Tess touched him, his mind slipped loose of that frantically spinning hamster's wheel of anger and regret, frustration and guilt. It floated unexpectedly free, into a vast open space that he exhaled his whole self into, with a rush of relief so intense it almost made him want to cry. Though thank God, it had never come to that.

He was strung out on her. Look at him, running straight from the hospital to the massage center like a toddler running to his mommy to get his owie kissed. Throwing a goddamn tantrum in the waiting room, for Christ's sake. His out-of-control desperation was kind of freaky.

And his crush on Tess had gotten way out of hand, too. When he was all loosey goosey and dazzled from one of her massages, she looked like she was lit from within. Resplendent. The luminous, delicate flush on her lovely face, devoid of makeup. The wavy chestnut hair, wound into a braided bun so tight that he could never get a good sense of how long it was. Today, adorable fuzzy bits corkscrewed around her slender neck. Soft and tousled and sensual. Yum.

She kept blowing him off when he asked her out, but he couldn't seem to stop trying. To hell with dignity. The words just popped out of him. Whenever she leaned over him, he caught whiffs of her scent. Not like the nose-tickling, knock-you-on-your-ass Eau de Whatever that Cynthia drenched herself in. More like rain on a spring night. Cool, leafy. Lemon and mint, wood and water. Vanishing before he could pull enough into his lungs to satisfy himself, leaving him gasping for more.

And then there was the sweep of her eyebrows, with the little swirling snarl of darker hair marking the crest of the arch. The black, curling lashes. And her lips. Damn. His cock had just started to calm down to socially acceptable proportions, and he'd ruined it by picturing the crease down the middle of her plump lower lip, dividing it into two succulent, kissable pink cushions. He'd have to drape his jacket carefully over his crotch when he marched out front. As usual.

She was standing next to the Devil Receptionist from Mars, who was giving him the death-ray look. Time to bump back into reality.

The receptionist flipped her big hair and opened the appointment book. "Same time? Or do you anticipate any more *emergencies?*"

"Could I schedule an appointment for this weekend?"

"No way." Lacey was clearly delighted to thwart him. "Elsa could—"

"I am not interested in an appointment with Elsa," he snarled. He turned to Tess with the most coaxing, soulful puppy-dog look he could muster. "Couldn't you rearrange your schedule again? Like today?"

A rueful smile activated the little dimples at the corners of Tess's mouth. "It was a mistake, letting you get away with this. I've spoiled you rotten. Now there'll be no reasoning with you."

"Yeah," he agreed swiftly. "I'm completely ruined. So can you?"

She shook her head. "Not a chance. I won't even be here this weekend. I'll be working up at Cedar Hills Resort."

"All weekend? How much do they pay you for that?"

Lacey bristled in outrage. "None of your business!"

"Shall we put you down for the usual time?" Tess asked gently.

He nodded as he wrote out the check. Nothing more to be gained from talking to her while that extraterrestrial harpy looked on, but the thought of Tess giving massages at a resort planted an idea in his head.

He wandered out onto the street and turned it over in his head. Her car was parked across the street in front of a Starbucks. He would get a decaf, in honor of the fact that he'd just spent eighty bucks trying to relax, and let his plan develop while he waited for her to come out.

He got his coffee and checked out the surreal art that hung by his table. A painting of a floating, naked transparent guy with clouds inside him. New Age fluff, but it reminded him of himself during one of Tess's massages. Maybe she put him in a hypnotic trance. Some brain wave thing. He'd read articles about stuff like that, in health magazines that he found in the bathrooms of other people's beach houses. He imagined his body as a revolving galaxy of light, visited by a benevolent feminine entity with small, strong hands that glowed with life-giving heat. Yikes. He'd been catching too many late-night *Star Trek* reruns lately.

But being a relatively normal guy, and as such, having an

appropriately dirty mind, the next obvious question was, what would sex be like under such conditions?

Sexually, he was very skilled and aggressive. It was a game of conquest, a hot, sweaty duel, and orgasms were points he scored in the game. He liked to make his lovers have lots of them. That was how he won. And he wanted to win with Tess Langley. He wanted to kiss that luscious mouth, pop open the buttons on that kinky white dress, stroke and lick and suckle her until she screamed with pleasure. But as he stared at the naked floating guy, a suspicion began to form inside him.

The rules of the game as he knew it would be null and void in that magic landscape where he went with Tess. He would be brand-new, a bumbling beginner. Vulnerable and helpless.

The idea intrigued him as much as it alarmed him.

"Excuse me."

Tess stifled a squeak as she spun around. Her nerves couldn't take much more of this overstimulation. "Were you following me?"

"Just waiting." His voice was defensive. "That doesn't count as following. I have a business proposition, and I couldn't talk about it in front of your colleague. Let me buy you a drink. I'll tell you about it."

He waited patiently while she made repeated attempts to access that part of her brain that governed speech. Seconds ticked by. He frowned. "Got other plans? A date?" His eyes swept over her, taking note of the hideous white uniform under her jacket, the white shoes.

Date, hah. Just a half-formed plan to flop openmouthed on the couch and watch *Frasier,* or *Xena,* or whatever else she found channel surfing. Hardly a reason to not have a drink with the sexiest man she'd ever seen in real life. She shook her head. "No date."

"Great. There's a restaurant at the end of the block."

He got right to the point as soon as they were seated in the bar, and lucky for her, since she was too tongue-tied to handle chitchat.

"When you said you were working at a resort all weekend, it gave me an idea," he told her. "I want you to come up to my house at Cougar Lake, and do the same thing for me. Friday night."

"This Friday? For . . . you? But—"

"For my house party," he clarified. "I'm having people up this weekend, and I'd like to surprise them with something special."

She covered her confusion taking a nervous sip of her Dos Equis. "It doesn't sound very ethical," she said. "The MMC—"

"The MMC would never know. And it would be lucrative. I pay eighty bucks for a massage here. What percentage of that do you get?"

She hesitated, biting her lip.

He nodded, looking satisfied. "Exactly. I'll give you twenty-five hundred. A thousand a day, and five hundred for Friday night."

She was dumbfounded at the sum. "But that's . . ." She choked off the words *too much*. Such words didn't belong in the vocabulary of a future entrepreneur. "But I'm already scheduled to—"

"Get someone to cover for you," he cut in. "Get this famous Elsa who's so monumentally available to do it for you."

She set down her beer with a decisive thud. "Elsa is an excellent massage therapist," she said crisply. "Come to think of it, you might call her for your party. You would have no complaints if—"

"No. I want you." There was a bright, steely glint in his eyes.

Yeah, that's the problem, right there, she almost blurted.

"I don't think it would be a good idea," she said hesitantly. "I really don't like the idea of going behind my employer's back, and furthermore—"

"Four thousand." He gave her a winning smile.

She gasped. "But I . . . I wasn't bargaining with you! I can't—"

"I'll write you a check for two thousand now." He pulled out his checkbook. "I'll give you the rest when you get there on Friday night."

Her spine stiffened up, ramrod straight. "Money is not the point!"

He glanced up from the checkbook. "Money is always the point." His tone suggested that he was stating something painfully obvious.

Her chin lifted. "Not with me, it isn't."

And it wasn't. That was one of the vows she'd made when she left her old life behind. She'd left her old values, too. Or rather, the values that others had imposed upon her. Money would never rule her again.

Jonah studied her for a moment. He signed the check, ripped it out, and laid it on the bar, equidistant between their two beers. "So what is the point, then?" He sounded genuinely curious.

She stared at his jagged black signature. Two thousand dollars. Another two on Friday. With what she'd already saved, and a couple of loans, she'd be able to quit the MMC and open her studio right now.

She swallowed, and looked away. "I do strictly therapeutic massage," she said stiffly. "Going to the private home of a man I don't know seems to invite misunderstanding. You must know what I mean."

His sensual mouth curved. "Of course I know what you mean. I just get a kick out of watching you blush."

She leaped off the bar stool and backed away. "You know what? It's just exactly that sort of flirtatious, inappropriate comment that makes me nervous."

"Sorry, sorry," he said hastily. "Relax. My guests know what a professional massage therapist does and doesn't do. And so do I. I'm not inviting you to an orgy. Bring a friend, if it makes you feel better. Bring a squad of Ninja bodyguards. There's plenty of room." His expression was so winsome and contrite that her face ached to smile back. He put his finger on the check and pushed it toward her. Slowly. Inch by inch.

She looked away, flustered. "I have to think. And I have to see if someone can cover for me at Cedar Hills."

He fished a card out of his wallet and wrote two numbers on the back. "Home phone and cell phone. Call me any-time." He leaned forward and tucked his card and his check into the breast pocket of her denim jacket, ignoring the flinch and tremor that his touch provoked. "Take the check, too. Meditate on it." His eyes flicked down over her body. "I'm hungry. Can I buy you some dinner?"

She backed up another step, holding her purse in front of her.

His eyes gleamed with silent amusement. "Oh, yeah, I forgot. You've got something against having dinner with me. Wish I knew why."

"I don't have anything against you," she babbled, taking another step back. "I'm just not dressed for dinner, and I have to go. Right now."

"Hey. Tess."

The quiet force in his voice stopped her. She shot a ner-vous glance over her shoulder. "Yes?"

"I'm harmless," he said. "Really. I swear. A great big pussycat."

Pussycat. She imagined petting him, making him purr and stretch. Sinuous and sensual . . . and predatory.

"Yeah, right," she muttered. "Totally harmless."

She turned, and fled.

Chapter Two

"Yo, Tess. I just found your purse in the fridge. You going to tell your good buddy Trish what's up, or am I gonna have to nag?"

Tess looked up from her tepid mug of tea, and took the purse that Trish held out. The leather was clammy. "It's cold," she mumbled.

"Duh." Trish popped open her Diet Coke and sat down, fixing her roommate with an eagle-eyed stare. "So?"

Tess let the purse drop. "I got a business proposition today."

"So far, so good." Trish gave her an encouraging nod.

"From Jonah Markham. Remember the guy I told you about?"

"Oh, my God. The to-die-for handsome one who melts your brain?"

"The very one," Tess admitted.

Trish whistled. "How titillating. What's the proposition?"

Tess squeezed her eyes shut and braced herself for Trish's reaction. "That I go out to his house on Cougar Lake this weekend and give massages to his houseguests. For four thousand dollars."

Trish's cornflower-blue eyes widened. "Whoa! For four thousand bucks, I hope you're gonna give him a blow job, too."

Tess leaped up as if she'd been stung. "Trish! That's not funny!"

"So who's kidding?" Trish asked in a plaintive voice. "Come on, Tess, not even a hand job? With some of that perfumed oil you use? I can see it now, Mr. Pecs-R-Us with bedroom eyes, all tousled and ripped and bulging, just begging you to rub on his big, stiff—"

"You are incorrigible." Tess stomped into the kitchen and dumped the cooled tea into the sink.

Trish followed her in, undaunted. "That can't possibly sting you. You live like a nun, chica. It's high time you got some decent nooky. I'd pay four thousand bucks myself to get you some, if I could afford it."

Ignoring her was clearly not going to work. "Wasn't Tyler supposed to take you out on a dinner cruise tonight?"

"Not for another hour or so," Trish said cheerfully. "You're stuck with me, sweet pea. Let's discuss your outfit, shall we? You aren't going to wear the Vee Have Vays To Make You Talk monstrosity Jeanette makes you wear. Tell me that you're not."

Tess marched past her into the living room. "I haven't even decided if I'm going," she said stiffly. "And if I do, I'd better stick with the Vee Have Vays dress. It'll help me keep some professional distance and authority."

"Screw distance and authority. How about that flame-red stretch lace teddy that I got you for Christmas?"

"Trish." She gritted her teeth. "Read my lips. I am not going out there to have sex. No sex. None. Got it? If I go, it'll be for the money."

"Money's great, but money *and* sex are better," Trish pointed out.

Tess pretended not to hear. "With that four thousand, I could open my studio without making any . . . unacceptable compromises."

"Like asking your folks for help?"

Tess winced. "I'd only rather be dipped in boiling lead."

The phone rang. They stared at it, then at each other. "Speak of the devil," Trish said. "Whenever your family is mentioned, she calls."

"I wasn't the one who brought them up," Tess snapped. "Thanks a lot, Trish." She sighed and picked up the phone. "Hello?"

"Well, well, well. This is my youngest daughter, isn't it? I'm not quite sure, you see. I've forgotten what your voice sounds like."

Tess rolled her eyes at Trish. "Hello, Mom. How's everybody?"

"Oh, so so. We miss you terribly. Daddy wants you to know that your job is still open, honey bunch. Anytime you come to your senses."

Tess's stomach knotted with an old, familiar pain. "I'm not coming back, Mom."

"Oh, Tessie, honey, when are you going to grow up? My headaches are terrible since you left, and Larry's just pining away—"

"Oh, please. He can't possibly be pining, since he never cared about me in the first place. I was just the boss's daughter, that's all."

"Tess! That is unkind, and untrue! I know Larry as well as I know my own children! He's putting a brave face on it, but everybody knows you broke his heart, running off like you did. But know what I think, hon? I think there's still hope. If you came back, Larry would—"

"You don't get it, Mom." The weariness that Jonah's massage had dispelled crashed down upon her. She flopped onto the couch.

"What I don't get, darling, is why you're being so obstinate. What am I supposed to tell my friends? That my smart little girl, who did so well in business school and had such a lucrative career ahead of her, to say nothing of a dream of a fiancé, just threw it all away to work in a massage parlor? It's barely respectable! What's that, Bill? . . . oh, that's funny. Daddy says next you'll be reading Tarot cards!"

"Nothing wrong with that." Tess's words cut off her mother's tinkling laughter. "Some of my friends make a nice living reading Tarot."

Tess squeezed her eyes shut as she waited out the cold silence.

"You are deliberately missing my point, Tessie," her mother said.

"Therapeutic massage takes talent and training. And I'm very good at it." Tess felt like she was running a scratchy, worn-out promo tape for some unwanted product. "It's a very respectable career choice."

"Maybe for some people, but not for a Langley! You should be working in the family firm, like you planned ever since you were little!"

"Like *you* planned," Tess said, though she knew it was futile.

"You're just doing this to upset me, aren't you? You should get therapy, dear, really you should. Because the person you're actually punishing is yourself. You're barely scraping by. You work so hard you didn't even have time to come home for Melissa's birthday party!"

"Did she get the present I sent?" Tess tried to deflect her mother's relentless trajectory, to no avail.

"The point is that your current profession is a financial dead end compared to working for Daddy. Oh, Daddy just made Larry CEO, by the way. And if you come home, Daddy will give you a raise of—"

"I'm opening my own massage studio," Tess blurted.

There was another gelid silence. "I beg your pardon?"

"I've already got a client base," Tess said desperately. "I get lots of referrals. I'm very confident that it'll go well."

"Opening your own studio?" Her mother repeated the words as if she couldn't quite grasp them. "And where did you get the capital?"

"I've been scrimping and saving," Tess said, crossing her fingers.

Trish made a questioning gesture, asking if Tess wanted her to leave the room. Tess shook her head and waved her back down onto the couch. "This is something I've wanted for a long time, Mom."

The silence on the other end of the line made her want to scream.

"Well," her mother said. "I suppose there's nothing more to say."

"You could wish me luck," Tess suggested softly.

"I'm sure you'll need it. Good-bye, dear."

The line went dead. Tess lay the phone down, chin quivering.

All teasing was gone from Trish's face. "You've boxed yourself into a corner, chica. You're gonna need that gig out on the lake, now. She's for sure gonna check up on you to see if it's true. She never lets up."

Tess let the phone drop to her lap. "It'll be true," she said in a small voice. "With that money, I can do this on my own. I know it."

"Of course you can." Trish got up and rummaged through the clutter on the phone table until she found Tess's address book. She sat down next to Tess, plucked the phone off her lap and dialed.

"What are you doing?" she asked suspiciously.

"Helping you. You're too rattled to do this by yourself. You, like, just refrigerated your purse. Oh, hi, Elsa? Yeah, this is Trish, Tess's roommate. I'm her personal secretary tonight. Are you free to cover for her at Cedar Hills this weekend? . . . Yeah? Really? Oh, awesome. I'll tell her. Yeah, she really owes you one. Thanks, Elsa."

Trish hung up, her face glowing with triumphant satisfaction. "The coast is clear! Now you've just gotta call up Mr. Deltoids and tell him you'd be thrilled to get paid four thousand big ones for the privilege of running your hands all over his gorgeous bod."

Tess fished Jonah's card and check out of her pocket, and stared at them. She picked up the phone with cold, shaky fingers. "I need privacy for this call," she said faintly. "I'm going into the bedroom."

Trish bounced with glee. "Take all the privacy you need, cupcake!"

"Oh, stop it," she said halfheartedly. "This is a business thing."

Trish's voice followed her into the bedroom. "Sure it is, chica. Hey. Promise me you'll at least pack the red lace teddy. Pretty please?"

"Enough!" She slammed the door, and stood for a moment in the dark room, clutching the cordless phone. She fingered Jonah's card as she sank down onto her bed. Weak in the knees. Scared to death.

But it wasn't Jonah she was afraid of. Not really. All alone in the darkness, it was easier to admit to that what really terrified her was her own aching hunger for magic, for sensuality, for something real and shining. A real life. Maybe even . . . a real love.

That was why she'd run away from Larry, the picture perfect fiancé who had made her feel so small, she'd almost disappeared. It was why she had run from her suffocating family, and the lucrative job that she hated. She had been running toward a romantic dream of joy and fulfilment. It was that dream that made her so vulnerable. Jonah Markham shocked all of her intense romantic longings to life, along with knee-trembling physical desire. A devastating combination.

She wandered over to her dresser and flipped on the light, unbuttoning the white dress with a sigh of relief. The cheap synthetic fabric did not breathe. She gave her body a long, critical look in the mirror, and rummaged through her top drawer until she found the gift box that held the red lace teddy Trish had given her. It had been a while since she'd tried it on. It was time for another look.

She struggled out of the rest of her clothes, and pulled the fragile thing on, looking at herself from all angles. Wow. It barely covered her nipples with scalloped red lace, leaving the entire bulging top of her bosom bare. She struck a pose, and tried to look sultry. She looked almost aggressively sexy. It made her think of—oh, no. Please, no.

She tried to shake away the memory, but it had a will of its own. It rose up in minute, painful detail. That day in the department store fitting room, when her mother had tried to persuade her to consider breast reduction surgery. *"Really, hon, D cup breasts are ridiculous for a girl your size. They look disproportionate. Like you're trying to draw attention to yourself. Larry agrees with me, you know. And such a big bosom gives the impression that you're overweight, when you're really not. Not that much, at least."*

She put her hands on her breasts, covering them, and willed the memory away with all her strength. She was a different person from that luckless, stomped-upon, past Tess. She had recreated herself. And her bosom was just fine exactly the way it was, thank you very much.

She peeled the teddy off, carefully avoiding the sight of her own naked body. She yanked on an old, wilted flannel nightshirt, but sensual images kept creeping back into her mind. Herself in the red lace teddy, thrusting out her boobs as if she were fiercely proud of them. An arch in her back worthy of a Playboy bunny. And Jonah, on his knees, all bulging muscles and bedroom eyes, begging her to rub on his big, stiff . . . hold it. Don't do it, don't go there, don't lift that towel, her rational self pleaded. But the red-clad devil just used her little pitchfork to snag the edge of Jonah's imaginary towel, and flung it off him with a shrill cackle.

She imagined him stark naked. Staring up at her with that

hot, dark, no-turning-back look in his eyes. His body, hers to please herself with. A heaving ocean of pleasure and danger. She wanted to fling herself into it. Her lower body tightened with a restless ache that stole her breath, that made her want to whimper and squirm and press her legs together. This feeling was unfamiliar, almost frightening.

She had to keep in mind that she was no red-hot love goddess in bed. Larry had made that very clear. She was a good listener, she baked great brownies, and she gave unbeatable backrubs, but sex with her was like trying to light a fire with a wet match. She had counted herself lucky if she could get through it without too much discomfort.

And she would just die if she had to see that look of polite disappointment on Jonah Markham's face. Better a lifetime of celibacy.

She needed to think positive, to concentrate on her strengths, not her weaknesses. To remember how great it would be to open her own studio, to achieve autonomy, independence, success. To follow through on her own dreams and plans, and no one else's. To prove to her family, once and for all, that she was capable of making it on her own.

Nothing was going to stop her. Certainly not a silly spasm of lust.

Braced by that hopeful thought, she picked up the phone.

Four thousand bucks. Ouch. He'd officially lost his mind.

Jonah let himself into his apartment and dropped the takeout Chinese on the table. It wasn't that he couldn't afford it. He had plenty of money. He was just appalled at his own reckless extravagance. Just one more example of the unnerving desperation that Tess inspired.

Then again, the weekend with Cynthia at Lake Tahoe had cost a lot more than that, and he hadn't even come home relaxed. He winced, imagining what Granddad would've said if he'd seen the Lake Tahoe credit card bill. Granddad believed that frugality was a virtue. Too bad Jonah's cousins Steve and John, who were driving Granddad's company into the ground, didn't adhere to that philosophy. Dickheads.

Oh, fuck 'em. Why ruin his mood thinking about those brain-dead bozos when he could think about Tess instead? Her white dress had haunted him all the way home. The way it strained across her chest made him want to rip open those buttons, rub his face against that bulging cleavage, licking and kissing like his life depended on it.

She was so self-contained and mysterious, he couldn't predict what she'd be like in bed. His fantasies morphed and changed so often that he'd run the entire gamut. Maybe beneath that shy, subtle exterior, she was a hot little nympho sex fiend. What a concept; Tess astride him and riding hard, her flushed, beautiful face flung back, moaning in a rising tempest of pleasure, her wet opening clutching his cock with each stroke. Or maybe she was the sweet, mellow, earth mother type, hugging him tenderly and making soft, encouraging sounds as he rocked his hips, sliding lazily in and out. Relaxing and delicious.

The phone rang, and he knew with every cell in his body that it was Tess. He lunged for it, and stopped. Forced himself to wait, like a teenage girl afraid to seem too eager. Two rings. Three, and he couldn't take it anymore. He snatched it up. "Hello?"

"Hello. Is this Mr. Markham?"

A wave of anticipation made him dizzy. "Hi, Tess. Call me Jonah."

"Oh. Hi. How did you know it was me?"

"I've memorized your voice." What an understatement. Her low, golden voice brushed over his nerve endings like her hair would brush over his body if it were loose. Feathery, silky, sliding, soft. Like a kiss.

She hesitated, and he forced himself to wait. He didn't dare rush her. So far, the eager, panting puppy routine had gained him nothing.

"I just wanted to tell you that I'd, uh, like to take you up on your offer. If it's still open," she said hesitantly.

"Oh, excellent." He wanted to whoop with triumph. "It's about an hour and a half from the city. What time can you be there Friday?"

"Well, my final appointment is three o'clock, since I was planning to head up to Cedar Hills, so—"

"So you could be there by six." Excitement roughened his voice.

He sensed her sudden caution in her long pause. *Chill out, bonehead.*

"If you like," she murmured.

If he liked. Hah. If she only knew. "Let me give you directions."

He managed to dictate directions to his place and say good night without blurting out anything inappropriate or otherwise making an ass of himself. He had to keep reminding himself that she hadn't agreed to wild and crazy sex. She hadn't even agreed to a date. He had no reason to hope that he might get lucky.

Of course, he almost always did, but Tess Langley was unlike any woman he knew. The usual statistical norms didn't apply with her.

He knew that she was attracted to him. He'd seen it in her eyes. She got flustered and confused, she blushed often, she forgot what she was saying, all the signs were there. But she never flirted. He didn't know how long it had been since a woman had completely stonewalled him. He threw out lure after lure, and she just brushed them aside with her shy, mysterious smile, making him feel foolish and needy and obvious. And then she put her hot, strong, sorceress's hands on him and whisked him off to never-never land.

Weird. The massages weren't sexual, but they were so much more intimate than the sex he'd had lately with Cynthia. Sex with Cynthia was sweaty and pounding and highly athletic, but not particularly intimate. He always finished feeling like he'd played a really demanding set of racquet-ball. To say nothing of those fucking nails. He had to hold her down on the bed at all times to keep from getting hurt. Having to apply antiseptic ointment after sex got old really fast.

Tess's nails were short, buffed to a delicate pink glow. He wanted to kiss each one. And her lips, that same soft blush pink. She had him thinking about romance, enchantment. Not racquetball. Or Bactine.

Time to get that excess oil off his skin. He wandered into the bathroom and turned on the shower. He tossed away his clothes and got underneath the hot, pounding spray, specu-lating about the hidden details of her stunning body as he sudsed up with shower gel. He'd seen the perfect slender an-kles, graceful, rounded calves, and cute, dimpled knees. Then the skirt defeated him. He bet her thighs were sweet and soft and rounded, like her phenomenal ass. And she had a great belly, plump and Marilyn Monroe-ish. He would love to see her in low-slung jeans with a too-short tank top strain-ing over her breasts, and that cute belly pooching out a little, just begging to be nuzzled.

Oh, hell, if he was going that way, he might as well go to the end of the line. He scooped up some lather and took him-self in hand with a sigh of surrender. A guy had to do what a guy had to do if he wanted a hope in hell of sleeping tonight.

Forget the top, the jeans, the kinky white dress. He wanted her stark naked, standing in front of him. He would lounge in a chair, throbbing cock in hand, pumping himself slowly as she turned, arching and undulating. Showing him all the dips and curves and sweet mysteries of her body. Plump breasts that would be so soft and heavy in his hands. Nipples puckered and hard, aching for his mouth.

He would tell her to change position. Widen her legs, arch her back, lift her arms, toss her hair. Put her leg up on the chair, bend over and show him that sweet, round ass, all open and ready for him. The shadowy cleft, the crimson lips of her sex. He beckoned her closer, and the fantasy split into Version A and Version B. He couldn't decide between them. In Version A, she sank to her knees, green-gold eyes glinting flirtatiously up through long dark lashes, and gripped his cock in her strong, slender hands. Then she took him into her mouth, sucking him, taking all of him, deep and hot and wet. Fantastic. The image blurred and segued seamlessly into Version B, seconded by his pumping hand, his ragged breathing. She straddled his legs and very slowly sank down until the head of his cock nudged delicately into her wet, swollen folds, probing deeper and deeper, sinking lower until he was buried inside her. He would grip her hips, right on the lush curve, and cut loose, pounding himself heavily into her moist depths. Deep and hot and faster, faster . . . oh, God. The orgasm pulsed through him. He stood there for a long time, head flung back under the stream of water. Weak-kneed, sucking air, sputtering out water.

He turned off the water, hoping only that this exercise in self-indulgence had cleared his head enough to start coming up with a plan.

Damn. A house party. It was going to be tricky, to make his lie into a truth at such short notice.

To hell with it. A solution would come to him. That was his genius, finding solutions to problems. More important, and more fun, was to plan the menu. He had to schedule a trip to the gourmet grocery. Order the pastry from that kick-ass fabulous bakery next to his office. And he had to give some serious thought to the wines, too.

It all had to be perfect for her.

The sky was streaked with sunset pink when Tess peered for the last time at the directions taped to her dashboard, and made the turnoff into the driveway. She drove down a narrow road through towering pines and firs. She saw the glimmer of lake water, then the house, and was abruptly sure she'd gotten the right place.

It was a simple, angular place that blended harmoniously with its surroundings. Larger than it appeared, a subtle, weathered color like the rocks at the lakeside, it had a deep terrace and picture windows looking out at the lake and Mt. Hood. The only vehicle was a black Ford pickup, which seemed odd. Maybe his guests were late.

She got out and looked around, enchanted. The trees that framed the lake seemed at first glance to be an impenetrable dark wall, but when she looked deeper, she glimpsed vaulted depths, vast inner spaces. A fragrant mystery, redolent with tree resin, wood, and water.

The lake lapped tenderly against pebbles and tree roots that descended right down into the water. She saw no neighbors, no powerboats. The slosh and gurgle of the little waves was sensual, almost hypnotic. She gazed at the perfect reflection of the mountain in the lake water, blazing with wild colors and rippling in the soft breeze.

It was so beautiful, her throat tightened and her eyes stung. Nature beckoned to her with its savage allure. It didn't pretend to be anything. It had nothing to prove. It had no need to impress or placate or convince. It just was what it was, with serene indifference. Complete unto itself. Dear God, how she wished she could be like that.

The screen door squeaked. Usually when she was awestruck and torn open by the beauty and mystery of the ocean, or a sunset, or the stars, the feeling diminished when another person walked into it.

Jonah didn't diminish it. He deepened it.

She turned, composing herself. He stood on the porch, dressed in jeans and boots and a dark gray sweatshirt. They stared at each other.

"Hi," she said.

He nodded. "Glad you made it OK. Any problems?"

She shook her head. Social custom now dictated that she climb the steps, shake his hand, say polite, formulaic things, but the program wouldn't run. The screen in her mind stayed blank, cursor blinking.

He was so handsome. The sharp, austere planes of his face were warmed by the sunset's fiery glow. The jutting cheekbones, the shadows beneath his eyes. He looked wary. Apprehensive.

The place was silent but for the immense rustling of wind in the trees. Too silent. No laughter or talking from inside. No music.

"Have the rest of your guests not arrived yet?" she asked.

His eyes flicked away. He looked up at the sky, down at his feet, and came down the porch stairs, seizing her massage table and suitcase. He carried them up to the door, beckoning her to follow with a jerk of his chin. "Come on in. Let me get you something to drink."

The front room was dominated by picture windows and a flagstone fireplace. It segued into the kitchen at the back, with a rustic table dividing the two spaces. Delicious food smells wafted out of it.

No sign of anyone, no purses, suitcases, coats, voices. Nothing.

"Where are your guests?" she demanded.

His face looked tense with apprehension. "Uh, that's something I have to discuss with you. They, uh . . . canceled on me."

"Canceled?" Her jaw sagged.

"Yeah. Something came up."

She was bewildered. "But you should've called me. Obviously you'll want to reschedule if they couldn't—"

"No." He shook his head slowly.

"No?" Her voice rose to a terrified squeak.

"Nothing's changed. It's just that instead of giving massages to a whole bunch of people, you'll give them all to me."

She backed toward the door, pulling against the palpable tug of his hungry, possessive gaze. "You lied to me," she accused.

He scooted in front of her, blocking her flight to the door. "No, I didn't. I just—"

"I can't possibly stay here alone with you!"

"Don't worry about the money," he said. "The deal stands. I prefer not to share you anyway. As far as I'm concerned, it's for the best."

"I don't give a damn about the money. I'm not comfortable with this at all." She hated the way her voice quivered, the color rising in her face. She yanked open her purse and rummaged for her wallet. "I *hate* being lied to. Here, take back your goddamn check—"

Condoms exploded out of her purse and scattered across the floor. Over a dozen of them. All different brands and colors.

Jonah stared down at them, back up at her. A grin lit up his face as he crouched down and started gathering them up. "Wow. Talk about high expectations."

Tess dropped to her knees and wrenched the condoms out of his hands, shoving them into her purse. "These are not mine," she hissed. "My roommate plays practical jokes. I'm going to kill her, I swear to God."

Jonah plucked one off the floor and examined it. "This one glows in the dark," he remarked. "Very cool."

She snatched it from him. "Trish dies. And I am out of here."

She lunged for the door, yelping as his arms closed around her from behind in a gentle but implacable embrace. "Wait, Tess. Please."

"Let go of me." Her whole body vibrated with the electrical charge of contact with his body. It was such a hot, shivery rush, she almost burst into tears. She fought against a surge of blind panic.

"I will, I swear, in just a second. Calm down and listen. Please."

She twisted until she could see his eyes. So pale and penetrating. They saw too much. She couldn't bear it. "Talk fast," she whispered.

"First, let me apologize. I really wanted this, and I put it together at the last minute. That's why my guests fell through—"

"So you admit it," she challenged him. "You lied. When you lured me up here, there was no house party. You made it all up, didn't you?"

"There was a firm intention to organize one," he protested. "It just turned out that my friends had plans. I didn't mean to mislead you. I'm sorry if the situation is other than you anticipated, but I'll do everything in my power to make you feel comfortable. I swear, I'll be so good."

She glanced down at the thick, steely forearms that were wrapped across her chest. "Then why are you manhandling me?"

"To keep you from running, of course," he said patiently. "At least stay for dinner. I cooked this whole elaborate meal, just for you."

"You can cook?" She twisted to look at him again, startled.

"Yes. I'm a very good cook. And I've got a bottle of Chianti breathing on the table." His voice was soft with pleading. "Call your roommate, tell her the phone number, give her directions, have her call you every hour on the hour to make sure your virtue's still intact. Call your mother, call whoever you want. Please, Tess. You're safe here."

"You can let go of me now," she said quietly. "I won't bolt."

He released her with obvious reluctance, but he didn't step back. His body remained in contact, his heat kissing the surface of her body.

"You know, my colleagues warned me about you today," she said. "They say you're trouble. Too intense. That you've fixated on me."

"Maybe." His voice was elaborately light. "But you don't need them to tell you what to do. You can decide for yourself, right, Tess?"

She couldn't help but smile at his craftiness. That wily bastard instinctively knew just what buttons to push.

He smiled back, his eyes still wary. "You'll stay for dinner?"

"Just dinner," she murmured. "Then I'll see how I feel."

His face lit up with relief. He poured her a glass of wine and pressed it into her hand. "I'll go finish up the food, then. Call your roommate, like I said. It'll make us both feel better." He indicated the phone table near the door.

Trish picked up on the first ring. "Chez d'Amour."

"Trish, I suggest you enjoy your evening, because it's going to be your last," she hissed.

"Well, if it isn't the love goddess herself. How's it going, chica?"

"There is no house party! It's just him and me and a bottle of wine! And what on earth possessed you to fill my purse with condoms?"

Trish clucked. "As if! No way would I let my precious Tess go off on a provocative weekend massage-a-thon with a hot sexy love god without stocking you up with latex! I mean, like, duh!"

"Trish, damn it, I—"

"Friends don't let friends have unsafe sex, Tess," Trish lectured.

"But I'm not here for sex!" she shouted.

There was a stifled snort of laughter from the kitchen behind her.

She slammed the phone down and marched toward Jonah, her arms folded across her chest. She glared at him until he turned around with a nervous, what-have-I-done-now? look on his face.

"Why is it that every single person in my life assumes that I don't know what's best for me?" she demanded.

Jonah stirred something bubbling in a gleaming pot. "I'm not touching that one with a ten-foot pole."

"That's the smartest thing you've said so far," she observed.

His eyes gleamed with sly humor. "That's just because I don't know you well enough yet," he amended. "As soon as I do, I'll let you know what's best for you. In great detail. You can count on it."

She tried not to smile, but it was a losing battle. "You just had to ruin it, didn't you? Just couldn't resist, huh?"

"Nobody's perfect." An answering smile spread over his face; something fluttered inside her. His warmth pulled at her.

He felt it, too. His smile faded, and he took a step toward her. Something sizzled and popped in the pan behind him. He spun with a muttered curse and did something with the spatula.

"You're distracting me," he said. "Why don't you take that glass of wine and go out and watch the sunset fade off the mountain? By the time the colors are gone, dinner will be ready."

She looked out the window. The mountain had faded from pink to orange. She took another sip of wine. "OK," she murmured.

Jonah stirred the polenta with one hand, and roasted the sweet red pepper over the gas flame with the other. He felt off balance and weird. The only way to keep her here was to assure her that he had no lustful designs on her luscious bod, and lying made him nervous. He wasn't the devious type.

Usually disarming honesty mixed with beguiling charm was his winning formula. But he'd never encountered so much resistance before, and he'd never wanted anything so badly.

How strange, to listen to himself promising so earnestly to be good, while the rest of him stood by laughing its head off at the load of bullshit he was shoveling. He couldn't wait to get his hands on her. She was drinking her first glass of wine, at least, the horny bastard inside him noted. A great first step.

The fucking polenta was lumping up because he didn't have enough hands to stir it constantly. Like an idiot, trying to do three things at once so he could get on with the business of seducing her. He craned his neck as he stirred, struggling to see if she was still on the porch. He wished he could go watch the sunset with her, but this meal was too important. The mushrooms were ready, the parm was under the broiler, the cream for the chocolate soufflé needed whipping.

This grasping intensity wasn't like him. It dismayed him, but there wasn't a damn thing he could do about it. A beast had reared up out of the black lagoon of his subconscious, puffing out its chest and demanding its way, a thing with no manners, no self-control, no scruples. It wanted what it wanted, and since it wasn't acquainted with the concept of delayed gratification, it was therefore capable of fucking his chances of getting a massage or getting laid, either one.

He peeled the blackened skin carefully off the peppers, his mind considering and abandoning various half-formed strategies for controlling the situation. A delicious meal was the best he could come up with. He resolved to project an air of total harmlessness. A goofy, sort of feckless vibe. He had to seem awkward, anxious. It shouldn't be too damn hard. Put her off her guard, make her think, oh, yeah, I can handle this clown with one hand tied behind my back.

The blackened skin peeled smoothly away from the brightly colored flesh of the roasted pepper beneath. It had rendered up its crunchy stiffness to the searing flame, had gone voluptuously soft and lax. He sliced it into strips, dropped them onto the pool of olive oil and slivered garlic waiting on the plate. Swirled them till they were coated with oil, soft and moist and glistening. Some shredded basil on top, and that part of his seduction spell would be good to go.

Tess sipped her wine as she strolled down the twisting path that led into the forest. It was utterly dark. If she ventured inside, she could lose herself. The thought of a forest big enough, wild enough to lose herself in sent a thrill of excitement through her.

It stirred a buried memory. That trip, to see the redwoods with her parents, when she was ten. Long-forgotten details spread out like ripples through her mind. She had stared up at the enormity of those ancient, kingly trees, awestruck, and then tried to slip out of earshot of her mother's constant, anxious harping. Just far enough so she could hear the huge silence that embraced an infinity of tiny, harmonious sounds; rustling and quivering and chittering. Her ears strained for it.

She'd sneaked almost far enough to hear it when all hell broke loose, and she was hauled back to shrill, hysterical lecturing. *Stinging bugs and snakes . . . lost in the woods and wander for days . . . broken leg and starve to death . . . my poor nerves, where's my medicine. Look through my purse, my hands are trembling!*

Then it was back to the car, to look at the redwoods safely ensconced behind childproof auto-lock windows. *Sit straight in your seat and get your nose off the window, Tessie, there are* germs!

But she had never forgotten that moment of almost breaking free. That was how she felt right now. Something inside her was struggling to emerge, gasping for breath, for life. She drifted closer to the darkness of the trees. No one was here to shove her into a car with childproof windows. Nothing could hold her back, no one could save her, no one could stop her. She could do anything. The hugeness of her freedom crashed over her like a wave. Terrifying and wonderful.

Time was measured only by gradations of fiery light on the mountain. It faded slowly to softer and softer shades of mauve, dusty pink, violet. The dream of violet faded. The colorless shadows of twilight embraced her. The screen door squeaked. Tess turned away from the mystery of the trees and watched his dark silhouette move toward her. She sensed that he was nervous. Wary.

As well he should be. He had lied to her and manipulated her, and she did not owe him a damn thing. She could always throw his check back in his face. She didn't need to worry about pleasing him, or be anxious about offending him. Let him sweat to please her. Let him fret about not offending her.

She couldn't see his eyes in the dark. He was as impenetrable as the dark trees, yet she knew his beautiful body by heart. Muscle and sinew and bone and skin. She had absorbed him through her hands. In a way, he was already hers, and she wanted what was hers. A longing as sharp and urgent as the cry of an eagle in a vast, empty sky.

"Dinner is, uh, ready," he said hesitantly.

She took a deep breath of the fragrant evening air. The old Tess would have said something grateful and appreciative about him going to the trouble of cooking just for her.

The new Tess just took a leisurely sip of wine, and smiled.

"Good," she said. "I'm hungry."

Chapter Three

The dinner table left her speechless.

Candles illuminated a lavish culinary array that was ridiculous for two people. An earthenware crock of polenta with exotic sautéed mushrooms on top. Eggplant parmigiana, the golden mozzarella that topped it still bubbling. Roasted peppers adorned with fragrant shreds of basil. Crusty Italian bread, three different kinds of cheeses. Tender salad greens, baby spinach, watercress, endive. A heap of artichoke hearts, with a ramekin of melted butter nestled among them. Tantalizing odors made her head swim, her mouth water, her knees weak. It had been eight hours since she'd eaten a cheese sandwich.

"It looks incredible," she said. "It makes me want to cry."

"It's all simple stuff, really. Quickie recipes, except for the parm, and I put that together last night."

His casual tone was belied by the gleam of satisfaction in his eyes. She laughed at him, pointing an accusing finger. "You're patting yourself on the back for scoring points, aren't you?"

His lips twitched. "Maybe. We'll see. You haven't tasted it yet."

"Go ahead," she conceded. "Fifty bonus points for Jonah."

He made a move to refill her wineglass, and she put her hand over it, stopping him. "Do you want a massage tonight?" she asked.

His eyes flashed hungrily. "God, yes, if I can get one."

"Then I shouldn't have any more wine."

He frowned. "Don't be ridiculous. If you're too buzzed to give me a massage, I'll have only myself to blame. Let's be informal, OK? Otherwise I'll get tense and crabby, and the massages will be useless."

She lifted her chin. "You're a fine one to be making pronouncements and setting conditions."

The frown faded from his face. He looked uncertain. "True. But you're hungry, and we're celebrating. Have some wine, Tess. Please."

Slowly, she took her hand off the glass. The low gurgle of the liquid swirling into the gleaming bulb of glass was as tender and intimate as a kiss. He poured himself a glass, and set the bottle down.

They stared at each other in mutual shyness. "I've never met a man who can cook like this," she told him.

He swirled his wine around in his glass and took a sip. "I decided a few years ago that I needed a hobby, or I was going to turn into my grandfather. A workaholic steam engine with no life. I like food, so cooking was the obvious choice. And like you said, it earns me points."

"You made all this food just for me?"

He looked away from her, embarrassed. "Yeah," he said gruffly.

She fought the feeling, but everything he did, every word he said drew her deeper into his net. How sweet of him, to try so hard to please, with such attention to detail. She was utterly charmed.

"I decided to play it safe tonight, just in case you were a vegetarian, but I've got fresh steaks and fresh salmon fillets in the fridge. I brought along my kitchen pots of fresh herbs, and I've got pasta, and veggies, and six different kinds of cheese. I'll plan the menu around your preferences, of course. Whatever, you know, turns you on." He looked suddenly awkward, and shot her a crooked, apologetic smile. "So? Any dietary restrictions that I should know about?"

She was dazed by the variety, accustomed as she was to a diet of sandwiches, toast, fruit, yogurt, and Lean Cuisines. "No restrictions," she said. "It all sounds wonderful. I'll eat anything." The tense, meaningful silence that followed her words made them seem provocative, and she rushed on, blushing. "I do try not to eat too much chocolate, even though I love it. But that's my only restriction."

His eyes slid over her appreciatively. "You don't look like you need to restrict anything. You look perfect. And lucky for you, because there's a hot chocolate soufflé with fresh whipped cream for dessert."

"Oh, God," she said weakly.

"I didn't make it," he hastened to admit. "I bought it at the Sensual Gourmet Bakery. I haven't mastered pastry yet. Here, start with some peppers. They're good spooned over bread . . . like this."

She was a goner at the first bite. The peppers melted in her mouth, their sweetness set off by the spicy tang of the fine olive oil, the sensual hint of garlic, all soaked into the savory hot bread. She closed her eyes to savor it with a moan of pleasure, abandoning herself.

When she opened her eyes, his eyes were glowing with hot excitement. "God, I love it when you do that."

"Do what?" she asked nervously.

"Give in to pleasure. Wow. Here, have some more. Do it again."

She tried not to giggle and blush and slide under his spell, but she was failing, she was falling. The wine was making her giddy. Every new flavor, every succulent bite made her moan.

Jonah watched her decimate her loaded plate with evident satisfaction. "Tell me something," he said, dipping a chunk of steamed artichoke heart in butter. "That thing that happens when you give me a massage, does that happen with everyone? Here, try this."

She accepted the succulent morsel off the end of his fork and savored it with a murmur of appreciation. "What thing?"

"You know. That magic thing, like your hands are talking to my back. You do feel it, don't you? Or is it just me?"

"Yes, I feel it," she admitted softly. "And no, it doesn't happen very often. It depends on how receptive the person—"

"I've never been particularly receptive," he cut in. "Just ask any of my ex-girlfriends."

The claw marks flashed through her mind. She toyed with the salad greens on her plate. "I'd, uh, rather not," she murmured. "What you're feeling is probably just a light trance state. When you achieve deep levels of relaxation, your brain produces—"

"Don't spoil it for me by explaining it away."

Her mouth closed with a snap. "You know, you have a really bad habit of interrupting."

"Sorry. I'll try not to do it, if it bugs you."

"It's jarring," she said sternly. "Like having bad shocks in a car."

He looked abashed. "Ouch. Sorry. I'm kind of, uh, nervous."

She tried not to smile. "I thought that men liked scientific, logical explanations for things."

"Yeah. Usually I do like them. Just not when it comes to you."

Suddenly, there wasn't quite enough air in the room to

breathe. It was hot, immensely silent. Candles hissed and popped.

He got up and went into the kitchen, pulling something divinely chocolatey and fragrant out of the oven. He spooned steaming helpings of chocolate soufflé onto dessert plates and adorned them with towering mountains of whipped cream. He carried them to the table and laid them down, grinning. Immensely pleased with himself.

She giggled again, melting. "You've got to stop flirting with me."

"Do I?" His eyes took on a predatory gleam.

"Yes. You do. This whole situation is getting out of hand." She made a sweeping gesture with her hand, and almost knocked over her wine. Jonah's hand shot out, just in time, and gently put it in its place. "The food, the wine, the candles, the chocolate soufflé. It's over the top."

He shook his head. "No, Tess. This is normal for me. I like to treat myself well, and I have the means to do so. That's why you're here."

An image flooded through her mind. Herself, naked. Decked out in jewels and a sheer veil. Summoned to pleasure the lusty, sensual pasha. Commanded to fulfill his every erotic whim.

The image left her speechless. Her face felt damp and hot.

His glittering eyes seemed to read every thought that passed through her mind. "I like the way you massage me," he said softly. "I want to indulge myself, for hours. Is that so terrible? What's the crime? I'm willing to pay for my fun. I'm not stealing from anyone."

The harem maiden in her dream image threw off the sheer veil, and drew closer to the beautiful, naked pasha. Eager to prove herself. Desire sharpened to a dagger point that pierced through fear.

Nervous tension made her voice sharper than usual.

"You're spoiled, Jonah. You're used to getting exactly what you want."

He smiled lazily. "I do favor that scenario. Who could blame me?"

The arrogant, casual entitlement in his voice made her angry. "I could," she snapped. "The world's not like that, you know."

"It's not?" He picked up her dessert spoon and scooped up a mouthful of chocolate soufflé. He dunked it until it was heaped with whipped cream and leaned closer, holding the morsel out to her.

"Try this," he said softly. "Let yourself go. Open up."

She hesitated. He was projecting an intoxicating cloud of seductive energy. Pulling her effortlessly into his trap.

She opened her mouth, as if hypnotized, and accepted a mouthful of perfect bliss. Rich, creamy sweetness exploded through her senses.

"Welcome to my world, Tess," he said softly.

She sipped the espresso that Jonah insisted on making for her, but it did nothing to bring her back to earth. She was mellow and goofy from the wine, and trying very hard not to think about where this was almost certainly leading. If she thought about it, she would clench up and ruin it. She didn't want to ruin it. She was having too much fun.

He wasn't even coming on to her, just lounging his long, graceful self at the far end of the couch with a relaxed, lazy grin on his face, laying on the foolish flattery, exerting himself to make her laugh. It was working, too. She was giggling and snorting like a teenager.

She laid the espresso cup on the coffee table. "I'm a little tipsy, but I could still give you a back rub," she offered shyly. "It won't be one of those intense, mystical massages you like so much, though. Our stomachs are too full."

His eyes lit up. "Great. Fine. I'll take whatever I can get."

She set up the table and draped one of her flannel sheets across it, carefully keeping her back to him as he undressed. When she dared to turn around, she was surprised to see his jeans still on.

"You're going to leave on your jeans? I can drape a towel—"

"It's my back that needs work. Believe me . . . it's best."

She squirted oil into her hands and stared down at him. She'd never been the target of a strategic seduction before. She'd been tempted by food and wine and chocolate, mountain and forest and moonlight. Now the choicest bait of all was stretched out on the table in front of her, eyes closed in anticipatory pleasure. He couldn't wait to be touched. And she couldn't resist for another second.

She placed her hands against his hot, smooth skin. A shock of awareness went through them both. He drew in a sharp breath, his eyelids fluttering. Far from relaxed. She could feel his tense, coiled eagerness. He was waiting, with the patience of a seasoned hunter for . . . what? What did he want from her? What did he expect?

She ran her hands over his powerful back, leaning low enough to smell his subtle, unique scent beneath the perfume of scented oil. Clearly, he was either leaving it to her to make the first move or simply biding his time. She appreciated his delicacy and restraint, but she didn't have a clue how to begin. If only she could take a little time-out and call Trish for a quickie consultation. Should she follow her neck-kissing fantasy and find out where that led? Her heart pounded with excitement. Maybe she would hyperventilate. It would be so awful to flub this, to embarrass herself. To have him, God forbid, *pity* her.

She was monumentally untalented in the bedroom, after all. Larry's voice floated out of her memories, snappish and tense. "Can't you please at least *try* to concentrate?" She'd tried and tried to be less ticklish and tense, keep herself from floating out of her body and noticing odd, comical things that made her want to giggle—like the way Larry's skinny shoulder blades stuck out like wings.

Jonah's shoulder blades did not stick out like wings. He had the most beautiful, powerful back she'd ever seen. And she didn't feel ticklish or tense. She felt hot. Inflamed. Her hands were sliding over him purely for their own pleasure, not for his. She didn't have a therapeutic thought in her head.

She put both hands on his shoulders. She was leaning over, like she was actually going to do it, to just up and kiss that beautiful place on the nape of his neck that was so vulnerable and tender it just broke her heart and made her toes curl. She was inches away from the point of no return and drawing closer. Her breath came quick and fast and audible. He could probably feel it against his skin by now. The sense of anticipation, of waiting, swelled, like a wave about to crest.

She jerked back, and lifted off her hands. *Damn* lily-livered, scaredy-cat chicken. "What's going on, Jonah?" she whispered.

His eyes opened. He looked unsurprised at the question. "A back rub?" he ventured, clearly just for the hell of it.

She shook her head. "I'm not buying it."

He rolled onto his side and sat up, his legs dangling over the table. His erection strained prominently against his jeans. "Are we being truthful here?" he asked. "Totally honest and sincere?"

"I think . . . that's best," she faltered.

He reached out, very slowly, and seized her wrists, pulling her toward him. He lifted her glistening hands and held them up, close to his face, breathing in deeply. "What smells so good?"

"Almond oil." She stared at the size of his graceful hands. "With a few drops of essential oil. I change the oil according to the client."

"And what's my oil?"

"Sandalwood and coriander." She let out a silent gasp as he pressed her hands against his hot chest, splaying them out. Covering them with his own, sliding them around until his broad chest gleamed.

The clear purpose in his eyes made her breathless and giddy. "Jonah," she said, almost inaudibly. "What are you—"

"It's your own fault. You're the one who blew the whistle. I was going to be such a good boy. I was going to play it cool, all polite and refined. Get my massage, and then show you to a guest room with a lock on the door. But no. You had to unmask me. So here we are, Tess. Now you have to deal with naked reality. Whether you're ready or not."

"Jeans," she murmured. "Reality is wearing a pair of jeans."

He pulled her hands away from his chest and cupped them inside his own, dropping a kiss on her knuckles. "Your hands are so much stronger than they look. You're small, but I bet you're pure dynamite."

Larry's disappointed face flashed through her mind. She tugged at her hands with a pained, nervous laugh, but he would not relinquish them. "Uh, wrong. Sorry, but I'm not. Don't go building castles in the air about me. You'll just be disillusioned."

"How do you figure?"

She pulled again at her hands. "Past experience."

"Forget the past. I want you. And you want me, too. I can feel it."

It would be untruthful and undignified to deny it. "It doesn't matter," she said in a tiny voice. "It isn't part of the bargain."

"God." He rubbed his hand across his face. "This is driving me nuts. Can we change the bargain? What would it take?"

She straightened up to her full five foot two. "Some things can't be bargained for. Some things aren't for sale."

"Ah. Now we're getting someplace," he said, relieved. "I would never in a million years think that you were for sale, Tess. Why won't you let me get close to you? I'm trying so hard. I'm being so good. I'm being so charming and patient and goddamn careful, it's driving me insane. And I know that you want me. What is it about me that scares you so much?"

"You don't scare me. And it's none of your business."

"It is now," he said. He pulled her until she toppled against him, and trapped her between his thighs. "Nothing has ever been more completely my business. It's just you and me, Tess, and this thing we have between us. Our mutual business."

"We don't have anything between us," she protested weakly.

"We could. We could have something incredibly special."

She longed so badly to believe him, but it would be so much worse for her this time, if she let herself fall. She could really care about Jonah. She could fall wildly in love with him. She was teetering on the brink already. And when he got bored and moved on, it would sting and sear like the very fires of hell. It would make her feel so small.

She wrenched her hands away. "I don't need another rich, spoiled playboy walking all over me," she blurted.

His face froze. He dropped her hands. "Rich, spoiled playboy?" She stumbled back, unnerved by the controlled anger that smoldered in his eyes. He advanced upon her. "Where the fuck did that come from?"

"Uh, s-sorry," she stammered. "I shouldn't have said that."

"Sorry's not good enough. I did not deserve that, Tess."

"You're absolutely right. You didn't deserve it. Forget that I—"

"You can't erase what comes out of your mouth," he cut in. "Not in the real world. You have to face up to it."

She swallowed and pressed her trembling lips together.

"Rich, yeah. That I'll admit to. But I swear to you, I worked my ass off for it. Nobody handed it to me. Spoiled? I don't know. If I see something I want, I take it. But I pay full price. And I never whine. And I never for one second thought that the world owed me a goddamn thing."

"Jonah, I—"

"But playboy? What, do I come across like some pampered fop with a Ferrari and a pinkie ring? I work twelve fucking hours a day! I don't have time to be a playboy!"

"Oh, you find the time somehow," she lashed back. "I've seen the marks your lovers leave on your body. It wouldn't do my self-esteem any good to be part of your harem."

He looked bewildered for a moment, and then his eyes widened in dismayed comprehension. "Oh, God," he muttered. He closed his eyes, and opened them again, looking chastened. "You mean to tell me that the day I asked you out, I had, uh . . . claw marks on me?"

"They looked quite painful, actually. I tried not to get oil in them."

"Shit." He dropped his face into his hands and shook his head. "I should have canceled my appointment. No wonder you blew me off." He looked up at her, his face a dull red. "This may sound lame, but please believe me, I'd already ended that affair before I asked you out. I don't juggle women. My life is stressful enough as it is."

"You don't have to excuse yourself to me," she said hastily. "And I don't think there's anything morally wrong with seeing more than one person at a time, if everyone's aware and consenting. I'm just not wired that way myself. It would destroy me to be a notch in someone's belt."

He winced. "Ouch. Admitted, the timing and the claw marks make me look really bad, but that's still not fair, Tess."

"I'm just saying what pops into my head," she said. "I don't mean to hurt your feelings."

He didn't reply, just looked at her quietly. She became increasingly more aware of the crackling of the fire, the wind sighing in the treetops outside. Shadows played across the planes and hollows of his face. She didn't even see him move, but suddenly his warm fingers were wrapped around her wrists, and he was tugging her closer again.

"Let's take this from another angle," he said. "You said you don't need another rich, spoiled playboy, which implies that there have been other spoiled playboys in your past. Right?"

She remained stubbornly silent. He tugged on her wrist. "So?"

She sighed. "Just one. But I'd rather not talk about him. It just makes me depressed."

He nodded. His thumb moved against her palm in a tiny, soothing caress. "OK, foiled again. One last try. The playboy in question walked all over you, meaning he was an egotistic, selfish, oblivious asshole. Guess what, Tess? I'm not like that. I was brought up better. I would treat you like the queen of the universe."

"Oh, please." An unexpected giggle burst out of her.

His grin of relief was radiant. "Oh, yeah. Ever been treated like the queen of the universe before?"

A dull ache of old sadness pulled at her from below, and her smile faded. "I most certainly have not."

Jonah lifted her hand to his lips. "If you stay with me tonight, I promise you won't regret it. It'll be all about you. Your call, your rules, your pleasure, Your Exalted Majesty. You don't have to worry about anything. Just let me please you."

"Oh, my God," she murmured. Her hand tingled, shimmered with the heat, the tenderness of his soft lips.

"I won't do anything unless you say I can," he assured her. "Which is not to say that I won't make plenty of suggestions."

The teasing humor in his face warmed and reassured her. "How do I know you'll keep your word?"

He lifted his shoulders, let them drop. "You can't know," he said quietly. "You just have to trust me. Life's like that."

His calm, direct gaze, his warm hands, his gentle words, made something that had been tight and pinched in her chest relax and soften. She took a deep breath and for the first time, she let herself really look at him. Not through the lens of Larry or any of her past disappointments and heartbreaks and fears. Just at Jonah.

What she saw dazzled her. He was so solid. Beautiful and sensual, yes, but there was something fair and honest and stubborn in his eyes that was even more alluring to her.

He endured her long scrutiny with quiet patience.

"Do you really mean it, the queen thing?" she whispered.

He touched her cheek. "Is it so hard to believe?"

"For me, it is," she admitted.

He slid off the table and sank to his knees. "Oh, my queen. I am at your command." He smooched up the length of her arm until she shook with nervous laughter.

He pressed a hot kiss against her palm. His teasing grin faded, supplanted by naked desire. Her laughter abruptly stopped.

"Let me kiss you," he said hoarsely. "Then you'll understand exactly how it'll be tonight between us. Please, Tess. Can I kiss you?"

He rose slowly to his feet. His face was inches above hers, his eyes hot and pleading. She drifted closer and closer with the slow inevitability of clasped hands on the planchette of a Ouija board. The waiting, the breathless curiosity, and then the gasp of delighted terror when the oracle yielded its answer. Yes, or no? Yes, or no?

She drifted closer. Closer. *Yes.*

She touched his hot face as she had longed to do for weeks, running her fingertips over his skin, his high, elegant cheekbones. Tracing the strong, dark slash of his eyebrows, the faint rasp of beard shadow, the sharp line of his jaw.

The hot, thrilling, pulsing life of him beneath her hands.

She pulled his face hungrily toward hers.

Chapter Four

Her lips trembled beneath the light, brushing contact, which was all that he dared to allow himself. She was still poised for flight, and if he lost her now he would implode, self-destruct, disappear out of sheer frustration. He was as tormented by lust as if he were a young boy, everything brash and raw and unmoderated. No veils of hard-won self-control or calm experience to overlay the roar of need.

He tasted her lips, shaking with exultant eagerness. They were just as he had dreamed they would be, full and unimaginably soft. As fine-textured as a dream of silk or suede. Pansies, poppies, butterfly wings. Things too delicate to touch.

She was kissing him back now, praise God, and the sweet, liquid contact of her lips made him wild, crazy; first the pull, then the slide, then the tiny wet pop as her lips disengaged, panting for breath, and then another hungry, tender assault upon his mouth. One brush of her hot, eager tongue blotted out his ambitious promises. Her small, fragrant hands stole around his body with eager curiosity, stroking across his ribs, his back. He pressed the throbbing heat of his hard-on against her, hoping it wasn't too rude, too soon.

But it didn't seem to alarm her. She just stroked and petted and soothed him, opening to his kiss. Her response emboldened him to put his arms around her. He marveled at how small and deliciously curvy she was, her narrow rib cage with the pillowy softness of her bosom pressing against his chest. He clasped his legs around her, a grasping, possessive gesture that he couldn't control. His body spoke a language that needed no translating. *Mine, all mine.*

She murmured against his hungry, marauding mouth, and he forced himself to pull away. "I want—" He stopped, panting and unsure of himself. "I want to kiss you deeper, but I don't want to scare you." He barely recognized his voice, it was so shaky.

She smiled her mysterious smile that never failed to turn him inside out. Pure Tess, warm and unforced and achingly sweet.

"You're not scaring me, Jonah."

She let her head drop back trustingly into his cupped hand, going soft and pliant against him. Her response was like a match to gasoline, a heavy *whump,* and then flames roaring up. Careful, careful, pleaded the tiny voice in the back of his mind. This is the queen of the universe he was dealing with. He had promised to control himself, to indulge her utterly. But she was pressing her plump breasts against him, so lush and soft and tempting. He couldn't stop to ask, he couldn't help himself; he slid his hands over her, cupped her abundant curves through all those layers of clothing. He wanted to rub some of that scented oil on her breasts and bury his face between them. His mind was a mass of roiling sensual images. His mouth roved over her slender throat, fumbling desperately for buttons, zippers, anything. He became dimly aware that she was saying his name, over and over.

"Huh?" He lifted his mouth reluctantly from the hollow of her throat, groping for the curve of her ass through her voluminous skirt. That Little House on the Prairie outfit was pretty weird, but she could wear a burlap sack and he would be on his knees, salivating for her.

"I've decided my first royal command." Her tone was hesitant, but her green-gold eyes sparkled with challenge.

He tried not to pant like an animal. "Let's hear it."

"I want you to rub my feet," she announced.

He blinked at her.

She looked slightly defensive. "This might come as a shock to you, Jonah, but I've been on my feet all day long. And after a day like that, the most erotic, luxurious thing I can imagine is to have a big handsome guy kneeling in front of me, rubbing my feet."

He started to grin as the sensual potential of the situation dawned on him. Touching her delicate little feet until she purred and relaxed, and then moving slowly, inexorably upward. What an awesome lead-in.

She reached for the bottle of oil and smoothed some onto her hands, smiling up through her eyelashes as she rubbed them over his shoulders and chest. "Fantasy detail," she explained. "My love slave should be oiled up and gleaming."

He stared at her small, strong hands as they rubbed him all over with casual skill. His cock throbbed so hard it was a wonder there was enough blood going up to his brain to keep him on his feet. His tongue seemed to have dried out and adhered to the roof of his mouth.

"There," she said, with an approving pat. "You look perfect." She put the bottle of oil in his hands and raised her eyebrows. "Well?"

"Want me to be stark naked?" he suggested hoarsely. "You could oil up the rest of me, too."

Her cheeks flushed even pinker at the bold suggestion. "Let's take this one step at a time, shall we?" she said primly.

"As my queen commands."

* * *

She could hardly believe her luck. By some trick of amazing intuition, Jonah had come up with the one scenario that might not make her clench up and botch the whole thing. By declaring her queen of the universe, he had taken all the responsibility for the success of the evening upon his own broad, capable shoulders. She didn't have to worry about being skillful or responsive or creative enough. He had given her permission to be pampered and indulged, to think only of her own pleasure. And she was going to take him at his word.

Besides, he was tough. He was so supremely confident that she could bounce him around like a rubber ball, and he would never break. And such a sweetie, too, grinning at her like the idea of rubbing her tired feet thrilled him to no end. It was adorable.

She watched him pull the couch closer to the fire, hypnotized by the beauty of his lean torso. He crouched, silhouetted against the flames, and set another oak log on it. She took advantage of the moment to dart behind the couch to unlace her shoes. White rubber-soled sneakers did not belong in a sensual fantasy of the queen of the universe being pampered by her brawny love slave.

He was looking at her now. There was no graceful way to reach beneath the long skirt of her dress and tug down the black wool tights. She had to just do it.

Her fingers brushed across the scalloped lace of the red teddy. Dear God. She had forgotten all about the teddy. She had put it on this morning, just to give herself a jolt of confidence and have a naughty little secret against her skin. Now he would deduce that she had come up here intending to go to bed with him all along, and—

Or had she? Was this what she had wanted all along?

She didn't know, she couldn't tell. She felt like her body had been taken over by a mysterious stranger.

Oh, well. Too late to worry about it now. She peeled the

tights down, striving to perform the graceless act with queenly panache. Jonah indicated the couch with a gracious, sweeping gesture of his arm, and she settled into the soft cushions.

He sat down cross-legged in front of her and squirted some of her oil into his hand. "Any particular way you want me to do this? You're the expert, after all."

"Just follow your instincts," she said.

He cupped her foot tenderly in his big palm, and closed his fingers around it—and a heavenly chorus burst into song.

Oh, he was good. His hands were wise and warm and knowing. Strong when she needed him to be strong, gentle where she needed gentleness. Exquisitely slow and thorough. Her head fell back against the sofa cushions, her eyes closed. She abandoned herself to the feeling of being pampered and caressed. Almost . . . loved.

The foot that he wasn't massaging was resting on his thigh. A very hot, hard, long something was beginning to nudge against it. Then more than nudge. She could feel the heat, the pulsing energy.

Her eyes popped open. She remembered that the source of this sweet, heady bliss was a big, powerful, extremely aroused man.

"I read once in a health magazine that every part of the body corresponds to a point on the foot," he said. "Some kind of Chinese medicine thing, right?"

"Yes," she said. "Reflexology. Shiatsu and acupuncture are based on . . . ah . . . the same principles, as well."

He laid the foot he was working on tenderly on his other thigh, and rescued her other foot, his fingers sliding intimately around her arch. "So you know all these pressure points?"

"Of course. Oh, God, that's so wonderful, Jonah. You're incredibly good at this. You could be a masseur."

"Great. Nice to know that if the bottom ever falls out of my consulting business, I've got one more card to play."

She almost hummed with pleasure. "Don't be snide. A guy who looks like you could make a fortune rubbing women's feet."

"Yeah, right. How about you tell me what part of the body this corresponds to?" He rubbed the pad of her big toe, then tenderly manipulated the other four.

"Ah, the pads of the little toes correspond to the sinuses."

"So if I do this"—he lifted her foot and kissed each of her toes—"then it's like I'm kissing your nose and eyebrows, right?"

She laughed at his foolishness. "I suppose you could say that, if you wanted to be fanciful."

"Oh, but I do. And the big toe?"

Her brain was so swamped with pleasure, it was hard to concentrate. "The tip is the brain, and the inner side is . . . is the side of the neck. And the fullest point in the middle are the eyes and ears."

He kissed her big toe, sides, tip, pad, his mouth warm and soft. His hot breath tickled the delicate skin of her arch, and sensation shivered up her legs. He pressed hot, seductive kisses against the ball of her foot. "How about this part?"

"Lungs. Shoulders. Heart," she whispered.

"Yes. Heaving lungs, kissable shoulders, pounding heart. I love it." He kissed her foot repeatedly.

She giggled and tugged her foot, but his hand wrapped around her ankle. "Jonah, I—"

"How about this foot? I don't want to neglect it. How about this part right here?" He kissed the tender arch near the outside.

"That's, ah, the sciatic nerve, I think. And the appendix. And that should be . . . the ileocecal valve."

He covered the spot with tender little kisses and grinned at her. "You lost me there, sweetheart. I missed that day in eighth grade biology. But I'm sure yours is the cutest little ileocecal valve ever."

His butterfly kisses made her shake with laughter. "Jonah,

you're tickling me. Stop!" She pushed at his chest with her other foot, and he grabbed that one too, wrestling with her playfully.

Suddenly he let go. Both her feet shot out past his shoulders.

She froze. Her legs were wide open and draped over his hot, naked shoulders. And the look in his eyes was so purposeful. As if she were about to let him—oh, God. She scrambled back against the cushions, twisting and flailing.

"Hey, hey, hey. Don't panic," he urged. "You're still the queen."

She tried to breathe, to relax, to stop struggling. He was kissing her knee, making soothing noises, but she didn't feel soothed. She felt like she was going to fly apart in his hands, do something disgraceful and uncontrolled. It was scaring her to death.

"I love these dimples on your knees," he told her. "They're so cute. Hold still, let me put more oil on my hands. I want to massage your legs, too." He stopped, and looked doubtful. "That's OK, right?"

"Yes," she whispered. He pushed her skirt up. She jumped when his hands closed around her knee, and tension left her body in a long, shuddering exhalation. She closed her eyes, wanting, needing to trust him. His big, oiled hands crept higher, gentle and mesmerizing. He stopped and waited, motionless, until she opened her eyes. He stared into them for a moment, silently asking her permission, and pushed very gently against her inner thighs.

She opened for him with a soft, trembling sigh.

"I love the red lace panties," he said appreciatively. "They make your skin look pearly white." She gasped as he pushed her back against the cushions. "Shhh," he murmured. "I'm just going to touch these lacy underpants with the tips of my fingers. Like this."

The light, teasing circles against the dampening silk of her panties were sweet little flames licking against her. A heavy, aching desperation began to grow out of the pleasure. For the first time, she actually understood why people were willing to do dangerous, self-destructive, even immoral things in order to follow this impulse.

She invited him with her eyes to touch her wherever he pleased. She couldn't say it with words, but when he deepened the pressure and circled his thumb around her clitoris, she reached down and pressed his hand against her harder, with a pleading, wordless murmur.

He pinned her against the couch with his weight, his own breathing ragged and audible in the silent room, and she moved against his hand, her head thrashing back and forth, striving for something unknown and yet so seductively close, beckoning her.

When the hot oblivion pulsed through her body, she was so surprised, she actually fainted.

She floated back, dazed and limp. That was nothing like any orgasm she'd ever had—or rather, thought she'd had. She'd never understood what the big deal was about orgasms; to her they seemed no more than a sudden dissipation of whatever mild tension she had managed to build, a deflated sense that there was no point in continuing. Sort of like watching water swirl down a bathtub drain.

This had been . . . mind-shattering.

Jonah's arms were wrapped around her waist, the side of his face pressed against her belly. His breath had warmed her skirt. She put her hand in his hair and stroked it. Damp and silky and springy beneath her fingers. He was sweating, too.

He lifted his face, his eyes dark with wonder. "I've never felt anything like that," he said.

She licked her lips. "I think that's my line," she whispered.

"I felt it go right through me. Like a hot wind. You are incredible."

She tried to smile, but her muscle coordination was not

yet up to such a complex task. "Of course you have to say that," she teased. "It's in the script. Queens have to be flattered and adored."

He scowled. "Fuck the script. That was for real. And so am I. Don't you get that yet?"

She was startled at his harsh tone. "Um, yes," she conceded softly. "I think I get that."

"Good." He pressed his face against her belly again, his big, naked shoulders rubbing against her thighs. She clasped her arms around his neck, pulling him closer with a soft murmur.

He lifted his head, his eyes hungry. "And? So?"

"And what? So what?"

"I'm waiting patiently for you to command me to take the next logical step, and the waiting's killing me," he said.

"What step?" she hedged.

He shook his head. "You have to articulate your desires. The queen of the universe knows exactly what she wants. So go on. Instruct your eager servant."

She opened her mouth, but nothing came out. She swallowed. "I can't," she whispered.

He lifted his eyebrow. "You have to, Tess. Otherwise, we can't proceed."

She gathered her wits. "That's 'Your Exalted Majesty' to you. Don't you dare presume to tell me what I have to do, Mr. Love Slave, or I'll have you punished for your insolence."

"Ah. That's better," he said softly. He bent down to lick her thigh. She caught her breath at the warm, wet intimacy of the caress. "So? What does my queen command?"

She reached down and ran her fingers across the rasp of beard stubble that covered his jaw. She knew what she wanted, but the words were stuck in her throat, pounding against a brick wall. She bit her lip in frustration. "What do you want to do?" she asked.

"Everything," he said promptly. "But for starters, I want

to pull those panties off and lick you between your legs until you come again."

Heat pulsed through her at the image his words invoked: a tangle of lips and tongues and limbs, of kisses and caresses. Her breath jerked into her lungs, shallow and fast. "That sounds, um, interesting," she said. "My royal command is to . . . do what you want."

His eyes gleamed. "Whatever I want? You're sure?"

"Within reason," she amended swiftly.

He shook his head. "Can't have it both ways, sweetheart. If you give control to me, I'll take it and run with it. And I'm so turned on that I'm probably going to run long and hard and fast."

She let out a breathless laugh. "Are you trying to scare me?"

He shrugged. "Just being honest. If you can't tell me what you want, then I'm just going to have to show you what I want."

"Oh," she whispered.

"I'll let you off the hook now, but eventually, I'm going to get it out of you," he went on, kissing her thighs. "What you want, what you like, what you fantasize about. I want to hear the words. In explicit detail."

"I don't know how to talk about it," she said desperately.

"Then you'll learn." He lifted his head and gave her a slow, implacable smile. "Because I'll teach you." His hands moved over her, bold and skillful. "I'm going to make you come again now, Tess. Over and over, with my mouth and my fingers and my cock. Until you're begging me to let you rest. Until you've forgotten what it feels like to be shy or embarrassed. Do you want that?"

She nodded. She couldn't stop her lips from trembling.

"So, I'm taking over, then?" he said insistently. "You're sure?"

She pressed her lips together and nodded again.

He rose up with smooth grace, and pulled her to her feet.

"My first act as an emancipated love slave is to get these clothes off you."

Alarm went through her like an electrical shock. She clenched her teeth and tried to let it go. "OK," she whispered.

She tried to help him, but her hands were clumsy and ineffectual, just getting in the way of his swift, strategic assault on her clothes. Finally she just held her hands out, as stiff and passive as a doll, hoping desperately that he wouldn't be disappointed by what he found.

He got rid of the dress first, shoving it down off her shoulders. Then her loose fleece shirt, his deft hands making short work of her buttons. Her silk knit chemise sailed up and over her head into the shadows.

And there she stood, in nothing but the flame-red lace teddy. She squeezed her eyes tightly shut. She could not breathe.

He was silent for an agonizingly long time.

"My God," he whispered. "Did you wear that thing for me?"

She licked her lips, tried to speak. Tried again. "I . . . I guess I did," she admitted in a tiny voice.

Another maddening silence. She clenched her fists and waited.

"Thank you," he said simply.

She finally dared to open her eyes, and she was shocked by the look on his face. He looked moved, his eyes soft, dazzled.

He lifted his eyes to her face. "You're so fucking beautiful," he whispered. "You blow my mind. I'm afraid to touch you."

She let out a hitching little laugh that threatened to turn into tears. "Well, you better get over it."

They both laughed. He lifted trembling hands and placed them on her shoulders. Brushed them tenderly down her arms. He slid his fingers around her lace-covered waist. Splayed them over her hips with a sigh of approval, then cupped her bottom. She nudged herself closer, breathing in shallow little gasps.

One of his hands slid up to touch her breast. She nestled in his warmth as his fingers traced the pattern of the scalloped lace, brushing over her lace-covered nipple, making her heart pound. He pushed the stretchy fabric down over her breasts, until her nipples peeked over the edge of the fabric. She pressed herself against him, hiding her face against his shoulder.

"I hate to take it off you," he said shakily.

"I can always put it back on for you later."

"Promise?"

When she nodded, he began to inch the fabric down over her torso. He freed her breasts and peeled it down over her thighs. Gently lifted one foot, then the other. He smoothed the little garment in his hands and lifted it to his face, taking a hungry whiff. "Delicious."

She was laughing at his silliness when she suddenly realized that he was staring at her naked breasts. She made a move to cover them with her arms, and at the same moment realized how stupid that was.

She forced herself to drop her arms, closed her eyes, and tried to breathe. It had been so long since she'd been naked in front of anyone, and it wasn't as if she'd ever gotten very comfortable with it.

She jumped nervously as he reached around her shoulders, feeling for the thick knot of hair at her nape. His long fingers searched delicately for the pins, and he flung them away to join the rest of her discarded clothes and he let the knot unravel. It spiraled down to the small of her back. "I've been fantasizing about seeing your hair down since the first moment I saw you," he said, draping it across her shoulders like a shawl. "It's even more beautiful than I imagined."

He pushed her back, gently, until the backs of her knees hit the couch, and kept pushing until she fell into the cushions, staring up at him. Wide-eyed. He stroked her thighs, staring hungrily at every detail. He tucked a pillow behind her, and pulled her until her bottom was at the end of the couch cushion. "Your breasts are amazing," he said. "I wish my mouth could be everyplace at once, but the night's still young." And he pushed her legs wide open.

She tried to squirm, but she was pinned. "Jonah, wait—"

"What for?"

His mouth was on her, his tongue sliding boldly along her most intimate flesh. She was transfixed with pleasure.

Never. Never like this. She'd always been far too tense and self-conscious to enjoy this the few times that she had attempted it. This was utterly different. All she could do was stare at his dark head, her breath coming in harsh, audible gasps. His hands held her wide open as his tongue fluttered across the exposed, swollen bud of her clitoris. It rasped tenderly across the glistening folds of her labia, slowly up and down, lapping and licking with hungry abandon. He slid one long finger slowly inside her while suckling her clitoris, and looked up at her as he slid it slowly out. It glistened.

He thrust it again, harder. "You're so wet and tight," he muttered. "Clinging to my finger like you're sucking on it."

She barely understood what he said. Her body was lit up like a torch. Everything he touched was melting. Shimmering hot, liquid, lost. The center of the universe was the agonizing pleasure of his lips and tongue and clever hands. He brought her almost to the brink, and then drew back. Wave after wave, closer and closer, till she wanted to scream with frustration.

She clutched as much of his short, silky hair as she could grab. "Damn it, Jonah," she gasped. "Do it!"

His laughter vibrated through her sex. His tongue probing, teasing. "Trust me."

"Please," she begged. "Please, do it now."

"Soon," he promised.

"Now!" She swatted his shoulder, hard.

He thrust with his hand, bold and forceful. It almost hurt,

but then he was pressing tenderly against the hot, shivering sweet spot deep inside her sheath that she had never known existed, while his tongue circled the swollen bud of her clitoris. He drove two fingers into her flushed, swollen opening, and it all came crashing down. A throbbing explosion of rippling pleasure, widening out. A pulsating red glow that spread to every part of her body.

When she opened her eyes, he was on his feet, shoving his jeans down. She stared at the erection bobbing in front of her and suddenly remembered that she had ceded all control of their tryst to him.

He was impressive. Much longer and thicker than Larry. Rising out of a rich thatch of dark hair, thick and blunt, flushed to a deep, purplish red. Veins pulsing. He stood there and let her get used to the sight of him. He was so tempting and powerful and perfect.

He stepped closer. "Touch me there," he said quietly. "Please."

She put her hand against him, startled at how hot and smooth he was, how delicately soft the skin that covered his hardness. "Harder," he said. His hand closed over hers, squeezing and pulling, rougher than she would ever have dared to touch him on her own.

The pressure milked a gleaming drop of pearly moisture from the slit in the tip. She didn't stop to think, she just pressed her mouth against it, licking it away. Sweet and salty, heat and bursting pressure. She could get used to this feeling of power, the helpless groan of pleasure she dragged from him. She could learn to love it.

She gripped him, taking the whole tip of him into her mouth. It was big and blunt, and barely fit. She swirled her tongue around, moistening him, and was just about to suck him deeper when she felt his hands cupping her face, holding her in place.

"No, please," he said in a strangled voice. "I'll come in two seconds if you do that."

He pushed her back, and she stared at the thick hard shaft bobbing next to her face, radiating heat. Her eyes traveled slowly up his big, powerful body, saw his flushed face and dilated eyes.

Long and hard and fast, he had said. His size and strength were suddenly disconcerting. But she'd been so wanton, so selfish and eager and willing so far, there was no way she could draw back now. It was his turn, and she had to just relax and try to not be nervous and silly. It wasn't like she was a terrified virgin. She was twenty-nine years old. And the man clearly knew what he was doing.

·Jonah was moving briskly ahead, unaware of her spasm of doubt. He had already produced a condom out of thin air, and had rolled it purposefully over himself. His eyes dragged slowly, hotly over her body.

"I'm too big for the couch," he said. "Let's take this to the rug in front of the fire. It's nice and soft."

She was frozen in place, mute. He grabbed the fluffy afghan from the back of the couch and flung it out over the rug. He scattered a couple of the thick, fleece covered pillows onto the afghan, and held out his hand, a swift, imperious gesture. "Come on."

He was so overwhelming, she couldn't control her primitive hesitation, but Jonah had no intention of letting her pull back. He scooped her into his arms.

She protested, wiggling. "Jonah, you'll hurt yourself!"

He snorted. "Get into the moment. Do you think Scarlett said that to Rhett while he was carrying her up the stairs?"

She was startled into giggling as he lay her against the cushions. "So men fantasize about that scene, too? I thought that was a girl thing."

"You mean about what he does to her once he gets her into that bedroom? Hell, yes. At least I did. To start with, I think he throws her on the bed and rips open her dress, and goes like this—"

He lunged over her, covering her with his body, and pressed her breasts together, burying his face between them. He kissed and swirled his tongue against her curves, leaving a trail of wet, pulsing pleasure in his wake.

He looked up at her face as he suckled her nipple, and dragged his teeth gently across the sensitive flesh. The rasp of his teeth made her cry out, clutching his head to her chest. He lifted his eyebrows and hummed the theme to *Gone With the Wind*. She dissolved into giggles.

He lifted his head. "Then he rips open her bloomers or petticoats or whatever the hell else women wore back then, and he fucks her brains out. He tries to show her who's boss. Never works worth a damn, but it's fun while it lasts."

Her laughter cut off abruptly. She stared, transfixed, into his burning eyes as he pushed her legs wide, settling himself between them. The hot, powerful bulk of him was poised over her. No wiggling away, no second thoughts. Her fingertips dug into his upper arms.

He leaned down, covering her face with coaxing kisses. "Relax. I'm not going to hurt you. You're ready for me. I made sure of it."

"I'm sorry." She squeezed her eyes shut as she felt the smooth, blunt head of his penis sliding tenderly against her labia, probing, pressing. Then insisting.

"Open your eyes," he said. "I'm Jonah, and you're Tess, and this is no fantasy. This is for real. Right here, right now. Keep your eyes open, Tess. Look at me."

"I can't," she said tightly.

He cupped her face in his hands. "You have to," he said. "Now."

And such was the force of his will that her eyes actually did pop open. She stared into his face, lost and overwhelmed. A certainty was growing inside her, that opening herself up to this man was going to change her in ways she could not yet imagine. But there was no going back. She dug her hands into his shoulders and tried to relax. It had been three or four years since she last tried this, and he was so big and solid, stretching her tender opening to the point of pain.

"Stay with me, Tess." His voice was tense and strained. He stared into her eyes so intensely, she felt as if she were chained to him. His muscles flexed, and she cried out as he thrust all the way inside.

It was too much. She felt pinned, immobile. Stifled by his size, the force radiating out of him. The deep, aching pressure of his shaft inside her was a painful intrusion. She turned her face away, her breath getting short and strangled and panicky.

She felt his hands on her face again, wrenching her face back toward his. "Damn it. Look at me."

The steely anger in his voice stung her own anger to life. "What the hell do you want from me?" she spat out.

He shook his head, his eyes full of angry confusion. "I don't know! Be there for me! Meet me halfway! Tell me to fuck off, whatever the hell you want, but just be strong for me. Don't you dare slip away and leave me alone, like you're scared of me. I can't take that!"

She tried to wiggle beneath him, in vain. "Aren't you happy now?" she flung at him. "Isn't this what you wanted?"

He drew back and thrust slowly inside her again, holding her gaze. "No. I want more. I want everything."

"Great. Well, spell it out for me, then," she snapped. "Because I don't know just exactly what everything entails."

He cut off her words with a deep, plundering kiss that left her breathless. "I'm sorry I pissed you off, but I'd rather have you mad at me than slipping through my fingers like sand."

"This is your lucky day, then, Jonah, because I'm furious! I don't know why, but I am. You're too big, and too heavy, and you're making me nervous. Let . . . me . . . *breathe*." She wrestled her arms between them and shoved at his chest.

He arched himself up so his weight lifted off her, and

trapped her wrists and pinned them over her head. She could breathe, but having her arms stretched out over her head made her feel helpless and maddened. She heaved and bucked beneath him, but he wouldn't dislodge himself. He just thrust in again with a voluptuous surge that made her gasp.

Despite her furious tension, she was slicker and wetter and softer than she'd ever been. He sensed the exact moment that her body found the right angle to clasp him, move with him. The moment that the pressure of his thick penis sliding along the length of her humid sheath made a flush of excitement race like a grass fire across the entire surface of her skin.

She was burning up. Crazed and feverish. She tried to free her hands, but he was immensely strong. "Let go, God damn it," she panted.

He slowly shook his head. "No way. Be mad, Tess, if that works better for you."

"You bastard," she hissed. "It doesn't!"

"Liar," he said softly. "You're opening up to me, now. All wet and soft and scalding hot. You like it. Feel this." He drove himself deep inside her, a heavy lunge that shocked a wail of pleasure out of her throat. "See? Go on, spit some more venom at me. It turns me on, too."

"Damn you," she said shakily. Her face was crimson, and she couldn't stop her legs from twining around his, her sex from tightening around his thick, hard shaft. She couldn't control her own body, jerking up to meet his plunging hips.

He thrust again. "You're gorgeous when you're mad." He slid his arms beneath her shoulders, scooping her up to kiss her again. His tongue slid into her mouth, following the same slow, plunging, sensual rhythm as his hips.

She had been poised to tell him to stop, but the words wouldn't come. They receded, slipping back into the swirling pool of emotions, anger blending with desire and confusion, in a hopeless, muddled mix. "Jonah, please."

He kissed her face, her jaw, her ear. "Don't worry, sweetheart," he whispered. "I've got everything under control."

"Including me?" she snapped.

He grinned, delighted. "That's the spirit. Keep your eyes on me." And then he began to move.

She'd never felt anything like this before. Totally new sensations bloomed, one out of the other, and he watched it all, studying her face with heated fascination. The tension in her trapped arms, in her straining body, just sharpened her exitement, heating the volatile blend of feelings closer and closer to the edge. He reached down with a murmur of encouragement, toying with her clitoris while his hips pulsed and ground against her. Silently demanding that she take that blind leap, again.

His cry of triumph was the last thing she heard as she flew off the edge and lost herself.

He waited, motionless, for her to come back, while the aftershocks of her orgasm clenched him rhythmically. When she opened her eyes, he began again, and this time she sensed that he had given himself leave to seek his own completion. He was rougher, more urgent. The deep, slamming thrusts would have frightened and intimidated her before, but not now. She was changed. The wild, rebellious part of her, dormant for so long, had roared to life and found its equal. She wanted to lose control, to bite and scratch, to be taken deep and hard. She didn't even notice when he let go of her hands. She just found herself clutching his waist, holding herself up so she could see his thick penis, gleaming as he thrust and withdrew, his hard, ridged belly, his muscles flexing. She dug her fingers into him greedily, demanding without words for everything he had to give.

He shoved her down onto her back and rose up onto his knees, folding her legs up until she was spread as wide as she could go. "Is this what you want?" He lunged into her, deep and hard.

She grabbed his butt and dragged him closer. "Please."

"You'd better not punish me for this later," he warned.

Passion had changed her body, lengthening her sheath to accommodate him, waking up millions of nerve endings she had never known existed. She was made for this sweet, savage rhythm. Made for him, desperate for the sliding friction, and the deep, sweet pressure against the mouth of her womb.

Then pleasure burst, rushing over them and through them both, fusing them together like molten gold.

Chapter Five

He lay trembling on top of her, till he became aware of how hard she had to struggle to breathe beneath his weight. He lifted himself out of her tight, clinging depths, flopping onto his back.

"Jesus," he muttered. "I think you practically killed me."

He let his head flop to the side towards her. She licked her lips.

"That doesn't sound very complimentary," she whispered.

"Believe me, it is," he said solemnly. "Right from the heart."

"Not very poetic, either." Her voice was barely audible.

He would've laughed if he hadn't been so limp. "So you want mind-blowing sex, and then you want me to be poetic, too? Let me recover, OK? As soon as I can breathe, I'll be a perfect gentleman."

She rolled up onto her side. "You're not gentle," she said quietly. "I'm never buying that perfect gentleman line of yours, ever again."

A pang of guilt assailed him. "You didn't need gentleness," he said defensively. "I'd already done the gentleness bit. It did its job. If I'd kept on being gentle, you would have gotten bored."

She snickered. "Bored? With you? Hardly. So now you're the expert about what I need?"

He knew he was skating on thin ice here, but he had nothing to follow but his instincts. "Yeah, Tess. I think I am," he said simply.

She propped herself up on her elbow, her eyes shot through with gold from the firelight, wide with fascination. "So it was all calculated, then? Don't get mad, please. I just need to—to understand how this works. I didn't know sex could be like that."

His stomach clenched with apprehension. "Like what?"

"That it could go so far," she said softly. "Make me feel so strongly. It was scary."

"I didn't mean to scare you," he said roughly. "In fact, I hated it when you were scared."

"I know you did." She reached out and patted his chest, an unconscious, soothing gesture. "So you were deliberately trying to—"

"No. Nothing was deliberate. I didn't think, I didn't try, I didn't calculate. It just happened."

Her hair tumbled forward over her chest as she sat up, her eyes full of thoughtful speculation. "So you just lost control, then?"

His hand slammed down hard against the afghan. "Yes, I did," he snapped. "I lost control. I admit it. Sorry, OK? Are we done, now? Do we have to keep hashing this out? Can we please move on?"

She leaned over and touched his cheek gently. "I wasn't criticizing," she assured him. "I'm glad I wasn't the only one who lost control. It makes me feel less self-conscious."

Her eyes were soft, completely sincere. She really wasn't blaming him. She wasn't even angry. The look in her eyes was so sweet, he felt himself stirring again. He took her hand in his and pressed a kiss against it. "You really are innocent, aren't you?"

"Not anymore," she said primly. "You made like you were all harmless and docile. Pussycat, my butt. You're Attila the Hun."

The gleam of humor in her eyes reassured him. "It worked for you, though, right? I made you come, what, four times?"

"Don't be cocky," she reproved. "It's unbecoming."

He pulled off the condom, grinning. "Speaking of which. Anytime you want to try oral sex, I'm at the ready. Now that I've taken the edge off, I think I can risk it."

"Edge? I'm totally destroyed, and you've just taken the edge off?"

He got to his feet and held out his hand. "You didn't think we were done, did you?" he asked in mock horror. "Please, please, please, tell me you didn't think that."

She linked hands with him and let him pull her to her feet. "Are you a sex maniac?" she asked. "Or is this normal?"

"I don't know," he admitted.

They stared at each other, speechless and shy. He kissed her hand again, wondering how long this shaky, off balance feeling was going to torment him. "We'll see how you feel after a midnight snack," he told her. "Come on, let's go have some leftovers."

It was definitely time to lighten up, take a step back, he told himself. He'd shocked himself. He'd never meant to let things get so intense. He'd intended to be gentle, careful, endlessly patient. Not a sweating, pounding, screaming madman.

Even so, here she was, holding his hand, and padding stark naked and trusting alongside him into the kitchen. His erection bumped up another notch. Well over a forty-five degree angle, and heading up to ninety. She noticed it, her eyes skittering away. So cute and shy.

"I didn't know men could recover so quickly," she observed.

He washed his hands, waited while she did the same. "You make me so hot, I can't see straight," he said, opening up the fridge. "I've been fantasizing about that white dress of yours for months."

"Oh, please." She covered her smile with her hand. "You mean the Vee Have Vays to Make You Talk dress?"

"Is that what you call it? Grab some forks out of that drawer."

She handed him the forks. "My roommate Trish named it. The most un-sexy garment ever created."

He snickered as he pulled plastic wrap off the eggplant. "Not."

"A guy would have to have a truly dirty mind to find that dress a turn-on."

"That's me," he said cheerfully. He stuck the bread in the toaster oven. "I can already see myself, flat on my back, and you in that dress, standing over me. Legs spread. No underwear. Interrogating me."

She giggled, wrapping her arms across her breasts. He gently peeled them away, pushing them down to her sides. "You cold?"

"Not really," she murmured. "Just not used to being naked."

He touched her breasts with the tips of his fingers, light, tender strokes. "You're gorgeous," he told her.

She reacted to his touch with a little tremor, and a flush swept up over her chest, her neck. "It's sweet of you to say so."

He realized, with horrified dismay, that she didn't believe him. "I'm not particularly sweet," he said. "I don't give false compliments. And you're not just gorgeous, you're drop-dead gorgeous."

"Please, Jonah. Don't push it." She backed away from the intensity in his voice. He followed her, trapping her against the counter.

"It just gets me going, when you tell me not to push it. Did you know that I've been obsessing about every detail of you for months, now? I'm crazy about your hair, you know. I love all those little fuzzy bits that curl around your neck at the end of the day. I've been dying to unwind that bun and see how long it was. To put my face in it and just inhale your smell. God, what a rush."

Her face was tight with discomfort. "Jonah, you don't have to—"

"And your tits," he forged on. "God. You can't imagine how many times I thought about popping open the buttons on that white dress, one by one, and seeing those unbelievable breasts pop out—"

"I wear a T-shirt under the dress," she said, giggling.

He cupped her breasts in his hands and leaned down, kissing them. "Don't trample all over my favorite fantasy," he protested.

And before he even realized what he was doing, she was arched back over the counter, gasping, saying something in a pleading voice, but he was too swept up in a flare of unexpected lust to hear it. He licked and suckled her, reveling in her abundance, his erection pressing against her soft belly. He was rock hard, as urgently aroused as if he hadn't just had wild, wonderful sex on the living room rug, and her clutching hands, her flushed, shivering eagerness just egged him on.

She was so small, it would be easy to just push her up against the wall, spread her wide, and pin her into place with his thrusting body. And she was still soft from the last time, more than ready to—

"Jonah! The toast!"

He lifted his head and wiped his mouth, dazed. "Huh?"

"The bread! It's starting to burn! Don't you smell the smoke?"

"Damn." He let go of her and lunged for the toaster. "God

damn automatic timer's broken." He sneaked a guilty look at her. "I, uh, thought the smoke was coming out of my ears."

Nothing was going as smoothly as he had hoped, though it was a thousand times more interesting than he had imagined. Too interesting. Of all the sex scenarios he had envisioned, jagged, scary, on-the-edge-of-disaster sex was not one of them. The primal instinct to conquer and subdue. Caveman stuff. Wild. The woman really did it to him.

He fished the bread out of the toaster. Tess was staring down at his erection again. She made a nervous little gesture toward it.

"Wow. Are you always . . . I mean, do you already want to—"

"It can wait while you have something to eat," he said, with what he hoped was a reassuring smile. "This erection isn't going anywhere. Not while you're walking around my kitchen naked." He piled a tangle of roasted pepper onto a chunk of bread. "Come here," he urged. "It drips."

Her smile as she chewed made his chest practically puff out with self-satisfaction. He hand-fed her until she was laughing and begging for mercy—his cue for the coup de grâce. More chocolate soufflé. And he oh-so-clumsily let a big glop of whipped cream slide off the spoon and down over her breasts, leaving a creamy white trail for him to follow with his tongue. There were drops on her belly, and some slid lower to tangle in the luxurious nest of dark ringlets at her crotch.

And that was it. He had to taste her again, right here, right now. He shoved her up against the kitchen cabinets. Her small hands clutched his head, her thighs trembled as he forced his hand between them and opened her, sliding his tongue into her damp curls and seeking the delicious, delicate little bud of pure sensation. Loving it, worshiping it with his tongue. He lapped up her sweet, copious juice, sliding his tongue voluptuously up and down the slick, delicious folds of her tender cleft until she cried out and clenched around his thrusting finger.

She went limp. He caught her before she could fall to the floor, and swept her up into his arms. Time to take this to the bedroom. He didn't want to do anything creative or playful or fun, didn't want to show her the hot tub, didn't want to try any tricks. He just wanted to pin her down on his bed and bury himself in her, face to face, hips grinding, eyes locked. All his.

Staking his claim.

Jonah carried Tess up the staircase and down a corridor, into a large, moonlit bedroom. He laid her on the antique four-poster bed, shoving aside the thick down coverlet. He flicked on a bedside lamp, staring down at her, his eyes hot with predatory hunger.

When he had that look on his face, he made her very nervous.

He pulled a condom out of the bedside stand, rolling it over his erection with casual skill, and climbed into bed, pushing her down onto her back. "You're shivering," he said. "I'll warm you up."

"I just bet you will," she said with false bravado. "You're burning up."

She stiffened against him as he pushed her legs wide, but he had already gained entrance; there was no shutting him out. He shoved the smooth, blunt tip of himself into her and surged inside, in one smooth, seamless thrust. The wind tossed the trees outside. They sighed and moaned uneasily around the house. She splayed her hands against his chest. "Jonah," she said breathlessly. "What are you doing?"

"God. If you have to ask."

He thrust into her, hard enough to make her gasp. She shoved against his chest, suspicious. "Hey. Are you trying to show me who's boss?"

"Now why would I do a stupid, futile thing like that? I know better. Besides, I already know who's boss. I am, because that's how you need it to be. When you want that to change, let me know."

"You arrogant bastard." She writhed, and he responded with a deeper thrust. "You're doing it again. Making me angry on purpose."

"Yeah." His voice was matter-of-fact. "You were getting scared again. What am I supposed to do? Sing you a lullaby?"

"Are you challenging me?" she demanded.

"Do you need to be challenged? How's this for a challenge?" He reached down, hooking her knees with his arms. Spreading her wide.

She tried to gather her wits, but it was hard when he had that dark, volcanic look in his eyes. "Don't answer a question with another question," she said shakily. "It was OK the first time, to trick me out of being nervous, but now you're just pissing me off for the fun of it."

"Why are you afraid of me?" he demanded. "What did I do?"

"I am not afraid of you!"

He swooped down on her with a fierce, hungry kiss, as if he wanted to devour her whole. He lifted his head, panting. "Yes, you are. That's why you're angry. Because it's better than being scared. But there's something on the other side of your anger. I want to know what it is."

"You won't get to it by forcing me," she said sharply.

"Oh, I don't think I'm forcing you." He pushed both her legs to the side, and stared down at where his penis was squeezed between her trapped legs, hot and tight. He slowly pushed himself deeper. Pulled back. The intense friction made her whimper with terrified pleasure.

He found just the angle and pressure she needed. Everything he did was calculated to drive her wild. He was as skillful at manipulating her emotions as he was with her body. She hated him for playing her like an instrument. She loved him for being a virtuoso.

She flew apart around him, sobbing with yet another bursting rush of pleasure, but she felt him holding back his own release. His face was a grimace of concentration. He wasn't done with her yet.

He smoothed the damp curls off her forehead, his own breath shuddering with reaction to the little convulsions pulsing through her body. "You're fine," he said. "I'm not forcing you. Am I?"

She shook her head, her eyes squeezed shut.

"What is it?" he demanded. "Am I hurting you?"

She shook her head, helpless to explain. "Not exactly."

His face was rigid. "What do you mean, not exactly?"

"I don't know what I mean!" she said desperately.

He drove into her, letting her feel his anger. "So figure it out."

She didn't know why he pushed her, where he wanted to take her, what he was trying to force her to admit. But passion overpowered him, too, sweeping away his arrogance and rendering him as helpless, as desperate as she. They gripped each other, and the momentum of their explosion hurtled them unimaginably far. To the far side of fear or anger. Beyond words, beyond thought.

He gathered her into his arms afterward, wordless and trembling. They stared into each other's eyes. Tess tried to speak. An infinitesimal shake of Jonah's head stopped her.

Much later, he disentangled himself, just long enough to dispose of the condom. He slid promptly back into bed and grasped her tightly, as if he needed to assure himself that she was real.

Tess lay in his arms, wide awake, watching the moonlight shimmer on the lake, marveling at this new self that was emerging. Everything she had always taken for granted about herself had been thrown into question. Anything seemed possible.

Jonah's sleeping face seemed younger, innocent and vulnerable. His hand was tucked under his face like a little boy. She lifted the comforter to look at his body. He murmured in protest and rolled onto his back, seeking the lost warmth. She lifted it higher.

He was so beautiful, his broad chest tapering down to a lean, muscular abdomen. The dip and curves and hollows in the muscles of his flanks enticed her. She wanted to stroke them, explore them with her fingers and lips. This was the first time she had seen his penis soft. It was dark and curled up on its nest of hair. She touched it with the tip of her finger. Velvety soft, tender, and vulnerable. She touched the bulge of his scrotum, tracing a barely there caress, as soft as a kiss. Relaxed and vulnerable like this, he didn't intimidate her at all. Nothing stood between her and the impulse to lean forward and take his penis in her hands.

She caressed his balls, following the delicate tracery of veins, marveling at the unexpected fragility of his body. She stroked the graceful lines of his groin, his muscular thighs. Leaned forward to inhale his scent, musky and male, mixed with the smell of sex, of herself. He was already swelling, thickening. Fuller, longer. Quickening in her hand.

He jerked awake with a sharp exclamation, his body rigid with surprise, and stared at her, dazed with sleep. She smiled, and closed her hand around his penis, pulling slowly. "Oh, God," he said thickly.

She put her finger over her lips. "Shh."

He reached for her, but she shoved him down without ceremony.

He had woken up in the middle of one of his favorite adolescent wet dreams. She was a fantasy princess, gorgeous and stacked. All she needed was a little metal armored bikini, like Red Sonja. No, scratch that. To hell with the bikini. She didn't need a damned thing. She was naked. She was perfect. She was heaven.

She slid down his body with voluptuous slowness, licking and kissing him everywhere. She rubbed his cock gently against her silky soft, flushed cheek, kissed him with her lush lips, and then pulled him into her mouth, a warm, liquid, sliding, suckling bliss. She slid her clever little tongue all over the seething tension at the tip of his cock, making him sob with pleasure.

She pushed his legs apart and cuddled up between them, her eyes mysterious pools in the moonlight. She gripped him, a hard, strong grasp as he had shown her, and drew him deep into her mouth.

It was the sweetest, most delicious, explosively exciting thing he had ever felt. Heavenly torture. She lapped at him like a kitten lapping cream, sliding and swirling her tongue. He arched off the bed and cried out, begging her not to stop. But she wasn't stopping. She tried everything that came into her head—deep and slow, hard and fast. Exploring him, putting him through his paces, finding out what made him weep with pleasure, what made him scream.

She settled into a lazy rhythm of suckling bliss. Her other hand crept around his waist and caressed his ass, pulling him even deeper into her mouth. He flung his head back and stared up at the moon, his eyes filling with white light as his orgasm rushed through him, huge and uncontrollable. She let out a surprised sound at the long, wrenching spasm of pleasure. There was an astonished silence.

"Sorry," he muttered, as soon as he could speak.

She wiped her mouth and kissed his thigh. "What for?"

"I didn't ask if it would be OK. To come in your mouth, I mean. It just, uh, happened," he said cautiously.

"Don't worry about it," she murmured. "I think I communicated nonverbally that I had no problem with that."

He was still panting, dizzy with pleasure. "Do you want me to, uh, get you a glass of water?" he offered.

She reflected for a moment. "That would be nice."

He scrambled to his feet and stumbled, weak-kneed, to

the bathroom. Ran her a glass of water and brought it back to her. "That was amazing," he said as she drank. "A fantasy come true. Thank you."

"I liked it," she said.

"Anytime," he assured her. "I swear. Anytime."

He waited until he was sure she was asleep before he dared to close his eyes, but even then, they wouldn't close. He was too dazzled by the blazing moonlight to sleep now. Too astonished by the sweet passion of the mysterious woman in his arms.

He held her close against him and let the shape of the moon burn itself into his sleepless eyes.

Chapter Six

She woke up disoriented. Her body felt different. Sore, glowing, strangely alive. The air on her face was cold, but her body was incredibly, wonderfully warm, tangled up in the sleek, powerful limbs of—oh, God. It wasn't a dream. It was Jonah, holding her tightly against him. His muscular chest rose and fell beneath her cheek.

Memories flooded back, of what he had done to her, what she had done in return. She didn't even recognize the woman she had been; wild and desperate, out of control. At his mercy, body and soul. She had never been like that with anyone. Jonah had pried open doors she never knew were there. He had moved her to the core. And if Larry had been able to wreak such havoc with her feelings and her self-esteem, she could not even bear to imagine the damage that Jonah could do.

The mountain was glowing pink with dawn, and the spectacular beauty of it just scared her all the more. Her eyes were wide and hot, and her stomach ached with nameless dread. She jumped nervously as Jonah stirred beneath her and lifted his head. "What?" he said sleepily.

"How did you know I was awake?" she whispered.

"I heard you thinking," he said grumpily. "What's wrong?"

"Nothing." She wiggled out of his arms.

"Bullshit." He wrapped his arms around her and pulled until her back was sealed against the delicious heat of his torso. "You're upset."

She struggled away from him and sat up. The drawer of the little nightstand was open, a box of condoms torn open, used wrappers discarded on the surface. She covered her hot face with her hands and let out a harsh little laugh. "Condoms everywhere, huh? Living room, dining room, bedroom; do you keep them in every room in the house?"

"What the hell? You're upset because I have condoms?"

"It's not the condoms. It's the thought of being one of a crowd. Do you bring a different woman here every weekend?" She knew she was being bitchy and unreasonable, but the words just flew out.

His body stiffened. "Stop it. That's not fair. I told you that I'm not seeing anyone else, and my past is none of your goddamn business."

"You are so right." She scrambled out of bed. "I'll just grab my clothes and be on my way." She looked around. "Where are my clothes?"

"Scattered all over the living room floor." He lunged for her, hauling her back against him, and dropped down onto the bed, pulling her onto his lap, against his hot, prominent erection. He grabbed her arms and wrapped them around her waist, clasping her wrists and holding her in a breathless clinch. He pressed his face against the side of her neck. "What the fuck is the matter with you?"

She struggled against his tight embrace. "You," she spat out. "You're the matter with me, Jonah Markham. I want to go, and you're holding onto me like a vise. Let me go, and I'll be fine."

"No way," he said. "You're not going anywhere. Not in this mood."

She twisted around, staring up into his furious eyes. "You can't keep me here against my will."

"Watch me."

She went very still in his grasp, appalled. "But that's—"

She squeaked in alarm as he flung himself onto his back, taking her with him. He rolled over so that she was flat on her belly and he was on top of her, covering her. His erection pressed against her bottom, hard and urgent. If he dared, if he even so much as *thought* that he could—panic exploded inside her. She wriggled frantically.

"Jonah," she said breathlessly. "This isn't right."

"I've already tried to do the right thing. I did everything you said. I obeyed you to the letter—"

"Oh, sure! Like hell! You totally ravished me. I was not in control for one second," she said furiously.

"Only when you gave me permission," he pointed out.

She craned her neck up at him, glaring. "And when did I do that? I do not recall doing that!"

"Bullshit," he said impatiently. "Sex is messy and complicated. At least good sex. Good sex doesn't follow rules, it follows instinct. And the sex was more than good. It was incredible. I made you come till you fainted. And now you're acting like I'm Jack the Ripper."

She gasped in outrage. "I did not—"

"So fuck it. If following the rules doesn't earn me any points, then fuck the rules. No more rules, Tess, except for mine."

She froze beneath him. "You're scaring me now, Jonah."

He let out a snort of disgust. "Don't be stupid. I would never hurt you. I'm just not going to let you run out on me. I *will . . . not . . . allow it*."

"Damn it, Jonah—"

"This is just a spasm. It'll pass, and you'll thank me later."

The calm certainty in his tone sparked a burst of furious strength, and she made one more wrenching effort to throw him off. He shifted, trapping her legs between his and burying his face against her hair.

"Damn, but you're difficult," he muttered. "All I want to do is kiss you and pet you and tell you how gorgeous you are. I want to make you come again. Then I want to cook you an incredible breakfast. Why won't you just go with it and let me make you feel good?"

She couldn't think of a coherent answer to that. There was no good answer. The pleading tone in his voice confused her, made her heart ache and burn. She was so sick of the constant effort of staying clenched up like a fist. Exhausted from struggling to make it all alone, tired of the constricted feeling in her chest. Jonah was the antithesis of that, with his big, gorgeous body and his voluptuous appetite for pleasure, for laughter, and spontaneous delight. He had sneaked through her guard, and now he utterly refused to yield the ground he had gained. But the real problem was the burning ache of longing.

The real problem was her own reckless, treacherous heart.

To her embarrassment, she dissolved into tears. She pressed her face against the sheet to hide the silent scream of frustration, and sobs tore through her, out of control. A cynical voice in her mind pointed out that if she wanted to definitively scare him away, a good crying jag ought to do the trick. Heaven knew it always worked with Larry.

But Jonah just curled himself over her, nuzzling his face into the curve of her neck and shoulder. Breathing with her.

She cried for everything: for the shame of having disappointed her family, for the embarrassment of disappointing Larry. For how small and inadequate she had come to feel before she'd finally realized that she would never, ever satisfy them, no matter how hard she tried. For the desperation that had spurred her to run away, for the loneliness and the doubts, the hard work and penny-pinching, the effort of trying to build a life on her own, against all advice. It swept through her like a storm, thunder and lightning and a hot rain of tears.

Sometime later, she realized that she had stopped crying. A while ago. Maybe she had even slept for a while. She had cried herself to sleep with a big, live, warm Jonah blanket on top of her. She would have giggled if she had the energy.

Jonah dropped tiny questioning kisses on her neck, like he was afraid of scaring her. His breath was so warm and soft. He took the shell of her ear gently between his teeth and tugged at it. A soft, animal gesture, demanding, insisting, coaxing.

She felt renewed, reborn. Clear and light, but shivering, like she could melt into tears again at any moment. Full of light that flickered and changed with every breath, every thought. Her face buzzed with energy, as if electricity were running through it. She pressed her damp face on the sheet. "I need a Kleenex," she said soggily.

He reached out, and presented her with a Kleenex.

"I need my hand," she informed him. "To blow my nose."

They gazed at each other for a long, doubtful moment, and he let go of one of her hands, and watched her blow her nose.

"Are you OK now?" he ventured.

She made a little jerking motion that would have been a shrug if she hadn't been pinned to the bed. "I think so," she murmured.

He slid some of his weight to the side and stroked his hand very slowly, very tenderly over her hip. "So it wouldn't be a profound insult to your person if I did . . . this?" His fingers tangled tenderly into the thatch of ringlets between her legs.

She felt so shaky and melted and soft that her body was almost unbearably sensitive, but his touch was tender and unerring. She made a tiny, whispery little sound in the back of her throat and slowly parted her legs for him, letting him seek her pleasure.

And he found it. The rush of liquid heat was almost immediate. She clenched her trembling thighs around his hand. "You're taking advantage of my shaky emotional state," she accused him.

"With you, I'd better take every advantage I can get."

She laughed at him, and closed her eyes, squeezing her face against the crumpled sheets when the laughter started to blend into tears. She was so shaky and vulnerable, she felt like she were inside out. Every brushing touch, every kiss had a shocking, crackling intensity that shot through her whole body, jacking up the heavy yearning between her thighs into something hot and desperate.

She arched her back for him, opening wider and moving against his hand in silent pleading as he prepared her, spreading her slick juices across her vulva. She heard the tiny rip of the condom packet he was opening, the time it took to roll it over himself, and he slid his arm below her hips, raising her bottom. And then the relentless push and surge of his heat and hardness, sliding into her. Part of her.

He slowed down at the breathless sound she made, but he couldn't stop. He knew instinctively that if she bolted now, he would never pin her down again. And everything depended on keeping her here with him. He hoped he hadn't misjudged everything, ruined everything, but his sleep-fuddled wit failed him to think of any way other than seduction to soothe and persuade her.

The dawn revealed a whole array of new little perfect details, the pattern of scattered moles that set off the opalescent paleness of her skin, the sweet little dimples at the top of her buttocks. His breath caught in his lungs. She was the sexiest thing he had ever seen, the sensual curve and arch of her back, that round, rosy, gorgeous ass all spread out for him, the tight, glistening pink lips of her cunt clasping him, caressing him. Arching silently up, asking for more.

He settled into a deep, pounding rhythm, following the cues she gave him, the pulsing of her bottom as she jerked up to meet him, the rough sobbing of her breath. He curved himself over her so he could kiss her shoulders, her back, nuzzle her hair as he surged into her.

She twisted around, her eyes dewy and huge. "Jonah, wait."

Icy panic sped through his veins. He'd read the cues wrong, he'd committed the unforgivable sin, he was an unredeemable jerk.

He clasped her bottom in his hands and withdrew from her immediately. "What? Did I hurt you?"

She twisted around, and shook her head. "I just want to be able to move a little more. Can we change positions?"

Relief made him dizzy. "Hell, yes. Any position you want."

She scrambled up onto her knees. She had him right where she wanted him, if she only knew it. A panting puppy, desperate to please, terrified of making a mistake. She pushed him down onto his back and straddled him. He blinked, astonished, up into her cautious little smile.

"I'd like to try it this way," she said. "Is that OK with you?"

"Are you kidding? Anything is OK with me. Anything at all," he said shakily. From his position below, her luscious tits were full and enticing. He cupped them in his hands with a moan of delight. The plump heft of them, the tickle of her puckered nipples against his palms. Heaven.

He tried to be patient and let her figure out the mechanics of it, but she was adorably awkward and slow to find the right angle. It was driving him crazy. He gripped her hips, lifting her until he could nudge his stiff cock slowly inside her. He groaned in an agony of pleasure at the resistance of her tight, hot sheath as it clasped him, accepting him with tantalizing slowness. She slid down the length of his shaft, inch by delicious inch, eyes wide with discovery.

She braced her hands against his chest and began hesitantly to move, and he soon saw the realization dawning in her eyes, the hot flush of excitement as she shifted herself, rubbing against him with a purring moan of pleasure. She closed her eyes and flung her head back, and her hips pulsed faster and faster against him. It was so beautiful, and it squeezed his heart; it made everything inside him shake apart into a rushing torrent that swept them both away.

When he opened his eyes, he realized that she was crying again. But he could hardly object, since he was trembling on the brink of it himself. His throat was quivering, and his lungs hitched and shuddered dangerously when he tried to pull in a deep breath. He cuddled her and stared at the ceiling. "This is not normal," he blurted.

She snuggled against his neck. "Hmm? What's not normal?"

"For sex to be this good," he admitted. "I don't know about you, but this is not normal for me. I mean, I always like it fine. What's not to like? But it doesn't usually—" He stopped and shook his head, wishing he'd kept his big mouth shut.

She pushed herself up onto her elbow. "Doesn't what?"

"Blow my mind. Leave me all scared and humble and shaky."

She smiled. Her eyes were full of perfect understanding. "Like you've been run over by a herd of stampeding buffalo?"

He winced. "Ouch. I wasn't that rough, was I?"

"I meant that in a good way," she assured him.

He scowled. "What's good about being trampled by buffalo?"

"Oh, don't be so sensitive," she murmured. "You know exactly what I mean."

He yanked her back down against his chest and hid his face against her hair. She was laughing at him. The sound vibrated through his body. It was disturbing, to feel so doubtful and awkward and raw.

"Maybe I'm supposed to apologize for having been all macho and controlling just now," he said carefully. "But being as how it had the desired effect of keeping you in my bed, I'm not going to. You're still here, so I must be doing something right. I hope."

Tess extricated herself from his arms and gave him a slow, solemn nod. "So, uh . . . now what happens?" she asked.

He sensed that her question was fraught with importance, but he was too shaky to deal with anything heavy after being trampled by a herd of buffalo. He kissed the tip of her nose. "Now we go down to the kitchen, where I proceed to make you buttermilk pancakes. Fluffy and golden, with real butter and maple syrup. Bacon, or ham, or eggs if you want them. Fresh squeezed orange juice. Strawberries. Fresh ground French roast coffee with half and half."

"Oh, my God," she said weakly. "That's not fair, Jonah."

"My secret weapon," he said smugly. "The way straight to your heart. I'll keep you here with me in my seductive trap, baited with whipped cream and wild sex. You'll never want to leave."

"Hmm." She sat up and cocked her head to the side, studying him with eyes that were too solemn. "If I tried to leave, would you stop me?"

Tension gripped him. He tried to keep his voice light. "I'll use every resource I've got. Including maple syrup and whipped cream."

"And brute force?" She wrapped her arms around her knees and studied him intently.

He took her hand, pulling it up to his lips and kissing her knuckles. "Let's just say that I really, really hope that you won't put me to the test."

And thanks be to God, she let it go at that.

Breakfast was a resounding success, judging from the approving moans of pleasure and the amount that she tucked in. She tried to do the dishes, but he was adamant. "Nah. Forget it. You're a guest."

She giggled and stuck another perfect ripe strawberry in her mouth. "But I was supposed to work this weekend."

"So things change. Now you're a guest. Which reminds me. We have to think about dinner. Do you like steak?"

"How can you already think about dinner? Of course I like steak!"

"With herbed baby red potatoes? Stuffed mushrooms and grilled eggplant? Ceasar salad? Strawberry shortcake? Or should we go with the Dutch apple pie with the whipped cream and caramel sauce?"

She shook her head, laughing. "Are you trying to impress me?"

"Yes," he admitted baldly.

She sat on his lap, wrapping her arms around his neck. "It worked," she admitted. "I'm impressed. I'm charmed, my defenses are in ruins. You can relax. You don't have to go to such ridiculous lengths."

His cock started swelling beneath the sweet pressure of her ass. "Don't encourage me," he said. "I'll feel compelled to do my filet mignon with caramelized onions, so I can conquer you utterly."

"You always conquer me utterly," she said quietly. "Every time you touch me."

In a heartbeat, he found himself kissing her desperately. Hints of coffee, of cream and strawberries clung to her soft lips. He was on the verge of just lifting her up onto the table, shoving down his jeans and thrusting into her. He could already imagine every scalding, pounding detail: her soft thighs locked around his waist, her tender little cunt gripping him all the way to the screaming finish.

No condom. He hadn't put one in his pocket. God. He pulled back, panting and speechless, and hid his face against her chest.

She slid off his lap. "I'll just, um, run and take a shower."

He managed a speechless nod, his heart still thudding.

He was wiping down the counters when she came downstairs, a cloud of moist, perfumed air clinging to her. She was wearing the Little House on the Prairie dress again. It almost succeeded in hiding how sexy she was, but then again, he hadn't been fooled from the start.

"You shouldn't hide behind your clothes," he said.

Her face went so pale and stiff that he barely recognized her. "I didn't ask for your opinion of my wardrobe."

He cursed his own idiocy and searched for a remedy in the frigid silence that followed. "Uh, I wasn't criticizing. I only meant that—"

"I know perfectly well what you meant. *Let . . . it . . . go.*"

"Sorry, sorry," he said hastily. "Look, do you, uh, want to go for a walk in the woods? It's raining, and your shoes and clothes aren't great for it. They'll get muddy. But I think it's worth it."

Her face lit up like a torch, his gaffe forgotten. He was pathetically grateful for the distraction.

The dress got damp around the hem almost instantly, and the pristine white tennis shoes she wore with the Vee Have Vays dress would never be white again. In fact, at this point, they were barely recognizable as shoes. Thorny branches snagged the skirt as they pushed through the underbrush, and before long her face was beaded with rain, she was soaked from the waist down, and slimed with mud up to her ankles. She'd been let loose in a mythical fantasy world, pulsing with mystery and magic. She had never been so happy in her life.

Huge trees disappeared into the mist above them, their branches tipped with the bright, lambent new growth of spring. Pale yellow glacier lilies poked up out of the pine needles, jewel-like drops of rain clinging to their drooping heads. The earthy sweetness of the air made her dizzy. They could've been Adam and Eve in the garden, wandering through the breathless, vaulted hush of a forest cathedral, speechless with awe.

She stared at Jonah's tight, muscular butt from behind and finally understood what moved people to grope and grab and fondle, an instinct that had always struck her as vulgar. Hah. What a humbling surprise. She was so far beyond vulgar, she couldn't even remember what the far side of it looked like. She wanted to grab his butt, pet it, sink her teeth into it. Yank those jeans down and run her hands all over his big body, to feel every dip and curve, every muscle. The graceful way his sweater draped his torso, the long, clean, elegant lines of him made her so breathless with lust, it was impossible to think.

He smiled at her over his shoulder, and her knees almost buckled at his beauty—every delicious detail: the good-natured crinkles around his beautiful gray eyes, the sexy grooves that bracketed his mouth. He turned to go on. She lunged toward him. "Jonah. Wait."

"Hmm?"

"Hold still." She slogged heedlessly through the soggy undergrowth until she reached him, and laid a hand on his chest, feeling his warmth, the rise and fall of his breath through the damp fabric. She put her other hand against his face, smoothing the elegant planes and hollows with her fingertips. She ran her fingers through his glossy dark hair, along his strong neck, his broad shoulders.

Wordless comprehension dawned in his eyes. He understood the impulse that moved her. He waited quietly, letting her have her fill of touching him. Reassuring her of his warm, solid reality. Being there for her. Silently communicating his readiness.

He placed his hands over hers. "All yours," he said softly. "Anytime, anywhere, any way you like. Just tell me what you want."

She slid her hands around his waist, under his shirt. Gripped his lean waist, slid around to feel the taut muscles in his back. Then his butt, with a low, humming sound of approval. He drew in a harsh breath as she ran her hand over the bulge in his jeans, measuring the heat and length and hardness of him.

"I like this place," she told him. "It makes me feel primeval."

A hot flush burned itself high onto his cheekbones. "You're different today," he said. "You've changed. You take up more space."

"Yes," she agreed. "I do. I feel it, too."

He shoved her up against a tree, his hands moving eagerly over the sodden dress. "I like it," he said. "It turns me on."

She snickered. "Yeah, and what doesn't?"

He yanked up the waterlogged dress. "Primeval, huh? I guess that means you want me to be all macho and masterful and Neanderthal?"

She challenged him with her smile. "You really go for that, don't you?"

"With you, I go for anything." He plucked at the barrier of the wool tights with an exclamation of disgust. "Layers upon layers. Jesus. You do like to present a guy with a challenge, don't you?"

"So easily discouraged, Jonah?"

She abruptly regretted taunting him when he grabbed the wool knit fabric and ripped it open with one sharp wrench. "Wrong answer."

"Jonah! You're wrecking my—"

"Too bad," he said. Another sharp tug, and her panties gave way. Her most intimate flesh was open to the cool, damp breeze. "My primeval woman is always ready for me to tear open her fur robes, pin her up against a tree, and go for it."

She tried to steady herself by grabbing handfuls of his sweater. "It's dangerous to challenge you," she said shakily.

"You get off on it, though, don't you?" He parted the folds of her sex and caressed her tenderly with his finger, dipping into her liquid heat with a low growl of hunger. "You like pushing me to the edge."

He seized her mouth in a conquering kiss that did not coax or wheedle or charm. He claimed what was rightfully his. His savage ruthlessness was no game, and they both knew it. It was the truth between them, at its most elemental. He drew back, his eyes glowing with primal heat. "You want me to fuck you right here, don't you?"

She licked her lips. "Yes," she whispered.

"Say it. Say the words," he demanded. "I need to hear them."

Such a thing would have been impossible yesterday. But not anymore. She squeezed her eyes shut and took a deep breath.

"I want you to fuck me right here," she said clearly.

She was almost afraid to open her eyes and see the triumph on his face, but he didn't look triumphant. His face was a taut mask of need. "I love it when you talk dirty," he said hoarsely.

He shoved her back against the tree and plunged her back into the chaos of his kiss. She was pinned and breathless, her toes barely touching the ground, whimpering against his mouth, rubbing herself against his hard body. Reaching with every instinct for something shining just beyond her reach. He tantalized her until she couldn't take anymore. She groped for his belt, the buttons on his jeans. He hadn't bothered with underwear. His penis sprang out, turgid and ready, into her eager hands.

He had to set her down to retrieve the condom, and she took the opportunity to stroke and caress his engorged shaft, making him gasp and curse under his breath. He pushed her hands away just long enough to roll the condom on, and then scooped one of her legs up high, pressing his thick, blunt flesh against her labia, pushing slowly inside. She was tender from the unaccustomed sex, but so aroused that the sting was just a sharp definition around a hot, demanding ache of pleasure.

He forged inside until he had sheathed himself completely, and leaned against her, breathing hard. She could feel his heart pounding, his breath feathering her hair, his body trembling, his fingers digging into her bare bottom.

He stared into her eyes, holding her in a tight, speechless communion, and began to move. He withdrew with agonizing slowness, and surged in again, making her feel the sweet, licking caress of each stroke, inch by inch. It went on and on like that, until she began to pant. She was a live flame writhing against the tree, desperate for the plunge and slide of his thick shaft. She needed . . . she needed—

"Jonah," she gasped. "Please. More."

"More what?" His voice was as harsh and shaky as hers.

She clawed at his sweater, at his naked waist. "More everything! Move, damn it!"

He laughed triumphantly, and gave her what she needed. The power he had awakened swelled, bursting hot and golden in her chest and belly, surging like a fountain of molten liquid pleasure between her legs. Everything gave way to that blinding rush.

He waited for her orgasm to subside, nuzzling her neck, petting her bottom, murmuring against her hair. Then he eased himself out of her and let her slide down until her feet hit the ground. He caught her when her knees gave way, holding her until she found her balance.

And even then, he wouldn't let go. He held her tight against him, warm and panting and damp. Chest heaving against hers. He pushed her hair aside with his face and kissed the side of her neck as he arranged himself, zipping his jeans and buckling his belt. "You OK?"

She nodded, unable to speak. Her knees were weak, her legs still tangled in her ruined tights, her voice tangled in her throat.

He pushed back her hair, his eyes worried. "Sure?"

She didn't know how to express how she felt. She didn't even recognize the feelings roaring through her. Needs that could not be denied, emotions that blazed up like fires rushed through her like a flash floods, changing the landscape of her inner self in an instant, carving out canyons, mudslides, unexpected chasms.

She flung back her head. Drops of rain shed by the trees fell onto her face, pale sunlight pressed against her closed eyelids. She breathed in the heat, the light, the wild freedom of this new, changing self.

When she finally dared to open her eyes, he was staring at her face, fascinated. He didn't think she was crazy or hysterical or overwrought. His face was alight with triumph.

He knew exactly what was happening to her, and he liked it.

He pulled her close and sank his teeth gently into her throat with a fierce growl of approval. "You're fine," he whispered. "More than fine."

"I'm flying," she whispered back.

She abandoned the sodden dress and put on one of Jonah's T-shirts when they got back to the house.

When she came downstairs, he was building a fire. "Want me to make you some lunch?" he asked.

"How about a massage?" she suggested.

His eyes lit up. "Hell, yes. But only if you feel like it."

She gave him a misty smile, still euphoric from the forest. "I feel like it. I like pleasing you. But lie down on the rug this time, not the table. Otherwise it'll be too much like work, and I'll get confused."

He stripped and lay down with a sigh of blissful anticipa-

tion. She laid her oiled hands against him, and the strength
of the charge between them ran all the way up her arms,
made her shiver. She didn't have to soothe or calm him this
time. His barriers were already flung wide. Her hot, tingling
hands moved over him of their own volition. She had never
felt so powerful. She would have floated right up into the air
but for the immense gravitational force of his beautiful
body.

She had no idea how long she touched him. It could have
been hours. She would never have stopped if he hadn't rolled
over with a sigh of pure delight and reached for her.
"Please," he said simply.

He pulled the loose shirt over her head, flung it away, and
pulled her into his arms, pressing his face against her hair.
He squirted some of her oil onto his hands began to explore
her body with the same reverent attention to detail that she
had just given his. His hands slid slowly over her skin, as if
he wanted to memorize every inch of her. He kneaded her
shoulders and arms, hands, fingertips. He traced every verte-
bra in her back, brushed his fingertips across her ribs in soft,
feathery circular strokes. He explored the hollows of her collar-
bone, the muscles and tendons in her neck. He touched her
face, tracing every feature, following his caresses with kisses
like a hot, soft rain.

She huddled against him, lost in ever-widening ripples of
pleasure. She sighed as his hands moved lovingly over her
breasts, but he was just as fascinated with her belly button,
her throat. His touch soothed her into a state of perfect trust,
amazed by the luminous tenderness between them. His generosity made her want to offer him the best of herself.
Everything that was good and kind and true.

They were melted **into** one shining being when they
groped for the condom. Four trembling hands fumbled together, gleaming with scented oil and clumsy with eagerness
as they smoothed it over him. A sweet confusion of arranging limbs, kisses and sighs, and finally he settled her into

place, straddling him, her legs around his waist. The whole length of their torsos were in hot, kissing contact. Her nipples brushed against his chest. She wiggled carefully, reaching below herself to grasp him, seeking the angle that would permit him to nudge inside her soft opening. She let gravity do the rest, sinking down and enveloping him.

Joy swelled inside her, almost painful, but she welcomed the pain. He was so beautiful, it hurt to look at him. She hugged him close, leaning her forehead against his as they rocked together—sometimes almost motionless, locked together in a circle of shimmering perfection where neither dared to breathe, then melting seamlessly into pulsing, surging movement once again. She didn't want it to ever end.

The fire died down to embers, untended and forgotten. Light faded, but they stayed clasped together, afraid to break the spell.

But the room grew cold. Rain slanted down, gusting against the windows. She began to shiver, both inside and out, as she realized what she had done. She had flung herself wide open, held out body, heart, and soul in front of her like a sacrificial offering, and he had swooped down like a hungry bird of prey and taken them all.

If it had only been her body, that would have been perilous enough. But he had laid claim to all of it. He had devoured her, pleasured her beyond any fantasy with his sweet, ravishing tenderness.

He stirred against her neck. "No sunset tonight," he said with soft regret. "I should've grabbed my chance last night."

"Chance for what?"

"To look at you in the sunset. But that's OK. You're beautiful in any kind of light. Hey, you're getting cold. Wrap this around yourself."

She accepted the blanket without protest, but he sensed every shift in her mood, even in the darkness. He turned her face to what little light still glowed from the windows. "What?" he demanded.

She forced out a laugh. "Nothing," she said. "Hungry, I guess."

The tiny frown between his brows did not fade. "I'll make dinner."

"I'll help." She held up her hand, forestalling his protests. "Just let me chop veggies, set the table. I promise I won't get in your way."

Doing something mundane and practical might help this dull, scared ache taking hold inside her. At least she hoped it would.

Chapter Seven

They worked together silently. She washed salad greens, he prepared the steaks, put the potatoes on to boil, and stuck the stuffed mushrooms in the toaster oven. He opened a bottle of wine and poured her a glass.

"Tell me about yourself," he blurted out.

She was thrown off balance by the demand. "Tell you what?"

He shrugged. "Anything, everything. Hopes, dreams, plans. I've been so focused on getting you into my bed that I've gone about this whole thing backward. If you'd gone out to dinner with me when I wanted, I would've had all these facts straight by now. But no. You had to blow me off, string me along. Make me wait."

She relaxed a little and sipped her wine. "OK. I come from San Francisco, and I just moved to Portland three years ago and enrolled in massage school. I got my license last year."

"Last year?" He looked incredulous. "But you're amazing. I would have thought you'd been doing it for years."

She sighed. "I should've been, but I was too busy trying to make my parents approve of me. A losing battle if ever there was one, which culminated in my dropping out of my last term in business school. They still haven't recovered from that."

"Business school? You?"

She laughed at his expression. "Yeah, it's a concept, isn't it?"

He turned the steaks that sizzled on the grill. "So, to be a massage therapist, that's what you've always wanted, then?"

"I've always liked it. I was always good at giving massages, and it's something I never get tired of. The more I learn about the body, the more I like it. I'm opening my own studio, as soon as I can scrape the money together. I want to create a perfect environment for therapeutic massage. Maybe eventually expanding into a sort of mini spa."

He nodded his approval, and turned to the sink to drain the potatoes. "And?" he said expectantly.

She lifted her eyebrows. "And what?"

"I was hoping you would tell me about the playboy who trampled all over you," he said.

Her stomach knotted up. "Let's not and say we did, shall we?"

The potatoes sizzled as he tossed them into the hot pot with melted butter and fresh herbs. "Please, Tess," he said quietly. "Just the bare bones."

She sighed. "Larry," she said finally. "My ex-fiancé. The CEO of my dad's investment banking firm, which I was being groomed to join. And he wasn't really a playboy, to be honest. He worked very hard, and he's good at what he does. It's just that he has really high standards."

Jonah paused in the task of transferring the steaks onto plates, his face baffled. "Meaning?" he asked. "You're a goddess. Beautiful, smart, fascinating, sexy. What was his problem?"

She laughed at his gallant flattery, blinking away a rush of tears. "You are so sweet."

He frowned. "I am not sweet. High standards for what?"

"Larry felt that he deserved the best in everything," she explained wearily. "He wanted top quality, especially in his wife. He picked me out mainly because I possessed the sterling attribute of being the boss's daughter, but to do him credit, he truly did think that he could train me into being good enough. He told me once I was great raw material."

Jonah drizzled olive oil on the salad, waiting patiently for more. "And?" he prompted.

She shrugged. The memory of Larry's disapproval made her queasy and depressed. "I wasn't trainable," she said flatly. "In fact, I was a hopeless case. I was the wrong shape, I dressed wrong, I didn't laugh at the right places in the conversation, I wasn't witty enough, I couldn't—"

The wooden spoon froze in the act of tossing salad. "He didn't like your *shape?*" Jonah looked horrified. "What planet was he from?"

Trust Jonah to fixate on that. She was touched by his dismay.

"He wanted me to be more, uh, contained," she explained. "Larry was into control. Finally I just couldn't take anymore. I ran away. Like a coward, I guess."

"Like hell!"

She flinched back, startled by his tone.

"He didn't appreciate you because he was a brain-dead asshole! And you ran away because you're brave, and smart, and no matter what he said, you know your own worth deep inside."

She blinked at him, utterly taken aback. "Uh, well . . . thank you for defending me, Jonah. You are really—"

"Sweet, yeah. Right." He thumped the wooden salad bowl down onto the counter with such force that greens flipped into the air. Chunks of radicchio and arugula flopped over the sides.

She crossed her arms over her chest and studied his rigid face. "You're angry," she whispered.

"Sure I am. It pisses me off that people put you down. It

pisses me off even more that you bought into their bullshit. And you still do."

She closed her mouth with a snap and crossed her arms over her chest. "Oh. I see. How about if you tell me some intimate, painful details about your past now, so I can criticize you and judge you? Go on."

He opened his mouth to respond, but the cell phone on the counter rang, cutting him off. He checked the number on the display, and his face suddenly went blank of all expression. "I have to take this call," he said. "Stir the potatoes, would you?"

He walked out onto the covered side porch. Tess craned her neck to watch him as she stirred the sizzling potatoes and herbs. It was none of her business, but she couldn't help peeking. His face was grim and tense, and he listened more than he talked. Bad news.

After a few minutes, he came back inside and dropped the phone back onto the counter. He met her questioning gaze. "Work," he said.

She turned back to the potatoes without a word.

Jonah slipped his arms around her waist and took the spatula from her hand. He stirred the potatoes, turned off the flame, and kissed her shoulder where the neck of his T-shirt had slipped off, leaving it bare. "I'm sorry," he said. "It was none of my business."

"It's OK," she whispered.

"No, it's not. We were in a really fine place together, and I wrecked it somehow. I don't know what I said or did, but I—"

"It's not you." She spun around and hugged him hard, pressing her hand against his mouth when he tried to speak again.

His chest heaved in a heavy sigh. He kissed her fingers, and his arms tightened around her. She squeezed as hard as she could. Larry would have been horrified by her intensity, but Jonah seemed unfazed.

After a long while, he lifted his head. "Food's getting cold."

They smiled at each other carefully. "So let's eat," she said.

He'd broken the spell somehow. He could've kicked himself.

Good food was always a point in his favor, but it wasn't enough to bring back that perfect, shimmering intimacy of their magic afternoon. Now that he'd had a taste of it, he would forever be pining for more.

Half of his mind was reeling over the news Dr. Morrison had called to deliver. Triple bypass surgery for Granddad on Wednesday.

Ever ready to multitask, the rest of his brain churned right along, speculating on what the hell he might have said or done to pitch them into this awful downward spiral. They ate, chatting inanely. Both trying so hard to be neutral and nice that he wanted to scream. It was like a big, dark animal was sitting on the dining room table blocking their view of each other, and they were trying to pretend it didn't exist.

There had to be some way to dispel it.

He dished up the hot Dutch apple pie, scooped ice cream over it, and drizzled it with hot caramel sauce, and when he turned around she was cupping her stubborn pointed chin in her hands, looking stern.

"OK, Jonah. Your turn," she announced.

"For what?" He was pathetically relieved to see the sparkle back in her eyes. He preferred a difficult spitfire to a timid, careful mouse.

"Now you tell me something about you." She sat back in her chair, looking expectant.

He set her heaping dish of pie and ice cream before her. "OK," he said obediently. "I'm thirty-five. I have my own consulting business, specializing in problem solving and brainstorming techniques."

She rolled her eyes. "Blah, blah, blah. I read all that in your profile in *Northwest Business*. I was thinking a bit more personal, please."

"Personal?" He eyed her suspiciously. "What do you want to know about, my ex-girlfriends?"

She took a bite of her pie. "I was thinking more along the lines of family," she said loftily. "Basic historical detail. Are you a dog person or a cat person? Do you resemble your mother or your father?"

"No parents," he said. "They were killed in a plane crash in Chile. My dad was an archaeologist. I was eleven."

Tess's spoon froze in the air near her mouth. She slowly lowered it. "Oh, God, Jonah. I'm sorry. I didn't mean to—"

"It's OK," he assured her. "It was a long time ago. And I got through it. I had Granddad. He was the one who raised me. He was great. Strict, but great."

"He's still alive?" she asked cautiously.

"Yeah." *God willing and the creek don't rise,* he thought, silently willing her to change the subject.

They ate their dessert silently for a minute or two, both of them afraid of making another wrong move.

Finally Tess lay down her spoon and took a deep, audible breath. She touched his hand. "Jonah. That phone call. Was it bad news?"

He stared down at her hand. His throat tightened. He didn't want to talk about it. His stomach was knotted enough as it was, thinking about Granddad's chances. And then there were John and Steve, trying like hell to keep him out of the loop. Worried about their cut in the fucking will, as if he gave a shit about Granddad's money. He'd made plenty of his own, but that didn't help matters. His very success showed up their own lack of ability and made them hate him all the more.

It was all so raw that even at the thought of her gentle

sympathy, the questions she would ask, made him flinch. He would shove her away by reflex if she tried to comfort him, and that would cook his goose for sure. That was no way to get back to their magical union.

He took a deep breath and did what he had to do. He plastered on a bright, ain't-life-grand smile. "Work stuff. Nothing I can't handle."

Disappointment flashed across her expressive face. He felt guilty and stupid for lying, but he didn't want to burden her with the embarrassing truth. He wasn't on top of the world. He was scared to death of Granddad dying and leaving him all alone again. He remembered that empty, falling away feeling all too well, from when he was a kid. The awful, aching finality of it.

And no good-byes this time, either, since Granddad wouldn't talk to him. The stubborn old geezer was still furious with his grandson for turning down the chance to head up Markham Savings & Loan.

Oh, fuck it. He was just about to open his mouth and lay it all out there for her when the shifting play of emotions in her luminous eyes abruptly receded, as if she had closed a door in his face.

It was replaced by a dazzling, utterly impenetrable smile.

"Well. That's good, then," she said.

"Uh, yeah." He blinked at her, puzzled. "It is?"

She stood up and very slowly pulled his T-shirt up over her astounding tits. She tossed it behind herself. "I'm so glad for you, Jonah. Not a care in the world. It must be awfully nice for you."

"Uh, yeah," he said hoarsely. "It's . . . great."

There was a trap here, a bad one, and he was headed right for it, but with those perfect, puckered brown nipples right at eye level, his IQ was drooping in direct inverse proportion to the swelling in his cock. He would so, *so* much rather do this than talk about his deepest fears. . . .

She stuck her finger into the soupy vanilla ice cream that

was melted together with caramel sauce. She began to paint designs on her plump, full breasts with it. Deliberately glazing her nipples with creamy caramel goo. Loops and swirls, until she was wet and gleaming. She licked her fingers, one by one, and smiled. Not the shy, glowing smile, with all of her sweetness shining out of it. This smile taunted him, guarding its secrets. Provocative and bold.

Unreal, that after all the unbelievable sex he'd been having that he was ready to go at it again.

"You wanted me to articulate my desires," she said.

He tried not to pant. "Uh, so I did."

"Lick me clean, Jonah," she commanded.

He didn't have time to marvel over the sharp edge of command in her voice before he leaped to obey her. He was gone, lost, all over her, devouring her. She was sexy and syrupy and delicious, and if this was a trap, all he wanted to do was to dive into it headfirst, and stay in it.

For as long as he possibly could.

She had no idea what she was doing, or even why she was doing it. A powerful impulse had risen up out of the churning chaos inside her, and she had grappled onto it blindly. She wanted to be a goddess with the power to bestow pleasure or agony at her whim—a dark, tangled impulse, mixed with hurt and anger and fierce, animal need.

She wanted to make him beg.

It was going to be tricky. She had a tiger by the tail. He had pulled her onto his lap, licking the caramel and ice cream off her breasts with passionate thoroughness. Her panties had already sailed off into limbo, and his hand was between her legs, pressing with delicate skill against her clitoris. He shifted her so that he could shove his jeans down, and his penis sprang out, heavy and hot and straining.

He was going to be hard to master.

She reached down and wrapped her hand around his hot

shaft—and squeezed. Hard enough to make him drag in a startled breath.

"Whoa," he said. "Go easy with that."

"Slow down, Jonah. I'm running this one."

His eyes widened at the cool command in her voice. He lifted his hands in mock surrender.

"Kick off those jeans," she said. "You won't be needing them."

He did as he was told, his eyes locked on hers.

"Let's go to the bedroom," she said.

His head jerked in agreement. She suffered a stab of doubt at the foot of the stairs, reluctant to walk in front of him and wave her big naked bottom right in his face, in all its full-blown glory. But she couldn't think that way, even for a second, or she would lose the tenuous upper hand that she barely knew how to maintain.

She started up the stairs, back straight, hips swaying. He sighed with pleasure behind her, and then his big, warm hands were on her hips. His breath was hot against her skin. His mouth pressed against her backside. She spun around to tell him to stop, but before she could speak, he pressed his face against her mound, making her stumble back, almost falling onto the steps behind her.

"Give me a taste," he said. "Just one little sip from the fountain of life, to get me up the stairs. Or I'll fall down and expire right here."

She stared down into his pale eyes. The house was silent, and the staircase was dark, just the sigh of the wind and the lash of the rain against the windows. She clutched the banister and let her thighs unlock, widening her stance. A guttural exclamation of triumph vibrated against her sensitive flesh, and he parted the folds of her sex, pressing his face against her, his tongue thrusting.

He knew instinctively what she needed, the perfect, voluptuous blend of licking and suckling. His tongue fluttered and swirled against her clitoris, his teeth rasping, tugging, sucking her, bathing her in the hot cloud of his breath. He grasped her hips and devoured her as if he were starving. She was suspended in darkness and empty space, wind and rain swirling around her, and Jonah at the center, his mouth a hot vortex that claimed everything she had. She heard only the sounds of his mouth, saw only his broad shoulders, his dark head. She had no memory of sitting or falling, but she found herself sprawled on the stairs, legs draped over his shoulders, moving helplessly, eagerly against his face.

He knew her so well now, better than she had ever known herself. He could do what he pleased with her, and he damn well knew it.

No. The thought came from a cool, remote place inside her head that stood and watched her helpless pleasure, unmoved. If she let him unravel her, then the night would be his. The upper hand would be lost, and so would she. Undone, unglued. Conquered.

It went against every instinct, but she reached down and pushed his face away from her. He murmured in fierce protest.

"No," she whispered. "This is my show. I have to tell you when."

She couldn't see his expression in the dark, but she could picure the cool speculation on his face. He released her slowly, wiping his face on his arm, and let her struggle to her feet without offering to help.

They stared at each other in the gloom. He made an impatient, questioning gesture toward the head of the stairs.

She turned, trying to be dignified as she continued up the stairs.

Upper hand. Think upper hand, she repeated to herself as she led him into the bedroom. The upper hand really had less to do with physical strength than it did with confidence, inner power. Poise.

With Jonah, it was like walking a tightrope in a hurricane wind.

She flipped on the bedside lamp and made an imperious gesture toward the bed. "Lie down, Jonah," she said.

"What game are you playing, Tess?" he asked.

"You'll see." She flung open the closet and saw what she had hoped to see. Silk ties. Not a lot of them, but enough for her purposes. She pulled a handful off their rack.

His eyes narrowed in deep suspicion. "What's this?"

"Lie down, Jonah," she said coolly. "You've been very bad, luring me up here. Lying to me, seducing me, breaking our bargain."

"You drove me to it," he protested.

"No excuses," her voice snapped out. "You have to be punished."

He looked like he was trying not to smile. "You really . . . ?"

"Oh, yes. Really. Lie down. *Now.*"

He sat down slowly on the bed, his eyes fixed on hers. "I really, really hope I won't regret this," he said.

"Arms up, please."

He presented his arms, and she tied them to the posts of the old-fashioned bed. She knelt with her backside to him, and tied his feet.

"I don't know quite how I feel about this," he muttered.

"You will in a minute or two," she informed him.

"You're so unpredictable," he said. "Not like I expected."

"Expected?" Her voice was falsely sweet as she swung her leg over him and straddled his belly. "So you planned this all along, hmm?"

He scowled. "I didn't plan. I hoped. Are you going to punish me for that, too?"

She dragged her fingernails over his chest. "I'll punish you for whatever I feel like punishing you for. We'll see what comes to me."

He drew in a sharp breath, his eyes guarded. "You're in a dangerous mood," he murmured.

She reached for a condom, tossing it onto the rumpled

coverlet. Then she scooted down the length of his body and began to play.

She fondled his balls, and traced the veins that throbbed on the surface of his penis lightly with her fingertip. It lay against his belly, stiff and hard and twitching with every ragged breath he took. He hissed at her teasing, tickling touch.

"Tess," he growled. "Are you going to—"

"Shhh," she murmured. "Suffer in silence . . ." she leaned over, brushing his lips with her fingertip, ". . . or I'll gag you."

His face tightened. "Hey. Wait a minute. You really are mad at me, aren't you? This is no game. I can feel it. You're messing with my mind."

She didn't answer, just straddled his chest and shimmied down until her labia pressed against his stiff shaft, and began to slowly, deliberately slide her wet cleft up and down the length of him. She pleasured herself with the contact with his heat and power. Smiling at him, pitiless, as the realization of his plight grew in his eyes.

He struggled to nudge inside her, but she just rose up onto her knees, evading him easily. She reached down, holding his penis right where she wanted it. Rubbing against him. Hot, slick, slow torture.

He flung his head back, the tendons standing out on his neck. "Damn it. What did I do to piss you off this time? I thought we were a million miles past all that tedious crap this afternoon."

She smiled at him through her eyelashes and scooted lower. Licked his belly. Breathed softly against the thick, gleaming head of his penis, and then dropped the very lightest of maddening butterfly kisses on the tip. "You didn't think it was so tedious last night," she told him. "You liked it just fine, playing me like an instrument. Keeping all the control. Not risking anything."

He flailed beneath her, almost bucking her off. "What the hell do you know what I risked?" he snarled.

"Less than me," she said. "Way, way less than me."

He jerked as far up as his bonds would allow. "That's not fair. It's not true, either. And you are seriously pissing me off."

She gripped his penis, milking him as roughly as she dared. He arched beneath her again, lifting her right up off the bed. "That's the spirit," she taunted him. "Go ahead, Jonah. Be pissed off. You did this to me deliberately last night. Try a taste of your own medicine. See how it feels to be spread out and naked and helpless while somebody has her way with you."

She scrambled down over his tense, rigid body and bent low, flicking her tongue across the head of his penis and licking up the gleaming drop that had formed there. Just one teasing swipe of her tongue was all she offered him, then she drew back and gave him only the warmth of her breath, the slow drag of her hair as she brushed the heavy mass back and forth over his penis, his balls.

She straddled his chest again and gazed down with a secret little smile. She lifted up onto her knees, face flushed, showing him how wet, how soft and excited she was. Deliberately stoking the volcanic energy that was building up between them.

She undulated, parting the folds of her sex so that her clitoris poked out from the top of her cleft, flushed and crimson. She laid two fingers on either side of it and began to move them slowly up and down.

His eyes were locked onto her stroking hand. He panted, his face as flushed and damp as her own. "You're trying to drive me insane, aren't you?" he said. "You manipulative bitch."

She ignored him, caught up in her own pleasure. She caressed the undersides of her breasts, trailed her fingertips around stiff, taut nipples. She pulsed her hips against her hand, dragging in harsh little gasps of air. "Watch me come, Jonah," she whispered.

It was his eyes upon her, dilated with anger and desire, as much as her own hand, that catapulted her into climax. It was long and violent, different than the others. A wrenching blast of red and pounding black. She jerked back, mouth open in a soundless scream.

She opened her eyes, gasping for air. The fury on his face made her go very still. She had teased him mercilessly, given him no outlet at all. His stiff, empurpled shaft jerked with unfulfilled excitement. Long, glistening strands of fluid from the tip gleamed against his belly.

It occurred to her that she had to untie him sometime.

She didn't dare do so if he had that look on his face. She fell forward, catching herself against his damp chest, and searched the rumpled bed for the condom. She ripped it open with trembling fingers and smoothed it over his rigid penis and poised herself over him.

"Beg me, Jonah," she said. "I want to hear you plead."

His breath hissed through his teeth, his neck and arms corded with strain. "Stop fucking around, Tess. Do it. Now. Or else."

She guided the tip of his penis into her swollen wetness. Sinking lower with a gasp at the blunt size of him. She lifted up again, leaving just the tip of him kissing her opening. "Beg," she insisted.

"What the fuck do you want from me?" he exploded.

"Everything," she said rashly. "Everything you've got."

His face changed, as if she had flipped a switch. "Done," he said.

He wrenched at the ties, and yanked the knots loose with a few quick, violent jerks. He surged up off the bed, holding her against himself as he freed his ankles. He'd been able to free himself all along.

He had chosen not to. Now that restraint was swept away.

He flung her onto her back with a speed that left her breathless and disoriented. He shoved her thighs apart, and prodded roughly until he was lodged inside her, not bothering to remove the silk ties still clinging to his wrists. He shot them a quick, contemptuous glance.

"Girl knots," he said succinctly.

"I'm going to learn to tie knots you can't pull out of," she snapped.

He let out a harsh laugh. "You're not going to learn it from me."

He thrust himself deeply inside her and held her immobile. His face was rigid, mouth sealed, as if he didn't trust himself to speak.

She gathered her tattered bravado. "Don't be so huffy. You had all that coming. But go ahead. Tie me up, if it makes you feel better."

"I don't have to tie you," he said. "I can just hold you down."

Her nerve ebbed away. "Jonah, don't—"

"You said everything. You wanted it all. You didn't specify what that means, though, so I'll interpret it however I want. Anything, everything, anyhow, anywhere, as much as I want. I'm going to take you for everything you've got. Does that turn you on?"

She shoved against his chest, chilled. "Hey. I never said—"

"Or are you going to chicken out? Again?" he taunted. "You keep pushing me, Tess. If you push me right over the top, I have to assume that's right where you want me to be. Over the top. Out of control. Right? Go on, tell me that I'm right."

She swallowed. "Within reason," she whispered.

He laughed. "There is no reason out there in no-man's land. You push me farther away from reason with every breath you take."

She glared at him. "Stop trying to scare me."

"I'm not. I'm being absolutely straight with you. It's you who's fucking with my head. You betrayed my trust."

"Oh, please. Don't be silly and melodramatic," she snapped. "I didn't do anything to you that you didn't do to me last night."

"Bullshit. I might have teased you, but I was never cold," he said furiously. "Why were you cold to me, after what we shared this afternoon? What did I do to deserve that? Why, Tess?"

She winced away from the fury in his voice. A long moment ticked by. "I don't know," she said in a tiny voice.

He was silent, waiting for more, but she could think of nothing more to say that might satisfy him. She finally dared to look up.

The anger on his face was mixed with pain and baffled hurt.

"So figure it out, Tess," he said quietly.

He hid his face against her neck. When he lifted his head, it was a stark mask of pain. "If you don't want me, I won't force you," he said. "But decide, real quick. Because I'm right on the edge."

The rough, trembling honesty in his voice went straight to her heart, and her heart took over in an instant. Needing him, wanting him. All of him: his strength, his confusion, his anger. His unknown past, his untold secrets, whatever they were. Hers, damn it. All hers.

She wrapped herself around him. Squeezed him. "No," she whispered. "Don't leave me."

His breath escaped in a sob of relief. "Then stop playing games with me. I can't take it. Deal with me straight."

"That goes for you, too," she said.

They gave each other one last searching look. He nodded. "Deal."

He gathered her close and breathlessly tight into his arms, nudging and arranging her until her legs were twined around his. The look in his eyes made her want to cry. He kissed her, with heartbreaking intensity as his body surged into hers, and she accepted him.

All her tricks and games and efforts to protect herself seemed so vain and foolish now. Her heart was laid bare. There was no hiding from the fierce attention in his penetrating eyes. No denying the power he wielded over her. His very existence excited and moved her. His beautiful body, his strength, his restless intelligence, his sensitivity.

And his passion was like a key to a lock, opening up a whole new secret world inside her. A tidal wave began to gather, building higher and higher. They cried out together as it broke. It swept her under, and she felt him following her. Joined with her.

Reality crept back slowly. They were glued together by sweat, hearts pounding. He had gotten what he wanted. There was no going back. Too late now to put up walls or close doors. She'd taken her chances coming up here. She'd rolled her dice.

And she'd lost everything to him.

She dissolved into silent tears, her face against his chest.

He clutched her, alarmed. "God. What is it now? Did I hurt you?"

"Just shut up and just hold me," she snapped.

His arms tightened fiercely. "OK," he said. "That I can do."

Chapter Eight

A small eternity later she calmed down, and Jonah disentangled himself. He went out on the deck, tossed the plastic cover off the hot tub, and checked the water. Nice and hot against the evening chill. He flipped on the deck light to its lowest setting, a dim golden glow no more obtrusive than candlelight, and went back inside.

Tess was a lump under the covers and two shadowy eyes that regarded him solemnly.

"You OK?" How embarrassing that he should have to bleat out his insecurity by asking her that question, over and over.

"I don't know," she said. "I don't even know myself around you. All my demons wake up and go nuts."

"Oh." He could think of nothing comforting or cheerful to say to that. It didn't sound very goddamn promising. "Uh, sorry."

"It's not your fault," she told him.

"I guess that's a relief." He twitched the comforter off her and tugged on her hand. "Come try out my hot tub."

She sat up. "Oh, please. Is this another one of your tricks? Next you're going to show me your etchings."

He pulled her up off the bed. "Actually, no. To be honest, I'm kind of freaked out myself. I want to just sit in hot water and mellow out for a while."

Tendrils of steam rose up, illuminated by the underwater lights. They sank slowly down into the hot water, and silence spread out between them, becoming more vast and heavy with each passing minute. He took a deep breath, and forced himself to break it.

"It was perfect between us. Why are you so upset?"

She twisted her hair up into a knot, her eyes downcast. "Perfection is impossible," she said quietly. "No one knows that better than me. I want to hang on, but I know that I can't."

Vague, restless anger churned in his gut. "Why not?"

She looked away. "Because I can't. Things end. It's the nature of life."

Her bleak word foretold doom for this fragile, beautiful thing budding between them. She was jinxing it. It made him feel panicked.

"It doesn't have to end," he said. "I certainly don't want it to."

Her gaze snapped up to him. "Don't you dare dangle that in front of me, like all the other bait," she said, her eyes blazing with unexpected anger. "The foot rub, the chocolate soufflé, the queen of the universe. I won't bite this time. I may be stupid, but I'm not *that* stupid."

"Do not ever let me hear you call yourself stupid again," he said.

She sat up, her nipples just clearing the waterline. "Do not scold me," she said, enunciating very clearly.

They stared at each other, at a blind impasse. He'd never felt so baffled, so helpless. "What's happening, Tess?" he asked. "Tell me what I'm doing wrong. Tell me what you want from me."

Her eyes squeezed shut. "I don't know," she whispered.

He stared at her beautiful, averted face, praying to find

the right formula not to fuck this up. He was starting to need her. Her sweetness, her sharpness, her beauty. She made him feel so alive. And the more he wanted her, the more she seemed determined to slip away.

"Well, I know exactly what I want from you," he said rashly. "I already know what I want to cook for you, what I want to show you, how I want to touch you. I want to help you open your studio, too. I'll do a business plan for you—"

"Jonah—"

"Let me finish. I can give you double the money I was planning to give you this weekend right away. If that's not enough, then I can—"

"Don't be ridiculous!" She jerked back, horrified. "I can't take money from you! What would that make me?"

"Get real. You turned down paying work to come up here. I was the one who seduced you and turned everything upside down. You're entitled to that money. Call it a start-up loan if you insist, but—"

"Jonah. Not one more word."

The coldness of her voice stopped him. *Shit.* He'd bombed again.

"I can do this on my own," she said. "I don't need anybody to rescue me. I am not a child. Or an idiot."

He pushed his hair back off his forehead with a silent groan. Everything he said came out wrong, everything he did flew back in his face. It was like a bad dream. "I never meant to imply otherwise," he said stiffly. "Please don't be offended."

She hunched down in the tub, her arms wrapped across her chest. She looked so lost that his heart thudded painfully. He would offer her anything to make her smile again, anything. He stretched out his arms. "Please, Tess. Come here."

She drifted toward him, her chin lifted. He ached to soothe the proud hurt in her eyes. "Come home with me tomorrow," he urged. "Move into my apartment. I've got plenty of space. I want you in my bed. You can even have your own bathroom, if you want. I've got two."

Her eyes went wide and startled. "Wow. That's bold."

"Bold. Yeah. That's me," he said. "Will you? Pretty please?"

She opened and closed her mouth. "But I . . . my roommate will be expecting . . . and I'll need my clothes—"

"To hell with your clothes," he broke in. "I'm going to buy you a new wardrobe, anyhow. Enough of those ugly burlap dresses you wear, particularly if you're opening a business. You need stuff that—"

She sprang to her feet. Water sloshed into his mouth, blocking off the rest of his phrase, *"shows off how sexy and beautiful you are."*

She clambered out of the tub. "No way." Her voice shook with anger. "I dress the way I dress, Jonah Markham. I am what I am, and to hell with you if it's not good enough."

Oh, hell. He should have remembered. The clothes were a hot button, and he'd stomped all over it. He reached for her, but she wrenched her wet arm away from him with such desperate violence that he shrank back. "Tess, I'm sorry. I—"

"I mean it, Jonah. Don't touch me."

He stared at her trembling back. "I can't believe this. Dealing with you is like walking through a fucking minefield. I can see what your ex's problem with you was, if you were always this hysterical and unreasonable. I guess I've got some goddamn high standards of my own."

His shot met its mark, but the devastated look she shot back over her shoulder gave him no satisfaction at all.

In fact, it made him feel like five different kinds of shit.

Her clothes were scattered all over the house. She searched for them feverishly, pulling them on as she found them. This was worse than she had ever dreamed. Painful memories crowded through her mind: Larry gently suggesting a fitness trainer, to "help get rid of that puppy fat." An image consultant, for her clothes. A makeup expert, to teach her to compensate for her beauty problems. A wine-tasting course. Diction classes, to get rid of that lingering California college girl flavor in her accent. Larry believed in investing time, money, and effort in one's greatest personal resource: oneself; and Tess's mother had applauded his efforts. *"It's good that you have someone who pushes you to be the best that you can be, honey. A mother can only do so much."*

Well, wasn't that the truth, and thank God for it.

She had to get out of here, before she started to sink into the cracks in the floorboards, the incredible shrinking Tess. Embarrassed to take up space, apologizing for the very air she breathed. She thought she had worked through these awful feelings and left them behind, but here they were, stronger than ever, and it was Jonah's face, Jonah's voice superimposed over Larry's. And that was a thousand times worse.

Jonah appeared at the foot of the stairs, watching as she broke down her massage table. He hadn't bothered to dry himself. He just stood there, naked, a puddle forming around his feet. The silent reproach in his shadowy eyes tore at her. She had to get away before she shrank too small to even see over the dashboard of her VW Bug. There seemed to be no end to how bad she could feel about this.

"Sorry," she whispered.

He did not reply for a long moment. "Me, too," he said finally.

It took over two and a half hours in the rain to get home, sniffling all the way. Trish turned away from the TV and regarded her with blank astonishment when she stumbled in the door.

"What are you doing back already?"

"It didn't work out." Her voice was dull and flat.

Trish switched off the TV and stared at Tess with big,

worried blue eyes. "Are you, um, OK?" she asked cautiously.

"Let me give you the short version, because I can't handle a full-scale debriefing right now. Did I earn four thousand bucks? No. Did I have sex? Yes. Was it good? Yes, it was so unbelievably good that it practically destroyed me. Do I want to jump off a bridge? Maybe."

"Oh, dear." Trish bit her lip. "No money, hmm? How about the start-up? What are you going to tell your mom?"

Trish let the massage table fall to the ground with a rattling thud. "I'll tell her what I should've told her all along. That it's none of her goddamn business. I'll find the money some other way, in my own good time. And I am never, ever going to let anybody push me around, ever again. Not my parents, not Jonah, not Jeanette, not even you, Trish."

Trish blinked. "Not even me? That is some serious stuff, chica. I'm not sure whether to break out the champagne or dial 911."

Tess's chin started to shake. "How about you just give me a hug?"

Trish almost fell over her feet rushing to her.

It was a damn good thing he had more important things to occupy his mind, he kept telling himself.

Uh-huh. Yeah. Right. The fuck-up with Tess looped endlessly through his mind, whenever he wasn't worrying about Granddad.

It was driving him nuts. He didn't need a woman like that in his life. Too much trouble, too oversensitive, too quick to take offense. Life was too short to spend it tiptoeing around her tender little feelings.

But she was so sweet, and funny, and sensual. He'd never had sex like that in his life. He was ruined for normal women.

His office staff were whispering and circling around him

like he was a rabid animal. He kept calling the MMC, and slamming the phone down before it started to ring. He would have called her at home, if he had her number, but she wasn't in the book, and he didn't know the roommate's last name, and besides, why bother? She had his number. If she wanted to talk to him, she could call him anytime.

But she hadn't. She wouldn't. He had to get that through his thick skull, and let it go, and that left Granddad to worry about.

Sunday, Monday, Tuesday. Days ticked into nights that ticked relentlessly back into days again.

Wednesday morning dawned. The day stretched out ahead of him, long and bleak. He had to sit through the surgery sharing the waiting room with his asshole cousins and their bitchy wives. Oh, it wasn't that big of a deal. He'd survive. Those clowns didn't make his life bad, they just made it stupid. He didn't have the energy to deal with stupidity.

Hah. Then why did he keep dialing the goddamn MMC?

Maybe he could just drop by today, and ask her to wish him luck. There wouldn't be any other friendly face to pat him on the back today, and he was going to sit in a hard plastic chair in a hospital waiting room, clutching an outdated *Field & Stream* magazine, facing his deepest fears today for God alone knew how many hours. It would be really nice to get a hug first. Just to have those strong, warm hands on him for a minute would soothe that jittery ache inside him. He had just enough time to go down to the MMC on the hour and catch her between clients before he headed to the hospital.

He had to get over himself. Granddad was an old man; he had to go sometime. Everyone did. Just not quite yet. Please, not yet.

He got there five minutes early, and was doomed to deal with the Martian receptionist. Great. As if he weren't going to get enough hostile glares from his cousins at the hospital today.

"She's booked all day. And she's with a client now," the receptionist informed him, with a sugary, fuck-you smile. "And she can't bag somebody else's appointment for you, because Jeanette chewed her out for that last week. Big time. So don't even think it."

He glanced at his watch, exercising all the self-control at his command. "Just tell her I'm here, please," he said, rigidly polite.

The receptionist rolled her eyes and flounced into the back rooms. She came back moments later, with a long-suffering look. He grinned at her with all his teeth. She got very busy with her appointment book.

Tess came out a few moments later. Her hair was screwed into the most severe knot he had ever seen, and her face was pale, washed out by the white dress. Her rubber-soled shoes squeaked with every step. He glanced down at them. She'd either done a superhuman job getting the mud off, or she had more than one pair. They were snow white. As if the primeval sex in the forest had never happened.

Her face was just like her shoes. She had an it-never-happened expression: cool, polite, ever so slightly strained. With a professional, can-I-help-you-you-pathetic-bastard smile.

Dread gathered in his gut like an ice-cold stone. "Can I, uh, speak to you for a few minutes?"

"I have a client, Jonah."

He clenched his teeth and he swallowed, resolved to see this through, one way or the other. "Please," he said. "It's important."

She sighed and circled the receptionist's desk. The *squeak-squeak-squeak* of her shoes was driving him nuts. She stood in front of him in the waiting room, in front of everyone. Arms crossed over her chest. Waiting. Her foot would tap, if she weren't so fucking polite.

"Can we go someplace more private?" he asked.

Her sensual mouth tightened to a thin line. "I have a client in the back room," she said. "And if you want an emergency appointment, I'm very sorry, but I can't accommodate you. Welcome to the real world. I'm sure it must be a rude shock, but sometimes mundane reality just can't conform to Jonah Markham's whims."

Shields up, shields up. The red alert went off in his head, but it was too late. The torpedo had already gone speeding straight in, dead on the mark, completely trashing his main reactor. He had no way of knowing what expression he had on his face as he backed away. All that was important was getting out that door.

He jerked back as if she'd slapped him, his face going pale and stiff, and a horrible realization yawned open inside her, as if she had just stepped over a cliff. She was hurtling down, down, with a sick, scared falling feeling in her stomach. She had made a terrible mistake.

She lunged for him in a panic. "Oh, God. I didn't mean that. I'm sorry, Jonah. I just—"

He wrenched his arm from her, backing away faster. "Never mind. I'm out of here. Sorry I bothered you."

She scrambled to intercept him at the door. "No. Please, tell me what's wrong. Why—"

"Never mind. I got my answer. Out of my way. I'm in a hurry."

She watched him run down the stairs and stride away, as utterly wretched as if she'd just killed something beautiful, out of pure, blind stupidity. Her body exploded into movement, pure instinct taking over. It knew what it wanted, knew what was right. It could not be reasoned with, or cowed. She raced after him, legs pumping, and tackled him from behind. She clung to his slippery canvas coat like a monkey.

He cursed and tried to shake her off. "I don't have time for your weird mind trips today, Tess."

"I said I was sorry. I was a heinous bitch for saying that.

You didn't deserve it, and I'll make it up to you somehow. And you are not getting away from me until you tell me what you came here for."

He tried halfheartedly to detach her clinging hands. "You're strangling me, Tess," he said wearily.

She tightened her arms, pressing her wrist hard against his windpipe on purpose. "Tough titties."

His shoulders shook with silent laughter. He grabbed her forearms and pulled them down so that he could breathe. "My Granddad's getting open-heart surgery today. I was just going to . . . oh, shit, I don't know. Maybe ask you to come by the hospital later, if you have time. To sit with me while I wait. But you're super busy, I can see that, so whatever. I didn't have any reason to think you would want to. Just thought I'd ask."

"Oh, Jonah—"

"Let go of me, for Christ's sake. I feel bad enough as it is. And I want to get over there before they put him under."

"But Jonah, I didn't mean to—"

"No big deal." His voice cut across hers. "Get on back to your client. Let go, Tess. I really don't want to have to be rough with you."

She swung herself around, still clutching his arm. His face was like graven stone, turned resolutely away from her.

"Can you wait a minute?" she pleaded. "Just long enough for me to grab my purse and tell my boss what happened?"

"You don't have to feel sorry for me," he said. "I was an idiot to come here. I should have learned my lesson back at the lake."

She clung to his arm with all her strength. "Believe me, Jonah, there is nothing on earth I would rather do than go and wait at the hospital with you. Wait for me. *Please.*"

The anguished doubt in his eyes tore at her. He had always seemed so strong, vital, and confident. It hurt like hell to see him in pain. What a thick-skulled idiot she'd been; so intent on protecting her own heart that it never occurred to her that she actually had the power to wound his.

And the more jealously she guarded her heart, the more barren and cramped and arid it would be. At this rate, it wouldn't be long until there was nothing left in there to protect.

She raised his hand to her lips, dropping a supplicating kiss onto his knuckles. "Please," she whispered.

He closed his eyes. "I'll wait two minutes. Then I'm out of here."

She didn't even remember what she said in that mad flurry of explanations and apologies. Thank God she'd been lying about the client in the back room, and a quick glance at the schedule assured her that there was enough staff to cover her clients for the rest of the day. She grabbed her purse and ran, heedless of the protests that Lacey and Jeanette shouted after her. To hell with that stupid job. She'd been bullied, taken advantage of, overworked, and underpaid for too long, and she was sick to death of that ghastly white dress. She would find another job if her bridges burned this afternoon.

Jonah was more important.

She had to scurry to keep up with him as he strode through the corridors of the hospital. She clutched his rigid forearm and let him tow her along beside him. He beckoned her through a pair of big automatic doors, and finally they entered a room where a very pale elderly man with bushy white eyebrows and a hawklike nose lay on a gurney. His gray eyes glinted with anger, like a trapped animal. He saw Jonah, and his brows snapped together in a thunderous frown.

Jonah pulled Tess until she stood next to him, in the old man's line of sight. "Hi, Granddad," Jonah said, in a cautious voice. "This is my girlfriend, Tess. We just wanted to wish you luck."

The old man's eyes shot back to Tess, scrutinizing her

with fierce concentration. She smiled at him. "Good to meet you, Mr. Markham."

His grizzled brows shot up, and his gaze dropped appreciatively down the length of her body. She could have sworn that he winked at her, but a nurse hustled into the room, clucking with disapproval.

"Authorized surgical personnel only, at this point," she said sternly. "Out you go."

"Sorry," Jonah muttered to Tess as the nurse herded them out.

"For what?" she asked.

"For calling you my girlfriend. It just popped out."

She slid her arm around his waist. "I liked it," she whispered.

A flash of a smile crossed his pale face. "He likes you."

"How can you tell? He didn't say a word."

"Yeah, he's still pissed with me. I wouldn't take over for him at Markham Savings & Loan, so he still won't speak to me. Stubborn old bastard. But he likes you. Believe me, I can tell."

Shortly afterward, the waiting room began to fill. Two middle-aged men, one paunchy, the other thin and balding, and two women of the same age filed into the room, all talking in loud voices and staring at Jonah and her with what could only be described as pure hostility.

It was disconcerting. She glanced at Jonah, but he either hadn't noticed them or was pretending not to. His eyes were closed. She leaned closer to him. "Who are those rude, horrible people?" she whispered.

Jonah opened his eyes and shot them a weary glance. "My cousins, John and Steve, and their wives, Marilyn and Sandra. They're jealous of me, because I was Granddad's first choice to head up his company. Even though I turned it down and went my own way. They hate my guts. Long, boring story. Try to ignore them. That's what I do."

She slid a protective arm around his shoulder as one of the women came over, a well-dressed, strained-looking blond with a stringy neck. "Jonah, it's really very selfish of you to insist on being here when you know perfectly well that it upsets Frank to see you."

The woman's voice had the studied forcefulness that comes from assertiveness training workshops. Tess should know, since Larry had insisted that she take one "to increase her confidence and personal effectiveness." Tess tightened her arm around Jonah's shoulders and decided to put everything she had learned in that workshop to use.

"Why don't you just piss off?" she asked, in a calm, well-modulated voice. She gave the blond woman a dazzling smile.

The blond's mouth dangled open for a moment. It snapped shut. The nostrils of her pinched, narrow nose flared unpleasantly.

She glared down at Jonah. "Who is this person?"

Jonah looked at Tess. His weary, drawn face relaxed into a smile so radiant and beautiful that she almost burst into tears.

"Sandra, meet my girlfriend, Tess Langley," he said. "And she's just made a truly excellent suggestion. Piss off."

His arms wrapped around Tess, sealing them into a private space where the shrill, hostile voices squawking across the room were less important than the sound of faraway cars honking.

Time passed differently in their hushed, magical intimacy. She held his hand and contemplated the huge tenderness she felt for him, amazed that she had not allowed herself to acknowledge it until now. She wanted to protect, to heal, to comfort him. She couldn't fight against it, and she didn't want to. All she could do was hang on to his hand and try to breathe around the soft, melting feeling in her heart that kept getting bigger with each passing minute. She kept reminding herself that to cry would be self-indulgent and inappropriate. She had to keep it together, for Jonah's sake.

Hours went by. Cups of coffee, hushed conversation. Jonah's relatives looked glum and stressed, sniping at each other.

Jonah straightened up when the surgeon came out, relaxing visibly when he saw the smile on the man's face. Frank was doing well, the surgeon told them. The procedure had gone smoothly, his vital signs were stable, and they didn't expect any complications.

Jonah pressed his face against her shoulder, and her eyes overflowed. She couldn't hold it back any longer. The soft feeling in her chest made her feel strong. No more incredible shrinking Tess. She finally understood the puzzle that had confounded her for so long.

Her love for Jonah made her bigger, stronger. More of everything that was right and good and real.

She shifted, anxious not to let him think even for a fleeting second that she was pushing him away, and slid herself onto his lap. She fit his head under her chin, inhaling his warm scent. Delicious and satisfying.

He smelled like home.

He was out there, in orbit. Way beyond civilized, normal conversation. Emotions roared through him: relief at having the fear of losing Granddad lifted, and jagged, edgy exultation at having Tess in his grip again. She was looking at him with those glowing eyes that made him want to fling himself at her feet and clutch at her ankles.

He should be charming her, thanking her, he thought dimly. She'd been really sweet to him, sticking by him, defending him from Sandra and the rest. He should be making nice, thinking of something impressive to cook for her, being witty and urbane. Earning points.

It wasn't happening. All he could do was bundle her into his car, sweep her away to his lair, and use every trick that came to him to keep her there. Whatever it took to persuade her that she belonged with him.

He heard her ask where he was taking her, through the roaring in his ears. He snapped out "home," in a voice brusque enough to discourage any further attempts at conversation. So much for his boyish charm. And his converted warehouse apartment in the Pearl District, furnished with the sleek, postmodern chill of a well-to-do bachelor pad, was not homey. At least the fridge was full. He wished he could take her back to the lake, but it was too far away. He needed her now. So bad that it scared him.

The car alarm and door lock chirped behind him as he pulled her up the battered warehouse staircase that he hadn't had a chance to renovate yet. It was spooky-looking, but if he pulled her into the apartment really fast, she wouldn't have time to be creeped out.

The door swung shut behind them with an ominous, resounding, Dracula's Castle type of thud. At this rate, he was going to end up scaring her to death. He cast around helplessly for something normal, soothing, welcoming to say to her. No words came to him.

He gave in to brute necessity, and wrapped his fingers around her slender wrist, pulling her through the apartment. He couldn't be bothered to turn on the lights, to take her coat, to lay down her purse, or offer her a drink. He headed straight for the bedroom.

He shoved her coat off, letting it fall to the floor, and seized her. Kissing her like he was dying of thirst, and she was an oasis in the desert, full of sweet, life-giving water. She didn't recoil from his intensity at all. She pressed herself against him and opened for him, freely offering him all the springlike freshness of her soft mouth, her fragrant breath. The tender, wet assay of her tongue against his made him shudder with need. He didn't want to spoil this by being clumsy or rough, groping and pawing like a gorilla, but his hands had a will of their own. He couldn't stop touching her, cupping her lush curves.

She pulled away, and he was about to howl in frustration until he realized that she was just pulling loose the laces of her sneakers. She kicked them off and reached under her skirt to peel off the white hose. He couldn't wait to feel her pansy-soft skin sliding beneath his hands, the sexy swell of her ass. Every tiny detail thrilled him.

She shook with soft laughter as he wrenched her hose down to her ankles, and shoved the skirt up to her waist. Just what he was dying for—Tess all naked and soft and open. He could smell the humid warmth of her femaleness. It made him dizzy. He could barely make out the soft dark curls between her thighs, the graceful female curves in the dim room, but he couldn't bear to stop even long enough to turn on the light. He explored her with his hands, his face, his nose, his mouth, nuzzling and kissing her with desperate appeal. Assuring himself that she was real, she was here, she was his.

She grabbed his shoulders to steady herself against him, but he didn't want her steady. He wanted her flat on her back beneath him, wide open. With one well-placed push, he sent her pitching backward with a cry of alarm onto his bed, legs sprawled. He lunged to cover her before she could draw breath or protest.

Her eyes were wide, breath coming soft and shallow as he wrenched open the buttons of the dress. They yielded with a soft popping noise. No T-shirt under it, just a silk bra of indeterminate color, cupping the luminously pale bulges of her stunning breasts. She glowed like moonlight on his bed. Her fingers slid through his hair, touched his face. Cool and soft and caressing.

He buried his face against her bosom, rubbing it against the incredible softness and scent of her. Drinking it in, big greedy gulps.

She petted his hair as he nuzzled her cleavage. "You seem so desperate," she murmured.

Her thighs tightened around him as he licked the shadowy cleft between her tits, and his cock hardened even more, if that were possible. "I feel desperate," he admitted.

"You don't have to be," she assured him. "You've got me right where you want me." She stroked his hot cheek, soothing him, like he were some pitiable, maddened animal. He hated it and loved it, felt shamed and eager, like a trembling puppy grateful for every little pat.

He lifted his head, trying to calm down his ragged breathing, and noticed that her bra was the front-clasp type. He could have wept with appreciation for the convenience, but there was something he had to tell her, if his damn throat would stop vibrating long enough for him to use his voice. He swallowed over and over to make his larynx descend.

"I won't hurt you," he said.

She cupped her face in her hands, smiling at him. "Of course you won't," she told him. "I trust you."

His breath froze in his throat. "You didn't before," he said.

She kissed his jaw. "Give me credit for learning," she said softly. "I won't hurt you, either. You can trust me, too."

She squirmed beneath him until he realized that she was reaching back to undo the knot of hair—an enterprise he was absolutely willing to second and support. He plucked out hairpins and tossed them away with a disdain that bordered on hostility.

"You should wear your hair down all the time," he said.

A spasm of dread froze his insides. She was going to freak out on him for critizicing her hairdo. He'd fucked up again.

But she just laughed. "I will, if you like it that way. But you'd better get good at combing out my tangles."

"I'll be great," he promised her rashly. "I'll spend hours, naked, combing your hair. My new career. Naked hairdressing."

She looked like a pagan goddess with all that long, amazing curly hair spread over his pillow. He buried his face in it, letting tears leak out of his eyes and soak into her hair. He had to distract himself, quick. Sex and tears did not mix, at least not with him, and he wanted the sex.

So did she, thank God, if the focused attention she was giving to his shirt buttons was any indication. He undid the clasp of her bra and rubbed his face against her breasts with a moan of appreciation. He stroked the rich full undercurve with the soft, fluttering fingertip caresses that she loved, and pressed them together, kissing and licking until she writhed and moaned.

He unbuckled his belt, undid his jeans. She slid her hands eagerly inside the waistband of his underwear and gripped his cock, with the tight, slow pull that she knew he loved. He tried to keep his weight poised above her without going boneless with pleasure. Then it hit him. He collapsed against her, limp with dismay. "Oh, God, no."

"What?" Her eyes were wide with alarm.

"The fucking condoms," he groaned. "I left them at the lake. This is it. The final insult. I'm going to die right here, in your arms. Get ready for the tragic, tender moment. Move over, Scarlett and Rhett."

She started to laugh. "You're not going to die," she teased. "I've still got that stash that Trish put in my purse, remember? We can use the glow-in-the-dark one if you want. We'll probably have to expose it to light first, though, if we want it to work."

"Forget it. It'll take too long," he snapped.

"OK," she said cheerfully. "We'll save the glow-in-the-dark one for the third or fourth time. I'll get the chocolate and raspberry flavored one, instead. Just let me figure out where I dropped my purse, and—"

"Stay right where you are," he ordered. "I'll get them."

She lay back, apparently submissive, but he knew her too well to be fooled, particularly when she had that smile on her face. She opened her legs wider, the white skirt still crumpled around her waist, the bodice gaping open, her plump tits spilling out of it. Taunting him.

She put her hand against the dark tangle of hair on her mound. "It wouldn't make any difference if we had no condoms," she said huskily. "I'd just suck on you. Make you explode in my mouth. As many times as you want."

He was wide-eyed, frozen, and as stiff as a railroad spike. Hypnotized by the sensual pulse of her hips against his bed. "Are you pushing me again?" he demanded. "Playing games with me?"

She shook her head. "Oh, no. I just love the feel of your eyes on me. They press on me, burn me. It turns me on. And I love the feel of your, um . . . your cock. In my mouth. So hard, and yet so soft and velvety. Strong and sensitive. Delicious."

He dumped the contents of her purse heedlessly onto the bed, pawing through the assorted female paraphernalia until he found what he needed. He ripped open the condom and rolled it over himself. "I'm going to hold you to that," he warned. "For the third or fourth time."

He mounted her, guiding himself to her tender opening. It was too soon, experience and instinct all screamed at him that it was too soon, but he couldn't wait. He could only drive himself into her, deep and hard. The sound that jerked out of her throat as her body slowly yielded to him was not unmixed pleasure, but he pushed deeper, clenching his jaw. And withdrew, and drove in again, harder than he meant to. Her fingers dug sharply into his upper arms.

"I'm sorry," he said, his voice shaking. "I'm too—I can't—"

"Shhh." Her arms and legs closed around him tightly. "It's OK. I love you. I feel it, too. I love you."

Nothing but that hot blaze of joy and disbelief could have shocked him into stillness. "You do?"

She pressed her damp face against his. "Yes. I've never felt like this before. It's so huge, I'm lost in it."

He marveled at her words for another frozen, breathless moment. "So am I," he said. "But—the other night—"

She shook her head. "You have to forgive me for the other night," she said. "My whole universe was falling apart to make space for you. It felt like dying. I just panicked."

He pried his face away. "And now?" he demanded.

Her smile was luminous with joy. "Now I'm bigger," she said simply. "Now there's space. I finally figured it out today. I know I'm good enough, because I'm the best I've ever been, loving you."

He was so moved, he had to fight to speak. "I'm lost in it, too," he whispered. "I love you, Tess."

The triumphant joy inside him melted away every last vestige of his self-control.

Tess dug her fingers into the muscles in his shoulders and hung on. It didn't hurt at all anymore, after that first rough moment. Almost instantly she had softened to him, and now she was lost in bliss. Nothing was more perfect than this voluptuous give and take, the sweet, hot friction. He followed cues she didn't even know she gave him, shifting his weight up and pressing the length of his fingers on either side of her clitoris. Sliding them slowly up and down her slick cleft, exactly as she had shown him when she had tied him down and touched herself. His face was tense with concentration, eyes locked with hers. The power rose between them, higher and higher. It broke, and they collapsed into a sweaty, trembling knot of desperate tenderness.

They stayed clenched together, for a long time.

Jonah flung himself onto his back beside her and covered his face with his hand. "Don't run away from me again, Tess."

She rolled up onto her elbow. "Jonah—"

"I wanted to come see you at the MMC, but I was afraid I

would creep you out if I dragged my tongue around on the ground after you. So I tried to play it cool, you know? Stay away. But it didn't work. I can't be cool. I just can't do it. I'm madly in love with you."

"Oh, Jonah." Tears made her voice quiver. "I'm so sorry about the other night. I thought that you were . . . that you were trying to—"

"To what?" His hand dropped. He stared at her.

She plucked at the duvet. "I thought you wanted to . . . make me good enough to fit into your gourmet lifestyle," she confessed. "To bring me up to standard."

His face was expressionless. "Like the other guy did."

~~She sighed, and nodded.~~

~~He grabbed her wrist, tugging her until~~ she was eye to eye with him. "Can we make a pact, here and now, to never, ever—"

"Oh, God, yes," she said fervently. "I'm so embarrassed. I will never compare you to him, ever again. You are nothing like him, Jonah, nothing. He was just a hollow shell. You're for real."

He gave her a pleased, baffled smile. "Thank you," he said. He stroked his knuckle with reverent gentleness over her cheekbone. "And just for the record, I don't think you need fixing. I think you're perfect. But if we're going to be together, you're going to have to deal with me buying you clothes and jewelry without getting all huffy about it. Because I'm not going to be able to help myself."

She kissed his hand as it touched her face and snuggled closer to him. "I, um, think I'll learn to cope somehow."

"I can't wait to really introduce you to Granddad. He'll be out of his mind with curiosity about you. That'll motivate him to forgive me, if anything will. Granddad never could resist the ladies. And you're his type."

"What type is that?" she asked.

"*My* type," he said forcefully. "Strong, smart, sexy, sweet, fascinating. Challenging, complicated. And absolutely for real."

"Like you," she said. "For real."

His lips met hers, with reverent tenderness. "And forever."

Please turn the page for an exciting preview of
Shannon McKenna's next book,
EDGE OF MIDNIGHT.
Available next month from Brava.

"You're going down the drain, and we're sick of sitting around with our thumbs up our asses, watching it happen," Davy went on.

Going down the drain. Goosebumps prickled up Sean's back.

"Funny you should say that," he said. "It gives me the shivers. Kev said the exact same words to me last night."

Connor sucked in a sharp breath. "I *hate* it when you do that."

His tone jolted Sean out of his reverie. "Huh? What have I done?"

"Talked about Kev as if he were alive," Davy said heavily. "Please, please don't do that. It makes us really nervous."

There was a long, unhappy silence. Sean took a deep breath.

"Listen, guys. I know Kev is dead." He kept his voice steely calm. "I'm not hearing little voices. I don't think anybody's out to get me. I have no intentions of driving off a cliff. Everybody relax. OK?"

"So you had one of those dreams last night?" Connor demanded.

Sean winced. He'd confessed the Kev dreams to Connor some years back, and he'd regretted it bitterly, Connor had gotten freaked out, had dragged Davy into it, yada yada. Very bad scene.

But the dreams had been driving him bugfuck. Always Kev, insisting he wasn't crazy, that he hadn't really killed himself. That Liv was still in danger. And that Sean was a no balls, dick-brained chump if he fell for this lame ass cover-up. *Study my sketchbook*, he exhorted. *The proof is right there. Open your eyes. Dumb ass.*

But they had studied that sketchbook, goddamn it. They'd picked it apart, analyzed it from every direction. They'd come up with fuck-all.

Because there was nothing to come up with. Kev had been sick, like Dad. The bad guys, the cover-up, the danger for Liv—all paranoid delusions. That was the painful conclusion that Con and Davy had finally come to. The note in Kev's sketchbook looked way too much like Dad's mad ravings during his last years. Sean didn't remember Dad's paranoia as clearly as his older brothers did, but he did remember it.

Still, it had taken him longer to accept their verdict. Maybe he never really had accepted it. His brothers worried that he was as nutso paranoid as his twin. Maybe he was. Who knew? Didn't matter.

He couldn't make the dreams stop. He couldn't make himself believe something by sheer brute force. It was impossible to swallow that his twin had offed himself, never asking for help. At least not until he sent Liv running with the sketchbook. And by then, it had been too late.

"I have dreams about Kev, now and then," he said quietly. "It's no big deal anymore. I'm used to them. Don't worry about it."

The five of them maintained a heavy silence for the time it took to get to Sean's condo. Images rolled around behind his closed eyes; writhing bodies, flashing lights, naked girls passed out in bed. Con's predator, lurking like a troll under a bridge, eating geeks for breakfast.

And then, the real kicker. The one he never got away from.

Liv staring at him, gray eyes huge with shock and hurt. Fifteen years ago today. The day that all the truly bad shit came down.

She'd come to the lock-up, rattled from her encounter with Kev. Tearful, because her folks were trying to bully her onto a plane for Boston. He'd been chilling in the drunk tank while Bart and Amelia Endicott tried to figure out how to keep him away from their daughter.

They needn't have bothered. Fate had done their work for them.

The policeman hadn't let her take Kev's sketchbook in, but she'd torn Kev's note out and stuck it in her bra. It was written in one of Dad's codes. He could read those codes as easily as he read English.

Midnight Project is trying to kill me. They saw Liv.
Will kill her if they find her. Make her leave town today
or she's meat.
Do the hard thing.
HC behind count birds B63.
Proof on the tapes in EFPI.

He'd believed every goddamn word, at least the ones he'd understood. Why shouldn't he have? Christ, he'd grown up in Eamon McCloud's household. The man had believed enemies were stalking him every minute of his life. Up to the bitter end.

Sean had never known a time that they weren't on alert for Dad's baddies. And besides, Kev had never led him wrong. Kev had never lied in his life. Kev was brilliant, brave, steady as a rock. Sean's anchor.

Do the hard thing. It was a catch phrase of their father's. A man did what had to be done, even if it hurt. Liv was in danger. She had to leave. If he told her this, she would resist, argue, and if she got killed, it would be his fault. For being soft. For not doing the hard thing.

So he'd done it. It was as simple as pulling the trigger of a gun.

He stuck the note in his pocket. Made his eyes go flat and cold.

"Baby? You know what? It's not going to work out between us," he said. "Just leave, OK? Go to Boston. I don't want to see you anymore."

She'd been bewildered. He'd repeated himself, stone cold. Yep, she heard him right. Nope, he didn't want her anymore. Bye.

She floundered, confused. "But . . . I thought you wanted—"

"To nail you? Yeah. I had three hundred bucks riding on it. I like to keep things casual, though. You're way too intense. You'll have to get some college boy to pop your cherry, 'cause it ain't me, babe."

She stared at him, slack-jawed. "Three hundred . . . ?"

"The construction crew. We had a pool going. I've been giving them a blow by blow. So to speak." He laughed, a short, ugly sound. "But things are going too fucking slow. I'm bored with it."

"B-b-bored?" she whispered.

He leaned forward, eyes boring into hers. "I. Do. Not. Love. You. Get it? I do not want a spoiled princess, cramping my style. Daddy and Mommy want to send you back East? Good. Get lost. Go."

He waited. She was frozen solid. He took a deep breath, gathered his energy, flung the words at her like a grenade. "*Fuck, Liv. Go!*"

It had worked. She'd gone. She'd left for Boston, that very night.

He'd paid the price ever since.